At His Service

At His
Service

Suzanne Rock

St. Martin's Paperbacks

This is a work of fiction. All of the characters, organizations, and events portrayed in this novel are either products of the author's imagination or are used fictitiously.

AT HIS SERVICE

Copyright © 2015 by Suzanne Rock.

For information address St. Martin's Press, 175 Fifth Avenue, New York, NY 10010.

ISBN: 978-1-250- 05925-3

Printed in the United States of America

St. Martin's Paperbacks edition / June 2015

St. Martin's Paperbacks are published by St. Martin's Press, 175 Fifth Avenue, New York, NY 10010.

10 9 8 7 6 5 4 3 2 1

For my mom, who inspired and fostered
my love of reading.

Acknowledgments

It's hard to know where to begin. On the road to publication, one needs to navigate late nights, rejections, chocolate wrappers, rewriting, empty coffee mugs, and the occasional emotional outburst. It's easy for a writer to lose her way. Over the years, a few people have stuck with me through this journey, and I'd like to take a moment to express my gratitude here.

First, I'd like to thank my editor, Eileen, for helping me bring Leo and his family to life. The book is much stronger because of her input. I'd also like to thank my agent, Deidre, whose guidance and expertise helped me find a perfect home for the Perconti family and their friends. Then there is the Inkheart and Sirens and Scribes writer groups. It's hard to believe that I've known some of these lovely ladies for almost a decade. Where has the time gone? You all make the journey a little bit brighter. Thank you.

I'd be remiss if I didn't give a shout-out to my fabulous readers' group, who helped me brainstorm a bunch of details in Leo and Karin's world. I'm not going to tell you which items they contributed. Those "Easter Eggs" are placed in the story so that, when found, those awesome ladies know how much they are appreciated.

I'd like to thank my BFF and writer friend Lauren Hawkeye, who manages to keep me writing through the bad times, and is the first to congratulate me in the good times. I can safely say that I wouldn't be where I am today if it wasn't for her.

Finally, I'd like to thank my family. When I get play-dates mixed up, forget to cook a meal, or occasionally show up in the school yard in my sweatpants, they tend to take it in stride. They know better than anyone the highs and lows of being a writer, and their love and support means more to me than they'll ever know.

Chapter 1

Karin Norell shoved the cleaning cart inside the elevator and pushed the button in rapid succession to close the door. Once the doors closed and she slid her card for the pent-house suite, she slumped against the mirrored wall and let out a long breath.

Only twelve more weeks to go. Karin had to last just a few short months before she obtained the work credit needed for her hospitality degree. The second she finished her required internship, she was going to quit this lousy job and never think about the Palazzo again.

As the numbers above the door lit up, she pulled out her hotel-issued cell phone and dialed the housekeeping manager, Wes. It went directly to voice mail. *Lovely.* Sometimes Karin wondered why she even bothered. The owner of the ritzy Boston hotel, Marco Perconti, had gotten the entire staff phones to help improve communication. Since no one bothered *answering* theirs, the project had been a total waste of money.

Not that wasting money was anything new to the Perconti family. If the tabloids were correct, all six siblings had been fed with silver spoons since birth and wouldn't know a budget if it walked up and bit them in the ass. Just last week the gossip magazine *Whispers* photographed

Marco with two Kennedy cousins and some young, hot actress at the exclusive restaurant Magnifique. According to the article, that meal cost more money than Karin had in student loans.

"Damn it, Wes, where are you?" Karin asked after the voice mail tone. She leaned her head back against the mirror and held the phone a few inches from her mouth. "Dante got drunk again last night and trashed the ninth floor. 'The General' will be arriving soon, so we need to clean up the penthouse suite, stat." "The General" was what Marco had called his older brother, Leo, during an interview in a men's magazine last year. It was meant as a joke, referring to how Leo micromanaged the company and Marco's personal life, but the tone was less than flattering. The press picked up on the tension between the brothers and so had the staff. It wasn't long before each Perconti sibling had their own unique nickname.

"Voice mailbox, full," a mechanical voice responded.

Karin rolled her eyes at the loud beep and shoved the phone in her pocket. She loved Wes like a brother, but the man was a total mess. His personal life had more drama than a soap opera, and he preferred to flirt with upper management rather than do his job. Most of the time Wes's behavior was only a minor irritation, since his flirting often got the staff perks like fresh coffee and a new microwave in the break room. Today, it was just one more thing that made her want to scream and hit something, hard.

The entire hotel staff was on edge. Leo was arriving within the hour to ensure that everything was on track for their youngest sister's upcoming wedding. Karin understood that all of their jobs depended on impressing the oldest Perconti brother, but a little extra cleaning wasn't going to reverse years of neglect in a couple of days. Nevertheless, Marco was making everyone work overtime so that the hotel could put its best foot forward.

This morning the staff had received yet another order in a long line of outrageous demands. Marco had insisted on giving Leo the Palazzo's only penthouse suite for his stay. It didn't matter that the room had already been booked, or that Leo and Marco's younger brother Dante liked to crash there after drinking all of the top-shelf liquor in the hotel bar. They had to make sure that the suite was spotless for Leo's arrival. Normally this wouldn't have been a problem, but half of the housekeeping staff had called in sick that morning, and Wes was currently M.I.A. Since it was Karin's job to see that everything ran smoothly during Leo's stay, she was forced to leave her data-entry desk job to clean the three-bedroom, twenty-five-hundred-square-foot suite alone.

Some internship. While double-checking inventory spreadsheets wasn't her dream job, she didn't exactly want to clean other people's filth, either. Karin had hoped that this internship would give her some experience in management, but so far it seemed as if all she ever did was grunt work.

The elevator doors opened, revealing the large, open living area of the penthouse suite.

"Oh, fuck me." A tightness formed in the back of her throat as the stench of bad cheese and stale booze hit her full-on. She placed the back of her hand over her mouth as she surveyed the damage.

The beautiful, stately suite was in shambles. Empty liquor bottles and crushed take-out boxes littered the cream carpeting. The gold-toned couch and chairs were tipped over and half the decanters on the mahogany bar were smashed. Bar utensils were dangling from the ceiling fan and the poker from the large stone fireplace had been thrown through the glass of the television screen. The balcony doors were open and bedsheets hung over the lounge chairs and railings. The cool, late-April breeze did nothing to subdue the funky scent. It made her want to gag.

"Damn Perconti brothers." Tears filled her eyes as she picked up a fallen painting of a girl in a blue dress sitting on a swing. The late-afternoon sun shone on the picture highlighting the ringlets in her hair and her brilliant smile. She looked so free and uninhibited.

"That was my favorite painting," Karin muttered to herself. She had often daydreamed of being carefree like the girl in the picture. It had been a long time since she had been genuinely happy. After struggling on her own for so long, she had forgotten what it felt like.

"Hey, darlin'." Wes's voice drifted up from somewhere behind her. "I only got half your message, but—oh, damn." He came to a halt beside her. His long, blond locks fell into his eyes as he put his arm up to his nose. "What's that smell?"

"Bad cheese," Karin said as she lowered her hand. "Dante has been drunk dialing Sabrina's and ordering takeout again."

Wes let out a long breath as he rested his forearms on the top of his head. After a long moment, he relaxed his features and the playfulness in his bright blue eyes returned. "Dante sure knows how to throw a party, doesn't he?"

"That's putting it mildly." Karin wrinkled her nose and picked up one of the take-out boxes. "Just once I wish he'd fall asleep instead of ordering everything from that Italian place just to hear his ex's voice. He never eats what he orders, and it smells foul the next day." She dumped the leftover lasagna into the garbage.

Wes lowered his hands and straightened his white polo shirt over his torso. "Marco shouldn't let him drink so much. He knows how emotional Dante gets after a couple of Negronis."

"Are you kidding? They're Percontis. Restraint isn't part

of their vocabulary." Karin looked around the room as hopelessness and anger filled every crevice of her body. "Where have you been, anyway? I called you three times."

Wes picked up pieces of a broken decanter and winked at her. "Oh, sweetheart, you know I'm not one to kiss and tell." He dragged his gaze over her disheveled white blouse, black pencil skirt, and messy bun. "But maybe for you I'll make an exception. You look like you could use a good erotic story."

"Wes!" Karin smiled despite her frustration. They had met when Karin did her internship rotation with the housekeeping staff and had been close friends ever since. There was something about Wes's Southern charm and boyish good looks that always seemed to make her relax. Three years ago, he'd moved up north to be with his boyfriend. After the relationship had run its course, Wes decided to stay in Boston, saying that the New England weather suited him. He never spoke of his family or friends from his native Alabama, and Karin didn't press. She was just happy to have a friend in this place. She had tried to strike a conversation with other staff members, but had yet to find one she got along with as well as Wes.

He smirked. "You need some good ol'-fashioned sex, girlfriend. A little tickle with a pickle will do wonders for your soul." He dumped the broken glass in the garbage. "And a tumble with a Perconti brother will leave a smile on your face for weeks. I should know." He winked and made his way over to the cleaning cart.

Karin stared at her friend. "Dante?"

Wes scowled and waved his hand at her, making him look more like a teenager than a man in his mid-twenties. "Darling, give me a little credit. Even if the man wasn't as straight as an arrow, he just broke up with his girlfriend. He's still in mourning."

"I don't understand. If it's not Dante, then . . ." She

gasped and put her hand over her mouth. "Oh my God, Wes. Marco's our boss. You could get fired for that."

Wes chuckled as he searched through the items on the cleaning cart. "Don't worry your pretty little head about it. Marco's like me and lives in the moment. It's all in good fun with no strings attached."

Karin pulled the cleaning cart away from him, forcing Wes to meet her gaze. "You have to stop this. Marco is a billionaire who likes shiny new toys and right now you are the shiniest. He uses people. These things never end well for common, working-class people like us. Trust me." Memories of her former supervisor flashed through her mind. According to him, Karin was good enough to fuck, but not for anything else. She should have known better than to fall for the rich, spoiled man's charm. While she didn't love him, she had hoped to be treated with respect. His careless disregard for her feelings had made her feel less than human. Karin had put up with it for a while, but eventually his lack of common decency had become too much. On impulse, she'd stormed into her former boss's office and quit her job. It was hell trying to find another internship, and the delay had set her entire degree program on hold.

She cared about Wes and wanted to stop him from making the same mistakes she had.

Wes straightened and put his hands on his hips. "I know what I'm doing."

"But—"

"We have an understanding. It's only a little fun, nothing more." He lowered his arms and considered her for a moment. "Marco could help put a smile on your face, too. I'm sure of it." He flashed her a knowing grin and winked.

Karin frowned as she turned her attention to the cleaning cart. "No, thanks. I'd much rather have sex with you."

Wes widened his eyes and straightened to his full six-foot height. "Well, well, Ms. Norell. I had no idea that I was on your list of potentials."

"Wes—"

He waggled his eyebrows suggestively. "It's okay, honey. I know you frown on fun of any kind."

"Excuse me?" She put her hands on her hips. "I'll have you know that I *love* to have fun."

He raised his brows at her. "Really? When was the last time you had sex?"

To people like Wes and Marco, sex was a game, nothing more. Karin used to feel the same, but after the incident with her boss last year, she'd started being more careful. No longer did she have sex for physical pleasure. She was saving herself for something more meaningful.

And look where all of this holding out has gotten you. She was now alone and depressed. Karin wished that she could let go and enjoy herself like Wes did. Sex used to be fun and relaxing. Without it, she was stressed and irritable all of the time. It would be a dream to just give in to pleasure and not worry about her job, classes, or bills for a little while.

Maybe it was time to stop being such a hopeless romantic and have a little fun. Unfortunately, she didn't have time to find a partner to help her out. Her work hours had already doubled, and they'd stay that way until after the big Perconti wedding.

She waved her hand in the air between them. "Enough about sex. Just help me clean up this mess, okay? Marco's brother is supposed to be here any minute."

" 'The General' is already here." Wes took back the cart and looked through the cleaning supplies.

"What?"

"He came in a few minutes ago." Wes picked up the

mop and bucket. "The man is more gorgeous in person than on television, but also has a good dose of that classic Perconti temper."

"How do you know?"

"He was roaring so loud for Marco that it shook the chandelier in the foyer. I'm surprised you didn't hear it." He shrugged. "Anyway, I told Marco to keep him busy while we tidied up."

"You gave an order to our boss?" She shook her head as she remembered Wes's earlier confession. If Wes and Marco were sleeping together, then chances were that Wes could get away with things the rest of the staff couldn't. "Forget it. Just hurry."

Karin worked in the living room, while Wes started in the bathroom. They cleaned in comfortable silence until two of Wes's housekeeping team showed up to help. Between the four of them, they had the place put back together and aired out within a couple of hours.

"The suite doesn't have a television anymore, but at least it has curtains," Wes said after he dismissed his staff to attend to other duties. "I guess it doesn't matter. If 'the General' is anything like his brothers, he won't be watching much television, anyway." Wes winked at her as he loaded up the cart. "Now, let's get out of here before the big bad Perconti brothers show up." Wes made a face and shuddered.

Karin chuckled and shook her head as she followed Wes to the main elevators. Before she could push the button, a loud beep echoed through the foyer and the light above the door blinked on.

Karin's whole body froze with fear. "Shit, they're coming."

"What are we going to do?" Wes asked.

Karin ran through the floor plan in her mind. "There's

the service elevator off the office area in back. It goes down into the laundry room in the basement."

"I thought it was broken."

She shook her head and bit her nail. "Facilities fixed it yesterday. At least, I think they did."

"I hope you're right. When I left those two downstairs, they looked angry enough to start throwing punches at each other. I think the only thing keeping them in line was the reporter from *Whispers* peppering them with questions."

"Is that gossip queen still at the hotel?"

"Yeah. She seems determined to get some dirt on the Perconti wedding for her column. Wouldn't it be incredible if she found something? That family is just full of secrets, I know it."

Karin rolled her eyes. "You need to stop reading those tabloids."

"You need to start. How else are we going to find dirt on our bosses if it's not from the media?"

Karin listened to Wes go on about the benefits of reading tabloid magazines as they wheeled the cart into the office area in the back of the penthouse and pushed the service elevator button. As the doors opened, Wes's boyish features hardened. "I forgot my cell phone."

"You what?"

"My cell phone. It's still in the bathroom on the other side of the suite." His features twisted into pure panic. "We can't leave it there. I need it." He started to turn the cart around, but Marco's thick Italian accent rose up from the other room, freezing him in his tracks.

"Leave it," Karin said. "Remember what Marco said this morning about us staying out of Leo's way?" Leo enjoyed his privacy and lacked the patience of his younger brother. Rumor had it that Leo once fired a bartender for not knowing his favorite brand of scotch, and a concierge for booking an important dinner at the wrong restaurant. No one wanted to cross paths with the oldest Perconti brother and risk messing up and losing their jobs.

Wes rubbed his forehead and shifted his feet as Marco's voice became louder. "Fuck. I can't leave that work phone, Karin. It's got private stuff on it."

"You keep personal things on your hotel phone?"

He flashed her an angry look. "Not normally, no. Let's just say that if that phone is found, it wouldn't take Sherlock Holmes to know it was mine." He ran his hand over his face. "And then everyone will know how I got Marco to sign off on a new coffee machine in the break room."

"You have pictures of yourself and Marco on the work phone?" Karin widened her eyes in shock.

"He likes to be photographed. I was going to use my personal phone, but I was running late this morning, and left it on the kitchen coun—"

"Are you insane?"

"I was going to delete them, but *someone* needed me to help her clean the penthouse suite." He peeked around the corner as the voices got louder. "What am I going to do, Karin?" he whispered. "They can't see me. And if Marco's brother sees the pictures on that phone . . ." Wes shuddered. "I'm a dead man."

Karin bit her already-too-short nail as footsteps sounded on the hardwood floors. "Go," she said after a moment. "Take the cart downstairs. I'll go back for the phone."

"I can't ask you to do that."

"It's okay. I'm much smaller than you, so there are more places for me to hide." She grinned and motioned to her five-foot-three frame. "Just get out of here and send the service elevator back up so I can make a quick escape."

He hesitated, but then became resolved as the voices grew louder. "Bless your heart. I don't know what to say."

"Say 'thank you.'"

He beamed. "Thank you, darlin'." He kissed her cheek. "I owe you one." He kissed her other cheek. "Maybe two."

"Now go." She shooed Wes and the cleaning cart onto the elevator and breathed a sigh of relief as the doors closed.

The voices seemed to stay down the hall, thank goodness. Karin tried to remember the layout of the suite. She had to walk through the living area to get to the bathroom and the phone. Unless she could make herself invisible, she wasn't going to be able to pass by unnoticed.

Her heartbeat quickened as she weighed her options. If she left, then the cell phone would most certainly be discovered. If Leo saw those pictures, her best friend would be fired. Marco had pulled Karin from her regular office duties and given her the responsibility of making sure Leo's stay went off without a hitch. The months leading up to the Perconti wedding were where Karin would put months of learning to the test. If Leo found anything unsatisfactory, Marco would hold her personally responsible and report her failings to her advisor. Karin's degree depended on keeping the grumpiest Perconti sibling happy.

If she snuck back in, at least there was a chance that both she and Wes could emerge from this incident unscathed.

She crept to the office doorway and peered around the corner. Marco stood in the middle of the living room, waving his arms and talking. His medium-length hair hung in a mess around his face and his suit looked disheveled. Worry lines framed his gray eyes as he pressed his lips into a tight, thin line. Karin had never seen the suave man—nicknamed "Casanova"—look so out of sorts before.

A second man lounged on one of the couches with his feet up on the coffee table. *Leo.* Karin steeled her jaw as she thought about how hard she'd scrubbed polish into that coffee table only an hour ago. Clearly, none of the Perconti brothers had any regard for the furniture, or her hard work.

Marco turned his back to her and Karin knew that she had to move if she ever hoped to leave the suite unseen. She pushed aside her frustration and tiptoed her way through the living room. Luckily, the furniture was arranged to make a natural barrier between the comfy living space and the elevators. There was plenty of space for her to hide as she made her way across the carpeted floor. She hid first behind the chair, then the sofa, as she made her way to the bathroom to get the phone.

"You should have been honest with me, Marco." The commanding voice vibrated through the room and caused her to pause behind the couch. She looked up at the long, tanned fingers draped over the upholstery.

"God, Leo, it's been a nightmare," Marco said as he paced in front of the couch. "And it wasn't like you were accessible these past two years. You were with Gio in Milan—"

"Mother's idea. She still thinks that Gio will make it as a model."

"Will he?" Marco turned to face Leo, forcing Karin to crouch lower against the leather couch.

Leo let out a long sigh. "He might, if he focused his energy. Right now he's too busy throwing lavish parties and missing appointments to get very far."

"Such a waste. We could really use that money." Marco loosened the tie on his suit and took a large gulp of his cocktail.

"I couldn't very well order him to stop modeling without telling both him and Mother about the company's finances being in the red."

"You should just be honest with her."

"No." There was a note of finality in Leo's voice that gave Karin goose bumps. "She has been through enough."

"It's been years since Father—"

"I'll deal with it." Leo raised his hand and made a weary-looking gesture in the air. "Meanwhile, you need to get a grip on yourself."

"This hotel is not your concern. Father gave it to *me*. All I need is a little money to help fix it up."

"Good Lord, Marco, listen to yourself." Leo stood and walked over to the bar, giving Karin a clear look at his profile. "You may run this hotel, but I run the company that owns it. Mismanagement not only reflects poorly on you, but myself and the rest of the family. It is my responsibility that the Perconti name continues to be respected, not made fun of in some two-dollar tabloid."

"I swear to you, with a little more money—"

Leo held up his hand, cutting off his brother's words. Marco pulled his tie loose as his older brother moved toward the bar.

As Karin watched, she noticed that Leo was much leaner and more handsome than his younger brother. While Marco's face was round and smooth, his brother's was harder, more angular. His jet-black hair was trimmed short in a professional business cut. The touch of gray above his ears and the day-old stubble along his square jaw added to his commanding presence. She could see why Marco had told the paparazzi that his relationship with his brother was complicated. Leo's presence seemed to fill up the room. It was commanding and hypnotic. Karin was drawn to him and afraid of him at the same time. She found it difficult to look away.

Leo used the metal ice tongs to drop ice into his glass, then slipped his long, tapered fingers around the decanter as he poured himself a scotch. The man practically radiated testosterone. Karin held her breath and slid her gaze over his tailored suit, appreciating how the gray fabric hugged his muscular frame. The knot in his maroon tie had been loosened and the silky fabric hung loosely around his neck. The top few buttons of his white dress shirt had come undone, giving her a peek at the smooth, tanned skin of his chest.

Karin's heartbeat thudded in her ears as Leo brought his drink to his lips. Marco had told her Leo's favorite brand of scotch, but had she gotten the right year? A small twitch of his lips as he lowered the glass told her that she had succeeded. For the moment, her internship was safe.

As Karin slowly let the air out of her lungs, she noticed that there was something rather erotic about the way the older Perconti brother caressed the barware. Heat slid along her center as she imagined those long fingers caressing her pale skin, awakening parts of her that had been asleep for far too long.

"I can't give you any more money," Leo said as he stared at the contents in his glass. "There's nothing left."

"What do you mean, there's nothing left?" Marco closed the distance between them. "I thought that there were savings—"

"Lawyers' fees." Leo turned and faced his brother. His eyes were hard and his jaw set, as if he was daring Marco to challenge his authority.

"That bitch," Marco spat. "You should go public with whatever she has over you. That woman is killing us."

Leo glanced down at his glass. "I know." He swirled the contents around in his tumbler, but didn't drink. "I can't go public, however. She would ruin us."

"She's already ruining us."

Karin had no idea what they were talking about, but it didn't matter. She needed to get out of there before someone noticed her. Instead of going after the phone, she was crouched behind the sofa, drooling over the eldest Perconti brother and listening to a private conversation. Just the sound of Leo's voice made her body tight and ready. Perhaps Wes was right in saying she needed to get laid. Clearly, finding release by her own hand wasn't fulfilling her needs.

Focus. She needed to get out of there before she got in trouble. Right now, both brothers' backs were turned to her. She wouldn't have a better opportunity to get to the bathroom undetected than right now. Karin inched her way toward the bathroom as Leo spoke.

"Forget about her," Leo said. "All we can do is control our spending and hope that this wedding goes off without a hitch. With Arianna marrying that aviation tycoon, we'll be able to unite our companies and offer vacation packages that will bring in more income. The packages will undercut Stone's discounts and that bastard will finally get what he deserves."

Everyone knew of the famous feud between Leo and Jason Stone. Not only were they number one and two in *Whisper* magazine's top eligible bachelors list, but their businesses were the top two hotel empires in the world. When Jason learned that he came in second on both lists, he made a very public announcement that his goal was to better Leo both personally and professionally. Over the past few months, he had been rolling out a new publicity campaign that had left the people at both *Whispers* and *Travelers* magazines speculating that he might succeed.

Jason had begun offering bulk discounts to Web sites in order to gain customers and then kept them through their loyalty program. They had managed to steal approximately one-third of the Palazzo's repeat customers. Leo had been asked by *Travelers* magazine what Perconti Enterprises was going to do to stay competitive, and Leo had said that he was working on something that would please even the most finicky tourist. Karin wondered if the merging of families and offering vacation packages was what Leo had in mind.

The reporters downstairs would pay a lot of money for information like that. Not that Karin would tell them. No, she knew that if she told the reporters what the Percontis were planning, she'd make some fast money, but no one would trust her again. More than anything she wanted to run a hotel someday. It wouldn't be wise to start burning bridges before she even earned her degree.

"We'll be ready for the wedding," Marco replied. "I promise."

Leo placed his drink on the bar. "This hotel has to be perfect, Marco. Not just for Mother and Arianna, but for the press. Those reporters can't see the mess you've made of this place."

"What do you mean, mess?"

Leo grabbed his glass and faced his brother. "This place is an embarrassment to the Perconti name. While you've been spending your time partying, the hotel has been spiraling out of control."

Karin snuck into the bathroom, grabbed the phone, and paused. She peeked around the corner. Perhaps she could stay a few more minutes. It would be nice to see Marco get reprimanded for once. It was about time he got a taste of his own medicine.

"Leo, don't say that." Marco put his drink down on the coffee table next to the coaster, making Karin grind her teeth in frustration. If that glass left a mark on the mahogany wood, there was going to be hell to pay.

"Why not? It's true." Leo turned away from Marco and took a long sip from his glass. "No one likes to do any work around here."

Amen. Karin clutched the phone closer and took a good look at the handsome Perconti patriarch. His hazel eyes were hard, but they also held a weariness that Karin could easily identify with. As he continued to talk to Marco, Karin was drawn to Leo's rich baritone voice, falling deeper and deeper under his spell.

Marco placed his hand over his chest. "Leo, my staff has been working double shifts and—"

"Please, Marco. Spare me the sob story. This wedding is much too important for such theatrics. *Our sister* is much too important." He ran his fingers over his stubble and then pulled his hand away in disgust. "Until we can get this hotel running in the black, I'm taking charge."

"Perhaps if that woman wasn't bleeding us dry—"

"I don't want to hear it." Leo put up his hand, stopping Marco's words. "There's nothing that can be done, so we have to work around it."

"Leo, you're being unfair."

"Am I? You're the one who has been spending the company money on lavish outings with the Kennedy cousins—"

"I have not—"

"Don't act so shocked, brother. It's all over the tabloids."

Marco swallowed and fisted his hands. "That was a special occasion."

"The company credit card says otherwise." He held up his hand as Marco stepped forward. "I don't care what you have been doing. The point is you haven't been focusing on the business. Now Stone has managed to steal away our once-loyal customers. If things continue like this, the Palazzo will be bankrupt by the end of the year."

No. Karin put her hand to her mouth to cover her gasp. They couldn't go bankrupt. She had planned on leveraging this internship into a job once she graduated. All of her hard work would be for nothing if all of her references were no longer employed.

"You worry too much," Marco said.

"You don't worry enough."

Marco let out a long breath and pushed his hair from his face. "You need a break. Arianna said that you've been traveling for six weeks straight."

"Someone has to look after this mess," Leo muttered.

"You're worn out, brother." Marco pulled out his personal cell from an inside jacket pocket. "I'm well connected, as you know. With one phone call, I can get you someone to help relieve some of your stress," he offered. "Here's one. This woman likes to take charge."

"No." Leo's hazel eyes hardened as he narrowed his gaze. "No women."

Marco raised his brows. "Okay, then." He flipped through his phone. "If you prefer men, I know someone who—"

"Marco . . ." Leo closed his eyes and pinched the bridge of his nose. "No men, either."

Marco considered him for a moment. "A more submissive girl, then. I know one who is short, blonde, and eager to please. Some amazing sex with an experienced woman will—"

"I said no." Leo opened his eyes and lowered his hand. Karin saw the frustration flash through his features. "Marco, I really need to rest. I have a meeting tomorrow morning with my linguist, and—"

"You're not still trying to sound American, are you?"

"Americans spend the most money, and they're more comfortable around people who sound like them. It's in our best interests to assimilate as much as possible. You were supposed to take lessons as well."

"Yes, I know, but I've been busy—"

Leo held up his hand, stopping Marco's words. "I'm too tired to talk about this right now. If you don't mind . . ." Leo waved his hand toward the elevators.

"I'm going." Marco pushed some buttons on his phone.

"I'll send up the blonde for you, brother. Just give her a chance. That's all I'm saying."

Leo fisted his hands. "You need to stop spending so much time looking for a prostitute and spend a little more time fixing up this hotel."

"They're not whores, they're friends—"

"You keep interesting friends, brother. They might not be whores in the classic sense, but they are all using you to get something they want. Take the Kennedy cousins, for example—"

"I thought we might need the political connections." Marco slid his phone into his pocket. "And political connections aren't cheap."

"And the reporter? The police chief's daughter?"

Marco shrugged. "You never know when you might need to pull in a favor."

"I fail to see how that actress could possibly help—" Leo waved his hand in the air. "That is not important. What is important is that these outings stop and your focus switches to fixing this hotel. We won't need any connections if the building crumbles from disrepair."

"But—"

"Enough. No more money will be spent on these . . . connections." Anger sliced through Leo's features, causing Karin to move deeper into the shadows. The man looked positively venomous. There was something about the way he spoke and carried himself that suggested that this man was used to having his orders carried out. Karin guessed that not many people besides Marco questioned Leo's authority and hearing him put her boss in his place sent tendrils of heat sliding through her core.

Then the anger was gone, replaced by a weariness that reminded Karin of how she felt that morning when she learned that half her staff had taken the day off. "In the morning, I'm going to go over all of the Palazzo's financial statements from the past two years," he said.

Marco stopped in the doorway and stared at his brother. "But that would take days to pull together."

Leo narrowed his gaze. "My point, exactly. The squandering of our family money has gone on long enough. Tomorrow, we shall set out to make things right."

"But—"

"Good-bye, Marco."

Pain flashed over Marco's features before he schooled them into an expressionless mask. Karin didn't know when she had seen him look so upset. "Of course, brother. Father might have left me in charge of the Palazzo, but father left *you* in charge of Perconti Enterprises." Marco pushed the elevator button and glanced back at his brother. "But then again, he always did like you best, didn't he?"

The elevator rang and the doors swung open. Marco strode into the elevator and pressed the panel. The sound of the doors closing echoed through the silent penthouse.

"Damn," Leo muttered and downed the rest of his glass. "Political connections." He shook his head and turned toward the bar. "They're all playing him for a fool."

Oh shit. Karin had been so caught up in the exchange she'd forgotten to move. How was she going to get across the living area and back to the service elevator without him noticing?

Leo let out a frustrated growl and gripped his tumbler until his knuckles turned white. Tension filled the room, and Karin held her breath.

"Everyone in this family is so self-centered. None of them can see what their selfishness is doing to the company." He tightened his jaw. "Or to me."

Karin thought he was going to throw his glass, but he didn't. Instead, he placed it on the bar and pulled a small pill bottle out of his suit jacket pocket. Karin tried to focus on the writing, but couldn't make out the words. Leo placed the bottle on the bar next to the ice bucket and pinched the bridge of his nose. Dismissing the bottle, he let out a long breath as he refilled his drink and made his way toward the bathroom. *Toward her.*

Shit, shit, shit. Karin glanced around the bathroom. There was nowhere to hide. She clutched the cell phone to her chest and squeezed behind the door. Leo breezed past her into the room and turned on the hot water in the large tub. Steam rolled up from the marble basin, filling the small space. Karin held her breath as Leo undid the buttons of his suit coat and shrugged it onto the floor.

He's undressing. Karin tried to force her muscles to move, but they refused to listen. She watched as Leo placed his glass of scotch on the floor and then peeled off his layers of clothing, one by one.

For once, Karin didn't mind the mess. Wes was right, the Perconti brothers were sinfully handsome, and the oldest brother was the best looking of the lot. His tan stretched up his muscular arms, around his perfectly formed shoulders, and down his lean, angular back. Even his firm, tight ass was a golden color, putting delicious thoughts of Leo sunbathing nude in her mind.

She could easily picture his sleek body stretching out on some Italian beach, soaking up the sun. Karin wondered what it would feel like to press up against such a flawless physique and feel those solid hips between her legs.

She dropped her gaze down his torso as he turned toward the marble tub. Dark hair dotted his chest and lower abdomen, drawing her attention to his long, thick cock. Karin's heartbeat drummed in her ears as he stepped into the bath. Something fluttered inside her as she imagined crawling in alongside him and running soap along his athletic frame.

Oh God, she needed to focus. It had been far too long since she'd had sex, even longer since she'd had great sex. Looking at the grace and muscular beauty of Leo Perconti's body, she knew that a night with him would go a long way toward alleviating all of the stress that had been building up inside of her.

A dull ache formed between her thighs as she imagined straddling his hips and taking his hard cock deep inside her channel. She reached down her torso and pressed her hand against her mound and imagined his muscular body pressing up against hers. Embarrassment at her boldness heated her cheeks.

She bit back a groan of disappointment as Leo slid under the warm bathwater. His back was once again facing her and she knew that if she wanted to save her job, then she had to get out of there, fast.

Enough daydreaming. It was time to go. After one long, wistful glance at Leo, she slipped out from behind the door and edged out into the hallway.

"Stop."

Karin froze as the thick Italian accent rose up from the tub.

"Come here."

Karin turned back to the bathroom, unsure of what to do. She judged the distance from her spot to the elevator and wondered if she should make a run for it. Her escape depended on Wes having sent the elevator back up for her. If she had to wait for the doors to open, then she'd be caught. If Leo found cleaning staff in his room, she could get in trouble. Could she trust Wes to send the elevator back for her?

"I know Marco sent you."

Karin blinked. "Excuse me?"

Leo chuckled. "There's no need to be coy with me. I

know all about my brother's 'connections.' If the man
spent as much effort fixing up this hotel as he did bed-
ding socialites, we wouldn't be in this mess." He raised
his glass to his lips. "So tell me, are you the pushy one, or
the one who was willing to please?"

"I'm sorry, I . . ." Did Leo think she was one of the
socialite friends Marco had offered him earlier? She
scrunched her nose in disgust. She wasn't an empty-headed
socialite. And yet, there was something rather appealing
about the idea of pleasing him.

"Don't tell me you're a man," he said.

"I—no." She glanced back at Leo's long, lean form
as it lounged in the tub. Wes's words floated through
her mind. *You need some sex, girlfriend. Loosen up.* "Not
a guy."

"I thought as much. You don't sound like a man. Come
here and let me see if my brother's friends are as beautiful as he claims."

Leo Perconti was brazen. She should feel offended, but
that voice did things to her body that made her want more.
Karin wanted to obey his command and see where things
led. Besides, Leo didn't ever have to know her real identity. It was the perfect opportunity for a glorious night of
passion without consequence.

No, there was one consequence, a huge one. Leo was her
boss's boss. If he found out that she'd tried to deceive him,
then he'd take it out on Marco. Not only would she be fired,
but Marco could and probably would make the entire staff
suffer for her indiscretion.

But then again, wasn't she in charge of making sure Leo
had a pleasant stay? If the night went well and he was in a
better mood around his brother, then she would have done
her job. It wasn't like they'd be constantly running into
each other. The staff was supposed to stay out of sight as

much as possible. If by chance they should see each other again, she could always play ignorant. No one would have to know what had happened in this hotel room except her.

Karin looked from the hallway to the bathroom and back again. All she had to do was accept the night for what it was—pure physical bliss. No strings attached. If she could get away with this . . . it would be one hell of a night.

Resolved, Karin pocketed Wes's cell phone and straightened her skirt. She paused over the hem as a new revelation hit her. *Shit, my uniform.* Leo would mark her as an employee as soon as he saw her.

Perhaps it could be part of the game. She could tell Leo that she'd needed the uniform to get past the paparazzi downstairs undetected. All she had to do was come across confident in her abilities.

Confidence. Ever since she had caught her former boss fucking a politician in his office, Karin's confidence had remained hidden. She wasn't sure if she had it in her to pull something like this off.

"Are you coming?" Leo asked. "Or am I going to have to come out and get you?"

"No, I'm coming." She could do this, she just needed to stop overthinking.

Didn't Wes just accuse her of being too serious? This night was about de-stressing and relaxing.

Karin cleared her throat and adjusted her bra. Her breasts were on the small side of normal, but hopefully they'd be enough to please him. She undid the top few buttons of her blouse, revealing the upper curve of her breasts. After pinching her cheeks, she hid her shaking hands behind her back and concentrated on swaying her hips as she moved closer to the large, marble tub. *Here goes nothing.*

Chapter 2

Leo heard her footsteps on the white tiled floor behind him. The soft clicking of the woman's shoes on the tile stirred something deep inside, something he had buried years ago. The women he had bedded over the past year had always wanted to be taken hard and fast. While Leo didn't mind losing himself in a frenzied fuck, he preferred to take things slow. Tonight was different, however. The clicking of those shoes hinted at a woman who might like drawing out tension as much as he did. God, how he had missed the foreplay and exploration part of sex. He didn't realize how much until just this moment.

His cock swelled and he took a long sip of his scotch in an effort to gain control over his rising libido.

Perhaps Marco was right. A good fuck would go a long way to lighten his mood. He was just so damn tired of holding everything together. It seemed like the harder he tried, the closer things came to falling apart at the seams. He needed to numb his mind with a little erotic distraction for a while. Let off some steam. Then tomorrow he could go downstairs and start to fix the colossal mess his brother had made of their flagship hotel.

Leo set his drink down on the side of the tub as the woman came into view. *Well, now.* This was unexpected.

The woman had a beautiful, round face and creamy skin. Unfortunately, the drab hotel uniform covered most of her curves.

Hotel uniform? He raised his brows as he dragged his gaze up to her face.

She fidgeted with the sleeves of her blouse. "I know what you're thinking. I had to dress like one of the maids to get past the paparazzi downstairs." She offered him a shy smile. "I didn't want any of them to think that you were calling up women to your room."

Leo nodded his approval and noticed the tightness around her eyes. Interesting. He dragged his gaze down over her trembling chin and smooth, slender neck, then lingered at the swell of breasts peeking out from underneath her uniform. His stare must have been obvious, because she started to cover herself. At Leo's scowl, she returned her trembling hands to her sides.

Leo was pleased with his effect on her, but didn't want her to know that—at least, not yet. He wanted her to know that he was discerning, and in this moment, he was assessing her. He was the one with the power, the one in control. If this night was ever going to get off the ground, he had to make that point crystal clear.

He forced himself to keep his expression stern as he swept it down over her curvy hips and shapely thighs. He understood why Marco had sent her. Not only was this woman beautiful, but she didn't steel her jaw or look down at him over her nose. She was so different from the women Leo typically bedded. It was . . . refreshing.

"Turn around." Leo's voice sounded gruff to his own ears. This woman was affecting him more than he realized. Every inch of him was hard and needy. Perhaps Marco was right in his assessment. If this little woman was as submissive as her mannerisms suggested, then a night with her would go a long way to ease the tension of the last few weeks.

The woman hesitated at his command, as if unsure. A light pink stained her milky-white cheeks. She was embarrassed, he realized. Embarrassed and uncomfortable.

This knowledge captivated him. She looked like a fragile flower. He suspected under the right hand, she'd blossom into something quite beautiful.

Leo lifted his brow. "Having second thoughts?"

"No, sir. It's just . . ." She shook her head and started to turn in a slow circle.

Sir. The word pleased him. It stirred something possessive inside and only captivated him more. He started to ask her name, but then stopped himself. It would be better if they didn't use names. Names would only lead to feelings and complications. Leo's life was complicated enough.

The thought of her calling him "sir" in the bedroom was almost too much. His cock thickened as he wondered if she liked bedroom games as much as he did.

Leo clamped down on his rising need as he dragged his gaze back up over her body as she finished her turn. He met her questioning gaze.

"Nice." Nice legs, nice ass, nice . . . everything. Leo steeled his jaw as desire shot straight through to his cock. *Down boy.* It had been so long since he'd had a decent fuck.

She studied him with those wide, innocent eyes. It took Leo a moment to realize that she was waiting for him to give the next order. How . . . refreshing. Every day he was engaged in some battle with the family business. It felt intensely satisfying to have someone so obedient.

"Take off your clothes."

She widened her eyes, drawing his attention to her long, thick lashes. "Excuse me?"

"You heard me." He took another long sip of his drink. He thought a friend of Marco's would be more than willing to strip naked in front of a man, especially a Perconti, but this one seemed to be embarrassed by the thought. Still, he rather liked the faint pink in her cheeks. It allowed him to fantasize that she was untouched.

Her hands shook as she reached for her shirt. This woman was good, real good. Leo almost believed that she had never done anything like this before. He'd have to remember to thank his brother tomorrow for such a rare gift.

"There's no need to be afraid, *cara*. We're alone here," he said.

She nodded and pulled her shirt over her head, giving Leo an eyeful of creamy skin. He suppressed a frown as her plain white sports bra came into view. This woman really got into her role.

"Why do you wear such things?"

"Such things?" Her voice sounded shaky and unsure.

Leo forced his voice to be gentler. "Plain undergarments. A woman as beautiful as you should be wearing beautiful things."

"Beautiful?"

"You know." He waved his hand in the air between them. "Black lace. Silk."

"I . . ." She swallowed, clearly at a loss for words.

Leo grunted and waved his glass of scotch in the air. "Continue." It didn't matter what the little maid had on under her clothes. It wouldn't be on her body for long, anyway.

The woman unzipped her skirt and pulled it slowly over her hips.

"*Mio Dio.*" Leo ran a hand over his face. The woman was going to kill him. She wore white briefs to match her bra. Normally, he'd scoff at such a sight, but on her, it looked strangely erotic. The whole outfit supported the fantasy that this woman was an innocent, plucked from society and reserved just for him. *His.* Possessiveness surged through his bloodstream and left him dizzy.

She hesitated. "Is there something wrong?"

"No, *cara,* continue." When she didn't move, he struggled to get his emotions under control. "Please."

She reached for her bra with trembling fingers. Leo frowned as he watched. Perhaps he was wrong in his initial assessment. A woman wouldn't be shaking that much without feeling at least a little vulnerable.

"Are you new to this, *cara*?"

She stopped with her arms crossed over her chest and her fingers over her straps. "I—no."

"Haven't you undressed in front of a man before?"

"Not exactly. I've only had sex in the dark."

He raised his brows. "Even with Marco?"

Her eyes widened in shock, but then she seemed to recover. "I haven't slept with Marco." She lifted her chin as she spoke.

"But you have been with a man before, yes?"

"It's—it's been a long time."

Interesting. She was not new to the pleasures of sex, but rather uncomfortable because so much time had passed. Such a shame for someone that beautiful to be so unsure of herself. This was something he must rectify.

"I see. Well, you have nothing to fear from me. Please, continue."

The woman slipped her bra over her head, exposing her full, round breasts. She started to cover them with her hands, but a sharp frown from him caused her to drop her arms to her sides. He stared at her erect nipples as his cock thickened beneath the bathwater.

"Those men were fools to allow such beauty to hide in the dark," he murmured.

She must have heard him, because the pink in her cheeks fanned out over her body, covering her from head to toe. Leo frowned as she moved to shut out the light.

"Stop."

Once again possessiveness surged through his body. "Leave it."

She hesitated, then pulled her hand away from the light switch. His cock twitched and Leo fought the urge to touch it and alleviate some of his ache.

"You should know, *cara,* that I prefer to watch a woman while I fuck her. The more pleasure she experiences, the more satisfaction I feel. Because of this, we will leave the light on as you undress. Do you understand?" She nodded, and he hid a smile. "Good. You may continue." He raised his scotch glass to his lips and realized that his fingers were shaking as much as hers had earlier. Frowning, he set the glass on the floor beside the bath.

Soon her panties pooled at her feet, revealing a patch of blond hair a shade darker than that on her head.

"You have a beautiful body. Do not be ashamed of it," he said.

"Thank you." She averted her gaze from his and nibbled her lower lip.

Leo wanted nothing more than to have her join him in the tub, but not like this. Her shyness sparked something nurturing in him. She'd thanked him for his compliment, but did she really *feel* beautiful? He suspected she didn't and he wanted to change that.

He tilted his head and tried to decide on the best course of action. Each possibility brought new erotic promises, and hardened him to the point of pain. Unfortunately, before he could act on any of his ideas, he needed to learn more about her.

He waved his hand in the air between them. "You may pleasure yourself."

"I may—what?" She straightened and widened her eyes.

He draped his arm over the side of the tub and ran his fingers lightly over the marble. "Have you ever touched yourself?" He slid his fingers up the smooth skin of her outer thigh, causing her to make a beautiful, throaty sound.

"I—yes."

"Well, do it again now, so I can see what pleases you."

She covered her breasts with one hand and her mound with the other. "I—I can't."

He held her gaze and raised his brows. "Can't what?"

"Can't—"

He nodded in satisfaction. "There is nothing to be afraid of, *cara*. I just want to watch and learn."

"I know." She had no idea what *cara* meant, but the way the word rolled off his tongue, with affection and a touch of reverence, made her entire body tingle.

He inched his fingers up toward her thigh. "Then what's holding you back?"

She shivered at his intimate touch. Leaning forward, Leo laced his fingers with hers and removed her hand from her mound.

"Do you like it when I touch you?" he asked.

"Yes." Her voice came out as barely more than a whisper.

Leo suppressed a smile of satisfaction as he stared at her damp curls. "I can see that you *do* like it." He nodded at the tub's marble edging. "Place your foot up on the rim over there and make yourself come for me."

She swallowed and moved to do as he asked. Leo held himself still as she locked her gaze with his and put her foot up on the edge. The scent of her sex rose up into the air, teasing his senses. Slowly, she covered both her breasts with her hands and started pinching her nipples.

"Ah, you like that, do you?" he asked after a moment.

"Yes." She closed her eyes and tugged on the tips, teasing them into sharp peaks. Leo settled himself in the tub and fixed his gaze on her fingers, studying every movement.

She was pleasuring herself on his orders. The realization of this made him smile, and turned his muscles to stone. His cock ached to get in on the action, and it took a great deal of effort to not drag her into the tub with him right then and there. Never before had a woman been so submissive to him. This little maid was so hot and eager for his instruction. It made Leo wonder what else she'd do to please him.

The possibilities almost made him come right then and there. Leo steeled his jaw and reached for his glass of scotch. If he had any hope of maintaining control over the situation, he was going to need some liquid strength.

This was insane. Karin could get in serious trouble for what she was doing, and yet the idea of giving in to his demand was dangerously sexy. He looked so handsome lying there in the large marble tub. Hot water and soap covered his body, hiding everything from mid-chest to his knees. She imagined crawling into the tub with him and sliding her wet skin over his.

"Yes, that's it. Now move your hand lower, *cara*," he commanded.

She loved his sexy Italian accent. That term of endearment rolled off his tongue and made her whole body ache with need. She closed her eyes and imagined that it was *his* hands stroking her breasts, *his* fingers teasing her nipples. He'd kiss her and torment her body in the tub, stroking her desire until her whole body shook with need. Then, only then, would he allow her to take him. He'd grab his shaft and inch the head of his erection between her folds, stretching her muscles and filling her with pleasure . . .

"Open your eyes."

She did as she was asked and met his stern, disapproving gaze.

"Now keep them open for me, sweetheart." He held her gaze as she massaged her own nipples. "As I said before, I don't play in the dark."

Karin shifted her gaze to the water, remembering the full length of his cock. She imagined it sliding into her opening, rubbing against her inner walls as it plunged deeper and deeper into her core.

Before she realized what she was doing, she let out a soft whimper of need.

"It will happen soon, *cara*," he said as he reached under the bathwater and stroked his cock. "I want you ready to take me first."

Karin dragged her gaze away from his hand and up to his face. Leo nodded his approval as she slid one of her hands down her torso.

"Yes," he murmured. "Just like that."

She watched his gaze darken as he followed her fingers. He might be the one giving orders, but she was the one in control. Seeing him react to her made her feel powerful and wanton. She slid her hand through her curls and between her legs. Leo shifted in the tub and Karin became aware that touching herself was making him incredibly aroused.

No one had never wanted to look at her body like this. Her past lovers had said that the dark had made it more exciting for them, but it always made Karin feel ashamed of her body. Now, after seeing Leo's reaction to her nakedness, Karin felt sexy and beautiful.

Slowly, she slid her fingers through her wet folds until she found her clit. She pressed it, then rubbed the bundle of nerves in a circular motion. Need fanned out through her system, causing her to groan. The world around her became fuzzy as she focused on her pleasure.

"That's it, *cara*. Now moan for me."

She heard the clinking of ice on glass as Leo raised his drink to his lips. She stared, transfixed, as she imagined that mouth on her nipples, teasing them into hard peaks. She whimpered as pressure built deep inside her core.

Satisfied, he placed the glass on the floor outside the tub and moved his hand back and forth underneath the soapy water. She imagined him stroking his length, becoming more and more aroused with each passing moment. He held her gaze and her throat became dry as his hazel eyes flashed gold.

"Now, sweetheart." His voice was like a thunder in the distance: low, powerful, and thick with emotion. "Show me how you come."

Karin moved away from her clit and thrust her fingers deep inside her channel. She imagined Leo's cock stretching her inner walls and filling her with pleasure. Again and again he'd push into her body, possessing her with each needy thrust.

Her breathing quickened as her movements became more urgent. She bit her lower lip and tugged on her nipple. The sparks of pain blended with the stretching sensation in her core and caused her to whimper.

"Faster." Leo moistened his lips and shifted once more in the tub. Was he becoming uncomfortable? Good. With each stroke, Karin's fear slipped away and something more primal and hungry took over. Her strokes became bolder, her touch more rough. A low, guttural moan escaped her lips.

"Good. Now let it all go for me, *cara*."

His words were like a knife, carving away the last of her inhibitions. She shifted her hand and rubbed her clit with her thumb as she plunged her fingers deeper into her channel. Her breathing came out in short, rough gasps as pressure built between her legs. She watched Leo's gaze drop and focus on her hand over her mound. She noticed that his hand clung to the side of the tub until his knuckles were white, and he had steeled his jaw so hard it looked like it was going to snap. The water in the tub moved as he stroked his shaft, lapping against the sides with a steady rhythm.

Karin let out a low moan and shivered. Soon she was moving her hips in time to her thrusts, her body reacting to her newfound confidence and pleasure.

Her cries became louder, her hands, rougher. Insecurity, frustration, and stress melted away until there was just this man and this moment. Karin shivered as his tongue darted out over his lips. She imagined that wonderful tongue in between her legs, teasing and stroking her wet opening, flicking against her clit.

Karin came hard, harder than she ever had by her own hand before. She cried out as ecstasy filled her body, numbing it to everything but pleasure. Her muscles spasmed around her fingers and bliss crashed over her body in giant waves. She closed her eyes and tilted her head back, basking in the glow of the moment.

When the last ripple of sensation drifted away, she dropped her hands.

"Perfection." Leo stilled his movements under the water. She noticed that his body was still hard like steel, and his eyes, once golden, burned almost white with heat. "That was very . . . how do you say it . . . educational."

She lowered her foot and swayed as the room spun in circles.

Leo frowned. "Come here." He held his hand out to her. She grabbed his long, smooth fingers without thinking. Skin brushed skin and caused heat to build in her center once more. Leo curled his hand around hers and tugged her toward him.

"You want me in the tub?" she asked as she stumbled forward.

He furrowed his brow. "Yes." His voice sounded lower, sexier.

She stepped over the edge and placed her foot in between his legs.

"Sit down," he commanded.

She hesitated, unsure how to position her body next to his.

He sighed and rolled his eyes. "Turn around." Leo placed his hands on her hips and helped her turn until her back was to him. He ran his fingers lightly over her ass, causing her skin to tingle with sensation. Karin had always thought her backside was too large, but he didn't seem to mind.

"So beautiful," he murmured to himself. "Sit."

She settled her body in between his legs and felt his long, hard erection press up against her lower back.

"Good. Now was that so difficult?" he asked.

"No."

He coaxed her to lean back. As she inched toward him, he wrapped his arms around her body and splayed his hands out over her skin. "You have done well, *cara*. Now it's time to put my education to use." He slid one hand up over her breast and the other between her legs.

Karin gasped as he hooked his feet around her calves and spread her legs apart. Leo splayed his fingers over her abdomen, then slipped them between her thighs.

"Do you like this?" he asked.

"Yes." She leaned her head back on his shoulder.

"Good." He pinched her nipple with one hand and slipped the other over her curls. His long, hard erection pushed into her lower back and caused a stirring in her lower abdomen. She closed her eyes and groaned as he caressed her body, playing her like a musical instrument.

Leo had never felt anything so soft in his entire life. He shifted lower in the tub, allowing his erection to slide against the skin of her lower back. The woman gasped, but he gently massaged away the burst of tension with his fingers.

"Tell me, has any man ever taken you from behind?"

She shook her head and groaned as he pinched her nipple.

He slid his finger in between her swollen folds, just like he had seen her do with her own hand earlier. "We shall save that for another time, then. But I assure you sweetheart, once you try it, you won't want it any other way."

She shivered as he slid his finger deep inside her core. The woman was so wet, so ready. It would only take a few swift strokes to make her fall apart in his arms.

Not yet. This woman was completely at his mercy, and Leo wanted to make the moment last. He loved denying both himself and his partner pleasure. It made everything so much more intense when his release finally came. Leo liked to build the tension until neither one of them could stand it a moment longer. Only then would he watch her come undone in his arms.

He let go of her breast and flicked the elastic out of her hair. Within seconds it was on the bathroom floor and her long, blond locks tumbled onto her shoulders. *Much better.*

"You should always wear your hair down, *cara*," he whispered into her ear. "I want to be able to run my fingers through it." To emphasize his point, he slid his free hand through her hair, smoothing it away from her face. With his other hand, he moved away from her opening and pressed her clit, causing her to gasp and wiggle in his arms.

"Grab onto the sides of the tub for me," he whispered.

She did as she was told. Leo hooked his foot under her ankle and lifted her leg until both his foot and hers rested on the edge of the tub. Leo sank lower, taking her deeper into the water. Then he returned his hands to her body and resumed his exploration.

"*Sei incredibile,*" he whispered as he ran his hands over her skin. "My little temptress." He cupped her mound and dragged her back against his aching cock. With his free hand, he rolled her nipple between his fingers. She groaned and closed her eyes.

"Relax, little one," he said. "Trust me with your pleasure."

She leaned back against him, causing his desire to soar to new levels. Never before had a woman been so receptive to his commands. It was almost as if she had been made just for him.

Or she would be, just as soon as he prepared her.

Leo added pressure to his ministrations, pushing his little treasure closer and closer to the edge. She shifted her weight, and the friction against his cock drove him wild with need. Leo steeled his jaw and tried to focus on the task at hand. It was difficult. All he wanted to do was plunge inside that warm, soft channel and lose himself in a moment of bliss.

Leo shifted once more, pressing harder against her skin. Fuck, he needed to be inside of her, but not yet. *Not yet.*

He watched her twist with pleasure in his arms. He stroked faster, and was rewarded when she arched her back and groaned. A sense of urgency overcame him as he adjusted his hold so that he could rub her clit with his thumb. He watched her face as her muscles tightened and joy spread over her features. He continued to massage her inner walls, making sure every last bit of pleasure was extracted from her body.

Leo had never seen anything so beautiful in his life. To know that he was the source of her ecstasy, that it was *his* voice and hands that brought her joy, warmed his heart and sparked a protective streak inside his chest.

He stilled his fingers as she sank against him with a sigh. He was reluctant to leave her warm body, but knew he couldn't linger. His little woman had found her release, but he had yet to find his.

"See what wonderful things can happen if you trust me?" he asked.

She nodded and smiled contentedly in reply.

Leo turned his head and inhaled her fresh, clean scent. She smelled like the spicy bathwater and sex, a powerful combination. He was fully aware of how his own needs had yet to be met, and how much he yearned to be satisfied.

He waited as long as he dared, then removed his fingers. "Stand up."

She opened her eyes and flashed him a look of confusion, but then did as she was told. Leo stood as well. As the bathwater drained from his torso, he caught her gaze slipping down to his swollen cock.

"Soon, *cara*. Very soon."

She jerked her gaze back up to meet his. Leo offered her a seductive smile. "Come." He stepped from the bath and grabbed a towel from the nearby stack. "I don't want you to catch cold." He extended his hand. She took it without question, something that pleased him to his very core.

"Turn from me." Leo suppressed a groan as her beautiful round ass came into view. He glanced at his empty scotch glass, but then dismissed the idea of going for another drink. He didn't want to break the erotic spell that moved through the room by drinking his senses dull.

Slowly he opened the towel and began to rub the drops
of water from her hair. He started at the head, gently mas-
saging her scalp and neck. The woman whimpered as he
moved his long fingers through the fine strands of her hair.

Gorgeous. Most of the women he knew had hair the
color of coal or mud, or else they dyed it vibrant colors too
fake to be real. This woman was a natural blond, a rarity
in his world. Her skin was pure ivory as well. As he moved
to her shoulders and upper back, he couldn't help but notice
the difference between her skin tone and his. The contrast
was stunning, and made him picture how erotic their bodies would look intertwined.

He worked his way down her back, tracing the curve
of her spine and wishing that it was his fingers, not his
towel, that touched her skin. His movements were gentle,
like a caress. Her body responded to his touch. As he came
closer and closer to her ass, her arousal drifted up and tick-
led his nose. The scent was as beautiful as she was, and
Leo couldn't help but wonder if his shy temptress tasted
as good as she smelled.

When he reached her backside, his movements became
even gentler and more reverent.

"Spread open your legs," he commanded. His voice
sounded rough to his ears, but he didn't care. The woman
spread apart her thighs, and her perfume filled the air. Leo
dropped down onto his knees and focused on his task, listening to her moans and sighs, learning what pleased her
and what didn't. From his angle, he could see her delicate
folds. He paused as the urge to slide his tongue over her
slit overwhelmed him.

"Is—is something wrong?" she asked as she closed her
legs.

It took him a moment to regain enough self-control to
respond. "No, *cara.*" He stood and walked around to her
front. "Step apart and hold out your arms."

She hesitated, but then did as she was told. Leo watched her eyes widen in surprise as he rubbed the Egyptian cotton over her chest. He stroked in a downward motion, caressing first her upper chest, then the swell of her breasts. Despite the flash of desire in her eyes, the woman steeled her jaw and held his gaze, as if she was daring him to find something wrong with her. Leo realized that although she might be bending to his will for now, this little woman could be a little spitfire when she wished.

He ground his teeth as his erection became full and heavy to the point of pain.

Leo was the first to break eye contact. He slid the towel over her breasts, cupping them and feeling their weight in his hands. They were the perfect size. Not too big, but big enough to fill his large hands. The round globes were full, and felt natural. This pleased him. The women in his world were more plastic than human, but this woman, while not striking in the classic sense, had a natural beauty that eclipsed the others.

He ran his towel over her nipple once more, and watched it tighten under his touch. He glanced up at her reddening cheeks and touched her again.

"Never be embarrassed around me, *cara*," he said. "Every part of you is beautiful."

She opened her mouth to speak, but another caress from his fingers changed her words into a low, throaty moan. She closed her eyes and tilted her head back, inviting him to kiss her lovely neck.

Leo leaned forward slightly, then paused. No, he mustn't give in to temptation, not yet. If he only had one night with this woman, then he wanted to make it memorable—for both of them.

He dropped once more to his knees and stroked her belly, her hips, her thighs. Every caress elicited new sounds of pleasure from her lips. With each moan, fresh desire flowed through his veins, making it difficult to concentrate. When she threaded her fingers through his hair to steady herself, the effect was immediate. Leo's whole body hardened and moisture leaked from the tip of his cock. It would be so easy to give in to temptation, to lift her leg up onto his shoulder and run his tongue over her slick folds.

"Spread wider," he commanded.

She did as he asked. As she moved, he noticed how her aroma strengthened. Leo shivered and closed his eyes in an effort to stay in control. He had to extend the game as long as possible. The subtle give-and-take of foreplay was something Leo enjoyed immensely. There was nothing quite like the building of anticipation, or the heightened sense of awareness it caused.

He glanced up at the woman before him. Like him, this one understood the beauty in denying oneself, if only on a subconscious level. With her, Leo knew that he could bring them both to heights neither one of them had ever experienced before.

He held her gaze as he reached out with the towel and lightly brushed it over her folds. His caress was hard enough to stimulate the tissue, but soft enough to not provide any relief.

The woman nibbled her lower lip, trying to hold in her response. He smiled, silently taking up her unspoken challenge. He moved the towel back and forth, caressing her tender folds with the warm cotton.

She gasped and tried to sink down on his hand, but he pulled just out of reach.

"I have to dry all of you, *cara*." He continued to move over her skin, watching her face twist between pleasure and pain. His own body responded, and his sense of urgency built alongside hers. Somehow he managed to keep his hand steady, sliding the thick towel between her thighs with sure, even strokes.

"Please." She tightened her fingers in his hair, tugging on the ends in desperation.

Enough. He could tell she was close to the point of breaking, and he didn't want her to tumble over the edge. Not yet.

Leo dropped the towel and scooped her up into his arms. She let out a startled, feminine sound and threw her arms around his neck as he carried her from the room.

"Where are we going?" she asked as he took her down the hall.

He frowned and pulled her closer. "Does it matter?"

"I—no, I suppose not."

"You need to trust me, *cara.* I'd never take you anywhere you don't want to go, or make you do something you aren't ready to do."

She slid her fingers down his cheek, then turned her hand around and brushed her knuckles across his stubbled skin. "I don't know why, but I trust you." She shook her head. "It's crazy, I know."

He stopped walking, turned his head, and kissed her palm. "No, not crazy. Beautiful." He turned away and continued down the hall to the bedroom.

"Before this night is over, *cara,* I will push you to the very limits of your endurance, and bring you pleasure you never thought possible."

Chapter 3

Karin felt as if she was in some torrid dream. She loved the rumbling of Leo's voice and the way he took charge of a room. The man was like a sponge. He sucked all of the madness and stress out of her and allowed her to relax. It was addictive, and Karin wasn't ready to have the fantasy end just yet.

He brought her to the bedroom. Karin had seen this place many times before, but somehow this time was different. She was no longer hotel staff, but a patron. For a while, she could delude herself into thinking she belonged in his opulent world, belonged with him.

The bedroom was decorated in the same grand style as the rest of the suite. Dark woods and expensive-looking fabrics were fit for royalty. Gold accents set off the crimson walls in an effort to give the room a more masculine appearance. Red roses sat on the bedside table, their scent filling the small space. The thick curtains had been pulled over the window, but Karin knew that the Boston skyline stretched out beyond their room as far as the eye could see.

Leo placed her down on the cream-colored comforter and maroon pillows. As soon as her head hit the pillow, he was on top of her, easing his knee in between her thighs. "Open for me, *cara*."

Karin spread her legs on the bed, allowing him to sink closer to her center. He shifted his gaze to her mouth as she held her breath and waited for him to make the next move. Slowly he leaned forward and covered her lips in a hot, searing kiss. Karin wrapped her arms around his neck and pulled him close as he ran his tongue along the seam of her mouth. She opened to him completely, wanting to pull this man deep into her soul.

The kiss started soft, but soon turned hungry and possessive. He brushed his tongue against hers again and again, enticing little ripples of pleasure from deep inside her abdomen. She loved how his weight pressed her into the bed. It made her feel protected and safe. Karin groaned as she felt his cock swell and press against her torso. She lifted her legs as urgency pumped through her veins. The skin-on-skin contact felt wonderful, but she wanted more. She needed him inside of her, filling her.

With a gasp, he broke away from her lips and began kissing his way down her body, creating trails of heat in his wake. She threaded her fingers in his hair and held him as he worked, loving the way his whiskers rubbed against her sensitive skin.

When he reached her breast, he flicked the sensitive tip with his tongue and lifted his gaze to meet hers. Karin groaned when she saw all of her desire and passion reflected in his eyes. She moistened her lips as he bent down and took her nipple between his teeth and tugged. The spark of pain shot through her system, heightening her desire. He let go of her tip, then rolled his tongue over where he had just nipped. Karin tightened her fingers in his hair as pleasure fanned out through her body. He repeated the movements once more, teasing her until her nipple formed a sharp peak between his teeth.

When he was done, he broke eye contact and glanced down at his handiwork. "So perfect." He blew air across her skin. The chilling sensation shot through her body and made her weak with need. He placed one last long, leisurely kiss on her sensitive tip and then moved to repeat the same delicious torture on the other breast. By the time he was finished, Karin was hot, needy, and ready to burst with frustration.

It was then that he pulled from her grasp and left the bed. "Don't move."

"Where are you going?" His absence felt like a bucket of cold water. All of her insecurities came crashing back as she scrambled to get under the covers.

He didn't answer. She pulled the covers up to her chin and watched him retreat, his large, masculine frame moving from the hardwood floors of the bedroom to the carpeted area in the hall.

Karin replayed the past few hours through her mind, wondering if she had made a mistake. Then suddenly he was standing before her, his cock fully sheathed in a condom, and a long, dark piece of fabric in his hand.

"Close your eyes," he commanded.

"I—"

Leo twisted his lips into a disapproving frown. Karin considered his words for a moment, and then did as she was told. He placed the black cloth over her eyes and secured it to the back of her head.

"I need you to trust me," he explained as he tightened the fabric.

"I do."

"We shall see." He tied off the fabric and removed the bedsheet. Karin reached for him, but he moved out of her grasp and lifted her leg high in the air, forcing her head back onto the mattress.

"What—" Her thoughts scattered as he ran his tongue along her inner ankle. "Wow." With the blindfold on, her other senses became more acute, and her skin became more sensitive to his touch. She was hyperaware of his rough stubble and warm tongue on her calf. Slowly he moved his way up along her inner leg, kissing and stroking her body as he lit every nerve ending on fire.

"Leo." She groaned as he bent her leg in the air and slid his tongue in a long, leisurely line up her inner thigh, stopping just before reaching her mound.

"You taste wonderful, *cara*." He pulled his head back, took her hand, and curled her fingers around her own knee.

"Hold this." He backed away, leaving her holding her leg in the air.

The room got quiet once more. Karin felt a little silly lying there in such an exposed position. She shifted on the bed and heard Leo murmur his disapproval.

"I said, don't move."

Karin froze. She didn't know why she obeyed him except that there was something very . . . compelling about that voice. It was almost as if she was under a spell.

The room got quiet, very quiet. After a long moment, Leo picked up her other leg and repeated the same slow, torturous path up her inner thigh.

Karin arched her back and groaned as his hot, wet tongue moved over her skin. He felt so good, so right. She moistened her lips as he inched his way upward with agonizing slowness, gradually getting closer and closer to where she needed him to be. When he was inches from the part of her that ached for him most, he stopped, took her hand, and curled her fingers around her other knee.

As he retreated, Karin's heartbeat quickened.

She felt the bed dip, and then warm air puffed against her wet folds. Her insecurities vanished as fresh tendrils of need wound their way through her system.

"Talk to me," Leo said. "Tell me how it feels."

"How it feels?" She thought that was a little obvious. "It feels . . . amazing."

"Be more specific."

"Like—like a warm blanket is being wrapped around me."

"Good." There was another puff of air, making her shiver. "Now tell me what you need."

"I need—" Her words dissolved into a groan as a fresh sense of urgency welled up inside of her. "I need you inside of me," she whispered.

"Louder." He repeated his movements. Karin tightened her grip on her knees as he blew over her damp skin.

"Oh, God," she whispered as another wave of desire pumped through her veins.

"Tell me."

"I need you inside of me. Please."

Leo's hum of satisfaction rippled over her like a caress. "Like this?"

Karin groaned as his hot, wet tongue slipped in between her folds.

"Yes." Holy shit. *Yes.*

"Or like this?" He spread her apart with his fingers and flicked her clit with the tip of his tongue.

Karin bit her lower lip and moaned. She wished she could see him. She imagined his dark head between her legs, his firm lips closing around her and making her whole body light up with ecstasy.

"Or perhaps both?" He swirled his tongue around her opening, then dragged it up to circle her clit. "I have to confess, you didn't allow me a good look at where you touched earlier. I have to guess."

"That's . . . wow." She shook her head. "You're amazing."

"Am I?" He repeated his movements.

"Oh, yes." Was that insecurity in his voice? She nibbled her lower lip as she imagined him looking up at her, unsure. The image only made her want him more.

"Good. Now I'm going to do this again, but I don't want you to come until I tell you."

Don't come? The man must be insane.

Again and again he tortured her with his tongue, causing desire to surge through her body. Pressure built in her core and fanned out through her muscles, making them tight with need. He pressed his hands on her thighs and spread them wider apart.

She was completely and totally at his mercy, she realized. Her blindness made everything so much more intense. Karin could almost believe that she belonged here, with Leo, and that they were lovers.

Leo scraped his teeth against her clit and slid his finger along her slick inner walls. Karin groaned and contracted the muscles in her core, trying to get him to go deeper. He continued to nip her clit as he moved in and out of her body. Sweet friction heated her core, fueling her sense of urgency. Karin's nipples tingled and desire rippled along the base of her spine. The pressure inside her abdomen grew with each thrust until she found herself hovering over the edge of something vast and euphoric. She couldn't come yet, however. Not yet.

For a long moment she hung there, her climax just out of reach. Then Leo's commanding voice broke through her consciousness.

"Now, *cara*." His low voice rumbled against her skin, putting cracks in the pillars of her sanity. Leo shifted his hand and added a second finger. Karin cried out as he plunged inside her core, stretching her muscles and pushing her over the edge. She arched her back and gasped as her sanity melted away, leaving nothing but ecstasy. Never had she felt anything so strong. The world around her faded away as joy rolled through her body, leaving her boneless and exhilarated.

Reality came all too quickly. Karin whimpered as Leo

slowed his movements and the last ripples of pleasure slowly faded away.

Leo retreated. "Very good, *cara*." He shifted on the bed and spread her legs wider apart.

Her thoughts scattered as Leo lifted her hips off the bed and thrust hard and deep. Karin let go of her knees as he sank into her and covered her body with his own. He retreated and thrust hard once more, filling her with his passion. Despite her recent orgasm, she felt desire stir in her lower abdomen. Karin curled her fingers into his biceps and met his thrusts. There was this wildness about him. It was almost as if seeing her lose control made him reckless.

Karin dug her nails into his back as they came together hard and fast. She wished she could pull him inside her body and hold him there forever. Pressure formed once again in her core, making her light-headed. Higher and higher she drew up, until once more she felt her orgasm on the edges of her consciousness.

"Come for me, *cara*."

His words were like a lock opening a private door to her soul. Karin's climax crashed through her body with such amazing force, it left her breathless. She gasped his name as ecstasy once again filled her mind. Through the haze of her joy, she noticed his thrusts becoming jerkier and more desperate. Leo groaned as he stiffened and filled her with his passion. For one glorious moment, it was as if time stood still. Everything ceased to exist except for this man, and the wonderful moment they shared.

When the last threads of her ecstasy faded away, Leo retreated, leaving her feeling empty and alone. Karin curled up in a ball, wondering if it was okay to remove the blindfold.

Then he was back in bed, spooning her naked body with his own and pulling a blanket up over them.

Leo removed the blindfold and tossed it on the floor. "Rest now. We shall resume your lesson in trust in an hour or two."

Resume? Karin's mind blanked as he threaded his arm around her torso. Most of the time, her boyfriends had been satisfied with a quickie before bedtime. She'd loved the first "lesson" with Leo, and wondered what delicious torture he'd come up with next.

A soft click echoed through the suite, interrupting her moment of bliss.

"Hello?" A high-pitched female voice broke through the silence. Karin stiffened as Leo raised his head from the pillow behind her.

"Mr. Perconti? It's Kristi. Marco sent me. He said that you might need a little help relaxing . . ."

Tears stung Karin's eyes as reality crashed down around her. *No, not yet.*

"Relaxing?" Leo murmured.

"I need to go." Karin quickly slipped from Leo's arms and scrambled out of bed. Damn, her clothes were in the bathroom. She grabbed a throw blanket and wrapped it around her body.

"I'm so sorry," she whispered as she avoided his gaze. *I will not cry. I will not cry.*

"You have nothing to be sorry about, *cara.* I'll get to the bottom of this."

That was what she was afraid of. Karin risked glancing in his direction. Leo stared at her with open curiosity. The blanket had fallen, giving her a gorgeous view of his muscled chest.

"Please don't fire me," she murmured as she backed toward the open doorway, remembering the rumors of his temper.

"Mr. Perconti?" Footsteps echoed from somewhere out in the living area, triggering Karin's sense of urgency. She had to get out of there before she made an even bigger mess of things.

"Stay right there, *cara*. Don't move." Leo got out of bed, giving her an eyeful of male perfection. He scanned the floor. "Damn it all. My clothes are in the bathroom."

"I have to go," Karin choked out as she turned and crashed into something hard and stumbled back into the wall.

"Sorry." Karin looked up at the woman's flawless features and perfect platinum hair. *Oh, shit.* This woman was the sort of creature that would be plastered in the middle of *Playboy*. Karin felt so out of her league. It was ludicrous of her to think that someone as inexperienced and plain as she could ever please a Perconti brother.

The woman eyed her with curiosity. "Now this is interesting. Marco didn't say that his brother was into threesomes." She tapped her overly plump lower lip with her long fingernail. "It's been a long time, but I'm willing to give it a go."

Oh God, a *threesome*? This was getting wilder than one of Wes's crazy sexual escapades. She had to get out of there, fast. Unfortunately, the woman was blocking the path to the service elevator. That meant that the only way out of the suite was through the main foyer. While she didn't relish the thought of using the same elevator as the rest of the hotel guests, she also didn't want to embarrass herself by staying in the hotel a moment longer.

Without speaking, Karin gathered the ends of her blanket and sprinted for the main elevator.

"Wait."

She could hear Leo coming after her, but didn't dare look back. Karin grabbed her clothes from the bathroom and moved quickly down the hallway. Something slipped out of her skirt pocket and crashed onto the floor, but she had no time to go back for it. She raced through the penthouse to the open living area. Tears stung her eyes as she pushed the button over and over in rapid succession. When the doors flew open, she flung herself inside and slammed her palm against the button for the first floor. Karin peered back through the closing doors and saw Leo charge through the main foyer with a towel wrapped around his waist. He was heading for the elevators, but it was too late. He'd never make it in time.

Karin slammed her fist into the metal wall as the doors closed and the elevator headed down. "Damn it!"

Get a grip. She started counting to ten, but only made it to three before the tears streamed down her face. As the elevator descended, the enormity of what she had just done hit her like a cement block.

She had slept with a Perconti brother.

Not just any Perconti brother, but the head of the entire family. Leo owned luxury hotels all over the world and was famous for his temper. If she angered him, he could give her a one-way trip to the unemployment line. Worse still, he could ensure that she never worked in anything above a shabby two-star hotel ever again.

"I'm such an idiot." She wanted to scream and throw things, but knew that wouldn't bring her any peace. This disaster was entirely her own doing. Marco had specifically said to stay out of Leo's sight. Did she listen? No. Instead of following orders, she had to be impulsive and fun.

Wes was wrong. Having sex with a Perconti brother didn't put a smile on her face. Quite the opposite.

Karin took in a ragged breath as she thought of all the bills on her kitchen table. How was she ever going to get on-the-job-training credits for her degree and make ends meet if she got fired?

If by some slim chance she managed to hang onto her

position at the Palazzo, she'd have to steer clear of Leo
Perconti for the duration of his stay. It didn't matter how
sinfully sexy he was or how he could give her pleasure
unlike anything she had ever experienced before. Great sex
wasn't worth her job. No, she had to avoid Leo for as long
as he stayed at the hotel. Leo was like a hot, roaring fire,
and Karin couldn't afford to get burned.

"Mr. Perconti?"

Leo tightened his jaw in frustration as the elevator
started its descent.

What a nightmare. She wasn't someone from Marco's
little black book, but an honest-to-goodness member of
his staff. *A Perconti employee.* Leo pinched the bridge
of his nose as the full implications of his actions hit him
like a wall. Holy hell, he could get sued for sexual harass-
ment. That woman could take down his whole family.

And yet he knew instinctively that she wouldn't do
that. The employee, whoever she was, had had ample
opportunity to call off the evening and scream sexual ha-
rassment, yet she hadn't. If her response to his touch was
any indication, she had enjoyed their erotic interlude as
much as he did.

Leo knew that he should let it go. Thinking about it
would only stress him out, and he had another beautiful
woman ready and willing to help him forget the whole
thing ever happened.

Leo straightened and turned back to the living area, determined to put the whole unfortunate incident from his
mind. He found Marco's woman standing behind the bar,
sifting through the liquor bottles with wide eyes.

"Miss, ah . . ." Leo struggled to remember the girl's
name.

"Kristi." She picked up the bullet-shaped shaker and

flashed him a smooth and seductive smile. That smile looked so polished, so . . . confident. "Care for a martini? It should help you more than those little pills there." She nodded to the pill bottle on the bar and poured vodka and vermouth into the shaker.

Leo fisted his hands at his sides. "That medication is none of your concern."

"Hey, honey, I'm not judging. I take medicine myself, although mine goes up my nose." She giggled and poured the chilled alcohol from the shaker into two glasses. "You should try it. Works better than anything you can get with a prescription." She picked up the cocktails and sauntered over to his side. "I have some now if you want it."

"Thank you, but no."

"Suit yourself." She shrugged and handed him one of the cocktails. Unease slipped over Leo's spine as her blue eyes narrowed seductively.

"I have an idea." She moistened her lips as she held up her martini glass between them. "Why don't I pour these over my tits and then you can lick them off me." She slipped her gaze down to his cock. "Then I could make some more and lick it off you."

Leo grabbed her wrist and twisted her arm before she could grab his cock.

"Hey—that hurts," she complained.

He dropped her arm in disgust. "Not tonight, Miss . . ."

"Dawson."

"Miss Dawson." He put down his glass and stepped away so he could gather his emotions together. Frustrated, he ran his hand along his jaw and played back the events of the past couple of hours. The sharp stubble scratched his palm, reminding him of his disheveled state. He needed to shave. But first, he needed sleep. His mind needed to be sharp if he was going to get himself out of this mess.

"It's been a rather long day, Miss Dawson, and I'm ready for bed."

"So am I." She took a long sip of her martini and tossed it aside. It hit the coffee table and shattered, sprinkling glass in all directions. "Let's do it." She turned toward the bedroom.

"No, wait."

She glanced back at him and raised her brows suggestively. "Are you nervous?" She ran her tongue over her teeth. "Because I can help you with that." She swayed her hips from side to side and began to close the distance between them. "After I saw that photo spread of you in *Whispers* with those models in Milan, I knew I had to sample you for myself."

Once again he grabbed her wrist as she reached for his cock.

"Ow!" She ground her teeth as he twisted her arm.

"That was my brother Gio, not me." He sneered before he could stop himself. God, he was so tired of women like her. All they wanted was to become famous, and they believed that dating a Perconti would get them the notice they craved. It was self-serving and disgusting. Leo wanted no part of it.

"I suggest in the future, you learn the name of your mark before you go in for the kill."

"What?"

Poor thing, she looked honestly confused. "You heard me. Now, off with you. I've got a busy day tomorrow."

Leo couldn't get her into the elevator fast enough. Once the doors closed, he sighed and returned to the bar area. Marco meant well, but he needed to learn that there were people out there who would like nothing more than a piece of the Perconti fortune. People who would stop at nothing to take everything they had worked so hard to build and preserve.

Leo's thoughts turned to the blond woman who had run away earlier as he picked up the pill bottle off the bar and stared at the label. Had she, like so many others, wanted a piece of the Perconti fortune? It didn't matter. While tonight was wonderful—no, mind-blowing—it couldn't continue. The last time he had been so obsessed with his sexual partner it had ended in disaster. He couldn't afford to let it happen again.

Family was what was important. Leo's job was to preserve and provide for his mother and siblings, and tonight he had forgotten that. He was the backbone of Perconti Enterprises and as such, had to think about his image. Fraternizing with the help could undo everything that he had worked so hard to gain.

Leo made a frustrated growl as he took a pill and placed the bottle back on the bar. After trading scotch for water, he downed the pill and made his way to the easy chair next to his bed, determined to figure a way out of this mess.

Seconds passed and slowly the tension in Leo's shoulders eased. The woman's scent lingered in the room, as well as the aroma of sex. It was almost as if she was still there, sitting with him in the dark. The scent comforted him in a way that the pills and scotch never could. They might have been strangers, but she had responded to him like she knew what he needed. Her willingness excited him in a way he had never experienced before. He wanted to feel that way again.

Leo closed his eyes and relived every moment of the last few hours. He remembered how much she had pleased him, and how well their bodies fit together. Her obedience had awakened something dark and needy in his soul. Even now it cried out for her, missing her warmth and silent surrender.

No, he had to stop this line of thinking. Leo opened his

eyes and stared at the ceiling. The harder he tried to put the whole incident behind him, the more he longed for her soft skin and quiet voice.

"This isn't over, *cara*," he whispered into the darkness. Every inch of him wanted to search her out, but he didn't even know where to begin looking.

He didn't even know her name.

Chapter 4

Leo pounded on Marco's office door.

"Hold on, I'm coming, I'm coming." Marco's irritated voice rose up from the interior.

Leo steeled his jaw as he heard the moving of furniture and hurried steps. His nerves were already shot after the long, sleepless night. If his brother was fucking another one of those socialites in his office, he just might blow a gasket.

Leo tightened his grip on the cell phone he had found outside his penthouse bathroom, the only reminder he had of last night, and tried to be patient. It felt like an eternity before his brother came and opened the door.

"You're early." Marco curved his lips into a knowing smile as he dragged his gaze over Leo's frame. "And you look exhausted." He let go of the doorknob and turned his back on his brother. "Come in. I'm just getting set up."

Leo scowled. "I *am* exhausted."

"Then last night went well for you."

"Not exactly." Leo slipped inside the office and closed the door.

Marco sat in his oversized office chair and glanced at Leo's hand. "Planning on calling someone?"

"What?"

Marco motioned to the cell phone.

"Oh." Leo shook his head and placed the cell on Marco's desk. "No. This was left in the suite last night. It belongs to someone named Wes."

Marco's eyes widened in shock for a brief moment before his features smoothed over into an expressionless mask. "Did you see what was on it?" he asked as he grabbed the phone.

Leo let out a long breath. "No. The screen saver was locked."

Marco turned the phone over in his hand and ran his thumb over the label with the employee's name on the back. "I told them to stay out of sight," he muttered.

"Told who?" Leo approached the desk and took the seat opposite him.

"The staff." Marco slid the phone into his jacket and leaned back in his chair. "I didn't want you to be disturbed." He shook his head. "Wes should have known better." He returned his attention to the screen. "Don't worry. I'll take care of this. No one will bother you again."

His brother's words bothered Leo more than they should. The thought of not seeing the woman from last night made his chest ache. "That isn't necessary."

Marco lifted his brows and looked up from his computer screen. "Isn't necessary?"

"No." Leo waved his hand in the air and tried to appear nonchalant. "They are my employees and shouldn't be afraid to be around me. There's too much work for that nonsense."

"But you never wanted the staff around before . . ." Concern etched Marco's brow as he got up from his chair, rounded the desk, and put his wrist to Leo's forehead.

"What are you doing?" Leo asked as he pushed his brother's hand away.

"I'm checking to make sure you're not ill."

"I'm fine." Leo slapped his brother away again and scowled. "Why wouldn't I be?"

Marco sat back down in his chair. "Oh, I don't know. Just that you turned away a perfectly good woman last night in favor of one of my employees." Marco twisted his lips into a wry smile. "After lecturing me to be careful who I sleep with."

The look on Marco's face spoke volumes. He wasn't going to let Leo off the hook like he had hoped.

"How did you know—?"

"Kristi told me." Marco waved his hand in dismissal and smirked. "Personally, I would have gone for the three-some."

His brother was giving him a hard time, but for once, Leo didn't care. He deserved the shame. Throughout the night, he had obsessed over the woman in the white blouse and dark skirt, first wanting to hold her, then scolding himself for letting his emotions get in the way. He knew that he should just leave it and be thankful that she didn't file a complaint. Leo didn't have time for this, not when the family business was falling apart and his ex-wife was blackmailing him. And yet, he couldn't seem to let what had happened last night go.

Marco leaned his elbows on the table. "Who was it?"

"Who was who?"

"You know." Marco waved his hand in the air. "The woman you slept with."

Leo shifted in his seat. "I don't know her name."

"What?" Marco stood. "How could you not know her name? What did you call her?"

Leo thought about it for a few moments before responding. "I didn't call her anything."

Marco chuckled and slid back into his seat. "And they call *me* 'Casanova.'"

"What?"

Marco chuckled and leaned back in his chair. "Exactly what happened last night?"

"Nothing." Nothing he wanted to tell Marco, anyway.

Marco smirked. "I'm guessing that she was a welcome distraction?"

Leo ground his teeth. "I'm not here to talk about what happened last night."

"No, of course not." Marco waved his hand at the door. "And yet you bring the cell phone here, when you could have easily left it in your room."

"That means nothing." Irritated, Leo tapped his foot in rapid succession. When he had found the cell phone that morning, he had hoped it belonged to the woman who called him "sir" last night. His disappointment in finding out that it belonged to someone named Wes was almost overwhelming. He didn't want to admit to his brother that he had brought the phone here, hoping that Marco could piece things together and tell him the name of the woman he had slept with last night.

Marco grinned. "You're thinking about her, aren't you?"

"What?"

"I can tell." Marco chuckled. "The media might believe your poker face, but you can't fool family." Marco folded his arms across his chest. "Don't worry, my friend. I'll talk to Wes and figure out who was in your room last night."

Leo scowled. "You're just trying to distract me from the real reason why I'm here." He straightened in his chair. "Did you get the accounts I asked for?"

Marco's smile faded as he turned his computer screen so that they could both observe the spreadsheets. Leo could tell that Marco wanted to keep questioning him, but thankfully, his brother refrained. As Leo leaned forward and tried to listen, his mind kept drifting back to the woman from last night.

What is your name, cara? He wanted to search her out

and get some closure on what happened last night. The sex was amazing, but his company came first—always. Lying awake and thinking about her like he did last night would make him far too tired to do what was needed to save his company. Without his complete focus, Perconti Enterprises would be in financial ruin by the end of the year.

He'd give her some token for her time, of course, just to show his appreciation—and to make sure she didn't talk to that damn *Whispers* reporter who was always following him around. Then, once he finally closed the door on his little maid and got her out of his head, he could put this whole incident behind him and focus on what was really important—saving his company and providing for his family.

Karin wheeled her supply cart to the service elevators and pushed the button. Once again, the cleaning crew was understaffed. So once again, she was forced to go upstairs and clean Leo's penthouse suite—a job that made her incredibly uneasy. She didn't know if she wanted to go into that bedroom again after what happened last night. At least Leo wouldn't be there to make things more complicated.

Her mother had told her once that bad luck came in threes. Yesterday, half of her staff had called in sick. Then she had a dalliance with Leo that left her feeling awkward and embarrassed. It was only a matter of time before the third bad thing happened. She only hoped that it didn't mean that she was going to lose her job.

It was foolish to have sex with Leo, but she couldn't regret her decision. It was nice to be desired again. After her messy breakup with Jason, she had wondered if she was destined to be single her entire life. Leo had made her feel beautiful, and his words of encouragement had caused her to regain a little of the self-confidence she had lost when she had caught her ex kissing another woman in his office.

There was something about Leo's voice, about his commands, that spoke to this deep place in her soul. The man could order her to orgasm and that thick Italian accent would have her tumbling over the edge before she took her next breath. Despite her resolve to keep her emotions in check, every time Leo had spoken, every time he'd touched her, she'd felt part of her resistance slip away.

After she went home last night, she had mentally beaten herself up over her foolishness. According to the media, Leo used people to get what he wanted, then discarded them like trash. He spoke only in terms of money and power, and manipulated people to get more of each. He was a hard man, an unfeeling man, and there was no place for her in his materialistic world.

Just like he had no place in hers.

No, sleeping with Leo, while amazing, was a mistake. That meant one more bad thing was about to happen. She just hoped that it wasn't her losing her job.

"Hey, gorgeous," Wes said as he snuck up behind her and wrapped his arms around her shoulders. "Rough night?"

"No, not at all. Why?"

He let go of her shoulders and walked around until he faced her. "Oh, I don't know." He shrugged. "I sent the service elevator back up to get you, but you never came down."

She pinched her lips together as her heartbeat sped up. "I took the main elevators," she said after a long, tense moment.

"I heard." Wes bit his lower lip and furrowed his brow. He looked as if he wanted to say something more, but then the elevator doors opened, and she pushed her cart toward the open door.

She didn't like the look on Wes's face. It meant he was choosing his words, and she was quite sure she didn't want to hear anything he had to say. She pushed her cart half-way through the door before he spoke.

"I also heard that you left the hotel last night in tears with a bedsheet wrapped around you."

Karin froze as the enormity of what he said hit home. How many people had seen her run from Leo's room last night? It was late, but the staff at the Palazzo ran in shifts. Any number of the cleaning staff or front desk personnel could have seen her.

The elevator door crashed into her cart with a thud, shaking the contents.

"Here, let me help you." Wes opened the door once more and helped her push the cart out of the way. Karin watched as the doors closed, leaving them alone in the grand foyer.

"Emily at the front desk," he said in answer to her un-spoken question.

Karin closed her eyes. *Emily, of course.* The woman loved to gossip just as much as Wes.

"What happened?" Wes's voice was gentle and reassuring. "Darlin', if that man hurt you . . . I don't care if he's a Perconti or not. I'll—"

"No." Karin opened her eyes and forced herself to meet his gaze. "No, he didn't hurt me."

"Then—"

"Nothing happened."

Wes flashed her a knowing look. "I'm pretty sure some-thing happened. You aren't the type to run through the halls in a bedsheet. That's more my style."

His comment was meant to be funny, but Karin found no humor in his words. She broke eye contact and glanced around the foyer. The round, open space was decorated in the classic Italian style, with beautiful white marble floors, immaculate stucco walls, a cherry-stained front desk and sitting area, and bright, fresh orchids. Glancing up, she could see to the glass ceiling, nine floors above. Each floor circled around the foyer, and patrons could leave their room and glance down to the front desk. It looked like a gorgeous Italian hideaway for a monarch or celebrity. It was a painful reminder of just how out of place Karin was in the Perconti world.

As she swept her gaze down from the ornate railings, she spotted two men emerging from the offices on the opposite side of the foyer. They both looked tense, as if they had been arguing.

The first man was Marco. Even upset, he still had that familiar swagger. His pinched lips and furrowed brow revealed that he wasn't in a good mood. Karin made a mental note to avoid him until whatever had happened blew over.

The second man looked just as handsome as he did last night. Despite his expensive suit and perfectly combed hair, he seemed weary, as if the weight of the world rested on his shoulders. A familiar frown pinched his lips, and he tapped his fingers on the stack of folders under his arm with impatience.

Leo. She'd recognize those muscled shoulders and gorgeous ass anywhere.

"You took my advice, didn't you?" Wes said as he followed her gaze.

Karin ignored him and watched Leo take a second bundle of folders from his brother and put them on top of the ones in his hand. She focused on his fingers, remembering how they had brushed against her skin. His touch had been so gentle, and yet so commanding. A dull ache formed in her core as she realized that she wanted to feel them on her skin once more.

"Karin?"

As she watched Leo and Marco interact, memories flooded back of last night, and how Leo had brought her to orgasm again and again. Heat spiraled up through her center as she remembered his warm breath against her skin, and his firm fingers against her breast.

"Karin." Wes leaned over and whispered in her ear. "Please stop. People are already talking."

"What?" Karin tore her gaze away from Leo and stared at her friend. "What do you mean?"

Wes took a deep breath. "Emily wasn't the only one who saw you last night. That *Whispers* reporter saw you running from the hotel and she's been questioning the staff. You ran by too fast for anyone to get a good look, and no one knew you were supposed to clean the penthouse except Marco and me. I was able to put two and two together."

"Has Marco—"

"I'm not sure if Marco has pieced it together yet." He glanced through the large revolving door where two tabloid reporters were questioning the doorman. "It's only a matter of time before he figures things out. And if he doesn't, someone else might . . ."

"There's no story, Wes. The Perconti brothers share their bed with women all the time." Karin started to turn away, but Wes stopped her.

"That may be true, but those women don't normally run away from the sexual interlude in a bedsheet with tears streaming down their face. Honey, the Perconti brothers made the Hottest Bachelors Around the Globe list in *Whispers* two years in a row."

"The list." Leo was number one on that list last year. Of course the general public would take an interest in who he slept with. Since his divorce, Leo had female fans all over the world, all waiting to become the next Perconti conquest.

Karin glanced out the revolving door at the crowd gathering on the street. Two more tabloid people had shown up, and all three of them were closing in on the doorman like sharks, circling a school of fish. To his credit, the doorman was preventing their entry, but Karin didn't know how much longer he'd be able to hold off all of those people on his own.

"Build them up and tear them down. It's the American way." Wes shook his head. "All of those reporters would love to hear that the number-one most eligible bachelor in the world made a woman cry in the bedroom."

"Damn."

"By the afternoon, everyone is going to be wondering about the petite blonde running out of the Palazzo in a bed-sheet." Wes took a deep breath and let it out. "Sex sells." He tightened his grip on her elbow. "Especially when it involves the head of Perconti Enterprises."

"I'm ruined."

"Don't be so dramatic. They still don't know who you are." Wes glanced over her shoulder once more. "Does Leo know—"

"He doesn't know who I am. At least, I don't think he knows." She returned her gaze to Marco and Leo as the men said their good-byes. Marco reentered the office area and Leo turned toward the foyer and started closing the distance between them. As his gaze rested on hers, his steps slowed. Karin stared, transfixed, as recognition dawned in his hazel eyes. The tension vanished, replaced first by surprise, then something darker and hungrier. Shivers rippled down her spine as his gaze slid over the length of her body. Heat trailed over her skin, making it tingle with awareness. As his gaze slowly slipped back up to meet hers, a seductive, knowing smile touched his lips.

"Of course he doesn't know you." Wes's voice was thick with sarcasm as he returned his gaze to her. "Things look pretty dark, sugar, I know, but this is fixable." He grabbed her shoulders and waited for her attention to return to him.

"You just have to lay low for a while. Stay away from that gorgeous Italian and focus on your job."

Karin nodded and glanced over her shoulder at Leo. Dante had emerged from the restaurant looking his usual disheveled self and had intercepted Leo's advance. Karin guessed that Dante probably had fallen asleep underneath one of the stools from the bar. His jeans hung low on his hips and his black T-shirt clung to his broad shoulders and muscular chest.

"I mean it, Karin."

Karin dragged her gaze away from Leo and faced her friend. "Just like you stay away from Marco?"

"That's different." Wes shook his head. "Everyone knows that Marco's a playboy. He's sleeps with a different person every night. No one will notice if he takes on another lover. Leo, on the other hand . . ." Wes toyed with some of the cleaning supplies on the cart. "He's quiet and stern—and rather cantankerous. There are rumors that he drove his wife into the arms of another lover because he was so demanding."

Karin blinked at her friend and tried to digest all of this new information. She knew Wes was right. If there was anything going on in the glamorous lives of celebrities, he knew about it.

"Just be careful," he said. "If it was just a bunch of rumors from the other staff members, it would be one thing. But Leo's reputation precedes him, and you have a history of losing your heart. I just don't want to see you hurt again."

Karin's thoughts turned to her former boss, and what he had said to her when they first started having sex. *While I like our little arrangement, it can never be anything more than a pleasant diversion. You don't belong in my world, Karin, and you never will.*

Karin lifted her chin and met Wes's gaze. "I won't get hurt again."

Wes leaned forward and placed an affectionate kiss on her brow. "For your sake, I hope you're right."

Leo jerked back in surprise as someone touched him on his shoulder.

"Be careful, brother."

Leo turned around and saw his brother, Dante, standing behind him. Last night, Marco had told him that Dante was still hurting over his breakup with his girlfriend, Sabrina, much more than he let on in his occasional phone calls to Leo. Marco had mentioned that Dante was staying at the hotel until he got his life back on track.

His brother had changed since he'd last seen him. Dante was younger by ten years, yet in the time they were apart he seemed to age fifteen. Fine lines framed his thin lips and dark circles ran under his amber eyes, making them look haunted.

"Dante." Leo didn't know what to say. Leo knew how smitten Dante had been with Sabrina, and the breakup was messy and public.

Dante nodded toward where his little maid and another staff member were talking on the other side of the foyer. "Don't do it, brother. This will bring you nothing but trouble. I should know."

"I'm sorry about Sabrina," Leo said, desperate to change the subject.

Dante slipped his hand from his brother's shoulder. "Every day it gets harder and harder to stay away from her."

"It's for the best," Leo said.

"I know, but it doesn't make it easy." Ever since Leo's divorce, the media had been infatuated with the Perconti brothers' bachelor status. Leo, Marco, and Dante had had encounters with infatuated fans before, but all of those women had been harmless. None of the brothers had been prepared for the stalkerlike possessiveness one fan had over Dante, or how that obsession would lead to harassing Sabrina and trying to burn down her restaurant. The fan was currently serving time for her insane behavior, but Dante's guilt had driven him and Sabrina apart. The ordeal was sobering. It brought home the reality of their situation and how much damage they could inadvertently cause the ones they loved.

Outside of Sabrina's, standing only a few paces away from the fire trucks and a weeping Sabrina, the brothers had made a pact to never get close to anyone romantically again. Doing so would entice the interest of the tabloids, and open them all up to the possibility of something like that happening again. It was a steep price to pay, one that was the toughest on Dante, but the consequences of forming an intimate relationship were just too much.

"There have been rumors . . ." Dante hesitated, as if unsure how to continue.

"What did Marco tell you?"

Dante shook his head. "Not Marco, the reporters outside. I was accosted by that *Whispers* woman this morning before security found her and threw her out."

"Jesus."

"She wanted confirmation on a rumor that you had dismissed a maid from your chambers late last night because she couldn't satisfy you."

"What?" Leo couldn't believe what he was hearing. "That's not what happened."

"It doesn't matter what really happened. It only matters what seems to have happened. You, above everyone else, should know how important it is to keep up appearances."

Leo shuffled the folders from one arm to another and glanced over his shoulder at the gorgeous blonde, who was deep in conversation with her fellow employee. He didn't know if she was aware of the rumors, but supposed that it didn't matter. If people were talking about last night, the news would get to her eventually. Things like this had a way of spreading quicker than wildfire.

"But Marco sleeps around and it isn't the subject of gossip."

"Marco is different. Everyone knows that sleeping with him means nothing. They all know that what they do with him is nothing more than just a little fun."

"Just a little fun?" Leo glanced back at his little maid and her friend. Their conversation seemed to be getting more intense. He wondered if he was the cause of their tension, and if there was anything he could do to stop the rumors.

"But you—you're different. Your reputation precedes you."

Leo forced his gaze back to his brother. "I didn't know that I had a reputation."

Dante laughed. "Oh yes. You're an ogre and a cold-hearted bastard, didn't you know? And that poor little woman, running out of here with a bedsheet wrapped around her, crying, only solidified it."

Leo stared at him in shock. An ogre? He supposed that he had been rather hard on his siblings, but that was only because none of them cared about the company. They were spending money faster than they were making it and if something didn't happen soon, then they would all be out on the streets.

"Who started these rumors?"

Dante shrugged. "I have no idea, but we all have labels with the hotel staff."

"We do?"

"It's how they let off steam—they call us names."

"Names?"

"Marco is called 'Casanova' because he's always seen

with a different woman, and I'm called 'Martini' because, well, for obvious reasons . . ."

"What do they call me?"

" 'The General,' of course."

"Of course." Leo let out a heavy sigh as Dante searched around in his pockets and frowned.

"Where's my flask?"

"Flask?" Leo asked.

"The one Sabrina gave me."

"You're drinking? It's barely noon."

"That's the best time to drink, my friend." Dante went to hit his brother on the back again, but a sharp look from Leo gave him pause. "Look, I thought you knew about the nicknames. It's just tabloid talk." He lowered his arm and shrugged. "It's not a big deal."

Leo steeled his jaw. Dante was wrong. This was a huge deal, but his siblings were too blind to see it. Not only was the Palazzo a mess and the accounting a disaster, but the staff, instead of showing loyalty and working hard, were standing around the water cooler and poking fun at his family. Tabloid reporters were circling his beloved hotel like hawks zeroing in on their prey. Perconti Enterprises was no longer the great hotel conglomerate, they were a laughingstock.

Leo bent his head and pinched the bridge of his nose. Good Lord, give him strength. How was he ever going to get all of this straightened out by his sister's wedding? Everything had to be perfect. This was how they were going to turn everything around. The media was going to be all over the Palazzo, interviewing people and taking notes. It was Leo's hope to publicize the wedding and use it to pressure his sister's fiancé into using his aviation empire to help get Perconti Enterprises back on track.

"Aw, cheer up, Leo. At least they didn't name you after

a cocktail." Dante grinned. "Now if you'll excuse me, there's a bottle of Chianti over there with my name on it." He pointed to the restaurant behind him and started walking backward.

Leo thought about calling him back, but decided against it. Chances were that the restaurant was already a mess and one more missing bottle of booze wasn't going to change much. Besides, he needed to think and plan. Leo had no idea where to even begin cleaning up the hotel. It wasn't only the physical cleaning and updating. He had to stop the rumors surrounding his interlude last night, and get those tabloid reporters focused on the wedding once more.

All of this would take money, of course. Money the Perconti family didn't have.

He glanced over at the beautiful woman once more. She seemed so distraught. He hated to think that their one night of passion might have harmed her. He had to set things right, not only for her sake, but for his.

Stay away from her, Leo. Leo knew that talking to her at this point would only make things worse, but damn, he missed her. She was the only thing he could think about last night and this morning. He wanted to touch her again, to kiss her. Most of all, he wanted to know if she was okay. He didn't need Marco or Dante to tell him that he had upset her last night. He wanted to make it up to her.

I'll just check up on her. It wouldn't be anything sexual, just a quick conversation to make sure that there were no hard feelings.

Leo started closing the distance between them and stopped. He noticed how close she was standing to the man, and how her face had turned up to meet his. Their close proximity irritated him, and he quickened the pace, eager to put an end to their conversation and turn the woman's focus to something much more important—him.

"Mr. Perconti!" The voice rose up from behind, stopping him in his tracks.

Leo turned and stifled a groan as that damn reporter hurried toward him, recorder in hand.

"Mr. Perconti, about last night—"

One of Leo's security men swooped in out of nowhere and redirected the journalist toward the revolving door.

"There is a report of a woman running from your penthouse suite wearing nothing but a bedsheet—"

Leo fisted his hands as the security personnel took her out of the building and tried to break up the small crowd on the sidewalk.

Leo turned back to his woman and noted her shocked expression. His rational side told him to ignore her. Being seen together in public would only bring more unwanted attention and speculation from both the Palazzo staff and the media.

Dismissing her was the right thing to do, but every muscle in his body prevented him from walking away. While he was used to all of the media attention, she was clearly not. It must have been shocking for her to see the picture in the tabloid. It would be unfair of him to not talk to her and make sure she was all right.

As he started to close the distance between them, Leo dragged his gaze over her uniform, remembering how it had fallen to the bathroom floor last night. He knew every curve underneath that shapeless blouse, every dip and plane of her skin. With each step, the need to feel her naked body against his increased. Suddenly talking wasn't enough. Touching wasn't enough. Possessiveness rose up inside of him as he thought about taking her back up to his room and kissing away every last bit of embarrassment and hurt that article had caused.

Unfortunately, the woman had recovered from her

shock and was moving quickly away. As he watched that lovely ass swish back and forth, his irritation grew.

How dare she run from him. Those curves were his, damn it. He distinctly remembered telling her to wear her hair down last night and she had disobeyed him. He wanted to unhitch her bun and let her soft waves sift through his fingers. He wanted her to know who was in charge as he feasted on her mouth and felt her body against his.

A sense of urgency swept through him as the elevator doors opened and she navigated her bulky cleaning cart inside. He quickened his steps, desperate to get to her before the doors closed. There had to be some way to deal with this mess, a way in which he could have Karin and avoid the inevitable media circus that came whenever he or one of his siblings started getting serious with someone.

He caught sight of her through the closing doors. She was looking down and arranging the items on her cleaning cart. That damn cart was taking up the whole elevator. He didn't know if there was enough room for him, but it didn't matter. He'd climb up on top of that metal contraption if it meant that he could touch her once more.

He slid his hand in between the closing doors. The large metal panels stopped with a creak and reversed direction, making room for his long, lean frame.

Leo held his breath as he slipped into the elevator. *Thank God*. Someone up above must have taken pity on him.

As the doors closed them off from the foyer and the nosy staff, he turned and met her surprised gaze.

"About last night—" He stopped as he realized that he didn't want to walk away from this.. He remembered how she had been so eager to please him. With someone like that, Leo could be free to explore some fantasies he had been hiding all of these years.

They could start right now, in this elevator. He'd have

her take off her clothes—slowly. Then he'd order her down on her hands and knees. He'd take a slow walk around her naked body, drinking in every asset. He'd linger behind her of course, just to increase the tension. Perhaps, if she was good and kept her gaze forward, he'd caress the firm globes of her ass. Then he'd blindfold her and the true fun would begin . . .

"What floor?" a nasally feminine voice asked.

Leo jerked back in surprise. There was a second staff member in the elevator? *Damn.* He flexed his fingers and tried not to think about the beautiful woman standing next to him—or his rising desire.

"Mr. Perconti?" The woman snapped her gum and looked up at him with expectation.

"Err . . ." Leo realized that he had no idea where he was going. He didn't really care, one way or the other.

"He probably wants to go to his penthouse suite, Gloria," the beautiful blonde mumbled.

"Yes, the penthouse suite," Leo said a little bit too loud. Gloria snapped her gum and pushed the button for the ninth floor.

Gloria raised her brows and held out her hand. "I need the card."

"Of course." Leo fished around for his card and handed it to her. Gloria swiped it in the console next to the control panel and hit the button for the ninth floor.

"Thank you," he said as she handed him back the card. The elevator started to climb, and with each passing floor, the air in the stall became thick with tension. Leo wished that he could say something to alleviate the heaviness in his chest, but didn't dare. He had already made a fool of himself by running to catch the elevator. He didn't want to make things worse.

"There are a lot of reporters outside this morning," Gloria observed. "Did you notice them, Karin?"

The gorgeous blonde shrugged. "There are always reporters in front of the hotel."

Ah, Karin. He finally had a name for his little maid, a
beautiful name at that.

"One or two, yes, but not this many. It's almost as if they
were waiting for something to happen. Any idea why
they're there?" She flashed Leo a knowing look that suggested she knew exactly why they were there, and what
they wanted to know.

"I don't make a habit of indulging reporters," he said.

Gloria made a very unladylike sound and turned to face
the elevator doors. "It doesn't matter. It will be on the 'Dirt
Edition' tonight, I'm sure."

"I don't pay attention to such trash, and neither should
you." Dirt Edition, indeed. Leo found it hard to believe that
anyone would be interested in such a filthy television
show—or the magazine that was associated with it.

"Well, I—"

"If you have time to watch television, then perhaps my
brother isn't giving you enough to do."

Gloria opened her mouth and shut it again. The doors
to the elevator opened to the fourth floor. Seeing a route
of escape, she hurried off. As the doors closed behind her,
Leo resisted the urge to let out a long breath of relief. Finally, they were alone.

An uncomfortable silence settled around them as the
elevator began to climb once more. *Shit.* Leo had no idea
what to say.

A soft sniffle echoed from the other side of the elevator. Leo glanced beside him to see tears shining bright in
Karin's eyes. *Damn.* He had to make this right, but he
didn't know how.

"I'm . . ." His words stuck in his throat as a stray tear
slid down her cheek. She wiped it away with the back of

her hand and turned to face him, her face an expression-less mask.

"Forget about it," she said.

"Those reporters—"

"Are nothing I haven't dealt with before." She held up her hand as he tried to continue. "Look, I get it. What we shared was fun. I had thought that you had enjoyed it as much as me, but that's evidently not the case."

"Excuse me?"

"That reporter outside is telling people that you weren't satisfied last night. And it's okay. Really. You win some and you lose some. No big deal." She shrugged and picked at something on her cleaning cart.

No big deal? He could tell just by looking at her that she was lying. She was trying hard not to show that she was upset. Watching her struggle to keep her composure was breaking his heart.

Leo steeled his jaw as he pushed the emergency button on the elevator. The gears above ground to a halt, stopping them between floors.

"What are you doing?" she asked as she wiped another tear from her cheek.

That was a good question. This was insane. *He* was insane, but damn it, Leo couldn't let this woman go on like this. There had to be an answer to their situation, one that would satisfy both his need to have her, and his desire to keep the Perconti image intact.

"Bullshit." Leo turned to face her as an idea formed in his mind.

"What are you talking about?"

"What we shared last night might not have been a big deal to some people, but it was a big deal to *me*." He slipped his long, tapered fingers around her neck. "And I think it was for you, too."

Karin gasped as he pulled her over the cleaning cart and covered her lips with his own. As he worked his mouth over hers, memories flooded back of last night, and everything they had done together. He pictured her before him, pleasuring herself in his bathroom on his command. He wanted to know what else she would do on his orders, and how far he could push her.

He broke off the kiss and grasped her fingers. "I have a proposition for you." He led her around the cleaning cart, toward the elevator doors.

"A proposition?"

He kissed the back of her fingers and watched her through his long lashes. "Yes."

She started to speak, but he put his finger over her lips, stopping her. "Hear me out." As he continued to talk, he turned his hand and slid his thumb over her lower lip, imagining how good it would taste. "I'm guessing that what we did last night was new to you, yes?"

She nodded as her eyes became slightly unfocused.

He tipped his head and placed his lips right next to her ear. "That was just the beginning." He felt her shiver, and fought to keep the smile off his face. "I can show you more."

"More?" she whispered.

"Much more." He pulled away and let his gaze drag over her curvy frame. "Submit to me, and I will expose that side you keep so well hidden. Together, we'll push your boundaries and take you to heights you have only dreamed about."

"Hidden?" Her eyes widened as she inched back.

"Yes, *cara*." He inched closer. She was nervous, and that was to be expected, but she was also curious. He could sense it in the way the air seemed to electrify between them. "Together we can—"

"No." She shook her head. "This is wrong." She held

up her hand and Leo wondered if he had pushed her too far. He retreated into the control panel, and the grinding of the elevator gears began again.

"Relax, little one—"

"No, I can't." The elevator doors opened and she hurried off.

"Wait."

She stopped in the hall and turned to face him. "I'm sorry. Last night was wonderful and everything, but . . ." She shook her head. "This isn't me."

Leo placed his hand on the cleaning cart. "I was just going to say that you forgot this." He inched the cart toward her.

"Oh." She reached for it, and he covered her hand with his own.

"This isn't over, *cara*," he whispered into her ear.

She closed her eyes and shivered. For a brief moment, he thought he had her. Then she opened her eyes and jerked the cart away from his grip.

"It is for me." She pulled the cart through the doors and out into the hall. "It has to be."

"I know that isn't what you really want." His beautiful woman stiffened and glanced at him over her shoulder. Even with her nerves, he could see the raw desire in her eyes. As the elevator doors began to close, Leo's resolve strengthened, and he allowed himself a half-smile. "If you want to fight me, then I'll indulge you, but we aren't finished with this, *cara*. Not by a long shot."

Her whimper echoed through the hall as the doors finally closed and Leo was swept up to the penthouse suite.

Chapter 5

Karin paced back and forth in the break room of the Palazzo as her nerves jumbled into knots. For most of the day she had tried to keep up the calm, collected façade required to do her job, but the effort had left her drained. She needed to talk to someone about what had happened between her and Leo Perconti in the elevator, and she could think of only one person who would understand what she was going through.

She had only called Wes ten minutes ago, but each passing second felt like an eternity. She wished she had asked to meet him at a café after work, or at one of the benches in Boston Common. This break room was far too small, and the moldy bread smell from the refrigerator was just strong enough to set her stomach on edge.

"Hey, darlin'. What's going on?" Wes asked as he entered the room. "You sounded more uptight than one of my Catholic schoolteachers—" Noticing her agitated state, he stopped short and pushed his blond hair from his forehead. "Ah, hell. What happened?"

"Oh, Wes. I don't know what I'm going to do. I've made a huge mess." Karin fell into a nearby chair and leaned her elbows on top of the white circular table. "I feel like I'm drowning." She cradled her head in her hands as the full impact of what had happened over the past few days pressed down on her shoulders. "Marco's going to kill me."

"Come on." Wes slid into the seat opposite her and lowered her hands away from her face. "Things aren't that bad, I'm sure. Why don't you tell me about it?"

Karin stood, extracted her hands from Wes's fingers and walked over to the microwave. "I never should have slept with Leo. I'm going to get fired, I know it."

Wes leaned back in his chair and put his arms behind his head. "When we talked this morning, you told me you wanted to stay away from him. You had decided to pretend that nothing had ever happened."

"Things have changed," Karin said, remembering the words from the elevator, words she couldn't forget if she tried. She turned around and pressed her backside against the counter. "I didn't realize how hard it would be to avoid him when we both work at the same place. I see him everywhere and each time he looks at me I remember what we did together. Twice I had to hide in the bathroom to avoid talking to him. I—I think he wants to pick up where things left off."

Wes's face brightened. "That's wonderful."

"No, it's horrible." She let out a long breath and crossed her arms. "I can't have sex with him again."

"Why not?"

"Because I work for him!" Karin huffed and started rummaging through the cabinets. "Don't you see? I'm sure he wants to turn me into his plaything, someone who'll come running whenever he calls."

"Was the sex good?" Wes leaned back in his chair and folded his hands behind his head.

Karin stopped rummaging through the cabinets and turned to face him. "Well, yes—"

"I knew it." He smirked.

"And no."

He lowered his hands and leaned his elbows against the table. "What do you mean?"

"I mean that I can't do this, Wes. We come from different worlds. He's rich, powerful, influential . . . the list goes on and on. I'm just—"

"A gorgeous and desirable woman." Wes stood and began to close the distance between them. "Relax, honey. Sleeping with the head of Perconti Enterprises is like a badge of honor."

"What are you talking about?"

Wes pressed his hands on the counter on either side of her hips. "Do you have any idea how many people want to know what Leo is like in the bedroom? Especially after his ex, Danika, accused him of being a 'dominant lover' . . . Wait, he didn't hurt you, did he?"

The image of her blindfolded with her back arching in his bed flashed through Karin's mind. Heat crept onto her cheeks. "No." Leo didn't inflict pain, but he did other things, wonderful things that played over and over in her mind.

This isn't over, he had said. If Leo got her in his bed again, she knew that he'd continue to push her limits. Karin wasn't sure if she was ready for that. The man both frightened and excited her.

"I know you want to tell me what happened." Wes pushed away from the counter and folded his arms. "So spill it."

Karin hesitated for a minute, then sat back down at the break table. "All right, but you have to promise to keep this to yourself."

He collapsed into one of the chairs at the break table and crossed his heart. "Scout's honor."

She frowned as she slid into the seat next to him. "I thought they held up three fingers or something."

"Honey, I'll hold up all five fingers if it will get you to spill all of the juicy details. Tell me."

After a quick glance around to make sure they were alone, Karin leaned in close and lowered her voice. "It was amazing."

"I knew it."

"And scary."

"I told you it would be—what? How on earth could it be scary?"

Karin shrugged and looked away. "It just was."

"Scary—like how? Did he jump out of a closet or something?"

"No." Karin chuckled. "Nothing like that."

"Then what happened?"

She sighed and picked at her nail polish. "I'm not quite sure how to say this . . ."

Wes took her hands in his, stopping her movements. "Honey, sometimes blunt is best."

"You're probably right." She leaned back in her chair and decided just to come out with it. There was no delicate way to describe the amazing energy between her and Leo.

"Leo has this presence. The things we did together . . ." She leaned in closer to Wes and lowered her voice. "They were dirty."

Wes smirked and inched closer. "Oh yeah?" he whispered. "Like what?"

"Like . . . I was touching myself."

He stared at her, stunned. "Well, that's hardly scandalous." His voice sounded disappointed as he straightened in his chair. "Judging by the way you were carrying on, I thought that perhaps—"

"No." Karin shook her head. "Leo was a gentleman."

"I'm sorry."

"Wes, I'm serious."

Wes patted her hand. "So am I. No one wants a gentleman in the bedroom."

She rolled her eyes. "You don't understand. I've never done anything like that before."

He furrowed his brow in confusion. "You've never masturbated?"

"Shh," Karin said as a coworker entered the room. She shifted uneasily in her seat as he went to the refrigerator. "Of course I've done *that* before." She rolled her eyes as she whispered to Wes. "Just not at someone's command."

"Ah." Wes widened his eyes in understanding and leaned closer. " 'The General' likes to give orders, and you're frightened because of how much you want to obey them."

"Kind of." Karin watched the coworker leave the break area and thought about the erotic commands Leo had given her first in the bathroom, then later in the bedroom. The staff's nickname for the Perconti patriarch was appropriate. Like a general, Leo had expected his orders to be obeyed, and heaven help her, she wanted to please him. .

But Karin had fought hard to get where she was, and she wasn't going to throw away years of hard work to become someone's plaything. No matter how handsome he was—or how good in bed. She didn't want a sexual partner who ordered her around like a servant. She wanted a partner, an equal both in bed and out.

"What else did he do?" Wes asked when they were alone once more.

Karin felt her cheeks heat as she remembered how, after he had made her orgasm twice, he had blindfolded her. She could almost feel his hot, wicked tongue slide along her inner thigh. "Not much."

Wes chuckled and patted her hand. "Don't worry, you don't need to tell me. It's written all over your face." He tilted his head to the side and pressed his lips together for a moment in thought. "You liked it when he gave commands in the bedroom, didn't you?"

"Yes." She let out another relieved breath. "What I'm feeling isn't normal, Wes. It can't be." She should be appalled. Karin wasn't a child, far from it. Why did taking orders send her desire into overdrive? "I don't want someone to control me like that. I had enough of taking orders with Jason."

"Following commands between the sheets isn't the same as taking orders at work. Jason tried to control where you went and with whom. He thrived on pushing you away in public, and becoming closer in private. Jason was into mind games. This is different."

"Is it?"

"Of course." He leaned in and whispered conspiringly. "Marco used to order me around in the bedroom all the time. It was just part of the experience."

"He did?"

"Yes, and I loved every second of it." He leaned in closer. "In the bedroom, I'm submissive." He nodded, as if that explained everything. "We used to go to a club and hang out with others who did similar things, but Leo put a stop to it. He told Marco that it wasn't good for the family's reputation for him to be seen at a club that specialized in carnal pleasures with a male lover." Wes rolled his eyes.

"You've been to a club like that? With Marco?"

"Yes." He considered her for a moment. "He introduced me to it, and I was hooked. Once Leo forbid him to go there again, we started staging most of our scenes by ourselves, but sometimes I really miss the crowd, you know?" His features twisted into sadness. "Not that it matters anymore. Marco's still mad at me over what happened with the phone."

"Did you ever find it?"

"Leo found it in the penthouse suite and gave it to Marco. Thank God it was password protected. If Leo had seen those naked pictures . . ."

"You erased them, right?"

"Hell, no." Wes pulled out his phone. "I mean, Marco told me to erase them, and I will. Eventually." He flashed her a knowing smile. "I need something to help me get through the day, you know?" He frowned at the phone's screen. "Marco has been so busy. We hardly have any time alone together anymore."

"Wes, you have to get rid of those pictures." Karin covered the phone and waited for Wes to look up at her. "What if the paparazzi got them?"

Wes rolled his eyes. "Just give me a few days." He pocketed the cell and considered her for a moment. "Marco likes to live dangerously, and knowing I have those pictures on my phone is a turn-on. I can tell."

"How can you . . ." Karin shook her head. "Forget it. I don't want to know."

Wes chuckled as he pulled out his wallet. "When you sleep with a Perconti brother, you're bound to get more than you bargained for."

"What are you doing?" Karin asked.

"Here." He pulled out a card. "Take this."

"What is it?"

"It's a card from that club Marco and I used to go to. The first Friday of the month is newbie night."

"What?"

He grinned. "It's when people who are curious and want to learn more about 'the lifestyle' show up and ask questions. Doors open at nine. You should go."

"No, thanks." Embarrassed, she pushed the card back toward him.

"Do me a favor," he said, sliding the card back over to her. "Keep it and think about it for a little bit."

She pushed the card into his hands. "But Leo—"

"Forget Leo and go have fun with someone else." He pressed it into her fingers and stood. "And I won't take no for an answer. If you enjoyed yourself as much as I think you did, then you won't be satisfied with plain old sex anymore. You'll always be craving more."

"But—"

"You want to get Leo out of your system?" He nodded at the card. "Then go. I guarantee that you'll find the answers you're looking for there." Wes's work phone pinged, and he pulled it out to check his messages. "I'm needed on the fourth floor." He gave her a quick hug. "We'll talk more about this later, okay?"

She ran her fingers over the embossed navy blue lettering on the business card: DARK DESIRES. Even the name sounded seductive. What was she thinking? Never in a million years would she ever think of going to such a place.

Then again, she never would've thought that she would have enjoyed following Leo's commands in the bedroom, either.

Karin wasn't sure if she was ever going to visit a club. Unlike Wes, she wasn't into exploring her sexual side with a crowd. In fact, she couldn't imagine ever doing that with anyone but Leo.

This isn't finished, cara. *Not by a long shot.* Leo's words once again rang through her head as she ran her finger over the Web site address in the lower right-hand corner. If Leo was determined to make her part of his games, then maybe she should at least look into it.

Hours later, Karin collapsed into her cubicle chair and blew the hair out of her eyes. *What a mess.* In the hours since her talk with Wes, she had become more determined than ever to learn all she could about Leo's bedroom games. She was fond of Leo, but more importantly, she was addicted to what he could do to her body. Unfortunately, she had been too busy with Marco's tasks to follow up on her plan.

It would probably be better to wait until she got home to do her research, but she couldn't afford to take that risk. At any moment Leo could walk around that corner, and she had to have her defenses in place or risk succumbing to his charms once more.

Determined, Karin pulled out the business card and typed in the Web address. What popped up on the screen was a picture of a brick building a few streets over from Fenway Park. She squinted at the building and was impressed that it looked like any other club in Boston. There was a sign, tinted glass doors, and an overhang for people to wait under when it rained. Nothing about the building suggested anything lewd or crass. In fact, it looked classy.

The picture took up the center of the screen, and a large, beige border surrounded it. Underneath the picture in small type were the words "Click to enter."

As she clicked, a pop-up window appeared asking for a username and password.

"Damn." Wes hadn't told her that it was a closed Web site. Then again, he had wanted her to attend the club in person, not research the place online. Karin sighed and ran her finger over the mouse button. "Now what?"

She hesitated a moment, then went to Google. She typed in "BDSM," then "submissive." She found some interesting links, but when she clicked on them, they all were blocked by the Internet security system of the hotel.

This was ridiculous. She needed to stop searching for sexual kinks on the Internet at work. The hotel firewall wasn't going to let her get anywhere, and her browser history was going to raise questions she wasn't sure she could answer. Damn Leo, she was a good girl, a sensible girl. She should be focusing on her internship, not some sexual perversion. She cleared her browser history and cookies and tried to focus on her work.

It was difficult. She couldn't stop thinking about her interaction with Leo in the elevator, and wondered if he'd really meant it when he said that what was between them wasn't over. She hoped he was right. A part of her wanted him to come and carry her up the stairs to the penthouse suite, like some action hero in one of her favorite movies. Then, once they were alone, he'd command her body again.

It was too bad that the Internet firewall prevented her from learning more . . . or did it? After a quick glance around to make sure no one was watching, she went to Wikipedia. There, she typed a few choice keywords into the search engine. What popped up was an assortment of terms and pictures that made her blush.

"Oh my God," she whispered. Quickly, she scrolled down and skimmed information about safe words, bondage, and collars. She thought about the blindfold Leo had placed over her eyes. All of her senses had been heightened. Each touch felt more erotic, each kiss more intense. If Leo could take her to these amazing heights with just a simple blindfold, then what would happen if he used handcuffs, or a paddle?

Karin moistened her lips as she pictured Leo standing above her prone body, paddle in hand. She'd be chained to the bedposts, and her ass would be upright in the air, ready for punishment. He'd slap the paddle into his opposite hand, making a hard, cracking noise and filling the air with tension. Karin would brace herself as his low, sexy voice rumbled from behind.

"You've been a bad girl, *cara,*" he'd say. Then he'd rub the flat end of the paddle over her ass, stimulating the already sensitive skin.

"Karin?" Gloria popped her head over the cubicle wall. "Are you busy?"

Karin bolted upright in her chair, realizing that her hand had absently moved over her nipple. *Shit*. She lowered her arms and held her breath as she looked up at her coworker. "No, not at all. Why?"

"Good. I just got off the phone with Marco and he wants to see both of us in his office. Something about going over that spreadsheet you made for his brother's meeting this afternoon."

"Okay." Karin glanced at her computer screen and bit back a gasp of horror at the chained woman in leather. Thank God her screen faced away from the cubicle's opening and Gloria couldn't see it from her position overhead.

"We need to go now, Karin. You know what Marco is like when he's kept waiting." Gloria left her cubicle and walked around the divider. "He seemed on edge. I don't want to give him a reason to yell."

"Okay." Karin grabbed the mouse and slid it up to the far corner of the browser.

"Where are those numbers?" Marco bellowed from the far end of the cubicle farm. "Karin? I need those expense spreadsheets you've been working on."

"Yes, Mr. Perconti," Karin shouted from her cube.

"Now."

Karin clicked the button to minimize the screen, grabbed a stack of folders, and hurried to his office door. It was going to be a long afternoon.

Leo strode through the large office area toward Marco's office. Normally he took pride in his punctuality, but today he felt out of sorts. He couldn't stop thinking about Karin, or the sexually charged moment they had shared in the elevator.

As he wove his way through the cubicle farm, he wondered if he had pushed her too hard. When he had told her that things weren't finished between them, she had looked surprised, yes, but also intrigued. She was curious about their time together in his penthouse. He suspected that no one had ever given her commands in the bedroom before. It probably had confused and frightened her.

But it had also excited her. Leo could tell by the way she shivered at the sound of his voice, and the hitch in her breath when he had touched her. He was sure that the attraction he felt was mutual, but he wondered if she was ready for his intensity in the bedroom.

Pursuing her was a risk. If she wasn't ready, she could become frightened and then run to the first reporter willing to listen. Leo ground his teeth as he realized how much he could lose if Karin decided to end whatever they had and make their tryst public.

It would be disastrous not only for him, but his company. If he let her into his world, she would gain enough knowledge to ruin him and his family.

Common sense dictated that he leave her alone. There was simply too much risk involved in pursuing his little maid. Karin had no idea how to survive in his world, with jealous rivals and eager paparazzi. They'd eat her alive. One picture of her and Leo together, and it would be all over the news. People would be scrambling to find out every little dirty secret, and wouldn't hesitate to drag her name through the mud.

His name would be dragged through the mud as well. Leo knew that if given the chance, that reporter for *Whispers* magazine would splash his name all over the tabloid. Photographing a Perconti brother brought in big bucks, and learning juicy gossip could set up one of those reporters on easy street for most of the year. He had to be careful what he did. That was why, in his mid-twenties, he'd

decided to stop attending BDSM clubs. Even with their se-
crecy, the risk was just too great. If word ever got out about
Leo's kinky bedroom habits, his company would suffer.

His family would suffer as well. Each one of his siblings depended on the income that Perconti Enterprises
provided. Leo's actions had dire consequences. So he buried his natural tendency to dominate, instead partaking in
vanilla sex. Unfortunately, the encounters had always left
him unsatisfied. That is, until Karin.

With Karin, Leo saw the possibility of letting go of his
tight rein on his dominant side. He could be free to explore
and push boundaries, not only with Karin, but himself.
Whether she knew it or not, she had a submissive side to
her. It called to him. The only question left was if she was
willing to embrace it—and if he was willing to risk her
rejection and betrayal. Information about his private life
was valuable, and would translate into quite a bit of cash if
she talked to the right people.

As Leo reached Marco's office, voices rose up from
behind the closed oak door. He recognized the deep baritone as Marco and the soft, female voice as Karin. They
were talking about spreadsheets and expense reports.
Marco's voice sounded on edge and Leo smiled to himself. It would do his brother good to feel some of the
heat Leo himself had been feeling these past few months.
Perhaps it would motivate him to stop spending the Perconti savings on lavish meals and focus on the company.

Leo checked his watch. Perhaps he should let his brother
sweat it out a little more before he barged in on their meeting. The more prepared Marco was, the quicker this would
all be over, and Leo could turn his attention back to more
important things, like Karin.

Leo turned away from the door and wandered slowly
back through the cubicle area as he remembered how good
her naked body felt against him in the bath. She was ex-

quisite in every way—and so innocent. Everything was new to her, and Leo loved experiencing everything again through her eyes.

He paused outside one cubicle and stared at the name on the temporary plate. This was Karin's desk, her home at his hotel. He peeked inside and saw that it looked hopelessly sterile. Instead of photographs on her corkboard, Karin had lists and calendars. Instead of printed artwork, there were textbooks and notepads. There were no stuffed animals, no crumpled notebook paper, or empty cans of soda. The only sign of life was a small, half-dead plant she kept on the corner of her desk. It looked like it hadn't been watered in weeks.

Everything was neat, tidy, and organized. Nothing gave a hint as to who Karin really was. Oh, he knew she was a grad student and an intern, but what did she like to do with her spare time? Leo didn't know. Worse, it looked as if Karin didn't know, either.

Frowning, he moved the chair aside to take a closer look at a calendar and bumped the mouse of her desktop. Some internal fan started whirring, and the ancient dinosaur of a computer sprang to life.

Her desktop background, a sunset, flashed on the screen. There were a handful of folders lined neatly along the far edge, and a few shortcuts down below. Otherwise, the computer seemed rather clean for someone who spent a lot of time at her desk.

Clean and orderly, without a hint of fuss. The woman was in desperate need of letting loose, but was she ready to take the next step?

Frowning, he scanned the shortcuts and discovered that she had left her browser open. Intrigued, he opened the tab and stared at the screen. The Wikipedia page came into view and a slow smile spread out over his face as he scanned the page.

She was ready. More than ready. Her resistance to his advances didn't come from being appalled by his brand of kink, but from a denial of her true self. She had told him that she wanted no part of his games, but then turned around and started researching bondage on the Internet. Using a work computer, no less. The woman was so eager to learn more that she couldn't wait to get home before she attempted to appease her curiosity.

What intrigued Karin the most—bondage or role play? Perhaps a little of both. The more Leo thought about the possibilities, the harder he became.

He minimized the Web browser and opened up a blank document. After a quick glance around to make sure no one was looking over his shoulder, he began to type.

Karin was frazzled. She knew that Marco could be tough sometimes, but his edginess over the Palazzo's accounts had somehow gotten passed on to her. After twenty minutes of arguing, Marco finally dismissed her and said to send Leo in to see him.

Leo. Karin steeled her emotions as she exited Marco's office and met Leo's gaze. It did no good. Her insides melted over how his hair fell casually along his forehead and around his ears. She felt so small next to his large, six-foot frame. So helpless. She didn't want him to know that, so she raised her chin and forced herself to meet his hazel gaze.

"Mr. Perconti will see you now."

Karin was met with silence as he considered her for a moment. It must have been seconds, but it felt like an eternity. Finally, unable to take his all-knowing stare any longer, Karin averted her gaze.

"Ms. Norell." Leo nodded and headed into Marco's office, closing the door behind him.

What just happened? Karin felt as if it was significant,

but couldn't understand why. Leo, for the most part, behaved as if he had never blindfolded her, never commanded her to pleasure herself. She wasn't sure what to make of that, and as she settled back at her desk, she tried to tell herself that it didn't matter.

And this was a good thing. They both came from different worlds, and continuing to have sex would bring nothing but trouble. Besides, she had no time for such foolishness. She had classes to contend with, an internship to master, and student loans to pay off. Now if only she could get her hormones to agree with her head.

Karin put the stack of folders on her desk and opened her browser. Instead of seeing the familiar sunset background, she saw an open document. Her heart thudded in her chest as she scanned the words on the screen, then read them a second time.

Meet me in my penthouse at four o'clock. Come alone.

There was no name, but it was obvious who it was from. She considered his request. No, not a request, a demand. Every muscle in her body screamed at her to run up to the penthouse this very minute and wait for him. The more rational side of her thought that this was ridiculous. It would serve him right if she ignored it.

The more she thought about the note, the more conflicted she felt. Nibbling on her lower lip, she checked the time. She had three hours before he expected her to be in the penthouse suite. Three hours to decide if she was going to meet Leo's demand.

She closed out the document and opened up her Web browser. A woman tied up in rope stared back, her eyes wild with excitement. Karin wondered if this was what Leo wanted from her. More importantly, she wondered why seeing this woman, so helpless yet so aroused, sent tendrils of desire spiraling through her body.

Chapter 6

Karin stepped into the elevator and swiped her card for the penthouse suite at precisely four o'clock. For three hours she had been arguing with herself over whether this was a good idea and decided that she was just too curious to let this opportunity pass her by. Even so, apprehension slithered down her spine as the elevator started to rise. The sensible part of her wanted to ignore the note and focus on completing the tedious assignments Marco and Gloria had given her earlier that day. It was the right thing to do, and what was expected of her.

Unfortunately, if she did that, she'd never know why Leo had asked her up to the suite. He had left no reason for his summons, and he might not have had anything sexual in mind at all when he left her that note. Perhaps he just wanted to go over some spreadsheets, just like Marco had earlier that day. It was widely known by the staff that Leo had taken over the office area in the penthouse and made it his own temporary work space. If all he wanted to do was check some figures, wasn't it her job to see that he had the information he needed?

As the elevator came to a halt, she thought about what Wes had said about him and Marco going to Dark Desires together. She wondered if Leo had ever gone to the club, or if he wanted to take her tonight.

"Now you're just letting your imagination run away with you," she scolded herself. There was no good, rational reason why the head of Perconti Enterprises would want to take one of his interns to a club like that. Most likely, Leo would talk about the Palazzo with her for an hour, and then she'd go home. In fact, this was the most logical explanation, and why she had brought her coat and purse up with her to the penthouse suite. If he kept her late, she wouldn't have to swing by her cubicle—and face all of those curious expressions—before heading home. She could slip out the back.

Karin adjusted her wool jacket and switched her purse to the other shoulder as the doors opened.

"Mr. Perconti?" She took a cautious step into the empty foyer. "Sir?"

Silence was her only reply. She took a few steps more and hesitated. "Is there anyone here?"

No one responded. Frowning, she walked through the apartment room by room and confirmed that she was alone.

Confused, she returned to the living area and sat down on the couch. It was then that she noticed a plain, white envelope on the coffee table. Her name in some sort of hurried, masculine script decorated the front.

After a moment's hesitation, she picked up the envelope and opened it.

There's a dress and shoes in the hall closet next to the bathroom—wear them. I will arrive shortly to see how it fits.

Karin read the note again and rested it on her lap. *A dress.* It was probably expensive. For a brief moment, Karin thought that he might want to take her out, but then dismissed the idea. Leo would never be so foolish as to risk being seen in public with a member of the Palazzo staff. The reporters would fall over themselves taking pictures and asking questions.

No, he'd never take her out in public, so why the dress? Maybe the dress itself would give a clue. Leaving the envelope on the table, she stood and made her way over to the closet.

"What are you up to?" She opened the door, and instead of finding an elegant evening gown like she expected, she discovered a skimpy black and white outfit covered in a plastic bag. "What the—"

She pulled it out to get a better look. The piece appeared to be some type of uniform. Not just any uniform, but something impractical one would pick out for a costume. A quick look at the tag showed that it was in her size.

"God, is the skirt short enough?" Karin asked as she took the costume out of the bag and pulled on the ruffled fabric. The white skirt looked as if it would cover only half of her ass. The black bodice was skintight and low-cut. She guessed that it would barely cover her nipples.

As she turned the costume around to get a better look, something caught her eye. A small plastic bag was attached to the other side of the hanger. Inside were a pair of black high heels, a white feather duster, a maid's cap, and another note. She remembered how he had called her his little maid when they were together, and how it had made her burn with desire. Karin fought the ribbon of heat weaving its way through her core. Perhaps he wanted to dive deeper into some sort of maid fantasy. Surely he didn't expect her to clean up his suite in this outfit. Goodness, her breasts would pop out every time she bent over.

She hung up the costume, took the note, and opened it up.

Humor me.

It was just like Leo to be so direct. Karin smiled as she folded the piece of paper and ran her fingers over the ruffled fabric once more. Leo must have guessed that she'd have reservations about this. Karin sighed and tried to decide what to do.

This was . . . weird. No man had ever asked her to dress up before. It was simple enough to do, but she wasn't sure if she should indulge him in his strange request.

Karin knew what she *should* do—go back down to her cubicle and pretend that she had never been inside the penthouse suite. Being with Leo was wrong on so many levels. And this . . . she suspected that this was just the beginning of the odd things Leo would make her do before the night was over. No good could come of it.

Karin grasped the smooth skirt and realized that the material was of high quality. The bodice was real leather, and the white stripe down the front was decorated with fine lace. This outfit wasn't cheap, nor was it bought without thought. Leo had gotten this uniform with her in mind.

She pulled out the dress and walked into the bedroom. There, she tossed the bag on the bed and held the outfit up over her torso in front of the mirror. She imagined herself poured into the tight-fitting bodice, and Leo's hungry gaze sliding over her body. She bit her lower lip as she pictured him ordering her to turn around for his viewing pleasure.

"Oh, what the hell," she muttered to herself. Wearing a costume couldn't hurt. Besides, she was curious as to where all of this was leading. The last time Leo had taken control of a situation, Karin was brought to heights she'd never thought possible. She hated to admit it, but a large part of her wanted to know what a man like that would do for an encore.

The costume was snug, but not tight, and the skirt did cover most of her ass. If she didn't bend over, then all of her private parts would be covered.

She redid her hair into a twist, smoothing all of the loose hairs into place. After slipping on the cap and heels, she picked up the feather duster and turned to the mirror.

"This is ridiculous," she said. The outfit hugged her curves in all of the right places, but it was so impractical. Maybe he wanted to humiliate her, just because he could. Jason had made her do odd things as well, such as hide in closets or climb out windows and wait on fire escapes.

Billionaire playboys liked to play games, and Karin was starting to feel like a pawn.

Tossing the feather duster onto the bed, she grabbed her work clothes and strode toward the elevators. She had no time for such foolishness. This job was her life, her livelihood. It gave her a sense of purpose after her parents' tragic deaths. She wanted to prove to herself that she could stand on her own two feet and make it on her own. Karin wanted to make her parents proud of her.

This outfit was not helping.

Leo was going to be in for a rude awakening when he came up to the room. Karin would be gone, and she'd take the costume with her. Perhaps then he'd learn that he couldn't order people around on a whim. He might be in control of her job, but he didn't rule her life.

Karin slipped her wool coat around her shoulders and stepped into the elevator. After a moment's hesitation, she hit the button for the ground floor. It was close enough to quitting time. She'd slip out the back and head home to drown her sorrows in chardonnay. Then she'd burn the outfit.

She tapped her foot as the elevator came to a stop, impatient to be out of the hotel before anyone saw her. Unfortunately, her getaway wasn't going to be quite so easy. The elevator doors opened, revealing two tall men in expensive suits.

"Karin," Leo said.

Why didn't she use the service elevator? Karin steeled her jaw and looked up into Leo's assessing gaze. His brother Marco stifled a chuckle with the back of his hand.

Without taking his eyes off her, Leo motioned to his brother. "We will discuss this tomorrow."

"Of course," Marco replied. "Karin." He nodded to Karin and moved out of her range of vision.

Leo stepped into the elevator. The doors closed behind him, blocking the rest of the world from view.

Karin took a small step back in the elevator and bumped into the wall. Leo's gaze looked hungry, as if he wanted to tie her up to his bed and ravage her. Her skin heated and tingled all over. His gaze was hypnotic, so much so that she almost didn't notice his frown.

"You were to wait for me in the penthouse suite."

"I changed my mind." She lifted her chin in defiance.

He inched closer and raised his brows. The silence was deafening.

"You can't tell me what to do." Karin pressed her back against the elevator wall as her lower lip trembled. He looked so . . . intense. Her breathing quickened as he angled his body between her and the elevator doors. Leo reached behind him, swiped his card, and waited for the elevator to start climbing before he spoke.

"I can't?" He pocketed his card and hooked his finger under her chin.

"No."

He tilted his head to the side and dropped his gaze to her mouth. "Ever?"

"Ever."

He snapped his gaze back up to meet hers. "If you really meant that, then you never would have come to me the other night." His voice was low and seductive.

Karin shivered with desire as she remembered how he had heard her moving behind him and called her into the bath. Unable to say no, she'd followed his seductive command and given in to a side of herself she never knew existed. Images flashed through her mind of them both in his bath, and how focused he had been on her pleasure. Never before had a man been so focused on her needs. Karin found herself craving that kind of attention again.

Her resolve to teach him a lesson dissolved as she became hyperaware of how close they were standing together in the elevator. It *had* to be possible to be sexually intimate with someone and guard your heart. Wes had sex with Marco all of the time and their open relationship didn't seem to affect him. Perhaps a similar arrangement could be made between her and Leo.

"Well, maybe I like to take orders once in a while," she said, dropping her gaze to his firm mouth. She imagined it on her skin, tasting and teasing her senses.

"Like when?" He ran his thumb over her lower lip, causing her entire body to tighten with need. Before she could stop herself, Karin slipped her tongue between her lips and licked the tip of his thumb. Golden fire flashed through his eyes as he lowered his hand.

Never before had anyone looked at her with such hunger, such desire. Karin dropped her work clothes and gripped the sleeves of his suit as the world around them began to fade away. "Like now."

"Well, Ms. Norell." His voice rumbled as the elevator doors opened. "Come back into my suite, so we can finish what we started."

Before Karin could reply, he bent his head, and captured her lips with his own.

The kiss stole her breath. The man radiated strength and confidence. It was hard not to forget about her problems and lose herself in his rich, masculine taste. He leaned closer, and Karin inhaled his fresh, citrus scent. She tilted her head and invited him deeper. His taste burst in her mouth, making her weak in the knees.

Leo broke away from her lips and began creating a hot, wet trail along her jaw and neck. "Love the uniform."

"You should, you picked it out."

"It's perfect for what I have in mind."

Before she could ask what he was thinking, he kissed her lips again, sending her desire into overdrive. The cool metal of the walls pressed against her back and all six feet of hot Italian male rubbed up against her front. Desire rose up and bubbled through her body as she wrapped her arms around his neck and threaded her fingers through his thick, dark hair. The kiss became harder, more passionate. Karin gasped against his lips as his hands explored her back and sides, sending tingles of warmth along her skin.

"Wait," he gasped as he pulled away and placed his palms over her hips.

"What?" Karin tightened her grip around his neck to steady herself.

He reached behind and slammed his palm on the emergency button of the control panel. An alarm sounded, and the elevator doors froze in the open position.

Leo didn't seem to notice. He placed his palms back on her hips and bent his head until he was eye level. The look in his eyes was serious and intense.

"What happens in the penthouse must never be spoken aloud to anyone. You understand?"

Discretion. It was something Karin knew well. Jason had demanded it of her and although it made her chest squeeze with pain, she understood it. He was a CEO and couldn't afford to have his private life brought out for public viewing.

"I understand."

"Do you?" He leaned in closer. "I'm not kidding around. This is serious."

"I'd never—"

"Promise me." His voice was low and insistent as he searched Karin's face.

Karin started to reach out to touch his cheek, then stopped herself. "This is really important to you, isn't it?"

"More than you realize." He pushed away from her. "I've been betrayed before, Karin. I won't allow someone to do that to me again."

She reached up and brushed her fingers along the side of his cheek. "You have nothing to worry about with me. I won't say a word, to anyone."

"Thank you." He closed his eyes and let out a long breath. "If you want to stop, say 'red.'" He opened his eyes and inched closer. "Understand?"

Karin nodded and tried to kiss him, but he pulled back.

"Say it."

"Say what?"

"Say your safe word."

Excitement rippled through her as she remembered what she had read online. A safe word was something someone used when things got too intense. She realized that he was giving her an out. The fact that he'd do this only made her want him more.

"Say it." He tightened his grip on her hips and shook her slightly, as if emphasizing his words.

"Red," she whispered.

He closed his eyes and loosened his grip. "Good." He hesitated a moment before continuing. "All you have to do is say the word, *cara,* and I'll stop."

Karin ran her fingers over his cheek and waited for him to open his eyes. "What if I don't want you to stop?" Before he could respond, she stood on her tiptoes, and brushed her lips against his.

Leo slid his arms around her waist as he teased her lips open and slipped inside her mouth. Karin whimpered as she trailed her fingers over his head, neck, and shoulders, feeling every inch of his skin. She wanted to touch more of him and feel his skin next to hers. Desperate, she slid her hands around to his front and attacked the buttons on his dress shirt.

Leo pulled back and picked up her clothes. "Hold this." He tossed the work uniform to her and Karin caught it before it could hit the floor.

"But I can't touch you if I'm holding this."

"That's the idea." The air in the elevator grew warm as Leo kissed her neck and slid his hands down over her ass. After a quick squeeze, he lifted her off the ground. She instinctively wrapped her legs around his trim hips as he turned their bodies so her back pressed against the elevator wall. He held her up against there with his weight, freeing his hands to grip the back of her head and drag her once more to his lips.

She quickly thought about the last man she had sex with, and how different he was from Leo. Jason had never confided in her, or become emotional. Leo trusted her enough to tell her about being betrayed and when she looked in his eyes she saw vulnerability, something Jason had never shown. Things had gone from physical to emotional so quickly. It was hard to keep her head from spinning, yet she wanted more of the real Leo, not the icy general that the public saw.

Leo slipped his hand back down and cradled her as they kissed their way into the penthouse suite. They made it through the small foyer and around the furniture in the living area. Karin had no idea where they were going, but she didn't care. All she wanted to do was to be with Leo, to feast on him and pull him deep inside her body until neither one of them knew where one person ended and the other began.

She tossed her work uniform aside and tore at his clothes, fumbling with the buttons on his shirt as he rubbed his thick cock in between her thighs. A sense of urgency overcame her as he captured her lips once more. She ripped open his shirt and slid her fingers underneath the fabric. His chest felt smooth and hard, as she eased her hands over the dips and rises of muscle, loving the way his warm skin felt against her fingertips.

Leo set her down on something cold. She opened her eyes and tore her lips away from his.

"What are we doing?" It was then that she realized that they were outside. Cool air brushed her skin, making her shiver.

Her question seemed to have brought Leo back to his senses, at least a little bit. He eased away from her and helped her down from the balcony edge. Karin glanced over her shoulder and saw that the sun was nearing the horizon and was starting to set over the large skyscrapers of the Boston skyline.

"When I came back from my meeting this afternoon, my penthouse was a mess."

"What?"

"The suite was filthy."

"I . . . I'm sorry. I wasn't assigned to this floor—"

"Oh, I think you were." He raised his brows and slid his gaze over her body.

Karin glanced down at her disheveled clothes. *She was in a maid's uniform. Was this a scene like the one she had read about on Wikipedia?*

"Although," he said as he removed her work clothes and purse from her hands and tossed them on a nearby chair. "If you don't want to do the work, all you have to do is say the word."

This was it, if she accepted the scene she knew there would be no going back. And right now her excitement was overshadowing her fear. Looking at Leo, she knew that she was the one with the control. One word from her and everything would stop.

All of her life she had done what was expected of her, or at least tried to. She had taken some risks, but they had been calculated, her decisions based on research or weighing her options. Even her dalliance with Jason had been a careful choice, albeit a poor one.

She needed to just relax and enjoy the moment.

Karin looked at Leo's handsome face one last time and made up her mind. "No, I don't want to stop."

A hint of a smile touched his lips. "Good. Then you should know that I don't tolerate staff who are lazy."

"Yes, sir." She tried to curtsey, but it was difficult in the restrictive clothing. Still, pretending to be someone else was exciting. Desire surged through her body as she straightened and met his gaze.

His smile dissolved into a stern frown. "You will have to be punished, of course."

"Punished?"

He considered her for a moment. Karin's heart beat double time as he made a show of assessing her every feature.

"Turn around and place your hands on the stone wall," he commanded in a low, rough voice. The devilish gleam in his eye left no doubt in hers what he meant to do.

Karin hesitated, then turned around and put her hands on the balcony railing. The position placed her body at a forty-five degree angle, and caused her backside to jut out behind her. Leo shifted his stance and placed his palms on her ass. Karin's skin tingled with awareness as she looked over her shoulder to see what he was doing.

"Keep your eyes forward," he said.

Karin jerked her gaze forward and stared out at the city before her. Everything looked so quiet, so peaceful. The evening rush was starting to wane, and pedestrians hurried along to their destinations on the sidewalk below.

Leo's body heat surrounded her as he leaned forward and placed his lips inches from her ear.

"Look at all of those reporters down there, waiting to catch me in a compromising position." He placed his hands over hers on the wall and pressed his long body against her back, cocooning her in his warmth. "If only they could look past the one-way privacy screen that separates us from the rest of the world." He scraped his teeth along her outer ear, making her shiver.

"No one can see us?"

"No one, *cara,* but I see how the thought of being discovered excites you. Imagine it, those reporters looking up and seeing us together . . . but they wouldn't see me, would they? They'd only see you, and how aroused I can make you."

Karin's breath caught as Leo moved his fingers up her arms and then around her waist, splaying them out over her lower abdomen.

"Imagine someone rolling back the privacy screen and seeing me touching you." He inched his hands lower. "Undressing you." He flicked open the buttons on her outfit.

Karin moved to stop him, but he caught her wrist and placed it back along the railing.

"Leave them there," he commanded. "It's part of your punishment." He ran his fingers along the outside of her naked thigh.

Karin groaned as she felt the soft fabric move down her thighs and pool at her feet. Leo slid his rough hands over her skin as her panties fell, setting every nerve ending on fire. Her breath caught as he slid his fingers up and cupped her ass.

"I know you are curious. Before this night is through, I'll have you begging me for release." He squeezed her backside, sending tingles of sensation running through her body.

Karin moaned and closed her eyes. This was insane—and very wrong—but oh God, it felt amazing.

Abruptly, Leo slipped his hands away and stepped back. Confused, Karin listened to the rustling behind her. She wanted to turn around and see what he was doing, but remembered that he had ordered her to keep her gaze focused straight ahead. Anticipation rippled over her skin as she tried to guess at what he was doing behind her.

She shivered as Leo returned and placed his hands on her ass once more. "Now, for your first lesson." His touch was so gentle, so featherlight. It stimulated her skin and fueled her desire. Karin arched her back, pressing her backside into his hand. Leo made a low, throaty sound and placed a hard slap against her skin. Sparks of pain flashed through her like lightning, making her feel wanton and animalistic.

"Hold still." His voice was hard and commanding, but Karin couldn't miss the excitement in his voice.

Karin moaned and curved her back like a stretching cat, sticking her lower half in the air and allowing him better access.

"You like that, don't you?" When she didn't answer, he slapped her again, causing her to groan with need. His voice thickened. "Answer me."

"Yes," she whispered.

"Lesson one: I will tolerate nothing but honesty between us. Understand?"

"Yes."

He slid his fingers over her ass, caressing where he had previously hit. "Now, lesson two . . ."

Karin gasped as he slipped his finger in between her cheeks. The sensation was new, but not unpleasant.

"Lesson two is that you trust me with your pleasure."

He slid his finger down and around the sensitive tissue around her opening. Karin stiffened at the new sensation and tried to wiggle away.

Leo put his hand on her lower back, steadying her. "Relax," he soothed.

Karin relaxed, and Leo's murmur of approval made her feel hot and needy. He slid his finger around her opening until she arched her back once more, eager for . . . something, but she had no idea what.

Just when she was about to ask him for more, Leo withdrew. For a moment she thought he was going to leave her there on the balcony. Confused, she started to turn her head, but then he returned and slipped his finger in between the cheeks of her backside once more. It felt different this time. While before he was rough, this time he was warm and slick.

He leaned over her back and whispered in her ear. "Keep your gaze fixed on the reporters. Imagine their surprise as they look up and see us together."

"Yes." Karin widened her eyes as she watched the reporters talking to one another below her. None of them knew what was going on above their heads. One look, and she'd be exposed for the world to see. It was exciting and incredibly hot.

He resumed the circular motion around her opening. With each rotation, she felt her desire surge.

"As your punishment, you will wear something here while I take you." As he spoke he pressed the tip of his finger against the sensitive opening in her backside. Karin moaned and bit her lower lip as she pressed her ass deeper into his eager hand. Below her, a few more reporters gathered, and she imagined them looking up and seeing both her and Leo.

"It's called an anal plug. It might bring you some pain, but it will also give a lot of pleasure." He pushed his finger harder against her skin, slipping the tip just inside her opening. "You are not to make any noise, understand?"

"Yes." Karin tightened her muscles as he moved the tip of his finger in and out of her backside. She looked down and kept her gaze fixed on the reporters below. Knowing that only a thin privacy screen prevented her and Leo from becoming a tabloid headline made everything more exciting.

"Relax, *cara*. Trust me."

Karin groaned as he inched deeper.

"That's it. Now, concentrate on my hand."

She did as she was told. Back and forth he went, inching deeper and deeper into her body. Karin moistened her lips and concentrated on the friction of his movements. With every thrust, moisture began to gather between her thighs. With every caress, need roared through her veins, causing the hum of voices and traffic below to fade. She focused on his voice as he murmured encouragement. She wanted to please him, just like he was pleasing her. She imagined running her fingers over his tanned skin, and taking his large cock into her mouth . . .

When he slipped his finger into her backside up to the second knuckle, she whispered his name and arched her back, urging him deeper.

"Finally, you are ready," he murmured. Leo removed his hand and replaced it with something else, something cool, hard, and unyielding. It was covered in the same slick substance as his finger was moments before. Karin stiffened.

"What is it?" she asked.

"This might be uncomfortable at first, but relax and you will soon find it pleasurable."

Karin tried to do as he commanded.

"That's it. Trust me to care for you."

He worked the object back and forth just like he had

his finger. Karin felt her muscles stretch as it plunged deeper and deeper into her body. She whimpered as new waves of pleasure blanketed her system.

"Do you like how it feels?"

"Yes."

"Good." He slipped the object in as far as it could go. "I had Roberto get this along with the uniform."

She didn't know who Roberto was, and felt a little uncomfortable with Leo talking to someone about what had happened between them.

"Don't worry," he said, sensing her distress. "He is discreet. I'd trust him with my life." Leo slid his fingers over her ass cheek. "Remember, don't move, and don't make a sound."

She heard the rhythmic clicking of a zipper being undone, and then something tear. Before she could ask what he was doing, he reached around the ruffles of her skirt and eased his finger in between her folds. Karin groaned and whispered his name as he traced a seductive line around her opening. She wanted more, so much more. It was maddening how he teased her body like this.

"Please . . ."

"You will have to beg better than that if you want relief." His voice was low and sexy, but also laced with humor. Karin's whole body shivered with need. If he wanted to, he could make her orgasm with nothing but that sexy Italian accent. It was that powerful, that erotic.

"Leo . . ." She needed more from him. Her entire body had begun shaking, desperate for his touch.

Leo didn't speak, but instead slid his hand up through her folds and found her clit. He rubbed it in an up-and-down motion, causing spirals of pleasure to radiate throughout her body. She whimpered as he pushed his hips against her backside. His thick, condom-covered cock slid in between her cheeks and pressed against the object, causing it to inch deeper.

Karin bit her lower lip as pleasure spiraled out through her core and blanketed her body. She wanted to move, but didn't dare.

The tension built, and her muscles tightened with need. Karin steeled her jaw as she felt herself stretching, reaching toward that unseen goal.

When she felt herself on the edge, just shy of toppling over into oblivion, Leo removed his hands and straightened. Karin whimpered as he placed his lips against her back and positioned the tip of his erection against her slit. "Open your legs for me, Karin."

She spread her legs wider in invitation. Leo slid the tip of his cock just inside her and held it there, teasing her with its presence.

"Keep your focus forward." He slid his hands around her body, spreading his fingers out over her lower abdomen. "I want you to feel. Feel me. Feel us." He leaned over her back, cocooning her with his warmth. "I want you to realize how good we fit together, and how wonderful everything can be when you let me take control." He pinched her nipples through the fabric of the uniform, sending sparks of pain through her body. She felt trapped, wonderfully trapped beneath his massive frame.

"Feel both the pain and pleasure." He freed her breasts from the restrictive bodice and cupped them with his large palms. Karin made a low, throaty sound as she lowered her chest and pressed her breasts into his hands. He teased her nipples, all the while keeping his hips still.

Soon, Karin realized what he meant by torture. Her body drew up tight, straining for release. Every time she wiggled and tried to get him to move his hips, he'd remove his hands from her breasts and slap the side of her ass, causing her grip to tighten on the balcony wall. Then, once she stopped fidgeting, he'd return and tease her breasts once more.

"Let it build," he commanded. He pinched her sensitive tips, and she gasped as longing filled her body.

"Please." Her voice came out in barely more than a whisper.

"More, *cara*. I want more."

"Please, Leo."

"You know what I need from you—trust. Nothing but complete and total trust will bring you release." He shifted his hips, sliding his cock a fraction of an inch inside her. Karin moaned and gripped the wall harder.

"Give yourself over to me completely."

"Please," she whispered. He was going so slowly. She didn't know if she could take much more of this sweet torture.

He stilled his movements until nothing but her heavy breathing filled the space between them. "Honesty, *cara*. Tell me what you want." He inched forward until his torso rubbed up against her back and his head was next to hers.

Wasn't it obvious? Confused, she turned her head and met his gaze.

It was in that moment that she saw it. His features may have been hard, but his eyes gave everything away. Not only was he holding her back from the edge, but he was holding himself back as well. Instead of taking what he wanted, he denied both himself and her, waiting for her to trust him with her care.

In that brief, wonderful moment, she finally understood what he was asking of her.

"I want what you want." She eased toward him and brushed her lips against his. "I trust that you know what's best for me."

His features softened as he pressed his lips to her forehead. "What's best for us."

Leo straightened and grabbed her waist. Before she could process what was happening, he was pushing himself deep into her channel, filling her to the hilt.

Karin cried out with pleasure as his hips slammed against her backside. His body flush with hers, edging the object deeper into her ass. Karin groaned as she was filled from both the front and back. Once fully seated, Leo held himself still and let her body adjust to the intrusion. Her mind blanked, filling with desire and need. She wanted to move, but had been punished earlier when he told her to hold still.

She tightened her inner walls, causing him to groan.

"*Cara,*" he whispered in her ear. "You must wait. Denying ourselves pleasure now will only heighten our response." He bent over her once more and played with her breasts, pinching and stroking them until they formed sharp peaks beneath his fingers.

And yet still, he wouldn't move his hips.

Karin tightened her grip on the railing. Her breathing quickened and her heartbeat sped up. She wanted to move, oh God, she wanted to move. She craved to feel the sweet friction of their skin rubbing together. She longed to hear the sound of their bodies coming together in erotic bliss.

Desire swirled through her veins, filling her, possessing her.

"Leo, please."

Instead of relenting, he pinched her breasts harder, sending fresh sparks of pain through her body. It infused her with desire, pushing her closer and closer to the edge. She moistened her lips and tightened her pussy around his cock, silently urging him to action.

"Can you feel it, *cara*?" His voice sounded breathy, urgent. "Concentrate on the building of sensations." He tugged her nipples and Karin bit her lower lip as urgency swept through her body. "Feel how my fingers caress your breasts, how the plug stretches your muscles and causes you to tighten around my cock."

"Yes."

"Just let it sweep you higher and higher."

"Oh, Leo." Karin opened her eyes and looked out over the cityscape. The setting sun outlined the buildings, casting a red and yellow halo around the structures. Down below, people rushed along the street, hurrying home after a long day of work. She imagined one of those pedestrians glancing up to find her watching him. She imagined the erotic picture she and Leo must make.

A tingling sensation formed in her lower abdomen. "Oh God, I'm going to come." She couldn't believe it, but it was true. This man was going to make her orgasm without moving an inch.

"Not yet." Leo leaned back away from her body and grabbed her hips. "Let the sensations drive you, but don't go over the edge until I say, do you understand?"

"Yes." Before she could ask what he was doing, Leo began to move. His thrusts came hard and fast. Each time their bodies came together she cried out. Leo was large, and the plug in her ass made him feel even larger. He filled her channel, stimulating her from both the front and back every time he drove himself home.

The man was relentless. Her mind fogged as tension built throughout her body. It wound its way around her muscles, tightening her limbs and causing her to groan with desire. The primal sound of their bodies coming together filled the air. It felt so animalistic, having sex out in the open like this. The added sensation from the plug put her in sensory overload.

The man was amazing. Never before had she felt anything so good. Again and again he filled her, pushing her closer to the point of breaking.

"God, Leo. Please, let me come. I'm so close."

"Not yet." His voice sounded strained, as if he, too, was holding back from the edge.

She moved against him as her mind plunged deeper into the erotic haze. "Leo, I can't hold on."

"Then let it go, *cara*." Leo reached around her and found her clit. "Let it go." He rubbed it, just like he did before. Once, twice, on the third time her world exploded. Pleasure crashed through her body, filling her with joy. She cried out as her pussy hugged his cock and ecstasy swam through her veins.

Leo's movements became jerkier as his low, throaty groans filled the air between them. He pushed harder, faster. Suddenly he stiffened and whispered her name. With long, urgent strokes, he filled her as he tumbled over the edge into oblivion.

They both stayed in that space where time stood still and they became numb with ecstasy. As Leo wrapped his arm around her torso, Karin felt their connection deepen. It was like a fantasy, a great torrid fantasy that she never wanted to leave.

"Karin." Leo placed the kiss on the side of her neck as he withdrew his cock. "My lovely little maid." Within moments, he had removed the plug as well. She had no idea what he did with the sex toy or the condom, nor did she care. All that mattered was that he came back. As he lifted her up into the air, Karin slid her arms around his neck. He pressed his lips against hers as he carried her back inside the penthouse suite. The kiss was soft and reassuring. Karin felt a little dizzy as he carried her back through the suite toward the bedroom.

"You did wonderful, *cara*. Each time we're together, I'll

push both of us a little further, and you'll learn to trust me a little more."

Each time? Karin's heart sang at the prospect of doing this with him again. Her body had never felt as wonderful as it did in that moment. As Leo let her down on the bed, she wondered if this was one fantasy that didn't have to end.

Leo started to climb into bed next to her, when the sound of ringing pierced through the air.

"What's that noise?" he asked.

Her phone. Karin silently cursed Marco's staff-issued phones and sat up in the bed. "Where are my clothes?"

Leo hesitated. "Back on the balcony. Why?"

"That's my phone." She gathered a throw blanket around her body and hurried out onto the balcony. After a quick search, she found her work uniform and stuck her hands into the pockets.

"Is everything okay?" Leo asked from behind.

Damn, it was Wes. "Yeah," she called out over her shoulder. "I'll just be a minute." She walked out of earshot as she flipped open the phone and put it to her ear. "I'm here."

"Darlin', where have you been? I've been looking everywhere for you."

"I'm . . . I'm still here."

There was a slight pause. "Marco told me that you and Leo were pretty hot for each other in the elevator . . ."

"It's not like that."

"It's not?"

"No . . . it's complicated."

"Oh my God. You're starting to have feelings for him, aren't you?"

"I'm almost done here. I'll be right down." Karin started to disconnect, but something Wes said made her hesitate.

"Karin, if there are emotions involved, then you have to stop this. Now."

"Stop it?"

"Seeing Leo."

Anger pierced her chest. "You were the one who told me to go for it."

"That was when things were just physical. Now you're emotionally attached. You're starting to develop feelings for him, I can tell by the tone of your voice. If you keep seeing him, you're going to become more and more attached, and that means it's just going to fall harder when he finally tires of you—and he will tire of you eventually. Trust me on this. I should know."

"Why?"

"Because . . . because I caught Marco with someone else."

Karin's chest tightened as she remembered catching Jason in his office that night. Why were people who had everything sometimes so cruel? It was as if the more money they had, the less compassion they felt.

"Oh, Wes, I'm sorry. What happened?" she asked.

"I went to his office to ask about the status of our new vacuums and caught him naked with a socialite on his desk. I think—I think he wanted me to find them. The bastard always liked to be watched."

"Oh, Wes."

The worst part was that she had the nerve to act all uppity and possessive. The bitch told me that I better stay away from *her* man." He took a deep breath and let it out. "It doesn't matter. I knew what I was getting into when I started sleeping with him. From day one Marco had made it clear that it could never be anything more than sex between us."

"Where are you?"

"In the main conference room—where you should be."

"But it's after five o'clock."

"Since when has our boss let us work normal hours?"

Wes's voice sounded bitter and angry. "I've been trying to get ahold of you for the past thirty minutes."

"I'm so sorry."

"It's okay, just hurry up. Marco is mad that I made an issue about his having sex with other people. He said that I knew the terms of our relationship—no emotions involved."

"Things change—"

"Not for the Perconti brothers. He mentioned something about a pact with his brothers and how he could never get romantically close to anyone without destroying everything. Now he's riding my ass about some wedding guests arriving next week. I need you to get over here, fast."

"I'm coming."

"Good. Oh, and Karin?"

"Yeah?"

"Do yourself a favor and end whatever you have with Leo. Someone told me once that these relationships never work out for people like us. She was right."

Tears stung Karin's eyes as she glanced over her shoulder at Leo. *Too late.* "Okay. Bye."

Karin pocketed the phone and wiped the tears from her eyes. What the hell was she doing? Memories came back of her relationship with Jason. She had caught him with a politician in his office. Now Wes had caught Marco doing the same thing.

"Are you all right, *cara*?"

It was too soon for love, but she was falling pretty hard and fast. The possibility for something more was there. She tightened her grip on her phone as Leo stepped out onto the balcony, wearing nothing but a white bathrobe with the crimson Palazzo emblem. God, the man was beautiful. Power and confidence radiated from him, even when his brow creased with concern. Karin couldn't help but feel drawn to him. He might not have broken her heart yet, but she knew it was only a matter of time before he did.

"Karin?" Leo held out his hand, but Karin inched back from his touch and picked up her pants. "Come back to bed. We have much to discuss—"

"I have to go."

He lowered his arm and frowned. "Is everything all right?"

She stripped out of the maid uniform and shoved on her old clothes. "Yes, it's fine."

"It doesn't look fine."

She jerked her hands into her pockets and moved past him into the living area. What was she doing playing out these fantasies with Leo? Not only could she lose her job, but she could lose both her sanity, and her heart.

"Karin, look at me." Leo touched her shoulder and turned her around to meet his gaze. "What's going on? Who was on the phone?"

"No one—a coworker." She waved her hand in the air in dismissal. "I have to go. Marco wants the conference room cleaned up before we can go home. I . . . I was supposed to be there an hour ago."

"*Cara*." Concern etched his features as he studied her face. "Remember lesson one—complete honesty."

Karin stepped back and held up her hand. "Don't, please."

"Don't what?" He dropped his hands.

"Pretend you care."

"Karin—"

She reached behind her and pressed the elevator button. "Let's just leave this as it is—a pleasant afternoon."

Leo's jaw stiffened. "That's all that you think this was—a pleasant afternoon?"

"Of course." She forced herself to laugh as she blinked back tears. "You don't think that this was something more than sex, do you?" When a pained expression crossed his features, she hit the elevator button behind her once more. "Leo, don't think I don't appreciate . . . everything." She waved her hand in the air as tears formed in her eyes. "But let's not make this out to be more than it is."

"And what exactly is this, *cara*?" Something dark flashed over Leo's features, but she didn't have time to dwell on it.

The elevator doors opened, and Karin slipped inside. She placed her hand on the doors, stopping them from closing. She inhaled a shaky breath before saying the words Jason had said to her, the cold, hard words that brought reality crashing down around her ears. "This is just sex, Leo. It can never be anything more than that."

"Just sex?"

She plowed over his words, paraphrasing the speech Jason had branded on her heart. "We come from different worlds, you and I. I'm sorry if I led you on, but you can't possibly think that what is between us could ever be anything more than casual sex. It just isn't possible. I would be an embarrassment to you and your company."

"Now wait a minute—"

Karin lifted her chin and tried like hell to hang onto her dignity. "This isn't some game, Leo. It's my job you're playing with. My life." Karin blinked back tears. *I will not cry.* "Things like this never work out for people like me."

He took a step forward, then paused. "You sound like you speak from experience."

She focused on his fisted hands and stiffened her resolve. "I am. It's been fun, Leo, but now it has to end." She let go of the elevator door and allowed it to close.

"Why?" Leo jammed his body in between the doors, preventing her from leaving. "Karin—"

"The rumors have already started, and it's only going

to get worse. We need to end it now before we are both destroyed by our foolishness."

Surprise etched his features. "There are rumors?"

She lifted her chin. "There will be."

He shook his head. "So you want to destroy what we're building because of what *might* happen?"

Karin struggled to keep her voice level and confident. "I can't do this anymore, Leo."

"But there is still so much to learn."

"I'm done learning." She pushed Leo back out of the elevator, allowing the doors to close once more. "Good-bye."

"Karin—"

The doors closed and the elevator started to move. Karin wiped the tears from her cheeks and tried to regain her composure.

Breaking it off with Leo was the right thing to do. She was sure of it. Wes was correct in saying that nothing good could come of their sexual interludes. Best-case scenario, she'd end up hurt. Worst case, she'd lose her job and have to start over again, just like what had happened with Jason Stone.

Karin knew that she was doing what was best for both her and Leo. She just wished that it didn't hurt so damn much.

"Karin. Wait!"

Leo threw himself at the elevator as it closed. The machinery inside started up, and he slammed his fist against the sliding doors as the elevator moved away from him, taking Karin with it.

"Karin." He hit the door once more, but only succeeded in putting a dent in the panel. He rested his forehead against the cool metal and closed his eyes.

He couldn't have screwed things up any worse. She

should have laid in bed with him and talked about what happened. He should have learned what she liked about the experience and what she didn't, so that next time he'd know how to push her more.

She had been so responsive to his voice and touch. Not since his club days had he found a woman so eager to please. Something had been said to her during that phone conversation. Rage caused his chest to tighten as he thought about strangling whoever was on the other end of that line. He had to talk to her. With his business, his family, and now this wedding falling apart, he needed her.

He needed her, but he had to be careful. She was right. The rumors that had started when she ran from his room in a bedsheet would only get worse unless he brought things under control. There was so much he had to do, and he could almost feel time slipping through his fingers. He needed to speak to his staff about gossiping, and he had to make Karin see that she was worth more to him than a passing fling. Karin kept his sanity in check, for crying out loud, more so than any of those damn little pills.

Speaking of which . . . Leo retreated to the bathroom and opened the cabinet. A small row of pill bottles stared back at him. Sleeping pills, anxiety pills, depression . . . fuck, he was a mess. Karin was right to break it off with him. He was a fool to think that he had anything to give anyone.

With shaking hands, Leo popped open the bottles and took the required dosage, no more, no less. He normally took his anxiety medication when he first woke up, but his mind had been elsewhere this morning. The behavior wasn't like him. Leo had prided himself on adhering to a strict schedule and keeping his emotions in check. *Discipline. Control.* No woman had ever made him so crazed and forgetful before. Not even Danika.

That last, sobering thought broke through his helpless

stupor and cleared his head. He had given his heart to Danika once, and she had tossed it away like yesterday's trash. He should know better than to become so emotionally dependent on a woman. That path led to nothing but trouble.

He steeled his jaw as he put the pill bottles back in the cabinet. He knew that the best thing he could do was to let Karin go.

But as responsible as he was he didn't always do what was best. The weight of his responsibility was suffocating him, and Karin had become his only release. There had to be some way to make their arrangement work, but how?

Chapter 7

The Next Morning

"Wes, I'm sorry I'm late," Karin said as she hurried into the conference room and closed the distance between them.

Wes looked up from the coffee supplies he was arranging. "Thank God."

"What do you need help with?"

"Sit down for a minute, we need to talk."

"Are you sure? You sounded panicked on the phone. I thought Marco—"

"This is more important."

Karin started to retort, but something in his voice gave her pause. "Okay." She sat down as he pulled some sort of magazine out of his cleaning cart and strode over to the table.

"Did you notice the increased number of reporters outside this morning?"

Did she ever. There were so many reporters, in fact, that Karin was forced to slip in through the back entrance. "Yeah. It's probably for the wedding. I heard that Leo and Marco's sister will be arriving in town this week." She waved her hand in dismissal. "Everyone loves a good story."

"Yes, they do." He dropped the magazine down on the table with an ominous smack.

"What's this?"

"The latest edition of *Whispers*. Check out the cover story." He pushed the magazine toward her.

Karin hesitated, then glanced down at the article. "Holy shit," she whispered.

"And now you know why I called you."

Karin snatched the magazine from his hands. "No. No, no, no." She stared at the grainy picture of Leo's penthouse balcony and the lone woman, obviously some maid, leaning over the edge. Large male hands rested on her shoulders and her back arched in bliss. Above the picture were the words, "Party in the Perconti Penthouse."

"Yes." Wes hooked his finger over the edge of the magazine and tugged it down far enough to study her face. "Care to confess something?"

Karin looked up from the picture and met Wes's gaze. "It was a scene." *And he told me there was a privacy screen.* Considering the angle and the poor quality, it seemed as if someone had used mirrors to get around the screen. *Some people will stop at nothing to get a story.*

"Everyone is talking about who that maid could be. It's only a matter of time before someone snaps a picture clear enough to identify her."

Karin looked back down and started to read the article underneath the picture.

Mounting financial woes and rumors of bankruptcy circling Perconti Enterprises doesn't seem to stop CEO Leo Perconti from sowing his wild oats, and can you blame him? A man that handsome was made for sex. Women can rest assured that Leo knows where his priorities lie. Instead of giving his staff the updated supplies they desperately need, or the cost-of-living raises they

*have gone without for the past three years, he deflects
complaints by showing them why he was named* Whispers
*sexiest bachelor. Yes, my friends, who needs money for
food when you can party with the Perconti Enterprises
CEO in his penthouse suite? While this little maid might
be getting her "raise" from the company's owner, not all
staff members share her excitement. Earlier this week a
blond woman was seen running away from Leo's room in
nothing but a bedsheet and in tears. Perhaps our famous
bachelor's technique is slipping? I don't know about
you, but this* Whispers *reporter is determined to locate
these special women who have caught Leo's attention and
find out . . .*

Karin dropped it on the table and made a grunt of disgust. "I can't believe that's news."

"I know." Wes turned the paper to face him and scanned the page. "This reporter seems determined to interview you. She's offering a fair amount of money for you to come forward."

"I'd never do such a thing."

"Even for six thousand dollars?"

Karin raised her brows. "How much?"

Wes turned the magazine to face her and pointed at the figure. "She is offering both the woman in the bedsheet and the maid on the balcony three thousand each to come forward with their stories."

Karin wrinkled her nose. "That's disgusting."

"And that number is only going to go higher."

"I don't care. I'm not giving that interview."

"Perhaps you should reconsider."

"What?"

Wes shrugged. "There's been talk among the staff . . ."

"Talk about what?"

He considered her for a moment before responding. "The staff is fed up with the poor treatment they've been getting. Some are talking of walking." He steeled his jaw and glanced down at the tabloid. "I might go with them."

Karin stared at her friend as words escaped her. She had known that Wes had been hurt by Marco, but she'd had no idea just how much Wes was suffering until this moment.

"You'd really throw our bosses under the bus like that?"

Wes shrugged and averted his gaze.

"God, Wes, I know Marco hurt you, but—"

"I don't want to talk about it, Karin." He worked his jaw as some indescribable emotion passed through his features. "Not now, not ever."

"It isn't as bad as it seems, I'm sure—"

"Not bad? Not *bad*? *Saying* our relationship means nothing is one thing. *Seeing* him stick his dick into someone else is something different altogether." He shook his head and steeled his jaw as his eyes shone bright with unshed tears. "I'm done with the Perconti family, Karin. Every single last one of them." He picked up the magazine and waved it in the air as he talked. "Those Percontis are used to getting their own way. One word, and we're all scrambling to meet their demands. Then, when we ask for something simple, like a cost-of-living increase, they turn their backs on us."

"Wes—"

"No more, Karin. I'm tired of them fucking around with our emotions and our livelihoods. Let them fend for themselves for a while and see how the rest of the planet lives."

"You may have a point." Karin thought about how she'd almost orgasmed from Leo's commanding voice alone and cringed. Wes was right, the Perconti brothers were used to getting whatever they wanted. They acted without thinking about consequences, and it was high time that they learned to be less self-centered.

It was just unfortunate that teaching them this lesson was so painful.

"So what are you going to do now?" she asked.

"What else can I do?" Wes shrugged and turned back to the cart. "The economy is tight. It isn't like I can exchange this job for another. You, of all people, know how competitive it is out there."

"Yeah." After her blowup with Jason, Karin had been forced to give up her internship. She just couldn't stomach seeing Jason flirt with other women day in and day out. She'd needed to make a clean break from him to heal her heart and had made the impulsive decision to quit. Soon after, she realized that there were no more internships to be had. It took her forever to find a position again, so long that it set back her graduation date by eighteen months.

"Wes, think about what you're saying. Talking to reporters goes against the confidentiality agreement we signed when we got hired. We could lose our jobs."

"We might lose them anyway."

"What do you mean?"

"Leo and Marco have more problems than just this reporter." Wes put down the magazine. "I meant to tell you about this earlier, but with Leo coming, it slipped my mind."

"Tell me what?"

"You know how Marco put our raises on hold again until after the wedding?"

"Yeah."

"I guess a lot of people are upset about that. I mean, three years without even a cost-of-living increase is too long. They were counting on that money to survive."

"Yeah, me, too."

Wes studied her face for a moment. "There's talk of a strike."

"Over raises?"

"It's more than that." He shook his head. "You've been

so busy with school and work that you haven't noticed, have you?"

"Noticed what?"

"That everyone is overworked."

Karin shrugged. "It's because of the wedding."

"Think about it. This has been going on for much longer than the past few weeks. Marco and his siblings are working us until we drop."

"Once their sister Arianna gets married—"

"Have you really drunk the Perconti Kool-Aid?" Wes frowned. "One look at all of those limousines and society parties tells me different."

"What do you mean?"

"I mean . . ." Wes raked his fingers through his hair. "Marco tells us that there's no money, but then he replaces all of the furniture Dante destroys. He buys lavish gifts for his friends and takes his siblings out on spending sprees."

"But he's not using company money for that."

"Yeah, well, that's the thing."

Karin widened her eyes. "He can't be using company money. I've seen the expense reports."

Wes let out a chuckle, but it seemed forced. "He doctors the books."

"He what?"

Wes let out a long breath. "At least, he implied as much when he said that he wanted to take me away for the weekend up to this exclusive place in Vermont so we could be alone and salvage the relationship."

"Oh, Wes."

"When I said that I didn't know he owned a place in Vermont, he said that he didn't. He was thinking about renting it for the season and using company money as a security deposit. He had every intention of paying it back, but . . ." Wes shook his head. "It doesn't matter. What matters is that he's using company funds for private outings and letting his workers suffer."

"I don't know. Are you sure about this? He doesn't seem the type to be so cruel."

"He may not be doing it intentionally, but he's doing it nonetheless. Dante is so self-absorbed that he doesn't see how destructive he is, and Arianna has been too busy with her charity work and her wedding to pay attention to what's going on with the family business."

"But now Leo's here."

"Yeah, Leo." Wes slowly rolled up the magazine as he spoke. "There was hope that Leo would set things right, but now it's become evident that he is interested in more . . . carnal pursuits." He waved the magazine in the air and tossed it in a nearby trash can.

Karin felt her cheeks heat, but refused to look away. "I don't know what to do."

"I don't think there's anything you *can* do. The gears were set in motion the moment that tabloid hit the stands." He sighed. "That reporter is the driving force behind this. She has been stirring up the pot . . ." He steeled his jaw and looked away.

"Well, at least she won't get any more pictures. Leo and I are over."

"Are you sure?"

Karin's chest constricted as she thought about Leo's frustrated expression as the elevator doors closed. His hurt voice still rang in her ears.

"Yes, I'm sure."

Wes let out a long breath. "Good, because your relationship with Leo would only get caught up in the strike—"

Karin straightened in her chair. "So the strike is definite? Before you said it was just talk."

"Not definite, but if things don't change soon . . . I don't know, Karin. Things could get ugly, fast. I don't want to see you become collateral damage in this."

"But the wedding is coming up. Marco said everything will change after the wedding."

"You really want to gamble your paycheck on the whim of a young socialite and her desire to enter a loveless marriage?" He shook his head. "It would be perfect timing, really. The strike would show Marco just how much he needs us."

Karin opened her mouth and then shut it again. "You're really going to join them, aren't you?"

Wes shrugged and grabbed his cart. "I don't know yet. You have to admit, the idea has merit. It isn't like Marco has been treating us well over these past few months."

Yeah, and Marco broke Wes's heart. Karin ached for her friend. She knew what it felt like to be tossed aside. It hurt like hell, and it was obvious that Wes was still trying to cope with it all. "God, what a mess."

"Yeah. It's intense." He bit his lower lip for a moment in thought. "What time is it?"

"Five thirty."

"What are you doing after work?"

"I have a paper to write."

"Not tonight you don't." He smiled and elbowed her arm. "Tonight we will go out and blow off some steam."

"I don't know."

"Ah, come on, Karin. We've both been through a lot. Let's go out and have a little fun. We'll drink and curse the Perconti brothers and these foul jobs."

Karin giggled as she fell into step with her friend. "Where should we go?"

A wicked gleam lit his eyes as he met her gaze. "Sabrina's."

Karin smirked. "You can't be serious."

He shrugged. "Why not?"

"That's Dante's ex-girlfriend's restaurant."

"I know." He leaned in and lowered his voice. "That's why I think it's the perfect place. Think about it. Who better to serve us drinks than Sabrina? It will be a party of Perconti castoffs. Come on, say you'll go."

"I don't know. The end of the semester is coming up and—"

"You work too hard." He nudged her toward the door. "Come on, it's just one night. What harm could there be?"

Wes was right. The more she considered his offer, the more she realized that she could really use a night off. Wes was offering the perfect opportunity to forget her troubles with Leo. She'd be a fool not to take advantage of it.

"Okay."

"Really?"

"Yeah."

Wes grinned. "Great. I'll meet you out front in the foyer in ten minutes." He wheeled his cart away before she had a chance to change her mind. Karin shook her head and smiled after him. While it would have been wiser to go home and work on her paper, she knew that she probably wouldn't have gotten very far. After what happened with Leo, she'd probably ditch her work in favor of drowning her sorrows with a bottle of chardonnay and reruns of bad reality television. At least this way she wouldn't be alone. Knowing Wes, he'd make sure she'd have a little fun as well.

More importantly she needed to get rid of the nagging feeling that breaking it off with Leo was the biggest mistake of her life.

Leo was in a mood, and it had everything to do with Karin.

Twice today he had tried to contact her, but both times his inquiries had been deflected. He couldn't keep pressing her, not without people noticing, so he left her alone and tried to focus on his work.

It was difficult. Karin had reopened the door to new possibilities, one where he could quit pretending to be something he wasn't. With her, he could dispense with his public persona and be free to rediscover a part of himself he had buried long ago. In truth he had buried so much of himself for so long that he had forgotten who he really was.

It had been forever since he had been able to act on pure instinct. What she had done for him that afternoon on the balcony was more than sexual gratification, it was a peek into what his life had become. The job of CEO had been draining the life out of him, but he had been too preoccupied to notice. Karin had single-handedly pulled back reserved layers he had cloaked himself with and given him back a piece of himself. He remembered the good times he used to spend with Marco and Dante carousing in Italy, long before he took on the responsibilities of Perconti Enterprises. He longed for those days again.

Unfortunately, today's issue of *Whispers* reminded him just how risky letting his walls down could be. It didn't matter that he wasn't in the front-page picture. He still felt violated. He could only imagine what Karin had felt when she had seen it. That was why he had searched for her this morning. He didn't want to apologize—he'd never apologize for something that felt so right—but he did want to assure her that he'd do what he could to deflect the reporters and to see if she was all right. Unlike him, Karin hadn't been reading about her private moments in the papers for over a decade. She must have found it jarring.

Leo took out the small package from his suit pocket and stared at the white box with a red bow. It was both a peace offering and a promise. When he saw that tabloid article, he knew that the situation would take a little finesse to smooth over. He had talked to his driver and done some investigating. This present was his best chance at smoothing things over with Karin and returning things to the way they were.

When the elevator doors swung open, he stepped out and scanned the reception area. Karin stood by the front doors, wearing a pastel peacoat around her shoulders and talking to the blond staff member he had seen earlier. Jealousy rippled through him as the man put his arm around her and led her through the revolving doors. She refused to talk to Leo about what had happened between them, but was willing to lean on one of the cleaning staff? Leo pocketed the small box in disgust and started to close the distance between them. The thought of Karin confiding in someone else didn't sit well. He should be the one she turned to, especially in this instance. No one besides him had associated her as the maid in the picture. If she started talking to the staff—or worse, reporters—his whole company could suffer the fallout.

"Whoa there." Marco grabbed his arm, stopping his advance. "What do you think you're doing?" his brother asked.

"Going after them," Leo growled.

"No, you're not." Marco shook his head slightly and let go of Leo's arm. "You can't just go barreling over there like some crazed animal. You'll only add to the gossip." He nodded to the door. "And people are watching."

The doorman and two others made a path for Karin and her friend through the reporters, and they slipped into the crowd. The reporters barely noticed them. All of their attention was focused on Leo. Cameras snapped and shouting could be heard through the doors, but Leo was doing nothing out of the ordinary. Thanks to his men, the reporters were nothing more than unpleasant background noise, noise that he was all too used to having around.

He relaxed his shoulders and let out a long breath. "You're right."

"Of course I'm right." Marco glanced over Leo's shoulder and then moved them both so that they were out of sight from the reporters out front. "Look, I'm not going to tell you *not* to have sex with her. Lord knows, I've had sex with enough people to not be pointing fingers." He steeled his jaw as some indescribable emotion crossed over his features. "But the hard truth is that people like you and I can't have serious relationships. Remember what happened to Dante . . ."

Leo glanced over his shoulder at his staff, and the difficult time they were having holding the reporters at bay. "I know."

"Do you?" Marco gently shook Leo's arm and waited until their gazes met. "You're playing with fire, my friend. This isn't Italy. Once those reporters hear we are interested in someone, then that person's life is splattered all over the papers for the world to see. You don't want what happened to Sabrina to happen to her, do you?"

"No."

"People like Karin and Wes . . . they don't understand this life, what we put up with. Those reporters are just the tip of the iceberg and you know it. If their names become associated with us, the public would eat them alive."

"Why us, Marco?"

"Excuse me?"

"Why do you think the public is so interested in us?"

Marco sighed. "Because we are rich and powerful, I guess."

Leo snorted. "*Were*. If this wedding doesn't happen, we may not be any of those things anymore."

"Ah, but the public doesn't know that, do they?" Marco grinned and clasped his brother's shoulder. "It's the cross we must bear, I'm afraid. No person can resist an opportunity for money and privilege. The fact that we have remained unattached for so long only makes us more interesting." He chuckled and pulled his arm away. "Every woman thinks that they'll be the one to tame us." He winked. "And we can take full advantage of it."

"But—"

Marco shook his head. "No buts." He eased back and glanced over to where Karin and Wes were standing. "Like you told me when you first arrived: we need to focus. The staff is on edge as well as overworked and underpaid. Some, I suspect, are close to quitting. Let's not give them a reason to act impulsively." He lowered his hand. "Instead, let's give them a united front—one that is focused on saving this company."

Leo studied his brother for a moment. "Something happened today, didn't it?" When Marco's grin faltered, Leo's concern grew. "Was it because of the tabloid? Tell me."

"It's nothing. I've already dealt with it." Marco averted his gaze.

"Marco . . ."

"Leo." Marco waved his hand between them in dismissal. "We can't obsess about our staff. We have Arianna's wedding to plan."

"Are you sure it is nothing?"

"Absolutely. Everything is under control."

Leo studied his face for a moment before responding. "Okay, thanks."

"You'll stay away from her?"

"Only if you stay away from your socialites."

"Deal." Marco smiled and stepped back. "Because I'd hate to lock you up in that penthouse suite until our sister arrives."

"When is Ari due, anyway?"

"She's in London now, working on some event for that charity of hers. When that's over, she promised to focus on the wedding. Speaking of which, we have one more mess to clean up before Arianna arrives."

"Yeah? What's that?"

"Someone needs to go over to Sabrina's and tell her to stop taking Dante's calls."

"Why don't you go do it?" Leo asked.

Marco shuddered. "Sabrina and I have never gotten along. You know that." He hesitated for a moment before continuing. "Tell you what. If you go over tonight and talk to her, I'll speak with my staff and have them stop serving Dante. Between the two of us, we should get our brother relatively sober and together for the wedding."

Leo considered Marco's words for a moment. "Agreed. I'll head on over and talk to Sabrina later tonight." He glanced at the reporters outside. "Although if I go, there's sure to be a circus."

"Nonsense." Marco grinned. "Take my Jag. Roberto can bring it around from the garage." He nodded toward the front door. "You can sneak out the back and they'll have no idea you're gone."

"Until someone recognizes me at Sabrina's."

"You worry too much, my friend." Marco put his arm around Leo's shoulder and steered him back toward his office. "I'll make all the arrangements and you'll be in and out before anyone is the wiser. You'll see."

Leo let his brother lead him back toward the offices. With every step he tried harder to push Karin from his thoughts. There was no time to focus on his own selfish desires. He had to do what was best for his family, and that meant reining in his family and making Perconti Enterprises viable once more.

Family was what was most important, and it would serve him well to remember it.

Karin had forgotten how much fun Wes could be. As soon as they had entered the restaurant, the owner, a red-haired, pixie-faced spitfire with the same name as the restaurant, rushed over and gave Wes a hug. He introduced Karin as another Perconti castoff, and before Karin could remove her coat, both she and Wes had been whisked away to a corner booth and given the royal treatment.

"Here you go, honey," Sabrina had said as she set down the glass of her favorite brand of chardonnay. "It's on the house."

When Karin had tried to pay for the glass, Sabrina only shooed her away, saying that all Perconti castoffs had to stick together. A quick glance told Karin that the place was abnormally sparse for prime-time Friday night, but she didn't argue. Quite frankly, she was glad she didn't have to pay. Her credit card bill was overdue and she had gotten her second warning just that morning.

By the third glass of wine, Sabrina had joined them for a round, and that was where the real fun began. The three of them laughed and talked as waitstaff brought in fresh calamari and bread. The conversation remained light and upbeat, as if they all had made an unspoken vow not to mention their troubles with a certain family. When Sabrina's favorite Frank Sinatra song came on, she pulled Wes up from the booth to dance with her, who in turn grabbed Karin's hand. Soon all three of them were bouncing between the tables to the beat of "Come Fly With Me" and "You Make Me Feel So Young." Karin had never heard the old songs before, but it didn't matter. The tunes were catchy, and she'd had more than her fair share of wine. She couldn't remember the last time she'd had so much fun.

Between Sabrina and Wes, Karin was beginning to feel better. They danced, then ate, then danced some more.

Wine flowed freely until Karin lost count of how many drinks she had consumed. While they partied at the far end of the room, a few other patrons entered and left the restaurant, but otherwise the place seemed undisturbed. In fact, the staff hung around and gossiped more than they worked, which left Karin wondering how Sabrina managed to keep the business afloat.

"You two seem to be close," Karin said to Wes as they fell back into their seats, exhausted. It was almost closing time, so Sabrina excused herself to go in back to start the cleanup.

"We were close. When she was dating Dante, she was at the hotel all of the time." He sighed wistfully at her retreating form. "To tell you the truth, I miss it."

"Whatever happened between her and Dante?"

Wes scowled at Karin. "Oh, no, you don't. Not tonight." He raised his glass. "Tonight we only talk about happy things."

Karin laughed and clicked her glass with Wes's. There was something about the owner of the restaurant Karin found intriguing. Wes found her intriguing, too. Karin couldn't help but notice how his gaze followed her back and forth across the room as she chatted with customers.

"How come you never asked her out?" Karin asked when she caught Wes staring at Sabrina's backside.

"Huh?" He dragged his gaze away from the feisty redhead and focused on her.

Karin grinned and dipped her bread into the olive oil. "Sabrina. How come you never asked her out?"

"Oh, our relationship isn't like that."

"It could be."

Wes waved his hand in the air. "I wouldn't be above admitting to a certain fantasy involving her, Marco, and myself, but no. Despite her bravado, I know that she still carries a torch for Dante. And it's obvious that Dante still cares about her. It's the only reason why he places all of those orders."

Karin widened her eyes in surprise. "What are you talking about?"

Wes focused on her. "You know how Dante places those enormous orders from this place when he's drunk?"

"Yeah."

"Well." Wes waved his hand around the almost-empty restaurant, as if their surroundings explained it all. When Karin didn't respond, he chuckled and leaned in close so that only she could hear. "Dante places those orders to keep this place afloat." He glanced at Sabrina. "She's too proud to accept his money, so he orders her food, dishes he helped her to create, to feel close to her and to keep her dream alive."

"Wow." Karin played with the stem of her glass. "And she doesn't suspect it's her ex?"

"He doesn't use his real name, darlin'."

"But the Palazzo—"

"You think that the penthouse suite is the only place that orders?" Wes shook his head. "No, that is only one room in his rotation." He took a sip from his glass before continuing. "That boy drunk dials from all over the city."

"I had no idea."

"No one does." Wes shot a sideways glance in her direction. "He feels guilty over their breakup."

Karin blinked. "No way."

"Yeah, he and Sabrina were great, until the tabloids got ahold of her name and exposed her checkered past." He leaned closer and whispered in Karin's ear. "She did a stint in juvie for assault."

"Jesus." Karin followed his gaze to where Sabrina was standing. "I never knew."

"No one did until that reporter uncovered it. You would

think that she'd tell the whole story, that Sabrina was part of a protest against tearing down a local park to build a parking garage and things got ugly, but no. All the reporter was interested in was that Sabrina hit a police officer. No mention of the frenzied atmosphere, or how the police officers used pepper spray to disrupt the group of protestors. All Sabrina knew was that someone grabbed her and she fought to get away. Her fists were flailing and one connected with an officer's jaw."

"Wow."

Wes shrugged. "It was a short stint, but enough to create a lot of drama with the press. Then there was that crazy fan who read the article about Sabrina's past and decided Dante was too good to date someone with a record. She tried to burn down her restaurant as a warning to Sabrina to stay away."

"No way."

Wes nodded. "She didn't succeed, but Dante felt so guilty that he broke off the relationship. He made a pact with his brothers to never get serious over anyone again. They all believe that loving someone would only bring them pain."

"You found this out from Marco?"

"Yeah. The man likes to talk after sex." Wes took a long sip from his glass. "Anyway, even though Sabrina calls Dante a stubborn ass who doesn't listen to reason, I know she still loves him. Even if she didn't, I'd never provoke Dante like that. Those Percontis can have fierce tempers." He flashed her a knowing grin.

Karin considered his words for a moment. "We need to find you someone new," she announced as she held up her wineglass with authority. "Someone who isn't Italian, preferably."

"You, too." He grinned and took a healthy slug of his martini. "Although I have to admit, it's damn hard to do much of anything when Marco has us working around the clock for the wedding."

"Tell me about it." Not that she could ever look twice at anyone after being with the Perconti patriarch.

Leo. Even with all of the distractions, he was never far from her thoughts. Karin kept coming back to the way his touch felt on her skin, and how his kiss felt on her lips. Just remembering that moment out on the balcony gave her shivers. Every fiber in her being wanted to experience it again.

"Oh shit," Wes said, closing his eyes.

"What?"

He grinned and pointed to the speaker mounted in the corner of the ceiling behind them. "She's playing Dean Martin." He opened his eyes and waggled his finger at Sabrina, who flipped the CLOSED sign on the door and grinned at them.

Wes started bobbing to the beat. "Sabrina knows that I can't resist singing when this song comes on."

"You're kidding." Karin glanced around and found the restaurant empty. Still . . . "You can't be serious."

"That's amore . . ." Sabrina said as she approached and held out her hand to Wes. He took it, stood, and the two of them broke out into the chorus.

The lyrics weren't too complicated, and before she realized it, Karin was pulled up onto her feet and began singing with them. Wes pulled her close and slid his arms around her hips as Sabrina got up on a nearby table. The wine and the music pumped through Karin's veins, causing her to rock back and forth. Wes spun her into a twirl, making her giggle.

As the twirl finished, a faint rush of cold air caused the fine hairs on the back of her neck to stand on end. Her smile faltered and she glanced over her shoulder. Leo's cold, disapproving gaze met hers, causing her to stumble. What was he doing here?

Wes was quick to catch her, pulling her into another twirl. Her head spun, and she tried to think clearly. As she and her friends moved to the music, Karin felt Leo watching her, as if he was waiting for something. Awareness tingled over her skin as Wes finished the twirl and pulled her into an intimate hug. Karin knew that Wes was just being playful when he rested his hands on her ass, but that didn't stop her from feeling Leo's fury shoot across the room and snake down her spine. Her dancing slowed, and her singing faltered. Leo's presence didn't seem to damper Wes or Sabrina's fun. They belted out the chorus one last time as Wes dipped Karin back and spun her again. Leo's angry features flashed through her line of vision once more, making her uncomfortable. As the last lines of the song played out through the restaurant, Wes wrapped his arms around both her and Sabrina, resting his hands on each of their hips. Karin tried to join them in their fun, but had lost her voice. All she could do was watch Leo as he became angrier and angrier by the second.

When the music finally ended, Wes slapped them both playfully on the ass, causing Sabrina to giggle. Karin eased out of Wes's embrace as a strange, tension-filled silence filled the room. She turned to Leo, who continued to stare at her as if she was the only person in the room.

"Oh fuck me." Sabrina threw the linen napkin she was holding down on the table and quickly closed the distance between her and Leo. "We're closed."

Leo let his gaze linger on Karin for a moment, his disapproval evident in his features. Then he turned to Sabrina. "I didn't come for the food. I came to talk."

"I don't want to talk to you. Get out." Sabrina crossed her arms and lifted her chin.

"I will, just as soon as I speak with her." Leo shifted his gaze to Karin, his implication clear.

Karin's skin heated, and her legs felt weak. She took a step forward and stumbled.

Wes hurried to take her arm. "Easy now."

"No, I'm fine, just tripped over the tablecloth." She looked up and saw Leo begin to close the distance between them.

"You can't just barge in here like you own the place," Sabrina said.

"It seems like I do."

"What?" Sabrina hurried over and placed herself in front of him, stopping his movements.

Leo scowled. "Excuse me." He moved, and Sabrina moved with him.

"Don't use your intimidation tactics on me. They won't work." Sabrina crossed her arms and looked him in the eye. "What do you mean, you own this place? That's my name on the sign outside."

"Yes, but it is my brother's orders that are keeping you in business." He started to move around her, but she blocked his path.

"What do you mean?" Her voice sounded as shocked and angry as she looked.

Leo sighed, clearly exasperated. "Dante has been drunk dialing this place from every hotel in Boston and placing orders so you could keep the restaurant open."

"How . . ." Sabrina shook her head. "I don't fill orders for him. He's never called."

"Oh, he's called all right. Gives some fake name." He moved past a shocked Sabrina and grabbed Karin's arm. "Come, *cara*. We're getting out of here."

Chapter 8

Leo couldn't believe he had gotten caught up in this circus. All he'd wanted to do was tell Sabrina to stop filling orders for Dante and go home, but seeing Karin here, having the time of her life, pricked at his ego. She was supposed to be with him, damn it.

Wes took Karin's other arm, preventing her from moving. "Us Perconti castoffs stick together."

"Castoffs?" Leo's gaze narrowed. "What are you talking about?"

"Wait a minute," Sabrina said, raising her hand. "Dante has been placing orders here? How often?"

"Twice a week at least." Leo tugged on Karin's arm, but Wes held her firmly in place.

"That bastard." Sabrina shook her head. "Now what am I supposed to do, not fill any phone orders? That's insane."

Leo flashed Sabrina a frown and hoped she'd take the hint and get out of his way. "Dante won't be calling here again. I'll make sure of it." He returned his attention to Karin. "Let's go."

Karin glanced at Sabrina, then Wes.

"You don't have to do anything that man tells you," Wes said. "You aren't working right now, so your time is your own."

Leo glared at Wes. "I don't have time for this. There is much we need to discuss." And should have discussed a while ago.

"I was about ready to go home anyway . . ." Karin glanced from Wes to Sabrina, then pulled away from Leo and picked up her things.

"Then let me drive you home." Leo helped her put on her jacket.

"Karin . . ." Wes's voice was filled with warning.

"I'll be fine," she said over her shoulder as Leo steered Karin out of the restaurant.

"Leo, stop," she said when they got to the sidewalk. The air was cool and crisp for a spring evening, and she shivered underneath her jacket. "What are you doing?"

He hesitated, unsure of what to say. He wasn't about to tell her how her behavior had affected him. Seeing her so free and uninhibited had cut him to the core. He was *jealous,* damn it. As a CEO he had to watch what he said and did in public. People were constantly watching.

"You're freezing. My Jag is just around the corner." He wrapped his arm around her and started in that direction.

He looked up, and recognized some of the reporters from the hotel lingering in the opening of the alley where he had parked Marco's jag. He dropped his arm from around Karin and pulled out his phone.

"What are you doing?"

"Texting Roberto to bring the limo." His driver was quick to respond. Satisfied, Leo slipped the phone in his pocket. "He'll only be a few minutes."

"What did you want to talk to me about?" she asked.

"Not here," he said, keeping his eye on the group of reporters. Hopefully Roberto would hurry and get there before they were noticed.

"Then where?"

In my bed. Leo inhaled her fresh, clean scent and tried

to push back his rising desire. He missed her, and seeing her have fun in that restaurant only reminded him of all the things he was missing out on, all the things he could not have.

"No." She shook her head. "I'm not going anywhere with you." She stepped away from him, and the absence of her body heat left him cold. "Tell me what you want to say."

When he didn't immediately respond, she shook her head and started to walk away. "Good night, Mr. Perconti."

"Wait." He wrapped his fingers around her elbow and tugged her back. "You've been avoiding me."

She flinched and looked away. "I have not."

"You have and we both know it." He tilted his head and studied her features. "Why?"

"You know why." She lifted her chin and he saw the fear in her gaze. "We shouldn't be seen together."

"Because of the magazine," he added. She nodded, and he let out a long breath. "People should really learn to mind their own business." He hesitated a moment before pulling the small box out of his pocket. "Here."

She furrowed her brow. "What's this?"

"It's for you. Take it."

She glanced up at him and then wrapped her fingers around the box. She brushed her hand against his as she took it from him, and something electric sparked between them. The air heated as she tore her gaze away from him and tugged on the ribbon.

"I wanted to give you something to show you how sorry I was for what happened with those reporters." He eased back as she opened the lid and spread apart the tissue paper. "This reminds me of my childhood. I always thought ornaments like this were beautiful."

"Oh, Leo," she said as she pulled out the glass ornament. "It's gorgeous." She held onto the red velvet ribbon as the heart dangled between them.

"It has your birthstone," he said, brushing his fingers against the smooth emerald in the center of the heart.

She quirked her brow. "How did you know?"

"The employee database," he confessed. "Do you like it?"

"Of course." She lowered the ornament carefully into the box. "But I can't take it."

"I want you to have it."

"No." She replaced the lid and held it out to him. "I can't accept gifts from you."

"Like I said, it's a peace offering." He lowered his hands and offered what he hoped was a seductive smile. "Christmas has always been very important to my mother. All of her children are expected to be home and by her side during the holidays." He slid his fingers along the box until they covered hers. "Each one of us has a special ornament to hang on the tree when we come to visit."

She looked up and met his gaze. "What are you saying?"

He shrugged. "Only that the ornaments are special. Each one is unique, and marks a different point in the owner's life. My mother has taught us all the importance of family and remembering each other over the holidays. I thought that something like this would be special for you, too." He glanced down at the box. "When you put it on your Christmas tree, you can think about the time we spent together." He brushed her fingers. They felt so smooth and feminine. He imagined them sliding down his back, touching his waist, then slipping lower . . .

He cleared his throat and forced himself to pull his hand away. "Hopefully you'll remember it with fondness and not regret."

"Of course I'd remember it with fondness, but Leo . . . I can't take this." She pushed the box into his hands. "I didn't spend time with you for money or gifts. I did it because I wanted to be with you. Besides . . ." She dropped the box into his hands and inched away. "I don't celebrate Christmas, or any holiday."

He raised his brows. "Don't celebrate?"

She stared at a spot behind Leo, as if gathering her thoughts. "I know that it might be hard for you to believe, but not everyone enjoys the holidays."

"That's impossible."

"I just don't like them, can we please leave it at that?"

"*Cara,* look at me." Karin looked up and Leo noticed that her eyes shone brightly with unshed tears. "You know you can trust me with more than just your body."

Karin took a deep breath. "My parents died a few days before Christmas and the holidays just bring back all the bad memories."

He studied her face for a moment, unsure of what to say. He knew what it felt like to lose one parent, but two? And so close together.

"Well." He pushed the box back into her hands. "Let's make an agreement then. No matter what happens between us, we'll spend the holidays together and make new memories. No one should hate the holidays."

Karin hesitated, then took the box back and toyed with the ribbon. It was a long moment before she spoke. "I really need this job. I have bills to pay." She took a step back toward the building.

Leo advanced, and she took another step back. Soon he was matching her step for step. This was ridiculous. He knew that she was right, that she should run away from him and never look back. It was what was best for both of them. She could go on with her life and he could go on with his.

Things weren't that simple, however. Leo had tried to let go, but forgetting about Karin had proved to be impossible. She had gotten under his skin. He smelled her scent everywhere, and found himself looking at the passing staff members of the Palazzo, wondering if she would step around the corner and into his life once more.

Then tonight, seeing her move on with her life, as if what they had shared together meant nothing to her . . . It was insulting.

"This is my life you're playing with, Mr. Perconti," she said.

"I told you, call me Leo." He twisted his lips into a half-smile as she backed into the brick wall of the restaurant. "I think after all we have been through, you've earned the right."

"I'm using this job as an internship for my degree in hospitality management. If I lose it, I will not only lose any income, but I'll have to start over—"

"Don't worry about your job, *cara*. Or your reputation. Both are safe with me."

"But—"

"You need to trust me, remember?" He placed his hand on the wall next to her head and leaned in a little closer. "Tell me this." He held her gaze and saw something flash in her eyes. She looked so beautiful standing there, cornered by his large frame. So . . . kissable.

He leaned in closer. "Did you enjoy our time together in the penthouse suite?"

She swallowed and gave a short nod. "Yes," she whispered.

Satisfaction rolled through him, and it took a lot of effort to hide his smile. "Would you like to experience it again?"

She shook her head. When she spoke, her voice shook, but Leo couldn't tell if it was from fear or desire. "I . . . I can't."

"I didn't ask you if you *could, cara*. I asked if you wanted to . . ."

Leo watched her consider his question. She wanted him, he could tell by the way she clung to his present and the quick glances she cast his way. The knowledge made his whole body rigid with need. Her answer was important to him. He'd not take her by force. Not now, not ever. He had to know if she thought about him as much he did her, if she craved him just like he craved her.

"I . . . yes. Yes, I want it, but—"

"That's all I needed to know." He bent his arm and rested his elbow on the wall, bringing himself closer. Nothing but a paper-thin wall of air separated them. Her lavender scent was stronger now, calling to him and awakening a need stronger than he had ever experienced before.

He slipped his free hand down and palmed her hip. She felt so soft, so inviting. If only he could remove that ridiculous-looking peacoat.

She placed her hands up on his chest, as if to push him away. "Mr. Perconti—"

He tilted his head and captured her lips, stopping her words. The kiss was soft and brief, just a taste of what was to come. She tasted fresh, like a spring garden, and it took every ounce of willpower for Leo to force himself back. *Not yet.*

Karin's gaze softened, and he knew he had her under his spell. Leo kissed her again, keeping it gentle and coaxing. He ran his tongue along the seam of her lips and waited for them to part. He wasn't disappointed. With a sigh, she opened to him, and he took advantage. Her warmth poured out through her mouth and entered his body, warming him in places he never knew existed. He wanted her, oh yes, he wanted her, but knew that he couldn't let himself give in to his need. *Be patient.*

So he contented himself in the slow, leisurely way he caressed her tongue, taking his time to memorize every quiver, every sigh. He knew that this was wrong—more importantly, it was dangerous—but he couldn't bring himself to care.

He spread his fingers out over her hip, touching her through her bulky clothes and wishing that instead of being on the sidewalk, they both were naked and in his bedroom. Images flashed through his mind of their last time together, how responsive she was to his fingers, his tongue. More than anything he wanted to experience them again.

"Mr. Perconti!"

Leo forced himself to ease back from the kiss. It was tough, and from the dazed look in her eyes, he knew that what they did affected her as much as him.

"Mr. Perconti!"

Leo looked up and saw that damn *Whispers* reporter quickly closing the distance between them.

Where was his damn driver when Leo needed him?

"Leo?" Karin asked. Leo glanced at her, and found her eyes still glazed over with desire. He angled his body to keep her from the reporter's line of vision.

"Mr. Perconti, if I may have a word." The reporter was quick, but Roberto was quicker. Leo spotted the limousine pulling up to the side of the curb.

"I'm sorry, sir," Roberto said as he started to get out.

"Took you long enough." Leo grabbed Karin's hand in his own and tugged her toward the limo. "Come."

She dug in her heels, forcing him to stop. "Where . . . where are we going?"

He flashed her a seductive grin. "Somewhere safe."

"But . . ."

"Trust me."

"Mr. Perconti!" The reporter was almost upon them, and her raised voice was triggering others on the sidewalk to stop and stare. It would only be a matter of time before both he and Karin would be swallowed up by those vultures.

"No comment." Leo grabbed her hand and dragged her toward the car.

"Just one question, Mr. Perconti. Is the woman with you now the same maid you had up in your penthouse suite?"

Karin's entire body went stiff beside him. Leo swore under his breath as he caught sight of the other reporters quickly approaching.

"Mr. Perconti!"

"Just a moment of your time."

Leo shoved Karin into the limo as camera flashes started going off around him. Ignoring the temptation to smash a camera over a reporter's head, Leo slipped inside the limo and closed the door.

"Drive, Roberto."

"Where?"

"Anywhere." It didn't matter, as long as it wasn't the Palazzo. No, if he took her back there, then the reporters would see them together. It would be like throwing wood on a fire. His little angel's fears might come to fruition, and their indiscretion could destroy them both.

He couldn't bring her back to his hotel, but there was another place he could take her, one where no one would think to look for them. A place where he could guarantee total privacy.

"Take us to the financial district," he ordered. There was a place not far from there where they would be safe.

Karin rubbed her arms and tried to shake off the fear that had gripped her out on the sidewalk. Did that reporter see her? She didn't think so, but couldn't be sure. There was a good chance that she had, and Karin would once again end up in the most popular tabloid magazine in North America.

The harder she tried to fight Leo, the more he seemed to drag her into his world. All of this fuss made her uncomfortable. She didn't want expensive cars or nights in a penthouse. All she wanted was a steady job and someone to laugh with. Someone to love and who loved her back.

She glanced sideways at Leo, who seemed to be texting once more. She thought about the reporter, and wondered if he was constantly fielding nosy people's questions. It had to be lonely sometimes with so many people hovering around, seeing you as their next meal ticket. It must be difficult for Leo to let his guard down and open up to someone. There was always a risk that the person he was confiding in would turn around and sell his secrets to the highest bidder.

He had opened up to her back in the penthouse, however. Now, for the first time, Karin was beginning to realize what a huge step he had taken.

"There," Leo said, putting away the phone.

Karin raised her brows. "There?"

Leo smiled and took her hand. "It's too dangerous to take you back to the Palazzo right now. Those reporters will be waiting for us there."

"My apartment—"

He shook his head. "Not until I can be sure that they didn't identify you back there." He squeezed her fingers. "If they learn your identity, they'll be waiting at your apartment as well."

"How long until we find out?"

"Not long." He thought for a moment. "If they know anything, it will be in tomorrow's edition of *Whispers*."

She nodded. "Where are we going to go until then?"

"Somewhere safe." He inched closer.

"Where?"

He slid his arm around her shoulders and flashed her a warm, seductive smile. "Trust me."

Trust him. Her entire body warmed as she thought back

to his kiss on the sidewalk. She loved the way his lips felt against her skin, and how his heady masculine scent penetrated her senses and filled her with desire. Leo was like a thunderstorm, shaking the foundations of her soul with his force. After being with him, she never quite looked at the world the same way again.

"You still have so much to learn, little one." He hooked his finger under her chin and shifted his gaze to her mouth. "But first you must trust me to take care of you."

"But the reporters—"

"I'll handle them."

"What if—"

Before she could finish her question, he pressed his lips against hers.

The kiss was slow and full of sensual promise. Heat flooded her veins, and her skin tingled with anticipation. As he slid his tongue into her mouth, her mind fogged with desire. She let out a low groan as she met his advance, stroking his tongue with her own.

"No, *cara,*" he said when she reached out to touch him. He let go and leaned back in his seat, away from her. "I don't want you to touch me."

She watched his eyes flash with hunger as he dropped his gaze to her breasts.

"No touching?" she asked.

He shook his head. "Not yet." He dragged his gaze back up to meet hers. "But I do want you to take your clothes off."

"In the limo?"

He flashed her a half-smile. "Roberto has been avoiding the paparazzi for a long time and knows he'll need to take the long way to our destination to lose them. He'll be driving loops for the next hour in the city traffic." He reached up behind him and knocked his knuckles on the window. "And these are tinted. We can see out, but no one can see in." His eyes darkened as he lowered his hand. "Now take off your clothes, *cara*. I want to see you."

Excitement rippled through her veins as she placed her gift on the seat beside her and moved to do as he requested. "How about you?"

"Soon." He moistened his lips as she removed her jacket and began to unbutton her shirt. "Very soon."

Memories flashed back to her first time with him in the penthouse, of how he had asked her to remove her clothing. He seemed to like watching her undress. She met his hungry gaze as she flipped her shirt up over her head. Something dark and predatory moved beneath the surface. Whatever it was, he held it in check and nodded for her to continue.

She unhooked her bra and watched his gaze drop to her breasts. After a brief hesitation, she slid the long straps off her shoulders and let it fall to the limo floor. His sharp intake of breath caused her nipples to tighten and desire to blossom in her lower abdomen.

"Beautiful," he murmured.

With each passing second, she felt bolder and more beautiful. Karin reached down and undid her skirt, taking her time with the buttons and zipper. She was teasing him, she knew, and judging by the way he fisted his hands, she knew that he was responding to her every move.

Tension built in the limo as she toed off her shoes and slid first her skirt, then her underwear down over her legs.

"I think I might need to find a better uniform for my staff," he murmured.

"The bland blouse and skirt not doing it for you?"

His eyes sparkled as he dragged them up to meet hers. "Let's just say that they don't . . . appeal to me as much as that maid uniform." He slid his gaze over her naked skin like a caress. "This, however . . ."

Karin giggled with embarrassment. "I can't go to work naked."

He snapped his gaze back up to hers and raised his brows. "No? Pity." He flexed his fingers and shifted in his seat. "Lean back and let me look at you."

Slowly, she reclined as much as the small space would allow, resting her head on the soft leather and stretching her body out so it spanned the length of the cab. "Like this?"

"Yes, *cara*. Just like that." His eyes flashed with need as he removed his outer jacket. "Now touch your breasts."

She hesitated. "Aren't you going to touch me?"

"Soon." He placed his jacket aside. "Touch your breasts, just like you did back at the hotel when we first met." She moved to obey his command. Karin locked her gaze with his as she pinched and tugged her nipples, sending sparks of pain and pleasure swirling through her body. After a few seconds, she groaned and nibbled her lower lip, causing something raw and needy to flash through his gaze.

"Yes, just like that. Don't stop." He removed his suit jacket and loosened his tie.

She should be ashamed of what she was doing, but instead, she felt brazen and wanton. Leo was handsome and rich enough to have any woman he chose, but instead she was the one he took into the back of his limo. *She* was the object of his focus, his lust.

The ache started low in her belly, and Karin rubbed her thighs together as tension and heat built in the confined space of the limo. Leo slipped his silk tie from around his neck and smoothed it between his fingers. The movement was mechanical, almost instinctive, as he kept his heated gaze on her.

"You're so beautiful when aroused," he said. "Like a sweet fruit, just waiting to be plucked and eaten."

There was something about the way he said "eaten" that made her skin tingle with excitement. Images filled her mind of him between her legs, sampling her desire. She moistened her lips and tugged on her nipples as he folded the tie over onto itself and slid it through his fingers.

"Good. Now lower your hands."

She hesitated, unsure.

"Karin . . ." His gaze hardened, like flint and steel. On instinct Karin did as she was told.

"You have to trust me, Karin."

"I do."

"But not enough."

She shook her head. "You ask a lot from me. I can't trust you when we barely know each other."

"We know everything we need to know, *cara*." He leaned forward and brushed a stray hair from her temple. Karin closed her eyes and turned into his hand, suddenly wanting more.

"For example, I know that, despite your misgivings about our relationship, you are responsive to my touch." He slid his fingers around to the back of her head, making her shiver. "And despite everyone telling me to stay away, I can't stop searching you out." He slid his fingers over her neck until he came to her pulse. "This day has been torturous for me—always watching you and never being able to touch."

She widened her eyes. "You've been watching me?"

"Do you mind?"

She thought about it. "I suppose not." It wasn't like she hadn't been looking for excuses to go up to the penthouse, hoping to catch a glimpse of the sexy Italian.

"Good. Now, lower your arms and sit up."

She forced her body to move. As she inched away from the seat, Leo slid his tie around her head.

"I can't see." Her voice trembled as she spoke.

"For what we are doing, you won't need your eyes." He brushed her hair from her face once more. "Now lean back."

She followed his hand, inching back down onto the seat. Karin sensed movement next to her, but her world was dark.

Then his heat was there, next to her, much closer than before. His dress pants brushed against her fingers as he slid closer.

"You can move your head, but that is all," he commanded as he picked up her hand. "I don't want these lovely fingers distracting me from my work." Karin whimpered as his warm, wet mouth surrounded and toyed with her pinky.

"Promise me you won't move." He moved to her ring finger and repeated the same, delicious torture. Karin groaned and turned her head to the side, toward him.

"Promise, or I'll stop," he said as he pulled away.

"No . . . I mean yes, I promise." Her words sounded panicked, but she didn't care. She didn't want him to stop, not yet.

He chuckled as he moved back and kissed the tip of her third finger. "Good. I want you to lay here and feel me." He took the finger into his mouth and gently sucked on the tip. "Feel me and listen to my voice."

His touch was like fire. Her fingers burned as he moved over them, one by one, sending waves of heat through her body. She moistened her lips, desperate to kiss him, to touch him, but every time she moved, he'd pause and wait until she was still. Then, once he was certain she wouldn't move, he'd repeat his movements, until all ten of her fingers had been thoroughly ravaged.

"I don't want to just be with you physically, *cara*," he said as he put down her hand and shifted in the seat next to her. "Anyone could do that. Hell, I could send you home right now and you could probably give yourself the release you need." He moved again, and Karin got the sense that he was preparing for something, but she had no idea what it could be.

"No, while that might be satisfying, it would also be too easy." He leaned closer. Karin could feel his warm, minty breath on her lips. She held her breath as he spoke.

"Tonight, I'm not only going to claim your body, I'm going to claim your mind." He shifted again, and he was there, over her, beside her, around her. His heat was everywhere, his scent everywhere. "Because I will never be satisfied until you are completely, and totally, mine."

She could feel the air move against her lips as he talked. He was close, so close. She waited for the kiss, but it never came. Instead he inched away and moved his hands over her body, not touching, but so close that the fine hairs on her skin tingled as he passed over them. It was enough to drive her insane. She could feel his body heat, smell his intoxicating citrus scent, feel the air move around her as he moved so close to her skin, but the devil wasn't *touching* her.

The result was incredible. The heat from his hands infused with her skin, heating it, sensitizing it. Everywhere he moved, her body responded. She felt as if he was a musician and she was his instrument. He slid his fingers over her shoulders and arms, causing the hairs on her skin to stand on end. Heat raced through her body, creating a sense of urgency. She wanted him to touch her, damn it, but she knew if she reached for him, the game would end.

He was moving down with agonizing slowness. She could sense his hands near her shoulders, sloping downward toward her full, round breasts. She knew she wasn't supposed to move, but the temptation was too great. As he reached lower, she arched her back and brushed her taut nipple against his palm.

He jerked back his hand, as if touched by fire. "I told you not to move." His voice sounded more surprised than angry.

She whimpered at the loss of his fingers on her skin. "I couldn't help myself."

"Hmm." He shifted off the seat and onto the floor. "Then I'm just going to have to prolong your torture." He slipped his fingers in between her thighs and inched them apart. "Just remember, if you move, you will only make it harder on yourself."

His voice sounded rough and strained. Karin wondered if the torture was affecting him as much as it was affecting her. It had to be. As he positioned himself between her thighs, she felt his warm breath quicken against her skin, and his fingers tremble on her legs.

"Now hold still." He slipped his hands from her thighs and began once more, starting once again at her neck and shoulders. This time she endured his almost touch, grinding her teeth as his hands brushed against the fine hairs on her skin. He was close, so close. It took every bit of strength she had not to wiggle under his presence. His strong, clean scent filled the limo, warming her skin. He moved his hands down her flesh, stimulating, but never quite touching her breasts and belly. Karin groaned and moistened her lips, but otherwise remained completely still. If she displeased him and he decided to start over, she didn't know if she could endure such torture a third time.

"Good, *cara*," he whispered against her skin. "Very good." His voice sounded breathy and excited, like a boy opening a present on Christmas morning. "I can see how my presence affects you." He slid his fingers down her abdomen to just above her curls. "I can smell it."

She began to close her thighs, embarrassed that her passion was so obvious, but his body was in the way.

"No *cara*," he said. "Never be ashamed of who you are, or what my touch does to you." He slid his fingers down and brushed her curls. Karin gasped in surprise, and groaned when she realized that the slight touch was all the contact he would give her.

"I want you to relax and trust me with your body," he said. "Spread out your senses and concentrate on the sensations." He moved his fingers lower, brushing them over her inner thighs, her calves, her feet. "Can you feel it?"

"Yes," she whispered.

"Then tell me what you want, what you need."

"I need—" She moaned as he touched her leg, just behind the kneecap. Carefully he lifted her legs and placed her heels on the edge of the seat.

"Tell me."

He slid his fingertips over her skin. His touch was featherlight, just enough to stimulate, but not enough to satisfy. He gently pushed her legs wider apart, until the scent of her arousal filled the air.

"Tell me," he repeated.

"I . . ." She didn't know what to say. Karin knew what she wanted, but to voice the words somehow seemed so . . . dirty. "I want you in between my legs."

He chuckled, and Karin shivered as his warm breath brushed over her folds. "But I'm already between your legs."

"I want you to touch me."

"Where?"

"There." She moved to point to her mound, but he grabbed her hands and placed them back on the seat.

"Don't move. Tell me." His grip was hard and demanding. It only made her want him more.

"I want . . ." She swallowed as she struggled to form a

coherent sentence. "I want you to taste me," she whispered. Oh God, did she just say that out loud?

"Your wish is my command." He bent forward and slid his tongue in between her folds.

That voice . . . Karin gasped and lifted her hips off the seat as his warm, wet tongue slid around her opening. "Yes."

The sweet agony wasn't like anything she had ever experienced before. Leo was relentless in his quest, alternating his focus between her opening and her clit, gradually building her desire and pushing her closer and closer to the edge. His hypnotic voice was almost as powerful as his touch. Both spurred her on, pushing her higher and higher. She felt beautiful and wild. Everything around her faded away as she focused on his mouth, and the wonderful things it did to her body.

Leo never let up, stimulating her sensitive skin until she was shaking with need. He seemed to sense when she was close, to know when she was about to stumble over into oblivion. He'd pull back then and wait, then start the delicious torment all over again.

When she tumbled back from the brink for the third time, she began to tear up from frustration. "Please."

"Please, what?" When she didn't respond, he sighed and leaned away from her body. "Tell me what you want."

"I want you inside of me." She spoke the words loud and clear, her embarrassment forgotten in the wake of her need.

"Which part of me, *cara*?"

"What?" She lifted her head off the seat even though she couldn't see him.

"Which part of me would you like inside of you? My finger, my tongue, or my cock?"

He was so brazen. She held her breath as she considered the possibilities. While she loved his tongue and fingers, there was one option she wanted more.

"I want to ride you," she said. Karin wanted to control the pace and give him a taste of his own medicine.

"Do you now?" She sensed him moving once more. He leaned back, closed her thighs, and slid into the seat next to her. "I hadn't considered the possibility, but now that you mention it . . ." Excitement rippled over her skin as she heard the sound of a zipper being pulled down. "Come here."

He helped her onto his lap. "Just a moment." She heard a tear, and then felt him moving his hands between them. "Okay. Now."

He positioned her until she straddled his hips and the tip of his condom-covered cock pressed against her opening. She pressed down, nudging the head of his erection past her folds and into her body. Her muscles began to stretch, and a wonderful awakening occurred within her core.

"Wait." His voice sounded heavy and strained.

Karin paused with only half of his cock inside her. Every fiber of her being screamed at her to move, and she shook with the effort to obey his command.

"I want you to see me, *cara*." He reached up and removed her blindfold. "I want you to look into my eyes when you come and know that it is me that's bringing you pleasure."

He framed her face with his palms and dragged her closer until their foreheads touched. Their gazes locked as he slid his fingers over her skin, brushing them over her chest, nipples, and belly before finally resting them on her hips. Karin swallowed the lump in her throat as the tension inside the limo built to a feverish pitch. Leo dug his fingers into her flesh, pinching her sensitive skin and heightening her desire.

"Go ahead, *cara*. Do what you want." He brushed his lips against hers. "I'm all yours."

She moved her hips down, sliding over his long length inch by inch, using the same agonizing slowness he'd used with her earlier. His features contorted to something between pleasure and pain, making her smile. It felt good to hand him back a little of the agony she had been feeling since she had stepped into the limo.

Finally he was fully seated deep inside her body. The rough fabric of his pants rubbed against her thighs and the cool metal zipper against her mound. While part of her wished that he was naked beneath her, having him partially clothed somehow made everything more dangerous and alluring.

She moved her hips, delighting in the wonderful friction sparking to life within her lower abdomen. Leo dug his fingers into her skin and met her thrusts halfway. Their bodies crashed together again and again. His hard and unyielding, hers soft and accepting. As he filled her and retreated, the friction they created heated her core.

Tension built as she rushed toward the edge once more. She was moving fast now, much too fast. She quickened the pace as she sensed her goal sitting there, just out of reach.

Never did they break eye contact, not once. She felt him stiffen beneath her, saw both pleasure and pain alternate over his features. He was holding back his orgasm, she could sense it. He was waiting for her, and God help her, she loved him that much more for it.

"Now, *cara*." He reached between them and pressed her clit, sending fresh sparks of pleasure vibrating through her core.

She cried out as her orgasm slammed into her, robbing her of strength. Every thrust, every movement, sent fresh waves of pleasure through her body, blinding her to everything but ecstasy.

Still their gazes locked. She could see his own orgasm cresting, getting ready to explode. She continued to move over him, helping him achieve what he so obviously needed. Leo dug his fingers deeper into her flesh and the pain he created pushed her pleasure higher. He jerked once, twice, and then thrust hard as he tumbled after her into oblivion.

They both hung there, suspended in time, as pleasure and joy infused every spare inch of her body. The world around them faded away, until there was only this moment, only him. Karin didn't know when she had ever felt so connected to someone, so happy.

When it was over, he slipped his hand around her neck and tilted his head.

"You are amazing, *cara*. Simply amazing." He brushed his lips against hers in a tender kiss, more loving than urgent.

Karin melted against him. Never before had she felt anything so incredible. She could die in this man's arms right now and be thankful for it. She had never wanted anyone, needed anyone more than she needed Leo in that moment. She felt closer to him than anyone. He was like her other half, anticipating her needs even before she spoke them. She didn't know what he saw in her, but she was grateful for his presence.

The limo rolled to a stop. Leo reluctantly broke the kiss and glanced out the door.

"We're here," he said.

"Where?"

He gently eased her off and onto the seat next to him. "Where we will spend the night with no nosy staff members watching us." He brushed his fingers along the side of her cheek. "You better get dressed."

Curiosity filled her as she threw on her clothes and attempted to do something with her hair. It was a lost cause, she knew. Karin just hoped that the place where they were going wasn't too fancy so that her disheveled look wouldn't raise too many eyebrows.

"You look lovely," Leo said as he pulled her hand from her hair. "Don't worry, I've arranged everything."

"Where are we?" she asked again as the driver opened the door.

Leo smiled at her as he lowered his hand. "A place where no one will think to look for us." He walked out onto the sidewalk and extended his hand. "Come."

She hesitated, then let him help her up onto the sidewalk. The streets were busy with late-night partiers, and Karin had to step to one side to let a couple pass her by. The pedestrians were distracting, so she didn't really see the building until Leo threaded his arm through hers and steered her toward the large, very familiar, brass doors.

"Oh my God," she whispered as she dug her heels into the sidewalk.

Leo stopped his advance and turned to face her. "Is there something wrong, *cara*?" he asked.

Karin swallowed and looked up at the sign over the door. "We are at Stone Suites," she said.

"Remember what we talked about in the limo. I'll take care of everything."

And the perfect place for her to be exposed. This was Jason Stone's territory. After everything that happened between them, he'd surely recognize her and use the fact that she was with Leo to his advantage.

Even if Jason was away on a business trip, there was countless staff who had all seen her behave more animal than human. Numerous people who could testify to her mental instability and make her seem like a jealous shrew in Leo's eyes.

And when Leo found out that she had slept with the enemy, well, she knew that she'd be back out on the street once more. History had a funny way of repeating itself, and Karin knew that it was only a matter of time before her heart would get broken once more.

Chapter 9

Leo glanced over Karin's shoulder and saw Roberto give an affirming nod. Good, he had gotten Leo's text messages and put everything in place. Stone Suites had an automated check-in through the room's television, something Leo wished to copy but lacked the funds. There would be no need to go to the front desk and risk being identified. The plan was perfect, and he couldn't wait to get Karin in his arms once more.

"Isn't Jason Stone your rival?" she asked as he steered her toward the door.

"Yes, but there is no need to worry, *cara*. Everything has been arranged. No one will recognize me while we're here."

His answer seemed to mollify her a little, and Leo was touched that Karin would be so concerned with his welfare. There really was no need, however. Even if Jason saw them at the hotel, it wasn't like he would blast their arrival all over the Internet. Jason loved women and was known for his serial dating and one-night stands. It wouldn't take much effort on Leo's part to even the score, and they both knew it. No, Jason would be discreet, if for no other reason than he didn't wish for his own name to be dragged through the mud along with Leo's.

Still, it would work out best if Jason never knew they were there. Hence, having Roberto call in the favor and make an advance reservation under a fake name.

"Good evening, Mr. Collins." The uniformed doorman handed Leo an envelope and opened the large glass door. "You'll be pleased to know that everything has been arranged in room 905, just like you asked."

"Thank you." Leo took the envelope and nodded to the man. "My limo driver will be back with our overnight bags. Please see that the bags make it to our room safely." He slid some bills into the doorman's hand.

"Absolutely, sir." The doorman pocketed the money and Leo swept Karin inside.

"Does the doorman always hand packages to the patrons?"

Leo smiled to himself. "No, just to me."

She cast him a sideways glance. "How does he know you?"

Leo smiled, but said nothing. Instead he made a mental note to give an extra bonus to Roberto. It was funny how he had come to trust his limo driver more than his own family.

"Roberto arranged everything."

"The limo driver?"

"Yes."

She glanced over her shoulder at the hotel entrance. "So Stone Suites' doorman is on your staff as well?" Karin murmured as they made their way over to the elevators.

"In a manner of speaking, yes. Most hotel staff's loyalty can be bought if you offer the right price."

She widened her eyes. "You're bribing the Stone Suites' staff? But Marco had said that we didn't have any money—" Karin abruptly shut her mouth. Pink stained her cheeks and Leo guessed that she was embarrassed for bringing up Perconti Enterprises' lack of funds.

"Not everyone wants money, *cara*. It is amazing how sometimes just a small word or gesture can get them eating out of your hand."

Karin stumbled on the edge of the carpet and Leo tightened his grip on her arm. "Is there something wrong?" he asked. "You look ill."

"No, nothing." She glanced around at the opulently decorated foyer. "I guess I've never seen anything this elegant before."

Leo frowned at the beautiful marble floors, fresh flowers, and brightly painted walls, noting how much cleaner and more expensive things were when compared to the Palazzo.

"Yes." He turned back to her. "Come."

He steered her away from the curious looks at the front desk and toward the elevator. As they walked, Karin turned up the collar of her coat, shielding her face.

"Don't worry, *cara*. The staff here is professional. They are well trained and know that if they talk to reporters, they'd lose their jobs."

"How do you know all this?"

A faint smile touched his lips. "Let's just say that while Jason and I are rivals, we do agree on one thing—a highly trained and discreet staff is essential in our line of business."

He led them to the elevators and pressed the button. While they waited for the elevator to reach them, Leo used the moment to study his little maid's face, or what he could see of it. She seemed agitated, although for the life of him, he couldn't understand why.

"Are you sure you're okay?" he asked.

She moistened his lips and stared at the elevator doors. "Is this what my payment is, then?" Her voice was so soft, he had to ask her to repeat the question.

She turned, pulled up her coat collar to cover her ears, and met his gaze. "Are you paying me tonight so I won't tell that *Whispers* reporter about us?"

Leo took a step back, surprised at the anger in her gaze. "What? No. How could you think—"

"Because I have to tell you, there's no need." She steeled her jaw and turned her attention back to the elevator. "I am already loyal to the Palazzo. The Perconti family pays my bills and is providing me with an internship that will secure my future. There's no need to have sex with me. Trust me, my silence about your family has already been bought many times over."

"What are you talking about?" Leo remembered his words from earlier and mentally scolded himself for being such an idiot. "No, *cara*. What's between us isn't bribery. You're different."

She rolled her eyes and averted her gaze. "Yeah, right."

He grabbed her shoulders and turned her to face him. "Whatever this is between us, it's not about buying your loyalty or silence." He reached up and turned down her coat collar so he could better see her face. "Try to give me a little credit." He brushed his fingers against her cheek. "Contrary to what some people may think, I do have a heart." He focused his gaze on his finger as he slid it down her neck and into the V of her coat, right above her breasts. "This . . . this has nothing to do with business." He let his hand fall away. "It has everything to do with me." He brushed his thumb over her chin. "With us."

The anger left her features, and Leo forced himself to look away. He was a liar. A liar and a bastard of the truest form. No, he wasn't having sex with her to buy her loyalty or silence, but he *was* using her. Karin was the only person who had managed to slip past his walls and touch the person inside. Not the CEO or family patriarch, but the real him. She was like a drug, and kept his demons away better than any of the little pills Roberto would bring up later in his overnight bag. She was the one thing that made sense, his sanctuary, and he couldn't imagine not having her in his life.

He'd never intentionally manipulate Karin, but as he stared at the numbers above the elevator doors, Leo recognized some truth in Karin's accusation. Subconsciously, he had manipulated her into having sex with him again. He did it because he needed her like he needed air. When everything around him was falling apart, Leo wanted to have sex with Karin so that he could feel in control of his life once more.

He was acting just like his selfish siblings, but perhaps this was a case where a bit of selfishness was warranted. Everything Leo had done in his life had been for his family. Even with Danika, his pursuits had been for *her* pleasure, *her* gain. Not once had he ever lived his life for himself. Karin was his one indulgence, his one selfish splurge. Judging by the reaction to his touch, she was getting something out of their little arrangement as well. He had given her ample opportunity to walk away, and yet here she was, with him, waiting for the elevator to arrive so that they could go up to their room and share a night of passion.

Perhaps, on some subconscious level, she was using him as well.

As Leo slid his gaze over Karin's curvy frame, he realized that he had to be careful not to let their relationship become anything more than a selfish indulgence. He had given his heart to a woman once, and now she was out to bleed his family dry. Danika had betrayed him and stabbed a knife in his heart. He'd be damned if he'd ever let himself become vulnerable like that again.

"Karin?"

Leo turned to see one of Stone Suites' cleaning staff approach them.

"Karin, is that you?"

Karin turned up her collar and looked away. Sensing her distress, Leo put his hand on her shoulder. "I'm sorry, you must be thinking of someone else."

The woman's gaze met his and she took a step back. "Oh." She placed her hand on her chest as surprise etched her features. "I'm so sorry. I just thought . . . she looked so familiar." She shook her head as the elevator rang and the doors opened. "I'm sorry."

The woman hurried away and Leo ushered Karin into the elevator. As the doors closed, he pushed the button for the ninth floor and risked a sideways glance at his little maid.

"Someone you know?" he asked.

Karin slowly lowered her collar and shook her head. "She must have mistaken me for someone else."

Leo sensed the tension radiating off Karin in waves, but he didn't press. There were any number of reasons why Karin and that woman might have known each other, and he didn't want to ruin their night with questions. Instead, he made a mental note to check into it tomorrow. If Karin was going to help him bury his inner demons, then it was only right that he helped her bury hers.

The sliding doors opened, revealing a long hallway. Leo ushered Karin outside and along the soft carpet to room 905.

"I hope you find everything to your liking," he said as he took the key card out of the envelope the doorman had given him and opened the door. "I didn't know what you would like, so I—"

Her gasp cut off his words and gave him pause. Karin covered her mouth with her hands and entered the suite, staring wide-eyed at the elegance before her.

"Oh, Leo," she whispered. "It's beautiful."

"Not as beautiful as you, *cara*," he said as he closed the door and walked up behind her. "But I'm glad you like it."

"Like it . . ." Karin turned around slowly, trying to take in the entire room. "It's amazing." The opulent room was decorated with all sorts of flowers: roses, orchids, and expensive-looking arrangements that Karin couldn't even begin to name. On the far side of the room a table had been set, and wonderful scents of beef and wine drifted over to her.

She shed her jacket and tossed it on a nearby chair. "Did you order this?"

"I thought you might get hungry," he confessed. "And I didn't want to have to leave the room."

"It's amazing," she said as she lifted the lid and stared at the steak, baked potato, and steamed vegetables.

"You're amazing," Leo said as he came up from behind and wrapped his arms around her middle.

She turned in his arms and met his gaze. "You didn't have to do this."

"I think I did." He leaned forward until their foreheads touched. "I wanted to apologize."

"For what?"

"For everything." He closed his eyes. "For the tabloid and—"

"The tabloid wasn't your fault. You had no idea that one of them would look up and see me."

"Nevertheless, I should have been more"—he opened his eyes and paused, as if searching for the right word—"*aware* of what lengths some would go to in order to get a story."

"Stuff like this happens to you a lot, doesn't it? You probably don't even see them half the time."

"I always see them," he said as he laced his fingers with hers. "I just choose not to react to them and feed their frenzy. You shouldn't pay any attention to them, either. They can't hurt you, *cara*. I'll make sure of it."

She lifted her finger to his lips. "Shh." When he widened his eyes, she slipped her hands around to the back of his neck. "I don't want to talk about reporters or what may happen tomorrow. There's nothing we can do about it right now." She hesitated, then added, "We can do something about this, however."

Karin brushed her lips against his, reveling in how firm and solid he felt next to her. It was a bold move. Since Jason, she had never tried to entice a man in the bedroom. He softened against her touch, molding with her body and tightening his grip on her waist. As she pressed harder against him, she knew that she was doing the right thing. It was pointless spending the entire night worrying. Instead, she wanted to use the opportunity to explore what was growing between them. This was probably her last opportunity to have him all to herself, so she wanted to make the most of the time they had together.

Karin tilted her head and deepened the kiss, tentatively sliding her tongue into his mouth, tasting, exploring.

He met her questioning advance with his own. A sense of urgency overcame her as the kiss turned hungry and desperate. His wonderful citrus scent rose up, kicking aside the aroma of food and making her hungry for something else entirely. He shifted his stance, and a desire rose up within her. Soon she was grasping at his clothes, desperate for the skin-on-skin contact.

He fumbled with her buttons, then released the clip from her hair. He groaned against her mouth as long, blond waves fell around her shoulders. Her effect on him fed both her desire and confidence. As they tore at each other's clothes, she pressed closer to his body, pushing him away from the table and closer to the bed.

"Karin." He dropped her bra to the floor and cupped her breast, causing her to gasp.

She loved how the syllables of her name rolled off his tongue like a caress. She groaned against his mouth and tugged at his shirt. "Say my name again."

"Karin."

"Oh God." Karin gasped as pleasure rippled through her body at his touch. She couldn't get enough of him.

He inched back just enough to remove his shirt, then covered her lips once more. Need wound through her veins as she ran her fingers over his bare chest, enjoying the feel of the fine hairs she felt there. His muscles flexed beneath her hands, and he whispered her name against her mouth as she slid down over the hard planes of his abdomen.

She grabbed his belt buckle and tugged. Within moments it was free and she was reaching inside his pants, searching. He mirrored her movements, stripping her of her Palazzo uniform and dropping the articles of clothing to the floor.

With a growl he turned their bodies until she was next to the bed. With a gentle push, he eased her back onto the soft mattress. She reached for him, and took her fingers and raised them to his lips.

"Stay like that for me," he commanded.

She looked up at him questioningly as he kissed her palm. "Is there something wrong?"

"No *cara*," he whispered. "Not at all." He let go of her hand and moved over to the table. Karin lifted herself up on her elbows and watched the muscles ripple in his back as he moved. The man must have been chiseled from granite. His dark, lithe form moved easily across the room as he strode over and lifted the lid on one of the food dishes.

"Don't tell me you're hungry," she said.

He glanced over his shoulder at her and raised his brows. "Aren't you?"

She shook her head. "Not for food."

"Oh, you will be." He turned back to the table and searched the contents, lifting the lids one by one.

Karin took the moment to admire his well-muscled shoulders. She traced each hard line as they made their way down his back and to his waist. She imagined her fingertips tracing the dips and rises, feeling his skin tense with excitement.

She dropped her gaze and focused on his tight, round backside. It was perfectly shaped, and she resisted the urge to get up off the bed and grab it. She imagined that ass shifting over her body, of how it would tighten as he moved his hips between her thighs.

He turned and a slow, seductive smile spread out over his face as he caught her looking at him. "Like what you see, *cara*?"

Her breath caught in her throat. The man was positively breathtaking, and the way he looked at her made her limbs feel like water.

"Yes," she whispered.

"I do, too." He turned, and she noticed that he was holding a decanter of wine. "Move up onto the pillow."

Her heart raced as she obeyed his command. Leo strode to the side of the bed and placed the decanter on the table, and tilted his head, as if studying her. "Now, we have had our little lessons on trust. I think it's time to move on."

"Oh?" Karin arched her brows.

A slow, seductive smile spread over his lips. "Yes. Now I'm going to teach you the beauty in serving."

She stifled a chuckle. "You are really into that maid fantasy, aren't you?"

He considered her a moment before responding. "This isn't about my needs, *cara*, but yours."

"I don't need to dress up and act as a maid to have sex."

"No," he agreed, picking up a linen napkin from the side table. "But what we are going to do is more than just sex." He shook out the napkin. "Now, close your eyes."

She obeyed. He wrapped a linen napkin over her eyes and secured it to the back of her head.

"Hold out your hands."

"What are you doing?"

"Are we going to have to go back and revisit our last lesson?"

"No." As great as it was, she wanted to know what he had in store for them next.

"Remember, this is about you, and discovering your deepest needs. I won't do anything without your encouragement." He hesitated for a moment before continuing. "Do you remember your safe word?"

"Yes."

"Say it."

"Red." She felt something long and smooth wrap around her wrist.

"Good." He lifted her hand up by the headboard, secured it, then mirrored the movements on her other side. As he moved around her, Karin trembled with anticipation. She remembered the picture of the bound woman she had seen online. Just thinking about being bound during sex made her ache with need.

After a few moments, he eased back from the bed. "Now you shall serve me as we dine."

She etched her brow in confusion. "But I'm tied to the bed."

"It doesn't matter. You won't need your hands for what I have in mind. Are you comfortable?" he asked.

The man was damn confusing. She tugged on her bindings, testing them. They were tight enough to prevent movement, but not so tight as to restrict blood flow.

She shook her head. "Yes." As comfortable as she could

be under the circumstances. Her heartbeat quickened as she wondered what he was going to do next.

"Excellent." She heard his footsteps echo on the hardwood floor as he walked around the bed. He was on the other side of her now, and she turned her head toward him and tried to pick up sounds that would hint at what he was doing. He stopped and the room became quiet.

Seconds passed with agonizing slowness. She had no idea what he was doing, or if he was still even there. Unease slithered down her spine, and she tested her bindings once more to see if she could loosen them. They didn't budge. She tried harder, wiggling her body in hopes the movement would loosen whatever was holding her to the bed. If only she could see . . .

"Do you want to use your safe word, *cara*?" The closeness of Leo's voice startled her. She was so focused on her bindings that she had forgotten he was in the room with her.

She stilled. So, he hadn't left her. Instead he was watching her, taking in her nakedness. The knowledge sparked desire. It wound like silken ribbons through her core, wrapping around her muscles and tightening them with need.

"No." Her voice cracked on the word. She cleared her throat. "No."

"I would never leave you, not intentionally."

"I know."

"Do you?" She heard him move around her. "My life is filled with people who lie to me, who don't trust me. I spend all of my time cleaning up other people's messes because they don't do as I say."

Karin's throat went dry as she sensed him coming nearer. "I do that, too," she said.

He paused in his movements, and she imagined him studying her. Tension filled the air, and she hurried to fill the silence. "Every day I show up to work at the Palazzo. I am ordered by your brother to clean the rooms and ready them for guests, but I'm not supported with fresh supplies. Our equipment is outdated and our morale low." When he didn't say anything, she continued. "Your brother hasn't given us raises in three years, not even for the cost of living. Instead he demands we work longer hours with no pay."

Karin sensed his anger. It was sitting there, ready to strike. She knew that she was taking a great risk in telling him about her work conditions, but there was something about being tied up, something about being blindfolded, that she found freeing.

"The staff at the Palazzo is angry," she said. "It's hard to get them to work when there is little reward. I end up doing most of the jobs myself because it's easier than trying to convince them to help."

Silence followed her outburst. Karin shifted on the bed, suddenly worried that she had spoken too much.

"I can't believe my brother would be so cold," Leo murmured.

"Not cold, just self-absorbed," she corrected.

"No wonder the place is a mess," he added. "How can he expect things to be kept up when he doesn't pay his staff?"

She moistened her lips as she remembered what Wes had told her earlier in the conference room. "On the morning of your arrival, some of our cleaning staff were told to clean up your room and prepare it for your arrival. Wes had dispatched them, but I found out an hour later that they had all mysteriously come down with the flu."

"Did you tell him?"

"I couldn't reach Wes." *Because he was having sex with your brother.* "I wanted everything to be perfect, so I went up there to clean it myself."

She felt the mattress dip under his weight. "It happens,"

he said. "Sickness can easily spread when people work together in close quarters."

"But all six of them contracting the flu on the same day?" She shook her head. "I have been working in hotels since high school and have never seen such a thing." She thought about how she had worked hard to get the position she held at the Palazzo, and how she'd labored tirelessly to convince her college advisor to give her class credit for life experience. He had only agreed to her suggestion on one condition—that her position be turned into an internship of sorts, and that he'd take part of her paycheck as a consulting fee.

The hopelessness of her situation hit her hard, causing her voice to shake as she continued to confess the burden she had been carrying around in silence all this time.

"For months, the staff has been coming in late and leaving early, forcing me to work longer hours to pick up their slack. Sometimes, when I have class, I have to leave and come back to finish up jobs that are only half done."

"Karin . . ."

Leo's voice was filled with concern, but it felt so God damn good to let it all out. Karin couldn't stop herself if she tried. "When there are papers to write, I pull all-nighters to get them done on time. A lot of days I come to work having had only one or two hours of sleep the night before." She had never told anyone that before, but Karin was so damn tired of burning the candle at both ends. Tears stung her eyes. Helpless, she let them soak the blindfold. Something had to give, or else she was going to lose her sanity.

"They will be punished." Leo's voice sounded hard and gravelly, as if he was speaking through a locked jaw.

"No." She shifted on the bed, desperate to touch him. "Don't you see? This is what it's like to work at the Palazzo. This is my life."

"We will change it. I will speak to the others—"

"Punishing them isn't going to solve anything. They're reacting this way because they feel like they are already being punished. When I was with Wes tonight . . ." Her voice caught in her throat as she remembered seeing Leo in the restaurant.

"The blond man, yes." Leo's voice was quiet and dripping with venom.

"Yes." She took a deep breath and tried to steady her thoughts. "He told me that there is talk of mutiny among your staff."

"Mutiny?"

"A strike."

"Karin, I—"

"They just want their cost-of-living increases, or at least better equipment." Karin tried to sit up, but the bindings prevented her.

"I see." He eased her back down onto the pillows. His touch calmed her frazzled nerves and reminded her of her nakedness—and that he was in total control of this situation. "You have no more need to worry. I'll take care of it."

"You will?"

He didn't answer her question, but instead asked one of his own. "And when will this strike take place?"

"I . . . I don't know." She gasped as his hand inched up and palmed her breast. "He didn't say. I don't even know—oh God—if it's going to happen." She arched her back as he rubbed his rough palm over her nipple, sending spirals of pleasure swirling in her core.

"Could you find out?" he asked as he slid his hand lower. "Tell me if and when they plan to have their strike?"

"Wouldn't it be easier to just give them what they ask for?" She gasped and spread her legs open as his hand dipped over her mound.

"I would if I could, *cara*." He slipped his fingers in

between her folds, easily finding her clit. "But there is no money to give."

"What?" She nibbled her lower lip and lifted her hips off the mattress as he rubbed her sensitive nubbin in a circular motion, sending waves of pleasure crashing through her core.

"There's no money. Thanks to Jason Stone, Perconti Enterprises has been losing income for the past three years. Thanks to my siblings, we have been spending more than we make for quite some time." He eased his hand away from her body and stood. "I have tried to rein in their spending, but it is difficult. They are, as you say, self-absorbed, and don't understand the gravity of the situation."

"But you understand."

"Yes. Like I said before, people can be manipulated without using money. You just have to know what they truly desire." He slid his fingers over her nipples, causing them to pebble. "Don't worry, *cara*. I will take care of your problems. By this time tomorrow, you'll have nothing more to worry about." He skimmed his fingers over her belly and hips. "And soon, my family will have nothing to worry about, either."

She listened to him move around the bed as realization dawned. "The wedding. It's an arranged marriage."

"Yes." He picked up something next to the bed and held it over her body. Karin could feel something shift above her, and her body tensed with anticipation.

"If you are wondering if she agreed to it, the answer is yes. I would never force my sister into a marriage that she didn't want for herself."

"Marrying to help the family doesn't seem very self-absorbed to me." Karin gasped as something cool and wet fell onto her chest. *The wine.* Suddenly his cryptic words became clearer. *You will serve me . . .* He didn't mean she would serve him like a waitress, but that her body would act like a platter for his food. Desire rose up through her bloodstream as she realized what he was getting ready to do.

"No, my sister is different. Less self-absorbed, more . . . frivolous. She has her own reasons for wanting this marriage."

Karin felt the mattress dip once more as he shifted onto the bed and straddled her hips.

"Did she tell you what those reasons were?" she asked.

"She didn't need to. Everyone knows how much she loves her charity work. Her would-be husband, Landon Blake, is a philanthropist as well as an aviation tycoon. She hopes that his infusion of money will help fund her pet project, which has been struggling since I cut it from our budget." He moved an object inches above her torso. "Hold still."

Karin tried to lie still, but the cool wine on her breasts caused her to gasp and arch her back.

Leo made a tsking noise. "Now look at what you did. We have wine all over the sheets." His voice wasn't laced with anger or malice, but rather humor.

"What's her pet project?"

"A ridiculous charity that helps poor and sick children learn how to use eyeliner and foundation." He dribbled the wine down her abdomen, creating a long, sensual line to her navel.

Karin bit back a groan and spread her legs as the cool liquid made its way down between her legs.

Leo leaned over her body, and his warm breath caressed her nipple as he spoke. "My sister teaches kids on their deathbed, kids who couldn't afford to buy ChapStick, let alone designer perfumes, how to make themselves over into models." Karin felt his warm breath rush over her nipple as he chuckled. "Her heart is in the right place, but the money would be put to much better use helping them with their medical care." He hesitated, then added, "She needs to put her energy into curing the diseases, not covering up their pain and suffering with designer cosmetics."

Karin opened her mouth to tell him that sometimes a little makeup made people feel better about themselves, and his sister's charity probably did more good than he realized, but then his tongue slid over her nipple and all coherent thought was lost.

"But no more talk of work." Leo scraped his teeth across her nipple, causing it to tighten. "Or my siblings." He shifted to the other nipple and gently ran his tongue over the taut peak. "Instead I want to focus on you, and how you can serve me." He nipped her breast, causing her to groan.

Karin tugged at her bindings, desperate to touch the man who made her soul sing. Leo was relentless as he licked and laved her sensitive tips, sending wave after wave of pleasure crashing through her body. The fact that she couldn't see him, that she couldn't move, forced her to focus on her other senses. Karin wiggled beneath him as he worked his way down her body, collecting the wine that he had poured only moments before.

"You taste so sweet, *cara*." He dipped his tongue into her navel, collecting the small pool of liquid that had collected there. "The perfect accompaniment to my favorite wine."

Karin gasped and wiggled her hips, eager for more.

"Hold still." He slapped his palm on the side of her hip, and the resulting sting vibrated through her body, fueling her desire.

"Yes, sir." She willed her body to remain still.

He chuckled and worked his way down, gently spreading apart her thighs as he moved. Karin's thoughts plunged into an erotic haze as he feasted, opening both her body and her mind to his presence. The world around her faded away, until there was only his tongue, his breath, and his fingers.

Leo was a man of experience, and it didn't take long before Karin found herself racing once again toward that unseen goal. He spread her folds apart and dipped his tongue into her opening. She whispered his name as a sense of urgency shot thorough her core.

"Please." She hated begging, but couldn't seem to help herself. Leo knew just how to tease her, using the perfect combination of stimulation and retreat to reduce her to a quivering mound of desire.

"Not yet, *cara*." He pulled back, moving his fingers and tongue with agonizing slowness. "We haven't even begun the first course."

The first course? Karin groaned and turned her head to the side as pleasure retreated from her system. Then he returned, and began decorating her body with bits of food. "I've never been one to enjoy salad," he said. "But who knows? Tonight, I might change my mind."

He alternated between food and wine, placing each on her body in strategic places and using his mouth to remove them. Every other bite he'd take a piece in his mouth and offer it to her, filling her with crisp asparagus and greens, rich bits of beef and warm roasted potatoes. Karin whimpered and moaned as she was assaulted by the lovely aromas of food and sex. Leo knew just where to touch, just where to lick and lave, to give her the most enjoyment.

"Lift your legs."

She did, and he placed something warm and soft on her mound. Before she could ask what it was, he bent over and ran his tongue over her sensitive folds. He worked fast and then slow, pushing her right up to the edge of oblivion before retreating and starting all over again.

"I don't think I can take any more," she said as he re-treated for what seemed like the millionth time.

His body stilled. "Do you want to please me?"

"Yes." She said the word without hesitation. After everything he had done to her, after everything he had made her feel, she could do no less.

"Then you will lay still and trust that I know what I'm doing."

Something warm and soft slid between her legs, and the aroma of chocolate filled the air. Before she could ask what he was doing, Leo began to lick up the sauce, teasing her sensitive skin as he moved. This time as he licked and laved, he pressed his finger into her channel, rewarding her with a delicious stretching sensation.

"That's it, *cara*," he murmured as she moaned and turned her head to the side. "Let me enjoy you in the way you were meant to be enjoyed."

He advanced and retreated through her channel, causing her desire to surge. It wasn't long before she teetered on the blink of oblivion once more.

"Come for me, *cara*," he whispered when she thought she couldn't possibly take any more of his sweet torture. "There will be no holding back. Not this time."

He plunged his tongue deeper into her channel, causing her to gasp. "Yes," she whispered.

He slid his fingers in between her folds and spread her open. She bucked against his hand. His tongue teased and tasted, stoking the heat building within her lower abdomen. Once she'd gotten used to a sensation, he'd shift his movements, alternating between both pain and pleasure to drive her closer to her goal.

"I'm close," she whispered. "Oh God."

Karin wanted to touch him. She wanted to hold onto his head while he feasted on her body. She tugged at her bindings, but they held fast, and she realized that she was helpless to do anything but enjoy the moment.

Leo removed his tongue and inserted two fingers, rubbing against a particularly sensitive spot deep inside her core. The move sparked her orgasm, and Karin cried out as pleasure poured through her body like rain. Leo shifted, placing his hands on either side of her torso and his hips between her thighs. One moment his cock was at her entrance, the next he was filling her to the point of breaking.

"God Karin, you feel . . ." He groaned as she hugged his cock. Karin spread her legs wider, allowing him to go deeper than ever before. As the last ripples of her orgasm faded, he began to move, sliding in and out of her body with quick, forceful thrusts.

His thrusts buoyed her pleasure, capturing her orgasm and lengthening the waves of joy. Karin fisted her hands in her restraints and wondered if she could ever survive such an onslaught of emotion. It didn't matter. She wanted him deeper, harder.

"Come again for me, *cara*. Let me feel you tighten around me."

Leo's movements became jerkier and more desperate. She tried to move with him, but her restraints and the angle of his body made it difficult. He plunged into her with wild abandon, as if he was a man possessed. He was losing control, she realized. The stern, unyielding head of Perconti Enterprises was letting go of the fierce hold on his emotions. She was witnessing a side of him that no one else saw, and the knowledge made her want him even more.

The sound of flesh-on-flesh filled the room, mingling with their voices to create an erotic chorus. With each thrust, she wanted more, needed more.

Karin arched her back and cried out his name as her second orgasm washed over her. Ecstasy filled her system, blanking her mind to everything but the ecstasy of the moment.

She felt him stiffen, then push harder, faster. Again and again he pistoned into her body, as if with each push he was trying to brand himself into her soul. On the next thrust, he shuddered and groaned her name as he joined her in oblivion.

Never before had she felt such bliss. She didn't know if it was the honesty before sex, the fact that she was bound and at his mercy, or that he had denied her release for so long. Whatever the reason, she had never felt closer to another person as she did to Leo in this moment. It was as if her entire life she had been searching for something, a special connection, and it wasn't until this moment that it had been found.

Tears stung her eyes as Leo removed her bindings and blindfold. Karin hid her face in his chest as he rolled with her on the bed until they were both on their sides. He wrapped his arms around her and rested his head on the pillow, clearly exhausted.

Karin struggled to get her emotions under control. She was falling for him, she realized, and falling hard. It wouldn't take too many more moments like this for her to start believing that they might have some sort of future together. Thinking about the future was dangerous. Jason Stone had taught her that lesson well.

For a long moment they lay there in silence, and Karin tried to content herself with listening to his heartbeat. It was so strong and steady, so sure of itself. Karin wished she could be just as steady and sure of their connection, but doubts concerning their relationship lingered. There was so much left unspoken between them, so much baggage.

But for now, there wasn't any baggage. Now there was just the two of them and this moment, and she'd hold onto it for as long as she possibly could.

Karin awoke to silence. Sunlight streamed in through the window by the bed. At some point during the night, Leo had pulled back the curtain to let the light shine thorough. The room looked bright and cheery, and she slowly blinked the fog from her brain, she realized that she felt better than she had in a long, long time.

With a soft moan, she turned in the bed and threw her arm around Leo—only to find that he wasn't there. Tangled sheets and rumpled pillows reminded her that he had indeed come to her bed last night. The sex had been amazing and she had fallen asleep in his arms.

She strained her hearing, listening for some sign of activity. There was no shower, no footsteps, no movement to suggest that someone was in the room with her. Confused, Karin sat up in bed and pushed her hair from her face. After a quick scan of the room, she found everything neat and tidy—just as it should be. Even the table of food from last night had been taken away and replaced with a carafe of coffee, a plate of pastries, and a table setting for one.

"Leo?" Wrapping a throw blanket around her, she stood and walked into the bathroom, but nothing had been disturbed. She padded back out into the room and checked the closet, bureau, and beds, but still found nothing. She fought the rising wave of panic as she turned in a circle and tried to figure out what had happened. Leo wouldn't just leave her, would he?

He would, if the room was any indication. He had taken what he wanted and left her. If the man thought a couple of pastries were going to make up for his actions, then he was sorely mistaken.

Bastard. She thought back to their conversation last night, but couldn't figure out where everything went wrong. The more she thought about it, the more she considered the possibility that this was Leo's intention all along—to use her as a one-night stand.

"Damn you, Leo." He had given her a gift and made her think that they had a future together. With hardly any effort, he had lowered her defenses and made her care.

Karin moved over to the table of food, picked up a pastry, and put it back down. She just didn't have the appetite. With a sigh of disgust, she turned away and accidentaly knocked the tented napkin from the place setting to the floor. A piece of paper flew from the napkin and landed at her feet.

Curious, she retrieved the paper and sat back down on the bed. After a quick glance at the signature to confirm it was from Leo, she unfolded the paper and began to read.

I'm sorry for the quick departure. Something came up that required my attention and I didn't want to disturb you. Do not leave this room under any circumstances. Please enjoy your breakfast and accept my apologies. When I return, we'll have much to discuss. Some things about our arrangement will have to change, I'm afraid. And those changes are going to have to start today.

Chapter 10

Leo stayed up half the night planning while Karin slept. He had to call in some favors with his media contacts, but the end result had been worth it. Not only did the tabloid picture of him and Karin outside of Sabrina's get brushed to the last page, but Karin wasn't even mentioned. For all the world knew, he could have gone out with any number of Boston socialites. No one had pieced together that the woman spotted on the balcony in his penthouse suite, the woman seen running through the foyer of the Palazzo, and the woman with him outside Sabrina's restaurant were the same person. Karin's anonymity had remained safe, and that was just how he wanted it.

They had been lucky. That *Whispers* reporter hadn't been able to get a good look at her last night, and Sabrina and Wes were too loyal to Karin to give the reporter any details. His luck was going to run out soon. Three times they had managed to keep Karin's identity under wraps. Leo didn't want to tempt fate for a fourth.

The sooner he set things in motion, the sooner he could have it all—Karin by his side, and those nosy reporters at a distance. With interest in the new lady in his life slowing down, public attention would shift toward his younger sister Arianna's wedding—right where he needed it to be.

Leo opened the door to his room at Stone Suites and paused in the doorway. Karin was sitting up in bed, wrapped in nothing but a throw blanket, and reading the note he had left her. Desire hit him hard as the previous night's events played out through his head.

She looked up from the note with an expression he couldn't read. Leo hesitated, realizing that he might have given her the wrong impression by leaving so suddenly and while she slept. He had mentioned that he would return, however, and that he'd explain everything when he got back. She should have trusted him not to run off on her.

He cleared his throat. "Ah, you're awake. Good." Hopefully he didn't sound as nervous as he felt. So much was riding on this moment.

Leo entered the hotel room, duffle bag in hand. He'd had his driver retrieve some things from the Palazzo for both him and Karin while he made his phone calls. He wanted to make sure that she wasn't wearing her Palazzo uniform as they left Stone Suites—just in case they were spotted by some nosy photographers while getting into the Perconti limo.

"What happened?" Karin asked.

He glanced at the table of food. "You didn't eat."

"I wasn't hungry."

He pulled out the chair. "Come, you must be famished."

"Not until you tell me what's going on."

He bit back a sigh and reminded himself that she still had much to learn. "You must take care of yourself, *cara*," he said. When she didn't move, he raised his brow. "You look pale, and I can't have you fainting of hunger before we finish our conversation."

She pursed her lips together and glanced down at the chair. "I'm not hungry." Her stomach growled, and Leo struggled to keep the smile from his face.

"Humor me," he said, echoing the note he had written

to her right before they performed the maid scene up in his penthouse suite. He hoped that his words reminded her of the lesson he had taught her there. Trust me.

She raised her gaze to meet his. After a long moment, she nodded and stood.

Leo waited until she sat and had taken a chocolate croissant from the plate. So, she had a sweet tooth. He made a mental note of it for later.

"So what took you away from the room this morning?" *And me* . . . She didn't say those last words, but the question was implied.

"Good news." He carefully avoided her gaze and instead opened up the duffle bag and pulled out a tabloid magazine. "That *Whispers* reporter wasn't able to get a good look at you. The only information they had was that I had attended a restaurant with a woman, which isn't really a story at all." He grinned. "We're a fuzzy picture on the last page." He opened the magazine and showed it to her.

Karin took the magazine from him and quickly scanned the article. "This doesn't really say much of anything."

"Right." He cleared his throat and went back to his duffle bag. "We got lucky this time, but I'm sure you realize that our luck won't hold out forever."

Karin put down the magazine and stared at him. "What are you saying?"

He glanced up from his bag. "I'm sure you are well aware that things can't continue like this. It's much too risky—for both of us."

This was it, Karin realized. She supposed that she should make it easy on him by telling him that she understood and letting him go. It was the quickest way to end this painful exchange and move on with her life.

She opened her mouth to do just that, then shut it again. Hell, no. She wasn't going to make this easy on him. Karin had had about enough of being used and then tossed aside. If Leo wanted to break up with her, then he was going to have to say it to her face. It was the least he could do.

"Things between us need to change, how?" Karin put down her pastry and watched him fumble with his toiletries.

"Yes, well." He stopped pulling items out of the duffle and stared at her. His features were hard, determined. "The only reason why people are interested in us is because they want to know who I'm involved with, and if she is a member of the Palazzo staff." He moved over to the edge of the bed, close to her chair. His knee brushed hers as he sat, sending tingles of awareness over her skin.

"Yes, this is true . . ." She drew out the word, trying to figure out where his thoughts were going.

Leo grinned. "Well, it's settled then. It wouldn't do if the media learned that I was involved with a Palazzo intern, so we will have to terminate your position."

"What?"

He took her hand. "I've talked to your advisor, and he agrees. Since you're going for a hospitality degree, you'll need to experience more than just cleaning hotel rooms and filling in spreadsheets."

"How did you know my advisor?"

"Details." He waved his hand between them in dismissal. "Instead of working numbers for Marco and cleaning up after Dante's messes, you should have a more high-level job where you can oversee different aspects of the business."

She pulled her fingers from his grasp. "And how do I do that? I can't be in charge. I don't have that kind of experience."

Leo grinned. "No, you wouldn't be in charge. *I* will be. You'll come and work for me, and in turn, I'll show you everything you need to know about running a hotel chain."

"But I already work for you."

"No, I mean you'll report to me directly." He stood and began to pace as Karin rubbed her temple in confusion.

"I don't understand," she said.

"It's really quite simple," he said as he poured two separate mugs of coffee. "You'll become my personal assistant."

She made a face. "I didn't work this hard to be someone's secretary."

"Consultant, then." He added sugar to one cup and waved his spoon in the air. "I'll think up some fancy title for you if you want. It doesn't matter. The point is, you'll follow me around and gain a top-down view of running a hotel conglomerate." He glanced at the cups. "Cream and sugar?"

Karin nodded and tightened her blanket around her as she watched him add cream to the cup. "Exactly what would I be doing for you as your consultant?"

He grinned and handed her one of the mugs. "I've seen how you pitch in and pick up the slack for your coworkers, and Marco gives your organizational skills high praise. I suspect you know the inner workings of the Palazzo better than most." He took a sip of coffee and set it aside. "You have an insider's knowledge about the difficulties the staff faces on a daily basis."

"True."

"You know what the Palazzo needs to run smoothly, and what improvements will have to be made to take it to the next level."

"But—"

"We'll start here, with our flagship hotel, and then move

outward." He returned to the edge of the bed, his expression intense.

"Outward?"

"Of course." He began to tick cities off on his fingers. "New York, Los Angeles, London, Paris, Milan—"

"Wait a minute—"

"I placed a few phone calls and made sure that you've taken the necessary management classes already. And you've seen this hotel." Leo waved his hand around the room. "It's immaculate."

"It's different," she agreed as she took a sip from her mug. "The coffee is better, too."

"It's full almost every night of the week," he said in disgust as he stood. "You can change that."

"You want me to steal visitors from Stone Suites?" she asked as she put her coffee aside.

"Not steal, necessarily, but offer them a deal that they can't refuse." He grinned and began pacing once more, fully caught up in his fantasy. "We'll beat Stone at his own game and put the Palazzo on the map once more."

"But I'm an intern. I don't have my degree yet."

He stopped pacing and raised his brows. "Many corporate CEOs have very little formal education. What you don't know, you can learn on the job."

"I don't know—"

"I've seen your resume," he said before she could finish her thought. "You have excellent grades, and your advisor told me that it's your dream to one day oversee the daily running of a hotel."

"Well, yes." She nibbled her lower lip. "But that's Marco's job."

"Yes. Yours will be different. You will be our management consultant."

"You want me to tell you where your brother has failed?"

"And offer solutions. Yes."

She nibbled her lower lip in thought. "Won't Marco be mad?"

"He's a big boy. He'll get over it."

She stared at him and tried to comprehend what was happening. He wasn't trying to get rid of her. In fact, if she was to become his consultant, they'd be spending more time together.

"I . . . I don't know what to say." Karin needed time to think, and she couldn't do that with him staring at her as if he wanted to kiss every inch of skin on her body.

"Say yes." He closed the distance between them and took her hand. "You won't get this opportunity from anyone else."

"You're not thinking this through. You can't just create a position and then have all of your problems disappear. What about the reporters? Won't they think it's odd that you're hiring an intern to help you do a major reorganization?"

"It's not the facts, but how you spin them that's important. You need to have a little faith in your abilities. I do." He raised her hand to his lips and kissed her knuckles, causing a stirring in her lower abdomen. The idea of spending so much time with Leo was appealing, but something about all of this didn't add up. What was he up to?

"This is insane . . ." she hedged.

"You already know that when a decision has been made, I don't like to wait."

"But a decision hasn't been made. I can't agree to this. It's too much—"

"It's not as if I'm throwing you to the wolves, *cara*. I'll be right there with you the whole time." He let out a long breath and squeezed her fingers. "Let me make this a little easier for you." He tugged on her fingers, pulling her closer. "I will handle all of the arrangements, including the media spin. I have a team already working on putting everything in place." He brushed a stray hair from her face and cupped her cheek with his palm. Karin's entire body heated, and a tightening formed in her lower abdomen as she remembered how good his skin felt next to hers, and the wicked things he could do with those lips.

"Has everyone agreed to this?" she asked. This was all happening so fast. "I don't want to anger anyone, or create a strain on the relationship between you and your brother." As appealing as this deal sounded, she couldn't see how this could work for his family. Even if Leo was right and her new position quieted the rumors, there was still his family to consider. His siblings would surely question his sanity by giving an intern such a high position in his company.

"Thanks to Marco, we have lost many of Palazzo's repeat customers to Stone Suites," Leo said.

"True, but—"

"And now you tell me that my staff is thinking about mutiny."

"Yes."

He slid his hand to her neck and brushed his thumb along her jaw. "If my staff goes on strike, then there will be no Palazzo left to run. We must act fast if we are to save the hotel." He rounded his fingers along the side of her face and hooked them under her chin.

It was becoming more and more difficult to think rationally with him sitting so close. Karin cleared her throat and tried to steady her voice. "Losing the staff could be catastrophic. Not only will things not be in place for your sister's wedding, but the resulting media scandal will tarnish the hotel's reputation and make our restructuring even more difficult."

He quirked his lips into a half-smile and rubbed his thumb over her chin. "See? You're already thinking like a consultant." He lowered his hand and took her fingers holding the blanket at her chest. With a gentle tug, he pulled them away, allowing the cotton fabric to slip around her waist and expose her tight nipples. She supposed she should be embarrassed, but the hungry look in his eyes as he glanced at her chest made her feel wanton and needy.

"Work with me, Karin," he said as he dragged his gaze back up to meet hers. "Together we'll find out where the Palazzo is failing and bring it back to its former glory."

He was so damn tempting, both his words and the excitement in his eyes. Karin wanted to believe that everything would work out just as he imagined it. It would be so easy to get swept up in his orbit, but she couldn't quiet the little voice inside of her head suggesting that this could end in disaster.

This was a huge step. There had to be a catch, but her brain wasn't functioning enough right now for her to puzzle it out. It all sounded a little too good to be true.

He glanced at his duffle, as if considering something. After a quick tightening of his jaw, he returned his gaze to her.

"It will require long hours alone with me," he said as he brushed a stray hair from her face. His touch felt soft, almost like a caress, but his fingers burned a trail of heat all the way to her core. "You'll be well compensated for your efforts." He lowered his voice when he spoke the last few words, making his implication clear.

"I—"

He placed his finger in front of her lips, stopping her words. "Think about it. If you take this new position, no one will question our time together. It will be expected."

"True," she said after he slid his finger away from her lips, around her jaw, and down the sensitive skin of her neck, causing a ripple of need to race down her spine.

"And your education wouldn't be just in the hotel industry. I will continue to teach you in other ways."

She nibbled her lower lip as a tightening formed in her core. "How long?" Her voice was soft and a little breathless.

As if sensing her crumbling resistance, he slid his fingers down over her nipple, barely touching her skin. "Don't worry. This is only a temporary position. If you wish, then after the reorganization of all of the Perconti hotels, you may return to your schooling."

There it was—the catch. Karin pulled away from his touch as his words dispersed the erotic haze in her mind. This wouldn't be a permanent position, but a temporary one. After she helped him restructure his hotel empire, he'd toss her to the curb.

"So this is only temporary," she repeated, just wanting to make sure.

"Yes, of course." Leo moved to his duffle to search for something, as if the matter had already been settled and he was moving on to other matters. "I've already arranged everything with your school. You will be able to keep all of your credits and pick up where you left off."

Pain sliced through her as she watched him rummage through the bag. She had hoped that he was offering more with his proposal, but she could see now that it was only a business deal. Karin was a little surprised at how hurt she felt. Then again, after the wonderful gift and intimate moment last night, she had thought that there was something more between them than just a business agreement.

"I'll need to go home, eventually," she said.

He glanced up from the duffle bag. "Why?"

"I'll need to shower and change."

"You can move your things into the penthouse suite, with me." He frowned and continued his search.

"But—"

"You have to understand, *cara*. This position will require you to stay at the hotel. We'll be working long into the night and it would just be easier for all of us." He gave up searching and straightened. "You'd have your own room, of course. The penthouse suite is large enough for two."

Another stab of pain lanced her chest. "That's good. I'd need my own space . . ."

"Think about it, Karin. You'd gain valuable work experience to put on your resume . . . and we could finish what we started last night." He sat by her side once more and allowed his gaze to drop to her chest. He brushed his fingers along the outside of one full, round breast, causing desire to pump through her veins and heat her skin. "We have only just begun discovering all you have to offer in the bedroom . . . Don't you want to see what else you are capable of giving?"

He lifted his gaze to meet hers and slid his fingers over her hardened nipple. "Give it a chance, *cara*."

The man was convincing, that was for sure. Leo was offering her an incredible opportunity. She'd be crazy not to take him up on it. For the price of a year off from school, she'd have an impressive resume that any hotelier would envy. When it came time to look for a permanent position, she'd have her pick of jobs. "I have to admit, it sounds intriguing."

Leo struggled to keep the triumphant grin from his face. "Of course." He squeezed her fingers. "So you understand."

"That this can only be temporary? Yes."

"That this is about your education and nothing else," he corrected as he stroked the underside of her wrist. After a long moment, he pulled away. "It cannot be anything more than that." The words were for his benefit as much as hers. The more time he spent with her, the more he started to feel, and those feelings made him more cautious.

If they spent every waking moment together for the next several months, then it was possible that Karin might come to expect more than he was willing to give her. While he had no problem sharing his business and body, he could never completely open himself up to her. He had only shared himself with one woman before and she had ruined him. In many ways he was still recovering. He could never let himself become that vulnerable again.

The familiar ring of his cell phone broke through the silence. He ignored it and focused on her. "You won't regret this, *cara*. I promise." He leaned forward and brushed his lips against hers.

"I didn't say yes yet."

"But you will." He pinched her chin between his fingers.

"Why?"

"Because I'm impossible to resist." He brushed his lips against hers. Her body immediately responded, pressing against his and silently begging for more. Damn, he couldn't get enough of her.

After the third ring, she reluctantly pulled away and nodded to the phone. "You might want to get that."

"This is more important." He steeled his jaw and tried to control his annoyance.

She glanced at his suit jacket on the chair. "Are you sure? It could be important."

"Very well, but this isn't over, *cara*." *She's stalling.* Leo scowled and grabbed his phone out of his suit pocket. The number that blinked back at him caused his chest to tighten with anxiety.

"Damn." He looked up from the screen. "I have to get this. Sorry."

"It's okay."

He considered moving out into the hall for some privacy, but decided against it. He might be seen and recognized by someone. Instead, he grabbed the duffle bag and went into the bathroom. After closing the door and setting the duffle on the counter, he flipped open the phone and put it to his ear.

"This better be important. I'm busy."

"I can't believe you went to Sabrina's." Dante's irritated voice rippled over the phone. "Are you insane?"

"No more insane than you ordering all of that food from her and leaving the empty cartons all over the penthouse suite."

"You've screwed everything up." Dante let out a ragged breath.

"Marco suggested—"

"Didn't you imbeciles consider for one moment that I order from Sabrina's because I might *like* her food? In case you've forgotten, I've studied with world-renowned chefs in Florence. I know my food and her technique is above reproach. Some of those dishes we even designed together."

Of course Leo hadn't forgotten. He had spent an exorbitant amount of money to send Dante to some of the best culinary schools in the world. After dropping out of places in Paris, Florence, Istanbul, and Barcelona, it seemed like the only thing Dante excelled in was knowing which flavor of alcohol got you inebriated the fastest.

Leo rummaged through his duffle for his pills. "Why would you order so much, though? Really, Dante, we have to be careful with our finances."

"Sabrina's dream is to run an Italian restaurant in the North End. She lives and breathes that place." Dante's voice was filled with venom. "The negative publicity I gave her hurt her business. This was the least I could do."

"I know." Breathing a sigh of relief, Leo pulled out his anxiety medication and struggled with the lid. Now if he could only get his brother off the phone so he could focus on more important matters—like his new assistant sitting in the other room. "I don't see how buying food—"

"Our pact was only one of the reasons why we broke up. Another reason was because she wanted to make it on her own, without the help of the Perconti name."

"I see." Leo wedged the phone between his ear and shoulder and pressed down on the medicine cap. He was so tired of dealing with his siblings' drama. Perhaps his first order of business after the wedding will be to take Karin on an extended vacation . . .

"No, I don't think you do see," Dante said. "She's not succeeding. I checked. She's up to her eyeballs in debt."

"I don't see how this is our problem." After multiple tries, Leo popped the top off and poured the little pills into his hand. Karin's indecision and the mess with *Whispers* was enough to cause a surge in his anxiety. Thank goodness his driver, the only one who knew of his diagnosis, had thought to pack his pills.

"Her restaurant is failing. Ever since the publicity of dating me died down, she has been struggling. There's too much competition, and while she's good, she can't compete with chefs who have studied in Italy. I was ordering the food to help her keep her restaurant afloat. I was doing it under a false name, so she wouldn't know that I was helping her."

"We have a hard enough time keeping Perconti Enterprises in the black—"

"That's not all. I ordered that food because the taste of it reminded me of *her*. We used to be so good together . . . but those reporters ruined everything."

Leo grabbed one of the small glasses left by the hotel

staff and pinched the bridge of his nose. "And now, after I talked to her, she knows that you were behind the food all along."

Leo filled the glass with water from the sink and swallowed both it and the pills. Closing his eyes, he focused on the medication as it slid down his throat and into his stomach. "Dante, I'm sorry but this can't go on any longer. You know our pact. What if one of those reporters discovered what you were doing? You don't want to give her more negative publicity."

Dante let out a long breath. "Yeah, I know. I suppose it doesn't matter anymore anyway. Sabrina called an hour ago and told me that she she's canceling her delivery service. She doesn't want to see any of us ever again."

"It's probably for the best."

Dante didn't seem to hear him. "I have to come up with a different plan to help her out."

"Why?"

"Because I love her."

Leo glanced at the door, then moved away from it to the far end of the bathroom and lowered his voice. "This family can't afford love. You know that. There are too many risks involved."

There was a brief moment of silence before Dante answered. "Sabrina isn't like Danika."

"All women are the same. They'll dump you in a heartbeat for a better offer."

"Surely there must be some exceptions."

"None." Leo thought of Karin in the other room. He really wanted to believe that she was an exception, someone he could trust completely. Unfortunately, his experience had taught him otherwise. No, as much as he longed to share his soul with someone, such things were not for people like him. There was far too much temptation to betray him to the paparazzi or his enemies, and Leo didn't think he could survive his heart being broken a second time.

So he had decided to settle on the next best thing. He'd made Karin an offer she couldn't refuse to keep her by his side, and he'd use that plan to enjoy her company and keep the loneliness at bay. The confidentiality agreement she had signed before becoming an intern would keep her from divulging any corporate secrets, and she had as much motivation as he to keep their bedroom games private as well.

Leo would allow her to learn his body and his hotel empire, but she could never touch the real person inside. Not even his family knew of his demons. Those he kept to himself.

But that was him. His brothers were different. Dante in particular needed to separate himself from this woman and focus on getting better. The man was making a fool of himself, and it was only a matter of time before the paparazzi made his pathetic behavior common knowledge.

"Trust me on this, Dante. Let a woman into your heart and you'll get nothing but trouble in return. You need to forget about her."

"I can't."

"You must."

"But—"

"Common men can afford such luxuries, but we cannot. Nothing good can come from giving your heart to a woman. Nothing."

"Brother, for a man who runs one of the largest hotel chains in the world, you can be a real idiot sometimes." He started to say something else, but his voice sounded like a garbled mess.

"Dante, is everything okay?" Leo asked.

"Can't you damn reporters leave a man in peace?" Dante yelled. It sounded like he had pulled the phone away from his ear. "Who the hell let them in here?"

"Are you still there?" Something crashed on the other end of the line and Leo ran his hand over his face. Christ, what the hell was going on? "Is everything okay?"

The phone went dead. Muttering a curse, Leo dialed a different number.

"Marco?" he said when his brother picked up the line. "I think we might have had a breach in security. Something's happened to Dante—"

Chapter 11

Karin blinked back tears as she stepped away from the bathroom door. She hadn't meant to eavesdrop, but she couldn't seem to help herself. Leo had looked so worried when he saw the number on his cell. She had only wanted to offer support.

Nothing but trouble. Leo's words rolled around in her head as she scanned the room around her.

She shouldn't have been surprised at his words. It had just confirmed her earlier assumption—that rich corporate CEOs were all the same. She was under no illusions as to his real intent. By day they'd work on the hotel, by night she would lay in his arms, bending to his will and his command. Even now, hearing his sexy voice through the bathroom door gave her shivers. To have him to herself every night would be like a dream come true.

But that was all it could ever be: a dream. While Leo was willing to use her mind and body, he wouldn't allow her into his heart. Those glimpses into his more personal side were just that—glimpses. He'd never let her get close to him. They'd never have a normal, functioning relationship. It wasn't until she had heard him say the words through the bathroom door that she realized how much she had hoped he was different. When he had given her that

Christmas ornament outside the restaurant, she could have sworn that he was hinting at something more, something deeper. Ever since her parents' deaths, she had felt so alone. Oh, she had friends and extended family, but nobody close. There was no one with whom she could share her thoughts and hopes for the future. No one she could truly confide in.

Leo was offering her everything, except the one thing she really wanted. That beautiful gift he had given her outside of Sabrina's wasn't a token of his affection and a promise of a future, but merely a trinket used to buy her loyalty. She'd thought she could live with their relationship staying superficial, but now she wasn't so sure.

After dressing, she glanced over her shoulder at the bathroom door once more. She could tell by the snippets of conversation filtering under the door that Dante was on the other end. As annoyed as he was with his siblings, Leo also cared deeply for them. They'd always come first in his life, and she a distant second.

Karin knew that she needed to walk away from this. She was in over her head. Already she was beginning to develop feelings for this man, and he had just said that he could never give her what she wanted.

She should walk away, but she couldn't. It was more than the wonderful carrot he dangled in front of her by letting her fix up the Palazzo. Sure, she'd get valuable job experience, but that wasn't the only thing that was attractive about the offer.

She wanted *him,* she realized. Leo made her feel special. With one possessive look, he made her feel cherished and wanted. The "education," as he put it, was just a bonus.

If she couldn't have Leo's heart, then she wanted him for as long as it could possibly last. Saying no to Leo's offer was the smart thing to do, but if she did that, then they would still have to work together. Knowing that she'd see him every day, but not be able to touch him or hear his

voice, made her physically ill. At least this way she would
be able to stay close to him. Perhaps, if they spent enough
time together, she could even change his mind.

Leo emerged from the bathroom fully dressed and
dropped his duffle bag on the floor. "I'm sorry, *cara*," he
said as he slipped his phone back into his pocket. "That
couldn't be helped."

"It's not a big deal." If she was going to guard her heart,
then the less she knew about his personal life, the better.

He offered her a wry smile. "Unfortunately, I have more
bad news. It seems as if there's some sort of crisis going
on back at the hotel. I need to return."

"What happened?"

"Nothing, at least not yet. The problem is with my
brother." He crossed his arms and frowned as he leaned
against the bureau. "It appears Dante has taken to smash-
ing the bottles of alcohol in the restaurant."

"Yeah, he does that."

"I know." He swept his gaze around the room and
dropped his arms. "But in this case, he did it because he
caught a reporter eavesdropping on our conversation about
Sabrina. If it ever got out into the tabloids that Dante still
loved her, Sabrina could be targeted again."

Karin thought back to her conversation with Wes and
shuddered. She couldn't imagine being the focus of some
crazy Perconti fan who wanted the famous brothers all
to herself. After the incident, Dante broke up with Sabrina to protect her, but it was obvious that he still cared
about her.

Leo shook his head. "At any rate, he hung up on me, so
I sent Marco in to check up on him. Even so, I need to be
there. When Dante is emotional, he can become unpredict-
able. The man is capable of anything."

"I understand."

He glanced down at the duffle bag on the floor. "It's

quite possible that Marco won't be able to handle this situation by himself. I need to go and assess what Dante has ruined and what can be salvaged."

"Of course."

He grabbed a dress from the hotel closet and tossed it on the bed next to her. "You're a similar size to my sister, so I had Roberto bring over a dress. I hope you don't mind."

"I have plenty of clothes, thank you."

Leo scowled. "Of course not. Don't be ridiculous." He glanced at her uniform. "If you're seen wearing your Palazzo uniform, it's bound to arouse suspicion when we leave."

She considered him for a moment and realized he was right. "I'll return it to you tomorrow."

He shook his head. "I'm sure my sister wouldn't miss the dress, she has so many, but if it makes you feel better . . ." He stepped forward, closing the distance between them. "Have you considered my offer?" His smile was warm and inviting. Heat spread out through Karin's body, warming her to her toes.

"Yes."

He hooked his finger under her chin and tilted her head up to meet his gaze. "And?"

The doorbell rang, saving Karin from answering. With a curse, Leo went to answer it. Karin let out a long breath and tried to calm her raging libido. It was amazing how much a simple touch affected her. Leo had single-handedly tied all of her emotions up in knots. The sooner she got away from him, the sooner she could think all of this through and come to some sort of rational decision, one that wasn't based on the rising need in her core.

"The car is waiting for us outside, *cara*. If you don't mind—" He stopped when he saw her fully dressed.

"Do you think it looks okay?" she asked.

"Darling, you look . . ." He blinked as he dragged his gaze up and down her body. "You look amazing."

She felt the heat rise to her cheeks. "Thank you." She shifted the low-cut edging to cover more of her breasts. "But it's a little tight in places."

"It's perfect."

"I feel as if I'm going to burst out of this."

"Here." He chuckled as he picked up her jacket and placed it over her shoulders. Karin shivered as his fingers brushed over her skin. "This will make you feel more comfortable."

"Thank you."

He adjusted her jacket, lingering over her breasts. "You are right," he said. "This dress will need to be removed at the first opportunity." He slid his fingers under the hem, brushing the skin right above her nipple. "I will make it a priority to find something more . . . suitable for your new position."

"I haven't accepted your offer yet," she said as he pulled away.

"But you will." He offered her his arm. "Shall we?"

"We're going out together?"

"Of course. We're both going to the same place, are we not?"

"Perhaps we should go down separately. I don't want to risk the paparazzi seeing us together." Or having Jason see them together. So far they had been lucky, but Karin had no idea how much longer they could get away with not being recognized.

"Don't be ridiculous." He held out his arm. "No one will think to look for us here. And if anyone does see us, it won't arouse suspicion. Without the uniform, we are of no interest. Come."

Karin hesitated for a brief moment, then took his arm.

As they stepped out into the hall, she glanced from side to side, watching the passing patrons to see if there was anyone she knew. With each step she felt more and more uncomfortable. Even if the reporters weren't lingering around downstairs, her former coworkers most certainly were.

Leo hit the button for the elevator and as it opened, one of the cleaning staff pushed a cart out into the hallway. Karin recognized him immediately and averted her gaze. Quickly, she dragged Leo into the elevator.

The staff member stopped and stared. "Hey, do I—"

Karin pushed the button for the ground floor and the doors closed before he could finish his sentence. Leo shot a thoughtful glance in her direction, but thankfully said nothing. Crisis averted—for now—but Karin wouldn't feel completely at ease until they were in the Perconti limo and far away from this place.

As the elevator doors opened to the front waiting area, she breathed a small sigh of relief. Besides a few lingering staff, the hotel was empty.

Leo whisked her toward the front doors as Karin pulled up the collar of her coat. With a little luck, she'd make it out of the hotel unseen.

"Ah, Leo, so great of you to join us," the loud, friendly baritone echoed behind them. *Shit.* She knew that voice. It appeared as if Leo did, too. He stiffened next to her, and Karin felt the tension radiate off him in waves.

Jason Stone walked around into their field of vision and shook Leo's hand. "So, what brings you to Stone Suites? Coming to check out the competition?"

Karin shrunk back and averted her gaze, hoping he didn't see her face.

"No, Jason," Leo said. "I came because I wanted to see if cheaply made hotels turned a profit." He made a show of looking around. "I can see that they don't."

Jason's smile appeared forced. "Ah, but profits are up

for the third straight year, my friend. I wonder, can the Palazzo claim the same?"

Leo pressed his lips together, but said nothing.

Jason chuckled. It was a forced, fake laugh that grated along Karin's nerves. "And who have we here?" He turned to focus his piercing blue gaze on her.

Jason Stone was just as good-looking as ever, but that handsomeness was tarnished in Karin's mind. Physical looks could do nothing to overcome a self-centered soul. While Jason might be considered physically handsome, inside he was nothing more than a selfish lump of coal.

Leo tightened his grip on Karin's arm. "She's none of your concern."

"Come now, Leo. Don't be so greedy." Jason crouched slightly to get a better look, and Karin had nowhere to hide. Slowly she looked up and met his gaze.

His smug smile faltered, and his brows shot up with surprise. "Karin?" He glanced at Leo and then refocused on her. "Well, well, now this is a surprise." He took her hand and placed a chaste kiss on her palm. "Now everything is perfectly clear."

"Jason, please." Karin didn't want to make a scene. More importantly, she didn't want her secrets revealed. She hoped that Jason would be classy enough to keep quiet, but judging by the mischievous look in his eyes, she guessed that she wouldn't be so lucky.

Leo raised his brows at her. "You two know each other?"

"I used to work for him," she explained.

"Work for me?" Jason's self-satisfied smile made Karin want to scream. He dropped her hand and adjusted his suit jacket. "I suppose you could say that, yes."

"Jason." Karin tried to silence him with a sharp look. The humor she saw in his eyes told her that she failed miserably.

"I see," Leo said.

"I almost didn't recognize her in the different clothes." Jason grinned and stepped back from them. "A word of warning, my friend. Playing with the staff is never as discreet as you think." He glanced at Karin. "Especially when the staff member has trouble controlling her emotions."

"I have total control over my emotions." Karin fisted her hands as anger welled up in her chest.

"Oh? Could have fooled me." He nodded to her and met Leo's gaze. "This one cost me thousands in damages when I finally cut the cord."

"You didn't break it off, I did." Karin ground her teeth until she felt Leo's hand on the small of her back.

"Right after you did three thousand in damages to my office."

"You deserved it for sleeping around."

"No, I deserved it for sleeping with the help." He adjusted his suit jacket. "A mistake I'll never make again, I assure you." He glanced at Leo. "Something you should do as well, my friend."

"You heard her," Leo said through clenched teeth. "I do believe that the woman is over you."

Over him. Leo was right. The urge to slap that smug smile off Jason's face was strong, but she was stronger. Karin knew that Jason was goading her. Making a scene would draw attention to the fact that Leo was staying at his rival's hotel—with her. The resulting media frenzy would boost Jason's company, while making it even more difficult for Leo to put the pieces of his hotel chain back together.

"Just be careful, my friend. No woman is worth losing your business over, no matter how fine her ass may be."

"I believe you owe the lady an apology." Leo's voice was low and full of warning as he jerked out of Jason's hold.

"Of course." Jason held his hands up in mock surrender and nodded to Karin. "This is neither the time, nor the place. My apologies." He refocused on Leo. "It just seems that there are much better ways to relieve some stress." He waved his hand in the air around him at the patrons as he spoke. "One can never be too careful with so many eyes open around us." Jason's grin faded as he lowered his hand and considered them. "And I wouldn't put all of your financial eggs in one basket, either."

"What do you mean?" Leo asked.

Jason leaned in close and nudged Leo's arm. "Weddings sometimes have a way of not turning out the way we plan." He winked and leaned back, flashing both of them a knowing grin.

"What have you done?" he whispered through clenched teeth.

"Good night, Leo." Jason offered a slight bow. "Ms. Norell."

Karin frowned and considered Jason. It was obvious that he was up to something, but what? The answer was there, just out of reach.

Leo growled and tugged Karin to the front door before she could piece it together. Her whole body went numb as Leo dragged her out into the cool night air, around to a deserted side street, and toward the waiting limo. Roberto lifted his brows in surprise as Leo motioned her inside and whispered orders to his driver.

Fear immobilized Karin as she waited for Leo in the backseat. He was angry, but she expected that considering the bomb just dropped on him. Jason Stone had a way of twisting words to suit his purpose. While Karin didn't know what the owner of Stone Suites was up to, she *did* know that he was up to something.

Leo climbed into the seat and closed the door. As the limo pulled away from the curb, tension filled the air, making Karin feel slightly claustrophobic. *Why won't he say something?*

"Leo, I'm sorry," she said when she could no longer take his silence. "I meant to tell you about Jason, but . . ." She let the words trail off, unsure what to say.

"It seems that you have forgotten your lessons."

"Lessons?"

He raised a gloved finger between them. "Lesson one. Honesty."

"I know I should have told you." She swallowed and looked down at her hands. What a mess. "We met when I was an intern at Stone Suites."

"I gathered that much."

Silence descended between them, making Karin uncomfortable. Leo's features were unreadable. It would have been better if he ranted and yelled at her. Hell, it would have been better if he slapped her. She certainly deserved it for keeping something like this from him. Jason was his biggest rival.

It was easy to see how the staff came up with Leo's nickname. Just like a general, Leo remained cold and aloof. Karin could tell he was thinking about something— calculating was more like it—but he refused to share his thoughts with her.

The kindness and affection he had shown her back at the hotel was gone. The emotional and passionate side of Leo was something she had gotten used to. This man, with his hard, calculating gaze assessing her, made her nervous.

"Are you still with him?" he asked.

"What?"

He shifted in his seat so that he faced her. Other than the small vein throbbing in his temple, there was no other outward sign of emotion. "Are you still with him?"

"No!" The word came out in a burst of emotion. She cleared her throat and tried to appear as calm and collected as he. "I mean, no. Our relationship was just a fling. It only lasted a couple of months." She looked down at her hands in her lap. "When I caught him cheating on me, I called off the relationship."

"And left there to work at the Palazzo." Leo turned toward his window, shielding his face from view. Karin had heard that Leo always kept his emotions and motives hidden. Up until this point she'd never believed it. With her, he had always been so open. Now she could see those moments for the gift they were. She didn't know if she liked this side of Leo, this cold businessman. She wished he'd tell her what he was thinking.

"Not right away," she replied. "I . . . I mean I couldn't work for Ja—Mr. Stone anymore, all things considered. I quit the internship that day and worked with my advisor to find a new position." She took in a shaky breath. "I didn't find a job right away, though. It was about a month later that I ended up at the Palazzo."

"Did my brother know of your past work experience?"

"No." She took a long, steadying breath. Leo continued to look out the window, deep in thought. He had to be angry. The feud between Stone and the Perconti family was legendary, and frequently played out in the media. She had just given Leo's enemy a way to further tarnish his reputation and proved that she couldn't be trusted.

"I never meant to hurt you." Her voice sounded weak and pathetic to her ears, but she supposed it didn't matter at this point. He was probably furious, and never wanted to see her again. When he dropped her off at the Palazzo, she'd take the Orange Line home and never speak to him again.

"So you had information that could ruin my rival, and yet you did nothing with it," he murmured.

"No."

He looked away from the window and faced her. "Yet

you had every reason to. After what he did, you owed him nothing." He didn't continue, but the words hung in the air between them. *If things should go poorly between us, would you talk to reporters about me?*

She lifted her chin. "I promised him that I'd keep our relationship a secret. I had signed a confidentiality agreement when I joined the hotel staff—"

"Such loyalty for someone so undeserving." He averted his gaze. "You should have told me about him, *cara*."

"My relationship with Jason has nothing to do with us—"

He held up his hand, stopping her words. "It has *everything* to do with us."

"I can't see how—"

"If this relationship is to continue, then your loyalty has to be with me, not Stone." His features hardened as he met her gaze. "I will not compromise on this, *cara*. There is too much at stake."

"I understand." She looked down at her hands in her lap.

"What else is there that I should know about?" His voice was quiet, too quiet.

She shook her head. "Nothing."

"Are you sure?"

She lifted her chin. "I'm sure. And . . ." She swallowed and tried to steady her shaking voice. "And if you still want to go through with our business arrangement, I promise that my loyalty will be to you—only you."

He stared at her for a long moment as tension filled the air between them. Karin fought the urge to look away and instead held herself very still. No matter what happened, she wanted Leo to know that she had no intention of hurting him.

"You want me to trust you, *cara*, but first, you must give me a reason."

She was losing him, she could feel it. Leo was pulling

away from her and if she didn't do something fast, she was going to lose more than this job opportunity. She'd lose whatever thing was growing between them. The thought of losing that special connection made her feel ill.

Karin fought a wave of panic as she searched for the right words that would cause him to change his mind. She wanted this job, she realized, and more importantly, she wanted to continue what had started between them. Leo promised an education both in and out of the bedroom, and she wasn't ready to give up that opportunity without a fight.

"We have both done things in our past that we've regretted," she said. "A wise person does not dwell on their mistakes, but learns from them and moves forward."

He raised his brows. "And you have moved forward, have you not?"

"Yes." Karen held her breath and searched his face, but his expression was unreadable. "I promise that if you take me on as your consultant, I will use what I have learned at Stone Suites to make the Palazzo the best hotel in Boston." She leaned forward. "My loyalty will be to Perconti Enterprises and to you." She lowered her gaze to his lap, hoping to make her implication clear. "Only you."

He waited for her to look back up at him and considered her for a long moment. Then a knowing smile spread out over his lips.

"In that case, my offer still stands, *cara*." He held out his hand. "Welcome again to the Perconti family."

As soon as they shook on their agreement, Leo pulled out his phone. "Excuse me. I have some arrangements to make."

"Of course." As she sat back and watched him text, she couldn't help but feel a little disappointed. She had expected more than just a handshake on their deal, considering how insistent he had been back at the hotel. It didn't sit well with her that Leo was being so calm about all of this. It just reaffirmed her suspicion that he thought of her as nothing more than a business deal.

She reached into her pocket and ran her fingers over the box containing the Christmas ornament. He had been so sweet before. He had made her believe that there might be a future for them both. Now it felt as if Leo had put up a wall between them. What she was witnessing wasn't the man she was falling for, but the cool, rational persona he portrayed to the world.

Aloof she could handle, at least professionally speaking. In the bedroom was a different story, however. If they were going to move forward with their relationship, then she had to make something clear.

"I need you to promise me something before we get too far into this," she said.

"Oh?" He didn't look at her, but instead continued to type into his phone.

Karin took a deep breath before continuing. "When you grow tired of me, you have to promise that you'll let me know. We'll part with nothing more than your work recommendation between us, and I won't breathe a word of what happens behind closed doors."

He frowned and lowered his phone. "I'd never—"

"You asked for honesty from me, and I ask it from you in return. Please." Jason was a smooth talker, a charmer, and so far Leo appeared the same. While finding Jason kissing another woman had been devastating, she had recovered. Something told her that recovery would be next to impossible if she caught Leo doing something similar.

"I know that this is just a business deal, so don't sugarcoat it," she said. "All I ask is that when you tire of me, you'll break off our arrangement before finding someone else. I . . . I don't want to find out from the papers that you're finished with me."

He studied her for a moment, his forehead wrinkling in thought. "If it means that much to you, *cara,* then yes, I will let you know. But don't count on that happening anytime soon—unless you give me a reason to doubt your loyalty again."

"I understand." He was still hurting, but Karin had no idea how to make him understand. Jason was her past.

"Good." He pocketed his phone.

She took a deep breath and nodded. "I also want to give you this back." She pulled out the Christmas ornament and handed it to him.

He frowned at the package in her hands.

"This is purely a business arrangement. I didn't think that you would want me to have something so personal." She tried to give it to him again, but his scowl made her hesitate.

"Don't be ridiculous. I gave it to you because I wanted you to have it."

"You belong to me now, and I like to take care of what is mine."

What was his . . . Awareness crept over her skin as the implication of his words hit home. His possessiveness excited her.

He leaned in closer and ran his fingers over hers on the box. "I saw how your face lit up when you saw it. I hadn't seen anything so . . . genuine in quite some time." He left her hand and curled his finger under her chin, lifting her head. "You are stunning when you smile." Something dark and hungry flashed through his eyes. "We will have to find reason for you to do it more often." He shifted his gaze to her lips, causing ribbons of desire to wrap around her body.

"I can't accept something so expensive," she said.

"Nonsense, of course you can."

"But—"

"I won't have this argument again. If you do anything

less than say thank you, I will think that you are un-
grateful."

"I . . . thank you."

He nodded and lowered his fingers. "Now, that wasn't
so bad, was it?"

"No."

"I mean it when I say that I won't tolerate secrets or betrayal. Having said that, I also enjoy spoiling people who
are valuable to me, and I always make sure that loyalty is
rewarded."

Despite his words, Karin still felt the wall between
them. He was protecting himself, she realized. He didn't
believe that she was giving him her full loyalty. She
stared at his profile and tried to decide how best to convince him that her relationship with Jason was over. A seductive smile spread out over her lips as she thought of an
idea.

"I'm all yours, Mr. Perconti." She leaned forward and
brushed her lips briefly against his.

It only took a moment for Leo to recover from his surprise and take control. The press of his lips was gentle, yet
firm. It was everything she wanted a kiss to be, and everything she would expect from someone who was used to
getting what he wanted.

Karin moaned against his mouth and shifted her hand
to his thigh. Leo dragged her closer as he slipped his
tongue past the barrier of her lips and into her mouth. Excitement rippled through her veins as Karin felt his muscles tense under her fingertips. She inched her hand up over
his thigh and discovered that he was already hard for her.
Her core tightened and her panties became damp. She
wanted to remind him of how good they were together, and
just how valuable she could be.

Leo had spoken of lessons in the bedroom, but perhaps
this was a time for him to learn a lesson of his own. Leo

had built up this wall of calm and order, one where he showed no outward emotion. More than anything she wanted to make him come undone in the back of the limo. She wanted to remind both him and herself that while she was agreeing to the arrangement, she still made her own choices. She was still in control.

Karin parted her lips in invitation as she undid the zipper on his pants. Leo took advantage, rolling his tongue against hers in a way that made her mind fog with lust. She ran her fingertips over his shaft, feeling the hardness through his thin, cotton boxers. A sense of urgency overcame her, and she imagined what it would feel like to have his erection between her lips, on her tongue.

As Leo slid closer on the seat, Karin removed her hand and placed her palms on his chest.

"Wait."

He leaned back and raised his brows. "Is there something wrong, *cara*?"

"No, nothing wrong." She pushed his chest harder, sending him back onto the seat covers. "I just want to make sure that you are happy with what you are getting."

"I can assure you, I—" Leo's words dissolved into a growl as she slipped his cock out from his boxers.

"You always tell me that I need to trust you. Well, if this arrangement is going to work, then you will have to learn to trust me, too."

"I do."

"No, not yet, but you will."

Before he could respond, Karin shifted his legs apart and eased herself between them. Keeping her gaze focused on his, she crouched until his hips were even with her head.

"There is no need to do this, Karin." His voice sounded strained, and she couldn't help but see the excitement in his gaze.

"I think I do." She wanted to be an equal partner in this

arrangement. That meant that he had to trust her judgment just as much as she trusted his. To do that, he needed to let go of that firm control around his emotions, at least with her.

"Last night, you wanted to show me that there was pleasure in serving you. Well, I think I've learned my lesson." She slid her fingers around Leo's shaft, eliciting a moan. "I want to see if you think so, too."

Karin wasn't sure, but she thought she heard him mutter something in Italian as she ran her tongue over the tip of his cock.

"Do you want me to stop?" she asked as she glanced up from her work.

"God no, *cara*. No." He closed his eyes and groaned as she slid her tongue over his swollen head once more. Moisture collected on her tongue, filling her mouth with his salty taste. With each rotation, she felt him tense beneath her. He was trying hard not to touch her, trying to let her have her way.

Karin paused and waited for him to open his eyes. "Show me what you want." She took his hands and placed them on either side of her head. "Teach me." She curved her lips into a smile..

"As you wish." He brushed back her hair, cupped the back of her head, and gently led her toward his cock.

"Karin." Leo gasped as she slid her lips down his length. Never before had he felt anything so satisfying. He tightened his grip on her head, forcing himself to pay attention to the lesson she had asked from him. Slowly, he guided her over his shaft, but soon realized that she didn't need any instruction. He slid his hands to her temples and held her hair back as she retreated slowly, running her tongue over the sensitive vein underneath. The air in the limo heated as she changed directions and eased down over him once more

What she was doing was a gift, he realized. She gave herself over to him of her own free will and never expected anything from him in return. Up until now, everyone Leo had met had wanted something from him, whether it was money, a job, his influence, or media attention. Even his siblings offered their loyalty in exchange for Leo's security.

Karin was different, wonderfully, beautifully different. It made him want to throw her down on the leather seat and possess her mind, body, and soul. She was unique, a rare treasure, and if she thought he was going to walk away from that once the renovations were complete, then she had a lot more to learn.

He watched her as she slid down his length as far as she could go. She felt so warm, so wet. As she retreated, Leo felt her tongue press against the underside of his shaft, stroking the sensitive vein there. Pleasure rippled up his spine, causing him to groan.

"You please me, *cara*," he whispered. "Only you."

She slid her tongue once more along the underside of his cock, then dipped it lower, over his balls. Leo gasped as her hot tongue branded his body. It was one thing to feel her against his skin. It was quite another to watch her. When both senses intertwined, it brought him more pleasure than he could contain.

"Karin." He dug his fingers into her temples as she took one of his balls into her mouth. Need roared through his veins, making him light-headed. "God, that feels good."

"You like that, do you?" Her warm breath rushed past his sensitive skin as she spoke.

"Yes," he muttered, unable to say anything more coherent.

Karin repeated her movements and shifted her focus to

his erection. She was concentrating, he realized. His little maid was trying to please him. She didn't need to work so hard. Just by agreeing to his offer, she had pleased him more than words could ever say.

Leo shivered as she slid her tongue over the tip of his erection, then groaned as she took him into her mouth once more. He dug his fingers into her head, enjoying the feel of her lips against his length. She quickly found her rhythm, and the steady advance and retreat were enough to drive him insane.

"God, *cara*." Everything was building too hard, too fast. Never before had he felt anything so incredible. Leo closed his eyes against the erotic scene before him, trying to prolong the sweet torture. It was no use. When the familiar tingling formed at the base of his spine, he knew that he couldn't hold back anymore.

"I'm close," he whispered.

Without a word, she slowed her movements, gently bringing him back from the edge. Slower, slower . . . Finally she removed her mouth, but kept her hand around his length. Leo's heartbeat drummed in his ears as he opened his eyes and found her looking at him.

"Someone once told me that taking things slow would make the pleasure more intense when release finally came." Karin inched her hand over his length, causing another wave of longing to wash through him.

His chest squeezed tight as he recognized the words. She was using his own tactics against him, and he loved every second of it.

"That's true." Leo's voice sounded raspy and raw, but he didn't care. In this limo, this moment, she could ask for anything and he'd give it to her.

"I see." She flicked her tongue over the tip of his erection. "I'd like to test that theory. If you don't mind." The look she gave him was full of humor, but also desire. She wanted this as much as he did.

"Of course." Leo steeled his jaw and tightened his fingers in her hair as she took him into her hot, wet mouth once more. The need was too strong, his instinct to possess too powerful. If he ever survived this sweet torture, he'd make sure that she'd experience his payback—many times over.

She scraped her teeth lightly over his sensitive skin, sending a jolt of desire to his system. Leo groaned and moved her head, silently urging her to quicken the pace. He couldn't seem to help himself. Despite her determination to keep things slow and steady, he found himself racing toward oblivion once more.

Karin seemed to sense his quickening. She slowed her movements until he loosened his grip on her head. When he finally eased back from the brink, she ran her tongue over his shaft, then caressed his balls again.

The sensation was good, almost too good. Leo rested his head back against the leather seat as a mixture of pleasure and pain infused with every muscle in his body.

"Karin," he whispered. He didn't know how long he could last, and he didn't care. If he died in the backseat of this limo, he'd be a happy man.

He curled his fingers into her head and tried once again to get her to quicken her movements. She refrained, instead torturing him with her own, leisurely rhythm. When he loosened his grip, she'd move a little faster, and he'd rush up to the edge of oblivion once more. He rode the emotional roller coaster up to dizzying heights and back down again until sweat beaded on his brow and his breath came out in short, rough gasps.

"I'm close," he whispered the next time he felt the familiar tingle at the base of his spine. "I'm not sure how much longer I can last." The firm control he prided himself on keeping was slipping, he could feel it. Leo curled his fingers into the back of the leather seat, determined not to lose himself completely to the moment.

Instead of backing away like he expected, she quickened her movements, causing every nerve ending to come alive with pleasure. Realizing what she wanted, Leo moved her head, urging her to go faster. He tightened his jaw and pushed his hips off the seat, desperate to get closer. She pushed harder, went deeper. Tears stung Leo's eyes as he hovered on the brink, his release just out of reach.

She groaned against his shaft, causing long tendrils of need to vibrate up his center and blast through his mind. The added sensation shoved him past the limits of his endurance. Leo groaned her name as his orgasm blasted through his body like a thunderclap. Joy rushed through his veins and filled her mouth, robbing him of his strength and breath.

He watched her swallow and tried to hide his amazement. Never before had a woman done that for him. Something tugged in his chest as he poured the last of his orgasm into her mouth. She continued to pump his shaft with her fist, taking everything he had to give. As a result, something shattered inside of him, and the wall he had so carefully erected around his heart cracked.

When she was finished, she placed him back into his pants and looked up with expectant eyes. He knew that she wanted him to say something, but words escaped him.

"I didn't please you," she said when he didn't speak. Her averted gaze tore at his heart.

"No, *cara*. You pleased me very much. I'm just—"

She glanced up and smirked. "Tired?"

"At a loss for words," he corrected, not willing to admit just how much she had drained him. He wrapped his hands under her arms and dragged her up into his lap. She squealed, the perfect sound of feminine delight. He buried his face in her hair and inhaled her strawberry scent.

"*Cara,*" he whispered. "It was perfect." He tightened his grip around her middle, never wanting the moment to end.

For a while they sat in silence, and Leo was content to just exist in the moment. Here, there was no failing family business, there were no bothersome reporters or hotel in disrepair. Here there was only peace. There was only Karin.

When the limo slowed to a stop, he reluctantly let her go.

"I want you to take this bag up to our room," he said as she shifted back to her seat. "Wait for me there."

"You're not coming?"

He smoothed his fingers down her cheek and brushed his thumb over her plump, kissable lips. "Not yet. I still have to deal with Dante, remember?" He brushed his mouth against hers. "But I will be up as soon as I can." He flashed her a knowing smile. "Then we can continue with our lessons."

"I . . . okay." She seemed a little disoriented, but there was no time to explain anything further. Roberto had opened the door, and Leo had to face the world once more.

Leo smoothed his hair and in doing so, slid his emotional walls back into place. Sadness pulled at him, and perhaps a touch of regret, but he pushed the useless emotions aside. Once he'd dealt with his family, he'd return to her.

Leo stepped out onto the sidewalk. "Hold this," he said as he passed his bag to the driver.

Roberto nodded and Leo held out his hand toward the limo's interior. "Karin?"

She hesitated.

"Is there something wrong?" he asked, trying not to let his impatience show.

"Where are the reporters?"

Leo glanced around on the sidewalk and noticed that the paparazzi was blissfully absent.

He turned back to her and shrugged. "Perhaps they have found a better story to tell." He held out his hand once more. "Come, there's much to do."

She studied his face for a moment, then put her hand in his. Once out of the limo, Leo placed her hand in the crux of his arm and led her through the revolving doors of the hotel in silence.

The cameras immediately started flashing, temporarily blinding him.

"Oh my God." Karin tried to slip away, and Leo reluctantly let her go. When he finally blinked the spots out of his eyes, he noticed that the place was in chaos.

Staff members ran this way and that, collecting broken items and cleaning glass off the floor.

"Where are my brothers?" Leo asked a passing staff member. She looked familiar, but for the life of him, he couldn't place her name, nor did he have time to dwell on it.

She nodded toward the restaurant, her dark hair falling out of her bun. "In there. One punched a reporter, and the other is swearing up a storm."

Leo let out a long breath and turned to Karin. "Roberto will see to your needs."

"I don't—"

He squeezed her fingers, silencing her words. "Let him help you, *cara*. I will return to our room shortly." Leo nodded to Roberto and hurried into the restaurant portion of the hotel. Hopefully he wasn't too late.

Chapter 12

"*Our* room?" Gloria raised her brows as Leo strode out of earshot. "Since when did the two of you move in together?"

"I want to know the same thing," said Amanda Vaughn as she quickly approached.

"I'm just an employee at the Palazzo," she told both of them. "If you want any questions answered, you'll have to speak to Mr. Perconti himself."

Amanda narrowed her gaze at Karin, considering. "Could I at least have your name? For the article."

Instead of answering, Karin turned to Roberto. "You don't have to show me upstairs. I have a passkey."

"You have your own key?" Gloria asked. Amanda started scribbling in her notebook.

"I clean the penthouse sometimes when the staff doesn't have the time," Karin reminded Gloria. She shot Amanda a nervous glance.

Sirens blared outside the hotel, drawing everyone's attention. An ambulance pulled up to the front doors, and emergency personnel poured out onto the sidewalk.

"Excuse me." Amanda hurried outside with the other reporters.

"Is everyone okay?" Karin asked.

"They're fine. I wouldn't put it past that Amanda

Vaughn to call the ambulance just to make more of a scene
for her story," Gloria said.

"Come, we must get you upstairs," Roberto said. He
frowned at the swarm of reporters gathering on the sidewalk. "I will get your clothes in a few hours, after things
calm down." He touched Karin's arm and steered her
toward the elevators.

"You're *staying* up there?" Gloria asked as she followed
in her wake.

Karin sighed as Roberto pushed the button for the elevator that went directly up to the penthouse suite. "I've been
hired for a new position and it's part of the requirement."

"Ah, a new *position*." Gloria made quotation marks in
the air with her fingers when she spoke the last word.

Karin met her gaze. "What's that supposed to mean?"

"What do you think?" Gloria nodded toward the restaurant. "While you've been wining and dining with Mr. Perfect, we all have been fielding a media shitstorm."

"We?"

"Marco mostly, but Wes, Emily, and I helped."

Karin closed her eyes as guilt washed over her body.
"What happened?"

"That reporter—Amanda Vaughn—pretended to be
one of the new waitresses and got past security. She found
Dante in the restaurant and started badgering him about
Leo and that maid who was up in his room." Gloria pressed
her lips together. "If I ever get ahold of that maid, I'm going
to throttle her. She could have very well cost us all our
jobs."

"What do you mean?"

"That reporter is relentless. She's convinced that there
is more to the story than Leo letting off some steam."
Gloria leaned in conspiratorially and lowered her voice.
"She believes that Leo is having sex with a hotel staff
member."

"What did Dante say?"

Gloria shrugged. "What could he say? He didn't know anything. None of us do. Leo is more private than all of his siblings put together." She sighed and glanced over at the chaos at the restaurant. "When she got in Dante's face, Emily tried to remove her from the premises, and got a black eye for her efforts."

"Oh God."

"Dante went crazy. Shouted something about people learning to mind their own business. Then he picked up Amanda, carried her over his shoulder and dumped her out onto the sidewalk on her ass." Gloria waved her hand at the chaos outside. "And that drew the interest of the other reporters. They overwhelmed the doormen and started swarming Dante. He accidentally hit one of them while trying to get out of the way."

Karin followed her line of vision out to the sidewalk and found Leo and Marco talking to the emergency personnel. Reporters poured out of the hotel and started taking pictures. Right in front was Amanda Vaughn, waving her microphone in their faces.

"Dante barely touched him, but that reporter is acting like he just went ten rounds with a prizefighter," Gloria said in disgust.

As much as Karin wanted to help, she knew that her presence would raise more questions than answers. She couldn't explain why she was hanging around, or her familiarity around the eldest Perconti brother. No, it was much better to do as Leo suggested. At least until the whole thing between Marco and Dante blew over.

"Must be nice," Gloria said, pulling Karin from her thoughts.

"What?" Karin asked.

Gloria frowned and dragged her gaze over Karin's body. "New clothes, fancy car." She tilted her head to the side.

"You don't happen to know who that maid was up in the penthouse suite, do you?"

"Of course not." The elevator doors opened and Karin slipped inside. "We can talk about this more later. I hope you understand . . ."

"You're busy. Of course." Gloria continued to stare thoughtfully at Karin as Roberto stepped into the elevator and swiped his card for the penthouse suite.

Karin nibbled her lower lip as the door closed on Gloria's pensive expression and the elevator began to climb.

"I wouldn't worry," Roberto said after a few moments.

Karin glanced at him, but Roberto's gaze was fixed on the elevator doors.

"Leo will have everything under control within a few hours," he said. "Your secret is safe."

Was it? Karin faced front once more as uneasiness settled in her chest. If word got out about her relationship with Leo, it would create even more unrest among the hotel employees. It might even push them over the edge and into striking.

The elevator doors opened and Karin recognized the familiar foyer of the penthouse suite. Roberto held open the door for her and waited for Karin to step inside.

The place was immaculate, and for once it struck Karin as odd. She was normally the one to clean this room, and knowing that someone else shouldered her workload made her feel self-conscious.

Roberto placed the duffle bag on a side table and folded his hands in front of him. "Will there be anything else?"

"No, thank you."

"No clothes or supplies from home?"

"If you're seen there, won't people start asking questions?"

"Not if the announcement of your new position is made." He shrugged. "If you wish, I can collect your things, and I can be discreet." When she hesitated, he continued. "I wouldn't have been on Mr. Perconti's payroll for so long if I didn't know how to avoid the press."

Karin nodded numbly. She handed Roberto her house key and gave him the proper instructions. After the limo driver left, she wandered through the suite, staring at the clean floors and dusted furniture.

What had she gotten herself into?

One thing was obvious. Karin had to stay busy, or she'd slowly drive herself insane. She made her way back to the foyer and decided to put Leo's duffle bag away. It would give her something to do instead of dwelling on the rumors and how Leo was faring downstairs. She took the duffle to the bedroom and placed it on the bed. After rummaging through it for a few moments, she pulled out his shaving kit, another jacket, a toothbrush, and a prescription bottle.

Frowning, she stared at the writing on the bottle.

"Anxiety medication?" She felt around inside the duffle and pulled out another prescription bottle. "Depression?"

She sat down on the edge of the bed and stared at the bottles in her hands. She knew that Leo's family and the business had taken its toll, but she had no idea just how deeply rooted Leo's stress had become. As she blinked at the bottles, she wondered what else Leo wasn't telling her.

Karin thought back to Leo's behavior and how he never outwardly displayed his emotions while in public. She supposed that was a defense mechanism, born from years of having the paparazzi follow his every move. After being the subject of speculation so many times, he probably learned that it was much safer not to show emotion at all.

But keeping everything bottled up inside had its consequences, as these pill bottles indicated. Karin wondered what else Leo was hiding from the world, and if, one day, it would bubble over and ruin the fragile relationship they shared.

Slowly, she rose from the bed and put the medication back into his duffle. *Your secret is safe with me.* She knew that this would all need to be addressed at some point, but now wasn't the time. Leo was far too busy saving his company and this wedding to deal with whatever was bottled up inside. Still, she was curious. Leo was a man of many layers, and part of her wanted to discover each and every one of them.

Karin brought the bag to the hall closet and set it on the floor for him to take care of later. Out of the corner of her eye, she spotted the maid uniform, cleaned and neatly pressed on a hanger. She ran her fingers over the ruffles, remembering their scene on the balcony. Leo had shown her a side of herself that she never knew existed.

Smiling, she took the uniform down from the hanger and brought it to the bedroom. Perhaps by gaining Leo's trust, she might uncover some of his layers after all.

Leo had one hell of a headache. True to form, Dante had gone off the deep end emotionally when that reporter started picking on the staff. After he had dumped Amanda Vaughn out on the sidewalk, she started kicking him and yelling obscenities. While threatening to expose his cave-man ways to the world through a lawsuit, she managed to draw the attention of several more reporters and create a small media frenzy. When Dante tried to get away from the hysteria, all hell broke loose. The chaos had allowed many of these reporters into the hotel, where they started peppering the staff with questions and making them uncomfortable. The brothers had finally gotten them all to disperse, but Leo was sure that none of them would forget the incident. He and Marco were going to have to spend another long night calling in favors to keep this latest scandal from hitting the papers.

Leo had gotten a couple of odd stares as he helped the cleaning staff pick up the shattered glass and overturned chairs in the restaurant. Their scrutiny made him uncomfortable. He didn't understand it. Did they all think that he'd leave everything for the custodial crew? No one wanted to see the place cleaned up more than he did. When it was a mess, they were forced to close, and when they were closed, they weren't making money. Leo knew better than anyone that they couldn't afford to have the hotel restaurant closed for long.

Once everything was cleaned up, Leo left standing orders with Emily to oversee the details of repairing the furniture and headed up to the penthouse suite. He wanted to get away from the suspicious stares and spend some more time in his little maid's arms.

As the elevator began to climb, his cock thickened with anticipation, though it wasn't just her body that he craved. Karin seemed to understand what he needed most, and was all too willing to give it.

He thought back to their time in the limo and remembered how good it felt to have her mouth around his cock. Leo desperately needed to forget his brothers and his troubles with the Palazzo. He needed to sink himself into a beautiful woman and feel nothing but pleasure for a while.

No, not just any beautiful woman. Karin.

When had Karin ceased becoming another warm body and started becoming something special? It was hard to tell, and quite frankly, Leo was too tired to think about it. As the elevator doors opened, he rushed into the penthouse, eager to see her again.

"Karin?"

"Over here."

He rounded the corner and found her standing by the bar in the maid uniform he had bought her. Seeing her there in the barely-there outfit made him instantly hard all over.

"I thought I'd make you a drink, but didn't know what you liked." She ran her fingers over the bar suggestively.

Leo shrugged out of his jacket and tossed it on the couch. So, she wanted to play out another scene, did she? He was more than ready for it. "Scotch, on the rocks."

"So simple," she said as she slipped behind the bar. "I would have thought that you liked your drinks more complicated."

"I might seem complicated, but I'm a simple man, with simple needs." Leo didn't really want the drink. He just wanted her. But playing the game was drawing out the tension and anticipation, which would only add to both of their enjoyment later.

Her hands shook as she took a glass from the bar and put it on top. Leo suppressed the urge to help and kept himself perfectly still. He'd go to her when the moment was right and not a second before. A wave of protectiveness rose up through him as he watched her fumble with the barware. She was so innocent. Leo was used to taking care of those close to him, and he wanted to care for her. She had to want him to do it, however. That was what it was all about: teaching her to trust him to provide for her needs. Only then would they be able to move forward and take this relationship to the next level.

When she spilled a little liquid on her hands, he recognized the opportunity and approached her. "You're doing it wrong, *cara*."

The words were so simple, but they caused a ripple of need to run down her spine. Karin carefully placed the decanter back on the bar. She went to wipe away the liquid, but he caught her hand.

"No."

"But—"

"When we're alone, you will let me take care of you." He bent his head and ran his tongue over the line of scotch on her hand. "All you have to do in return is trust me."

"I do trust you."

He made a noncommittal sound as he dropped her hand and rounded the bar. Tingles of awareness spread out over her skin as he came up from behind.

"What are you doing?" she asked.

"Showing you how to make a proper drink." He slid his fingers down her bare arms, causing her entire body to heat. As he covered her fingers with his, he inched closer and pressed his cock up against her ass. Karin felt his erection slide up against her backside and she shivered with anticipation.

"Here." Covering her hands, he slowly showed her how to pour a drink. Part of Karin wanted to tell him to stop it. She was a grown woman and a scotch on the rocks wasn't exactly a difficult thing to make—but as they moved together, she became hyperaware of how close he stood behind her, and how small her body was against his. As they reached for the decanter, she felt his biceps against her arms, and his abdomen against her back. Karin held her breath as they went through the motions, slowly realizing that this wasn't about the act itself so much as showing her the sensuality of the movements. Karin stood, transfixed, as he replaced the top on the decanter and lifted the glass.

"You see?" he whispered in her ear. "The perfect drink."

Karin shivered as desire wove its way through her bloodstream.

"Here, try it."

"I don't like scotch." She turned her head away as he brought the glass to her lips.

"Ah, but you haven't tried this scotch."

He held the glass steady, waiting. Leo didn't force her to drink, but she knew that he expected her to do it.

Let me take care of you. She sensed that this was about more than tasting the scotch, but didn't quite understand what he was trying to show her. Still, she didn't want to disappoint him, so she took the glass from his hands and raised it to her lips.

"Just a sip," he warned.

She was surprised at the smoky, complex flavor. It was smooth, not biting as she remembered. While not her favorite, it wasn't as terrible as she'd thought.

"What do you think?"

She glanced at him as he took a sip from the glass. "Not bad."

"Just not bad?"

She shrugged. "Not my favorite."

He took another sip. "Let me see if I can change your mind." He set down the glass and invaded her mouth, filling her with the heady mixture of scotch and man. As he slid his tongue across hers, she tried to turn to face him, but he placed his hands on her hips, holding her steady against him.

Karin resigned herself to being immobile, and instead of battling him for control, accepted what he was giving her. As her body began to relax, he pressed closer, and began to undo the buttons along the front of her uniform.

"What do you think now?"

"Better," she said. She leaned in for another kiss, but he backed away.

"Face forward."

Her core tightened in anticipation as she did as she was told. "What are you doing?"

"You need to learn not to question." Finishing the last of the buttons, he slid the uniform down her body and let it pool on the floor. Karin moaned with desire as he traced his fingers along her spine, moving them slowly down to the curve of her ass.

"You weren't wearing anything under your uniform. Good." He eased his fingers over her ass and squeezed. They were delightfully close to her center. Karin wiggled her hips, silently urging him toward her opening.

"Get up on the bar," he commanded.

"Excuse me?"

He shook his head as he took his glass of scotch and walked around the bar to face her. "What did I tell you about questioning me?"

She dragged her gaze from him and stared at the polished wood. "I'll ruin it."

"If you do, I will buy a new one." He tapped the bar once more. "Up."

Karin swallowed the lump in her throat and did as she was told. She had no idea where he was going with this, but she wanted to find out.

"Tell me. What type of things did you do with Stone?" He settled himself on the couch and rested his glass in his lap.

"That's . . . that's a little personal." *And embarrassing.* She didn't want Leo to know about that dark time in her life.

"Open your legs."

Karin spread her legs open along the edge of the bar, revealing herself to him.

"Wider."

"But—"

"Do it." His stern voice startled her. Before Karin realized what she was doing, she leaned back onto her hands and moved her thighs wider apart.

"Better. Honesty and trust, *cara*. I need them both." He set his glass on the coffee table and considered her for a long moment. "Now tell me, was there anything . . . unusual about your encounters?"

"No." She started to close her legs, but he raised his hand, stopping her.

"I will tell you when and how to move." He glanced down at her feet. "Hook your heels into the edging of the bar. I want you completely exposed to me."

Karin felt her cheeks heat as she did as she was told. "We only had sex a few times, and it was always rushed because he had to get back to work." But it was enough for her to become attached. Karin realized that what she had felt for Jason was nothing compared to her feelings for Leo.

He dropped his gaze to her mound. "Pleasure yourself."

Karin watched his gaze heat as she slowly slid one hand down between her breasts, gliding it over her soft abdomen and slipping her fingers into her opening.

"Not so fast."

She slowed her movements, thrusting her finger deep and then retreating once more. She nibbled her lower lip as her body tingled with awareness. He was watching her. More importantly, Leo appeared to be engrossed with her movements.

Again and again she thrust into her channel, letting the pressure inside of her build. All the while she kept her gaze fixed on Leo, pretending that it was his fingers touching her, his body pressing down against hers.

Karin leaned back on her elbow as her fingers became damp. Turning her body, she reached up with her free hand and pinched her nipple, squeezing it until cords of pleasure snaked around her core. Tension built, and Karin caught sight of Leo's hand fisting in the cushions of the sofa. He shifted slightly, allowing her to see just how much her actions were affecting him. Karin quickened her movements, and soon her breathing came in short, needy gasps.

Finally, Leo stood. "I have to get something in the other

room, *cara*. I want you to continue pleasuring yourself, but don't let go until I get back. Understood?"

Karin nodded and watched him leave. She had no idea where he was going, or what he was after, but she knew that she wanted to please him. Right now, in this moment, that was all that mattered. Anticipation built as she dipped her thumb into her moisture and rubbed her clit. Need wound through her body, pushing her closer and closer to the edge. She thrust harder, rubbed faster, but as she teetered on the edge she remembered his command to wait. Karin slowed her movements, drawing herself back. With a frustrated growl, she began the process all over again.

She glanced over her shoulder and wondered what was taking him so long. What could he possibly be looking for? When he returned, it was obvious that he was hiding something behind his back.

"What are you going to do?" she asked.

"Punish you."

She stilled her arms. "Punish me?"

He frowned at her fingers. "I didn't tell you to stop."

Slowly, she began pleasuring herself once more. "Why?"

"Because you keep questioning me, *cara*." He slid his fingers along her inner thigh, causing her to tremble. "Now you may stop."

Karin eased her hands away from her body and looked up at him in silent question.

Leo stepped back and nodded. "Get down, turn around, and put your hands on the bar."

She moved slowly as she obeyed him. As she curled her fingers around the edging, she started to ask him what he was going to do, but then stopped. Questions had gotten her into this predicament. Asking more might get her into more trouble.

"Move back." He placed his hand on her hip and guided

her until her torso was almost parallel to the floor and her arms were stretched out in front of her. "Good."

She bit her lip to keep from asking questions. It seemed as if an eternity had passed before he finally put both hands on her back.

"You're learning," he mused.

His fingers were warm and slick. Soon the scent of lavender filled the air.

"It's heated oil, meant to calm the nerves," he explained. He slid his fingers over her back in wide circles, touching every inch of skin.

Karin closed her eyes and concentrated on how Leo glided his hands over her body. The movements took on their own rhythm and felt surprisingly intimate and caring. She groaned and dipped her head as he eased his hands up and massaged her shoulders and neck. She had never had a massage before, and his fingers felt amazing. Gradually her muscles relaxed and tension she didn't even realize she had evaporated.

"I will not cast you away, nor will I betray your trust. You're mine now, *cara*. All mine." He eased his hands underneath her torso and rubbed her nipples, causing her to gasp. Gradually he increased the pressure, changing his gentle, relaxing strokes to stimulating tugs and pinches. Karin shook with need as he ran his fingers all over her breasts and abdomen, teasing pleasure from every crevice of her body.

When every inch of her was covered in oil, he straightened and stepped to one side. "Look at me."

Karin turned her head and noticed he was naked.

"This is what you do to me." He added more oil to his hands and rubbed them over his length. "This is what you've reduced me to."

She glanced down and watched him grip his shaft. "I'm . . . sorry?"

He smiled as he ran his fingers over the tip of his erection. "No, you aren't," he accused as he removed his hand from his erection and placed it on her ass.

Karin tensed as he rubbed his finger around the opening in her backside.

"Don't worry, *cara*. I won't hurt you."

She forced herself to ease her grip on the bar.

"Remember our time on the balcony, when I placed the plug here?"

"Yes."

"It was a test. I wanted to see if you would enjoy being taken from behind and you confirmed my suspicions." He eased the tip of his finger into her opening. "I'm going to take you here in a few moments, *cara*, and it's going to feel much more intense and pleasurable than what you experienced on the balcony."

Karin wasn't sure if she wanted to be taken from behind. The toy had been good, but it was only a fraction of the size of his cock. It hadn't moved as much, either.

He inched the tip of his finger into her opening, stretching her muscles. Karin gasped at the stretching sensation.

"Relax and enjoy the moment, Karin. Don't overthink it." He pushed harder, easing himself in up to the first knuckle.

Back and forth he moved, testing and stretching her endurance. Karin gripped the bar hard as he worked first one, then two of his fingers into her.

"Oh God." He was right. While the plug was good, his fingers were so much better. They were not only wider, but they penetrated deeper than the plug.

"Do you want more?"

More? Karin didn't understand how it could get any better. Desire pumped through her veins and a sense of urgency rose up from within her core. "Yes."

Leo retreated and placed the tip of his cock against her opening. He reached around her hips. As he eased into her backside, Leo thrust two fingers into her channel.

Karin whimpered and spread her legs wider, giving him better access. He advanced steadily and hard, filling her as far as their bodies would allow. Once he pushed his cock and fingers as far as they could go, he rubbed her clit with his thumb. Pleasure rolled through her mind, causing her to whimper and cling to the bar. Then he retreated and repeated the wonderful torture all over again.

Trust me . . . She widened her stance, silently urging him to go deeper. She loved the sense of fullness he provided. It was as if he was not only penetrating her body, but her mind and soul as well.

He quickened his movements, thrusting hard and deep. The sound of their bodies coming together filled the air, making her feel primal and wanton. Again and again he commanded her emotions, pushing pleasure through her system with each thrust. It wasn't long before she was losing herself to the moment, bucking against him as her body stretched toward release.

"Come for me, *cara*," he said. The words caused the muscles along Karin's inner walls to tighten. Leo made a low, throaty sound as he moved faster. Moisture coated his fingers, allowing them to slide more easily. He tightened his grip on her hips, digging his fingernails into her skin and branding her as his own. Karin tightened her hold on the bar and moved against him, wanting to take everything he had to give and more.

"Yes, Leo. God, yes." Her breath caught as her mind fogged with desire. "Take what you need from me."

Faster, harder. With each thrust, her nipples ached, and her pussy throbbed. Karin bit down on her lip as desire surged through her body, reducing her to little more than an animal in heat. A sense of urgency rose up within her, and her breath came out in short, hard breaths.

On his next thrust, her world exploded. Karin cried out his name as pleasure washed over her body, robbing her of her strength. White light spread across her vision and filled her core.

Leo groaned and straightened behind her, digging all ten fingers into her flesh. His breathing became more shallow and his movements more desperate as he slammed harder and harder into her backside. With a groan of bliss, he emptied himself inside her and tumbled over the edge into oblivion.

Karin didn't know a time when she had felt so complete, or so thoroughly consumed. As the last vibrations of her orgasm faded, she shivered with exhaustion.

Leo retreated and carried her to his bed. A warm cloth materialized in his hand, and he began to clean her body with gentle strokes. Time stood still, and Karin felt more protected and loved in that moment than she ever had before. When Leo had finished, he spooned her body, cocooning her with his warmth and strength.

"All you have to do is trust me, *cara*," he whispered into her ear as she drifted off to sleep. "And I will take care of everything."

Three Days Later
"Damn." Leo slipped his cell into his pocket and pinched the bridge of his nose.

Karin knew that look well. She had seen a lot of it in the past few days. "What happened?" she asked from her perch on the opposite side of the desk.

"The wedding caterer canceled." He sighed and dropped his cell phone onto a stack of papers. "I guess my brother was a little too much of a perfectionist."

"Dante?" Karin put her laptop up on the desk in front of her and took off her glasses. "Dante was being a perfectionist?"

"Yes, and I'm as surprised as you." He let out a long breath as he leaned back in his chair and looked up at the ceiling. "He said that the antipasti was too bland and the lasagna didn't have enough sauce. Everything that they made he sent back for them to fix. Finally the caterer hit his breaking point and gave back the deposit."

"Perhaps he really wasn't good."

Leo flashed her a frown. "Please, this is serious."

"Well, have you tried the food?"

"He is a five-star chef with his own restaurant chain and television show. He came highly recommended." Leo got up and began to pace. "Now what are we going to do? We only have a few weeks before the wedding."

"We adjust."

He stopped pacing and stared at her. "Adjust? How?"

Karin thought for a minute. There was a reason why Dante kept criticizing the menu, and it probably had nothing to do with the food.

"Is Arianna insistent on the menu being Italian?"

"Yes, we all are." He threw up his hands. "This is to be a celebration of our culture and what makes Perconti Enterprises unique."

"I see." She tapped her pen on her temple as she thought back to the day of Leo's arrival, and how it took hours to clean up the penthouse suite.

"See what?"

"Just a minute, I'm thinking." Ever since Dante's conversation with Leo, he hadn't been placing those large orders from Sabrina's. Without the large orders, the restaurant was probably struggling more than normal. Perhaps Dante was being overly critical not because he wanted perfection for his sister's wedding, but because he wanted to help his ex-girlfriend.

"I have no idea where we're going to find a caterer on such short notice." Leo sighed and began to pace in front of her once more. "Everything needs to be perfect—"

"I agree." Karin straightened in her chair and grinned. "Does Sabrina's offer catering?"

"Sabrina's? Why?"

She shrugged. "Perhaps Dante isn't playing nice with the caterer because he wants someone else to provide the food for the wedding."

He widened his eyes as he considered her words. "Possible." He walked around to his chair and pulled up his computer. "What do you suggest?"

"We should have Sabrina cater the wedding."

"She'd never agree to it."

"You're probably right. Unless . . ." Karin tapped her pen on the desk. "Unless we go about it a different way."

"How?"

"We say that having her cater the wedding was Arianna's idea, not Dante's, or yours."

"It might work, but this wedding is much too big for her. She wouldn't be able to handle the crowd with the staff she has."

Karin shrugged. "Dante has always wanted Sabrina to succeed in the restaurant business. Perhaps he could find someone to help her."

Leo considered the possibility. "Dante has had training. I'm sure when he was studying overseas he made a few connections."

"Connections that could help Sabrina improve her technique and make her restaurant stand out."

Leo's features softened, and his smile appeared genuine.

"You're right—as long as Dante personally stays away from the kitchen."

"Why?"

He hesitated before responding, as if he was choosing his words carefully. "We aren't like most families, *cara*. Everything we say and do is scrutinized by the media. Unfortunately, any person we show an interest in will be placed under the same microscope."

"And have their pasts exposed."

"Exactly, but the reporters aren't the only ones we need to watch out for. Ever since that tabloid put our names on that 'most eligible bachelors' list, there have been fans . . ."

"Fans who want to see you stay a bachelor."

He waved his hand in the air between them in dismissal. "It is easier to just not get involved with anyone."

"But if you love someone, aren't they worth the risk?"

"Our lives are much too complicated for such things. That is why my brothers and I made a pact to never get emotionally involved with anyone."

"Doesn't the person you love get a choice?"

"Not in this case, no. There is more to consider than the press or fans," Leo said, not aware of the rising tension in the room. "When news of Dante and Sabrina's relationship got out into the media, not only did they suffer, but Sabrina's business suffered as well." He typed a few more words. "And that wasn't all. Investors in Perconti Enterprises became anxious and wondered if Dante's erratic behavior would carry over into the boardroom."

"Wow, I had no idea."

Leo glanced up from his computer screen. "When we become emotional, we only hurt ourselves and the people around us. Unfortunately, my brother had to learn that lesson the hard way." He scrolled through the Web page. "Here we are."

"What?" Karin uncrossed her arms and reminded herself that what she had with Leo was a business relationship. They weren't dating, and therefore he had every right to feel the way he did. She just wished that it didn't hurt so much.

Leo tapped the screen with his knuckle. "You're right. Sabrina's does catering." He grabbed her hips and dragged her close. "Brilliant."

Karin fell into his lap and wrapped her arms around his neck for support. "Dante would never fight with her over the wedding menu."

"Because he'd know that he'd be helping to make up for some of the hurt he had caused her."

Karin frowned. "Would she reject our offer for work because it comes from the Perconti family?"

He seemed to consider her words. "Maybe, but I think if we send the right person, she could be persuaded." He kissed her temple. "The publicity alone would be worth it, but I'll double her going rate just to make sure."

Karin thought back to how Wes had looked at Sabrina in the restaurant, and how well they connected. "Send Wes."

"Your coworker friend?"

"Yes. He and Sabrina are close." Karin shrugged. "And the last time I saw them together, I sensed some chemistry."

"Amazing." He pressed his lips against hers. "I don't know what I'd do without you." He kissed her again, invading her senses and making her dizzy. "I must go."

"Go?" she asked as she stood.

"Yes, I have to talk to Wes, and I have to tell Dante of my plan so he can stop screwing things up." He rose and moved toward the door.

His plan. Karin's hurt and anger returned with a vengeance. "I want to go with you."

He stopped and turned to face her. "I'm sorry, *cara*. I need you to go over those expense reports Marco sent up this afternoon for tomorrow's meeting. You know that." He closed the distance between them and took her hands. Slowly, he loosened her fingers from the fist she had made, one finger at a time, stroking her hand and easing the tension out of her body.

"But I've been cooped up in this room for three days—"

"It's only for a little while longer. I know best how to handle my brothers. It would be better for you to go over those reports so I'm prepared when I speak with Marco about the requests for new equipment." He gave her a chaste kiss and dropped her hands.

"Yes." She was to find money from somewhere to supply the cleaning staff with new vacuums. Not just any vacuums, but the newer industrial-sized models that had just hit the sales floor six months ago. The vacuums they had now were dinosaurs, and in such poor shape. She didn't know if they were going to last until the wedding. "About that—"

"Later. The hour is getting late, and I must not waste time." He kissed her forehead again as his cell phone beeped. He picked it out of his pocket and frowned at the screen.

"Who is it?" Karin asked.

"No one important." He switched the phone off and moved to the elevator, but not before Karin noticed the worry creasing his forehead.

"Is it the same person who called you last night?"

"Don't worry yourself, *cara*. I'll handle it." He pushed the elevator button.

An uneasy feeling rippled through her as the door opened.

Leo flashed her a devilish smile, and all of the worry she had seen moments before vanished. "Keep the bed warm for when I get back. I have a feeling that I'll be in the mood to celebrate."

Chapter 13

One week had passed, and while Karin had become closer to Leo, she still felt as if there was something missing between them. To make matters worse, she had gone behind his back to heal the jealousy between her and her colleagues, and in the process, she might have made things worse. Everyone seemed to be avoiding her.

Leo had relieved her of her old duties, but as she watched her fellow staff struggle with the extra work, she knew that she couldn't leave them hanging. Besides, she needed to get out of the penthouse and feel useful once more.

So in the mornings, after Leo left her in bed to talk to Marco about accounts and numbers, she snuck downstairs and helped with the basic cleaning chores. She figured as long as she made her way back up to the penthouse suite before lunch, Leo wouldn't catch on.

Her double life couldn't go on forever, however. Arianna was flying in that afternoon, and the rest of the Perconti family would arrive the following week. Leo was insistent that the rest of the family not know how much he was struggling. Jason had taken an unusual interest in the wedding as well, asking enough questions to make people suspicious. Meanwhile, the staff members were becoming more and more disgruntled over being over-worked and underpaid.

"It's going to happen," Wes whispered to Karin as he inched closer with his duster.

"The strike?" Karin lowered her voice as she ran her cloth over the same spot on the table. "When?" She had asked Wes to be her ears with the other staff members. Lately, it seemed as if he was the only one who bothered to give her the time of day.

"In three days."

"Three days?"

Wes motioned for her to be quiet. "Three days?" she repeated in a whisper. "But it's so close to the wedding. The whole Perconti family will be here." Leo would be devastated if his sister and mother got caught up in this madness.

"We have to stop it," she said.

"Why?"

Karin stared at her friend. "You can't be serious."

Wes shrugged. "I have no loyalty to the Perconti family. They've given me nothing but trouble."

"They gave you a job." Karin shook her head and put down her cloth.

Wes considered her for a moment. "Be careful which side you choose, Karin. This is going to be big. I might not be able to do much to save your job—or your reputation—if you get in over your head."

"You don't think . . . you don't think that they would come after *me,* do you?"

Wes turned back to his dusting. "There's been talk."

"Talk?"

"Questions on where your loyalties lie." He glanced in her direction. "In fact, since I have been talking with you, people are starting to question me, too."

"If we can delay the strike until after the wedding,

then things will improve. You'll see. Leo and I have been planning—"

Wes held up his hand, stopping her words. "It's not a question of if we will strike, but when." He sighed and put his duster back into the cart. "I'm sorry, Karin. Things are beyond my control. You've been spending so much time with Leo that you're blind to what's been going on around you."

"Is there something wrong?" Leo asked as he approached.

Karin's stomach churned as Wes glanced up at him. "Nothing. Just cleaning, that's all."

Leo turned his attention to Karin. "What are you doing outside the suite?"

Karin took a small step back as she sensed his rising anger. "I wanted to help."

"But I arranged it so that you don't have to do your previous duties."

"I like cleaning, and we're already understaffed. Besides, I needed to get out of that room. I was beginning to get cabin fever."

Leo frowned. Of course he didn't let her out of the room, but that was because he wanted to shield her from those nosy reporters. He also didn't want her to find out just how difficult things had gotten with the staff. Everything he did was for a reason, and her standing here showed him that they still had a long way to go to build trust. He couldn't take care of her if she was blatantly disobeying his requests.

"You should have come to me if you wanted to leave the suite," he said.

Karin lifted her chin in defiance. "You can't keep me locked away anymore, Leo. I'm not some pet you keep in a cage. I can make my own decisions."

"Of course you can." Unfortunately, she wasn't making

the right decisions. "But every decision has a consequence. What do you think that *Whispers* reporter would do if she saw my corporate consultant dusting tables and vacuuming floors?"

"I . . . I didn't think about that."

"What will the other staff members think of your help? Would they appreciate it, or perhaps be jealous that you are trying to take away their jobs?"

"They wouldn't think that." Karin glanced at Wes. He averted his gaze.

"You seemed so happy cleaning, I didn't want to ruin it."

She widened her eyes in shock. "I thought I was helping."

"You were helping—up in the suite." Leo took her hand. "You have to learn to trust me, *cara*. I only make requests when I have your best interests at heart."

She turned away from Wes and focused on him. "But you have to see that keeping me locked away up there isn't the answer, either. I'm staring at the same walls day in and day out."

"It's just for a short while longer, and you have your work—"

"It isn't enough." She squeezed his fingers. "I need more to my life than work, Leo." She pulled her hand from his grasp. "I'm sorry."

He considered her for a moment. While it was true that he had kept Karin in the suite to shield her from the chaos, there was another, more selfish reason for keeping her there. Leo didn't want anyone else to discover how important she had become. It was more than her business ideas or organization, it was the comfort she provided. With her, he didn't have to pretend. He could fully relax and be himself. Leo didn't know how it happened but, somewhere along the way, his protectiveness toward Karin had blossomed into affection, and then dependence. If some nosy reporter got between them and he was forced to let her go, Leo didn't know if he could function.

"Come with me." He touched her elbow and steered her toward the door.

"But my supplies . . ." She motioned to the cart a short distance away.

"Hey—you there." He nodded to her cleaning friend. What was his name? It didn't matter. "Clean this up for her, will you?"

"Sure thing." The blond man glanced at Karin and gave her a questioning look.

"I'll be fine," she told him.

The exchange only angered Leo more. That guy honestly thought that he could hurt Karin? Steeling his jaw, he grabbed her elbow and dragged her out of the conference room.

"Where are you taking me?" she asked.

"To do something I should have done that night after Sabrina's. We're going shopping."

"Shopping?" She dug in her heels, stopping Leo in his quest. As he turned to her, she furrowed her brow in a way that he found totally captivating.

"Yes. You will need a new dress for what I have in mind," he explained.

She ran her hands down the front of her blouse. "There's nothing wrong with what I'm wearing."

Leo snorted. "It's a staff uniform."

"Well, I'm a staff member."

"One who will need a proper dress if she's to be seen with me in public." He raised his brows, daring her to argue.

She pressed her lips together and he could see the frustration run through her features. After a brief moment, she let out a long breath. "Fine, but only one dress."

"That's all I ask." He held out his elbow. She took it, and he steered her through the front revolving door.

"Mr. Perconti, may I have a word?" Amanda Vaughn materialized at his side. "Do you always give your staff rides in your limo? Or is this one special?"

Damn, he'd forgotten about the reporters. "No comment."

"Where to, Mr. Perconti?" Roberto asked as they neared the limo.

"Newbury Street," Leo said as he motioned Karin into the car. "Call ahead to that place my sister likes. We have some shopping to do, and I don't want to be disturbed."

"Shopping for whom, Mr. Perconti?" Amanda asked.

With Karin safely out of sight, he returned to the reporter. "To buy a gift for my sister."

"With a female friend?" Amanda raised her brows.

"A staff member," Karin corrected.

Leo ground his teeth. That reporter was too nosy for her own good. "She is close to my sister and has similar interests. She will help me choose an appropriate gift for Arianna."

"Is your sister the only person in your family your companion is close to?" Amanda asked as she scribbled in a notepad.

"Good day, Ms. Vaughn." Leo got in and scowled as he sat in his seat next to Karin. They never should have gone out the front of the hotel. He should have known better. *Whispers* now knew that he was taking a staff member around Boston in his limo. He had given the reporter an excuse, but it was a flimsy one at best. He could almost see the headline now: "Leo Plans a Private Outing with His Staff."

He was becoming careless, but that was something he'd have to deal with later. Leo watched Karin as she examined the passing landscape. Initially, he had been attracted to her beauty and submissiveness in the bedroom. Now, he was beginning to realize that she had so much more to offer. She was smart, and her ideas on how to stay competitive were always inventive and kept costs low. He had begun to admire her work ethic and organization. He didn't know what he'd do without her.

That last thought made him uncomfortable. With her, he found he needed less and less of his anxiety medication. At his last doctor's appointment, he had shown marked improvement. Even Marco commented on how Leo had seemed less on edge.

She was changing him, he realized, and Leo wasn't quite sure how he felt about that.

"We're here, sir," Roberto said as they pulled up to the curb.

"Excellent." Leo turned to Karin as Roberto got out and walked over to the passenger door. "Are we ready?"

Karin flashed him a skeptical look. "Why are we here?"

"I already told you—to go shopping."

Her eyes widened. "But this place is so expensive."

He tilted his head to the side and studied her face. "Did you tell me back at the hotel that you needed time away from the penthouse suite?"

"Yes."

"And you needed something more than work?"

"Yes, but—"

"Then you shall have it. But first, we need to buy you a dress."

"But that reporter—"

"Gossip is going to spread whether you stay in the penthouse or not."

"When I talked about leaving, I meant going out by myself, not . . ." Her words trailed off as she met his gaze.

"That is unacceptable, *cara*—at least for now. I can't let you face the paparazzi alone and unprepared." Before she could respond, he got out of the car and held out his hand. "Shall we?"

She hesitated, and Leo felt tension fill the air between them. He'd give anything to know what she was thinking. Was he pressing her too hard? She had to realize that if she was to enter his world, then she had to start acting like she belonged there. Any fear, any hesitation, and his investors and the media would tear her apart.

After a moment, she put her hand in his. "Okay, but I'm serious about only buying one outfit."

The tightness in his chest eased as he helped her up onto the sidewalk. "Only one outfit—I promise."

It was all so overwhelming. Karin couldn't help but stare as employees cleared out the store and pulled blinds so that they could have some privacy. With the public gone, Leo immediately began pulling items off the racks. Karin had been trying on dresses for thirty minutes and a small stack of clothes he had rejected had piled up next to Leo on the sitting room couch. She eyed them nervously as she modeled the last one for him. She would have to work for three years to be able to afford it.

"What do you think?" Leo asked from his lounging position on the couch. As Karin had been changing, he had opened his tablet and was Skyping with various business associates. Now he seemed to be finished, and he was looking at her with interest.

Karin ran her fingers over the sequined dress. "It's lovely, but too expensive." She glanced at the pile beside him. "Just like everything I've tried on so far is so expensive. Maybe they have a discount rack somewhere—"

Leo frowned and waved his hand in the air in dismissal. "I told you, don't worry about the price."

"But the wedding hasn't happened yet and the Palazzo—"

"You're right, this dress isn't the one." He stood and picked up an emerald-green designer sundress off the rack.

"You can put the rest back." He waved to the pile on the couch. "While you do that, I'll help her try this one on. The buttons in the back can be difficult." He picked up the matching heels on the display counter beside the rack.

"Certainly, Mr. Perconti. I'll be right out here if you need anything." The saleswoman gathered the items and disappeared from the sitting room.

Leo waited until she'd disappeared before he approached Karin. "Go on, try this one."

"Why am I trying on all of these dresses anyway?"

"I'm taking you somewhere."

"Where?"

"Away from the hotel."

"I thought this was our time away from the hotel."

"This is only the beginning." He reached around and squeezed her ass. "Everything will be fine. Now go change."

Karin's throat went dry as the realization of what he wanted hit her full-on.

"You're—you're going to come back with me?"

"Of course. Those buttons can be difficult." When she didn't move, he squeezed her elbow reassuringly.

Before she realized what she was doing, Leo had her turned around and heading toward the dressing rooms.

"We shouldn't be doing this," she whispered as they passed by a stall. The changing room appeared to be empty, but it was hard to tell.

"You worry too much." He directed her to one of the larger stalls at the end and ushered her inside. After locking the door, he glanced above them. "See? No cameras."

"I don't know."

He raised his brow.

Karin looked around the dressing area. There was a small bench, two hooks, and two mirrored walls. She clutched her dress and watched Leo put the heels on the floor through the mirror. He straightened and met her gaze through the glass, and the hunger she saw there caused heat to burn through her body.

"You aren't moving." His voice was low and filled with authority.

His tone caused her breath to catch and her pussy to ache. A quick glance down informed her that the thought of punishing her had affected him as well.

"We don't have much time." Leo's voice sounded strained.

Karin dragged her gaze back up the mirror until it met his. She held his attention as she stripped off her clothes with agonizing slowness. His eyes darkened with each inch of exposed skin.

His gaze didn't leave hers as she put on the lightweight dress. "Breathtaking,'" he said as he looked up and down her body through the mirror.

"It fits well." Not only was it the right size, but the style accentuated her breasts and curvy hips. The color went well with her hair and complemented her pale complexion.

Karin slid her feet into the heels and was surprised at how comfortable they felt. A low, throaty moan of pleasure escaped her lips. "They're like slippers."

There was humor in his gaze as he did up the buttons in the back. "Now, put your hands on the mirror."

Her hands shook as Karin moved to do as she was told. This was so risky—they could be arrested for indecent exposure—but there was something exciting about the danger and risk of being caught. The mirror felt cool against her fingertips, and as Leo tugged her hips back to place her at a forty-five degree angle, moisture pooled between her thighs.

"You are so beautiful," he whispered as he pulled down his zipper. The loud noise echoed in the quiet changing room and made her legs weak. "And I know how much you like to be seen."

"I don't—"

"Shh. I was on the balcony with you, remember? Admit it, it thrilled you to know that all of those people were below, and that all that separated you from them was a thin privacy screen."

It *did* excite her. It felt a little odd, having Leo know so much about her, but that was his way. He was always observant, always taking note of what pleased her and what didn't. His attention to detail often surprised and pleased her.

He leaned forward until his lips were hovering above her ear. "From now on, there will be no more hiding in the suite." He slid his hands up her sides, pulling the dress up with it. "No more pretending."

"Yes."

"I will take you out in public and touch you like this, so everyone will know you are mine." He slid his fingers along the curve where her leg met her ass. "Look at us, Karin. See what everyone in Boston will see."

Karin moistened her lips and watched him through the mirror. The look on his features was almost reverent as he ran his fingers over her ass.

"Watch and imagine—but remember to keep your voice low." He inched his fingers around her hip and under her thong, sliding them through her slick folds. Karin gasped and closed her eyes, enjoying the feel of his rough skin on her sensitive tissue.

He placed a steadying hand on her hip and slid his fingers up to press her clit. The movement caused his erection to press up against her backside. Karin whimpered at the intimate contact. Leo pushed harder against her ass in response, causing them both to groan.

"God, you feel incredible." He pressed her clit harder,

and she bit her lower lip to keep from crying out. He curled his body over hers and rested his chest against her back.

He kissed her neck as he moved his hand, building the tension and pressure inside her body.

Karin opened her eyes and stared at him through the mirror. What she saw took her breath away. He was so tall, large enough to fill the small stall. Leo's rugged good looks radiated testosterone, and were a sharp contrast to the pink floral wallpaper on the walls.

Leo was watching them through the mirror as well. As their gazes met, his eyes darkened with need. Karin nibbled her lower lip and glanced down to where his fingers pressed her small bundle of nerves. He shifted his opposite hand, smoothing it around her hip and sliding it in between them. He inched back, and then positioned himself at her opening.

"Spread your legs wider for me, *cara*. Let me in."

She adjusted her stance, and was rewarded with the tip of his cock pressed just inside her body.

"That's it." He inched his way inside her opening, then retreated. It wasn't long before they developed a primal rhythm. All the while he held her gaze, watching her as he filled her slick channel.

Leo kept the pace frustratingly slow. He slid his hands up her torso, under her dress, and cupped her breasts. Karin bit back a moan as he pinched and tugged her nipples.

"Arch your back for me."

She did as she was told. At the same time Leo pressed forward until his hips came flush with her backside.

"Yes, just like that."

They moved together, him thrusting forward, her arching her back. Their bodies crashed again and again, the primal sound filling the small space. Karin's breathing quickened as he slid one hand down from her breast, letting it travel over the delicate skin of her lower abdomen.

"Look at me, *cara,*" he commanded. "I want you to see me when you come. I want you to know that I'm the one who commands your body. I'm the one giving you pleasure."

Karin dragged her gaze up to meet his. Leo looked so intense and focused on her. Knowing that she was the object of his desire only fueled her need.

As Leo moved, he inched his hand lower and found her clit once more. Desire flooded Karin's mind as she focused on his face. In that moment she knew that he was right. Never before had she felt so thoroughly possessed and claimed. She was his in every way that mattered, every way that was important.

"Come now for me." He held her gaze as he pressed his lips against her neck. "I want to feel that lovely pussy grip my cock." He tugged her nipple and pressed her clit, sending her senses into overdrive. Primal instincts rose from deep inside Karin's core, creating a sense of urgency. Again and again he pushed into her, until all that existed was this man and this moment. She bit hard on her lower lip as the urge to cry out became stronger.

Things were building too fast, coming on too strong. One moment she was teetering on the edge, and on the next thrust, she was over it and falling into an ocean of bliss.

Karin watched Leo through her euphoric haze. As the tremors of his own orgasm shook him, he never averted his gaze, not once. Instead he held her there, reminding her that she wasn't alone. He'd always be there behind her, supporting her. Just like he was doing now.

When it was over, he rested his forehead on her shoulder and held her close. "God, Karin, you will be the death of me." He placed a chaste kiss on her neck and withdrew. "I think we shall take the dress, yes?"

Not trusting her voice, Karin nodded.

"Good." Leo's smile was full of satisfaction. He

adjusted himself and smoothed both of their clothing into place. "Meet me out front at the cash register, then." He placed a second kiss on her temple, pulled off the price tag, and was gone, leaving Karin alone in the stall.

Karin traced her fingers down the mirror and straightened. What just happened? It was too much to process. One moment Leo was so loving and devoted. The next he was all business. She felt off-balance. While she loved his attentiveness in the dressing room, the idea that she had to dress up in a fancy outfit before spending the afternoon with him made her feel a little uncomfortable. She wasn't really into dresses or fancy things. Karin was far too practical for that. Still, the fabric did feel nice next to her skin, and the style hugged her curves in all of the right places.

Karin had no idea what he had planned for this afternoon, but anything had to be better than sitting around in that suite, right? There was only one way to find out what Leo had up his sleeve, and it wasn't by standing around in the changing stall. Collecting herself, she smoothed her dress and went out to meet Leo by the register.

"I hope you don't mind, but this was the only way we could go out and I could guarantee some privacy."

"It's gorgeous," Karin said as she leaned against the yacht's railing. "I've never been on a boat before." Certainly never one as big as this.

"But you live on the coast." He walked up from behind and handed her a flute of champagne.

She shrugged. "My parents preferred the city, and my mother got horrible seasickness."

"How about when you were older?" He stepped up from behind and put his arm around her, shielding her from the light breeze from the water.

"There was school and work." She took a sip of her champagne. "I didn't have any time for myself, and even

if I did, I couldn't afford anything like this." She waved
her hand around the upper deck of the yacht. "It's difficult
letting people wait on me." In fact, the past few hours had
been a whirlwind. After the dress shop, Leo took her in
his limo to his family yacht. There, waiting for her was
his personal chef and a small crew, ready to take them out
for a lovely afternoon on Boston Harbor. Never before had
she been exposed to such luxury. It would be all too easy
to get used to living like this. It was getting harder and
harder to remind herself that all of this was temporary.

"You get used to it." When she arched her brows, he
chuckled. "I didn't always have money, *cara*."

"You didn't?"

He shook his head. "I came from a poor town just outside of Naples. My father was the first of his generation to
go to a university. At his first internship, his mentor saw
potential, and, as they say, the rest is history."

"I think I remember reading about how your father
bought his first hotel at twenty-one and then went on to be
the youngest hotelier in the world."

"Yes, there isn't much about my family that isn't public
knowledge." Leo took a long sip from his glass.

"I'm sorry. I shouldn't pry." Karin placed her glass on
a nearby table.

"No, it's okay. It comes with the territory."

She tore her gaze away from the Boston skyline and
glanced at him over her shoulder. "Is that why you take
your pills?"

"Excuse me?" He let go of her shoulders and stepped
back.

"The pills in the bathroom. Is that why you take them?
Because reporters are always trying to invade your
life?"

He turned away, but not before she could see the surprise in his eyes. "Ah, here we are."

A young waiter stepped up on the deck with a plate of delicious-smelling seafood.

"Will that be all?" he asked Leo.

"For now, yes."

"Very well." The waiter glanced at Karin, and his curious gaze made her slightly uncomfortable. She was glad when he finally retreated.

"Come," Leo said, pulling out a chair for her.

"What is it?"

"Oysters Rockefeller. I tried it for the first time when I visited New Orleans and have been addicted to them ever since."

She flashed him a speculative look. "You have expensive tastes."

"Of course." He pressed his lips to her bare shoulder as he helped her into her seat. "I always demand the very best."

She put her napkin into her lap as he retrieved his glass of champagne and took his seat across from her. "You didn't answer my question."

"Question?" He took an oyster in the half shell and motioned for her to do the same.

"Yes, about the medication." She took an oyster, but was unsure how to eat it. There was so much silverware, she didn't know where to begin.

Leo picked up a small fork from above his plate and waited for her to do the same. "Try this first. Then we'll talk."

"Okay, but this doesn't mean that you can get away with not telling me." She scooped a small portion of the oyster filling and placed it into her mouth. "Oh my God."

"Good, yes?" He scooped out his entire oyster and ate it in one bite. "I told you."

"This is incredible." The chef must have used a pound of butter in making this dish. Her hips were going to hate her in the morning, but for now, Karin cherished each and every bite.

"I knew you'd like it." Leo popped another one into his mouth. "Marco and I found this restaurant that makes the best oysters. I'll have to take you there sometime . . ." He cleared his throat and took another oyster. "Or not. Restaurants can be highly overrated."

"Why wouldn't you want to go? Oh." She put down her fork. "You just don't want to take me."

"No, that's not it at all." He sighed and put his napkin on the table. "You have to understand, Karin. I'm responsible not only for myself, but the welfare of my family. As head of Perconti Enterprises, I have an image to maintain."

"And I'm not part of that image." Karin put down her napkin and stood. "Is that why we're hiding out on your yacht? Because I don't fit some Perconti mold?"

"No, that's not it at all."

"Then why all of this hiding? Why can't we just go out and have dinner like normal people?"

Leo stiffened his jaw, but no sound came out.

Karin let out a long breath and walked over to the railing. "This is just it, Leo. You keep saying that I need to trust you with my secrets, but you have yet to trust me."

"I do trust you."

"Really?" She turned from the railing to face him. "Prove it. Tell me why you take those pills, and why you don't want to take me out in public."

Leo hesitated, then approached until he leaned on the railing next to her. As he stared at the Boston skyline, Karin watched a myriad of emotions cross his features. It was a long time before he spoke.

"I don't do it on purpose, Karin," he said. "You have to believe that."

She turned around until she, too, faced the water. "Tell me."

He took her hand, but kept his gaze focused on the water. He spoke slowly and deliberately, as if every word was being dragged out from some dark place inside of his soul.

"My siblings are much too young to remember how poor we were, but I remember. We lived in a small apartment while my father went to school and worked an hour away in Naples. Sometimes he'd be gone for days at a time. My mother did the best she could, but often we'd have to rely on extended family for food, clothing, and basic necessities. My mother was a proud woman, and it hurt her to ask her sisters for these things. Her sisters didn't make it easy, either. They saw her as the lesser sibling, always needing help with things her husband couldn't provide for her." He took a deep breath. "When my father finally did catch his big break, my mother swore never to have to ask her family for anything again."

"How awful," Karin said. "For family to treat each other that way."

He squeezed her fingers. "Money came easily after that. He was quick thinking, and was always planning for the future. His rapid rise made him popular, first with the local papers, then with the international community. He interviewed well, and was young and good-looking, which only added to his allure. Men idolized him and women . . ." He cradled her hand in his palm and stroked her fingers. "I suppose it was only a matter of time before he started having mistresses."

"I'm so sorry."

Leo shook his head. "He was very much like Marco, always craving the spotlight. He mistakenly considered many of these reporters friends and threw lavish parties for them. He would tell my mother that he had to work late and she, too busy raising three children on her own, had no reason not to believe him. That is, until one day she saw a photograph of my father and his mistress in one of the local tabloids."

"That must have been awful."

He shrugged. "They fought, but my father was a charming man, and she forgave him. Gio, Gianna, and Arianna were born soon after that. My mother preoccupied herself with raising us and would turn a blind eye to the tabloids and their articles as much as she could. When someone in town mentioned my father and his exploits, she'd laugh it off . . . but at night I could hear her crying." He raised her hand and pressed his lips against her palm, sending tendrils of heat down her spine.

"I'm sorry, Leo."

"She thought she could hide it from us, but we all knew. Especially myself and Marco, who were old enough at that point to understand." He let go of her hand and straightened. "My father would visit, and they would fight behind closed doors. When he said it was time for me to move with him to Naples to learn the family business, my mother refused to let me go, saying that I wasn't going to follow in my father's footsteps."

"What happened?"

"In the end it was my choice." He turned around and rested his back against the railing. "I wanted to go and see for myself firsthand if the rumors around my small town and in the tabloids were true."

"Were they?"

He nodded. "Although they were embellished greatly." He crossed his arms. "Yes, my father had mistresses, but they liked to spend his money more than be with him. He had friends, but they loved his lavish parties more than his companionship. My father was a great man, but he was a lonely one. At night he'd sit by himself and drink away his sadness, much like Dante does now. He'd drink away the pain of his failed marriage and estranged children. All of those reporters he had befriended had eventually turned on him, publishing wild tales of his drunken escapades for all of the world to see."

"He committed suicide," Karin said. She had remembered reading about it in some exposé on Leo and his family a while back.

"In the end, yes, but it was a long, downhill road to get to that point, and I got to watch him take every step." He let down his arms and braced his hands on the railing behind him. "I tried to stop it, but he would brush off my questions."

"That must have been terrible." She put her hand on his arm in an effort to comfort him, but Leo was lost in his memories.

"Some say that he couldn't handle being in the spotlight, but in reality, it was because the paparazzi had stolen his life and put it up for the world to see. He couldn't do anything without the media writing a report about it. The publicity alienated all of the people who had ever meant anything to him." He tore his gaze away from the table, where the same waiter was cleaning up the oysters and bringing out trays of lobsters, and faced her. "Even at his funeral, starlets showed up, hoping to get a few minutes on camera. It was disgusting."

"So you live your life away from the public eye as much as possible."

"I try to deflect the media attention toward myself, so my siblings can have as much of a normal life as possible."

"But what about you?"

He tightened his jaw and turned away. "I tried to have a life once, but it didn't work out."

"Danika." When he jerked his gaze back to hers, she felt her cheeks burn hot. "I read about how she used you in *Whispers*."

"Yes, she did. After our messy divorce, I decided to deflect all of the media attention off my siblings and on to me. This way I can control what is printed and what isn't."

"But being something you aren't for the press must be tiring."

"And lonely," he admitted. "But that is why I take the pills."

"The pills stop you from feeling lonely?"

"Loneliness, anxiety, depression . . . They help me stay in control of my emotions and not let anyone use my feelings against me." He sighed. "Like my father, I seem to attract people who love what I can offer them, but could care less about me." He pushed away from the railing and took her hand. "Until you."

She glanced down at their joined fingers as warmth spread through her body.

"You're different, Karin, and I don't want the paparazzi to hurt you, like they did me. That is why I try to keep you hidden."

"Because you don't want the media to find me."

"I don't want them to expose your secrets to the world like they did mine. I do it for protection."

"But shouldn't I be the judge of what is good for me and what isn't?"

"Sometimes, but in this instance, you need to trust me. It's for the best." He smiled and tugged her toward the table. "Come, the lobster is getting cold."

As they ate their meals, the conversation turned toward less weighty topics of music and art. As they talked, Leo showed her how to properly crack open and eat a lobster, introducing her to all of the new utensils and a second bottle of expensive champagne. Karin found Leo to be charming and smart, and the food exquisite, but throughout the entire day his words were never far from her mind.

I don't want them to expose your secrets to the world like they did mine. Karin couldn't imagine how different her life would be if she had reporters following her every move. Her heart went out to Leo as she realized how sad and lonely his life must have been.

"Hold still," Leo said, stopping the conversation.

"What?"

He flashed her a sexy grin and slid his thumb over her chin, collecting some butter that had dribbled there. "You missed."

"Oh, sorry." Appalled, she started to pull out her napkin, but he grabbed her hand, stopping her. Before she could collect her thoughts, he was up on his feet, tugging her up with him.

"I didn't get all of it." He pulled her close and nibbled her chin. Karin whimpered as he kissed a trail along her jaw toward her neck.

"You're the best thing that has happened to me in a long time, Karin," he said.

Karin threaded her arms around his neck as his mouth crashed down on hers. She tightened her grip around his neck as he invaded her mouth, filling her with his taste. Karin arched her back and pressed her chest into his, enjoying the way his hard body felt up next to hers.

Leo slid his hands down and cupped her ass, holding her close. Tearing his mouth away from hers, he kissed long lines of fire along her skin until every muscle in her body was quivering with need.

"Leo . . ." A bright light flashed, and before Karin could collect her bearings, Leo was on the move. He raced across the deck of the yacht with incredible speed and grabbed the camera from the waiter's outstretched hands. The young man let out a cry of alarm as Leo sent the equipment over the edge of the ship.

"Who do you work for?"

"That camera was expensive."

Karin yelped as Leo grabbed the man by the collar and shook him. "Who do you work for?"

"A-Amanda Vaughn, sir."

Leo ground his teeth, and then shoved the waiter into the table. Karin noticed that it was the same waiter who had been staring at her with interest all afternoon.

"Roberto!" Leo yelled as the waiter started to stand.

The driver seemed to materialize out of thin air. "Yes, sir?"

"Take this guy down below and hold him there until we're ashore." Leo pulled out a few hundred-dollar bills and tossed them next to the waiter on the table. "For the camera."

"It's not my fault," the waiter said as Roberto dragged him away. "A guy's got to eat, and a picture of your socialite girlfriend will pay my bills for months."

"Get him out of here." Leo roared as another staff member rushed to help Roberto.

"I'm sorry, sir," Roberto said. "They were all vetted prior to hiring. Something must have been missed."

"It doesn't matter now." Leo waved his hand in the air. "Just go."

Karin watched Leo push his hair back from his face, lean against the railing, and drop his head into his hands.

"I'm sorry," Karin said as she approached and put her hand on his back. He felt tense, as if at any moment, he'd leap off the railing and start fighting like a madman.

It was a long moment before he lifted his head. "We're almost to shore, *cara*. You better gather your things."

Karin hesitated. She wanted him to talk to her, to tell her what was going on in that head of his. In the end, she did as she was told, knowing that at the moment, Leo needed space to get his emotions under control.

Damn reporters. Leo felt so helpless. The one time he

had found someone to confide in, the one time he had opened up his heart, and a reporter was there to cheapen the moment. It had always been like this, even as a child. He didn't know why he expected this to be different. His life was a series of headlines being sold to the highest bidder. He had thought that keeping Karin hidden would protect her, but now he saw how foolish his thinking had been.

As the boat pulled up to the dock, Leo's phone vibrated in his pocket. He frowned as he checked his messages. He had muted his cell before getting onto the boat and in that short time he had seven new text messages. All of them were from his ex-wife Danika.

You can't ignore me forever.

This isn't over.

You will give me what is due or I'll go public.

Leo made a disgusted sound and deleted them all without answering. Danika was asking for money again. She and her lawyers had found a loophole in the divorce settlement, and now wanted more money. She wanted a seven-figure yearly income, not six, and threatened to take him to court if he did not agree. When Leo refused, she resorted to blackmail, telling him that he'd pay her for the misery of putting up with his kinky, selfish ways one way or another. If he didn't give her a monthly allowance that met her standards, she'd not only go public with their sex life, but also tell the world that the head of the Perconti empire was a suicide risk, just like his father.

"Is everything all right?" Karin asked.

"It's fine, *cara*. Come, let's get you back to the hotel."

"Are you sure? Perhaps we can talk about—"

"There's nothing to talk about, trust me. The reporter believed that I was dating a socialite. He has no idea of your true identity, so you won't appear in the papers."

"Yes, but—"

"Hush." He kissed her nose and placed her hand on his elbow. "Trust me. Things like this happen all of the time. I will deal with it." He directed her off the ship, flashing Roberto a stern look as he passed. His driver nodded, indicating that the reporter had already been bribed and sent on his way.

Leo ushered Karin into the limo as his phone beeped again. He growled and moved to delete the text, when he saw that it wasn't from Danika, but his sister Arianna.

Flight early. @ Logan Airport and need a ride. Send Roberto?

Leo couldn't help but smile. *Ari.* It had been so long since he had seen her. Months. He texted her back as he slid into the limo seat beside Karin.

I'll be right there.

"Who's on the phone?" Karin asked as the limo started moving.

"My sister. She just flew in to Logan Airport." Leo couldn't help but grin at the thought. "I'll drop you off at the Palazzo on the way. You can go to the penthouse suite and wait for me." He squeezed her hand. "Perhaps get out of that restrictive sundress . . ."

"Sure." Her voice sounded less than excited, but there was no time to dwell on it. He gave Roberto orders through the limo's intercom and felt giddy with the prospect of seeing his sister again. Soon everything would work out and his family would be provided for once more. *Finally.*

The car ride was quiet, and as the streets passed, Leo became more and more uncomfortable with Karin's lack of conversation. "Is there something wrong, *cara*?" he finally asked.

"No, nothing at all," she said as they pulled up to the curb. "Why?"

Leo frowned at her eyes. They seemed bright, too

bright, like she was holding back tears. He took her hand. "I already told you that I'd take care of that reporter."

"It's not the reporter."

"Then what is it?" His phone vibrated, interrupting his thoughts. With a curse, he dropped her hands and pulled it out once more. *Danika.* It looked like she had given up on texting when he didn't respond and decided to call him.

"Who is it now?" Karin asked.

"No one." Leo dismissed the call, knowing that he couldn't deal with Danika in front of Karin. More than anything he needed to silence his ex until after the wedding so that he could concentrate on family. Unfortunately, her increasing texts and phone calls over the past few days were making that close to impossible.

Roberto opened the door. Karin quickly said good-bye, got out, and took her bags. Before Leo could blink, she was walking through the entrance of the hotel. There was something about her that bothered him, but it was too late to question her. Within moments the limo door closed and they were on their way to pick up Arianna at Logan. His phone vibrated once more and he pulled it out to answer it.

"You're late with your payment."

Leo pinched the bridge of his nose. "Danika, so lovely to hear your voice."

"Cut the crap, Leo. I want my money."

"Why? Is your musician boyfriend not giving you enough?"

"Harrison is a free spirit who needs space to work on his art. Space that your money is going to provide him."

"Like hell." A throbbing pain centered right behind his eyes. Leo bowed his head and turned away from the windows, hoping the darkness would ease the ache.

"Oh, so you want me to go public that the head of the Perconti family is a suicide risk who likes getting freaky in the bedroom."

Leo covered his eyes with his hand as the pain got worse. Icy fingers squeezed his chest, making it difficult to breathe. "I can't do this right now, Danni. Just wait until after the wedding. I'll have the money then." He hoped.

"You better." Her laugh sounded false and forced. "Or I will not only take your family down, but that little intern you care so much about, too."

"How did you know—"

"You have your sources, and I have mine. Good-bye, darling."

Leo started to yell at her, but then realized that the phone had clicked off. Muttering curses under his breath, he shoved the phone back into his pocket and ran his hands over his face.

Karin. He had no idea how Danika found out about Karin, but it didn't matter. He'd die before he'd let his ex-wife hurt her—or anyone else he cared about.

"We're here," Roberto said as he pulled up to the terminal.

Leo gathered himself together and ran his fingers through his hair. He had just managed to plaster a smile on his face before Arianna threw open the limo door. She grinned from ear to ear. A rather perplexed Roberto stood behind her.

"Hello, big brother," she said as she tumbled into the backseat with her mountains of suitcases and packages. "It's so good to be home."

"You need all of that for the wedding?"

"Wedding?" She stared at him, wide-eyed. "What wedding? Is someone getting married?"

Chapter 14

Leo stared at her with horror. "What do you mean, 'what wedding?'"

"Just kidding." Arianna elbowed him in the arm. "Lighten up, bro. You look so serious."

Bro? Leo adjusted his tie and made a mental note to arrange for his sister to spend some time with their mother in Italy. Clearly, her world travels were beginning to muddle her brain. "That wasn't funny. You know that this wedding is—"

"Very important for the family. I know." She rolled her eyes and leaned back in her seat. "You've told me that at least a hundred times before." She frowned and stared out the window as Roberto pulled out into traffic. "I just thought this day would never arrive."

"Excited?"

She shrugged.

"Well, we've all been working very hard. Everything is in place and waiting for your approval." He listed the tasks one by one, ticking them off his fingers as he went. The more he spoke, the quieter she became. Confused at the tension radiating off his sister, Leo leaned forward in his seat. "Ari?"

"What?" She jumped, as if startled.

"You haven't been listening to a word I've been saying," he accused.

"I'm sorry," she said. "I guess I've just had a lot on my mind."

Frowning, Leo patted her hand. "Care to tell me about it?"

"No, it's nothing, and you have enough to worry about." She covered his hand with her free one and smiled.

Leo pressed his lips together in thought. He wanted to question her further, but then they arrived at the Palazzo, and the moment was lost.

"We're here," Roberto said.

Arianna glanced at the Palazzo. Her features seemed tense and strained. "Is the rest of the family . . . ?"

"Marco and Dante are here," Leo said. "Mama will be coming with Gio after he's finished with his photo shoot in Milan, and Gianna will arrive shortly after."

She nodded her head and Leo stepped out onto the sidewalk. "Are you sure you're okay?" he asked as he helped her out of the car.

"Sure, why wouldn't I be?" She smiled as she took his arm. "Before we know it, I'll be married to an aviation tycoon who will keep my charity organization afloat, and the family will be able to restore the Perconti name and gain the respect we haven't had since before Dad died."

"Yes. Exactly." It was what Leo had been working toward ever since he had taken over Perconti Enterprises. A respected family name brought business deals, and business deals brought in money. With money, he could provide security to everyone in his care.

Leo knew that Ari was aware that he was doing this for her, for them, and yet as he watched his sister's profile, he got the uneasy feeling that she wasn't completely happy with the situation.

Leo wanted to question her, but there was no time.

Reporters circled them as Ari moved toward the large revolving door of the hotel. Questions came from every direction and camera flashes created spots along Leo's vision.

Word must have gotten out about Ari's early flight, because everyone had been waiting for the bride's arrival.
Frustrated that they couldn't be left in peace, Leo ushered
her inside and past security, where Dante and Marco were
arguing over decorations.

"Tell me, dear sister," Marco said as they approached.
"Do you prefer lace or bows around the bridesmaids' flowers? We can't seem to agree on a decision."

"Oh, it doesn't really matter, does it?" Arianna held out
her arms to her brothers. "What matters is that we're finally all going to be in one place."

"I don't think that has happened since Dad died," Marco
said.

After hugs and affectionate kisses were shared, Dante
took her arm.

"Come," he said. "Let me get you a drink. You must
need one after your long trip."

Arianna shuddered. "Yeah, I've always hated flying."

Marco frowned in frustration. "But the bouquets—"

"Can wait," Dante said as he squeezed his sister's hand.
"We have a lot to catch up on first."

Marco grumbled and shoved some papers in a folder.
"Very well, but we need to make a decision soon."

"Don't worry, it will get done." Dante turned to Leo.
"Coming?"

"I have an appointment, so unfortunately, I'll have to
pass." Leo thought of Karin upstairs waiting for him.
Arianna should be okay with Marco and Dante for a while.
They could watch each other, and something told Leo that
he'd only get in the way. He gave her one last hug and
pressed his lips against her temple. "I'm sorry, but I have
a personal obligation to attend to."

"Yeah, real personal." Dante snorted, causing Leo to flash him a frown.

"Oh, is Leo seeing someone?" Arianna asked as she unhinged her arm from Dante's grasp.

Leo thought about it. "I'm not sure yet."

She widened her eyes. "Who is she, some heiress?"

Leo's chest tightened at the hopefulness in her gaze. "No, I'm sorry, Ari. You'll have to find someone else to do your shopping with. Karin is different."

Dante leaned over and whispered in Arianna's ear loud enough for his brothers to hear. "She's an intern—no wait." He smirked at Leo. "A *consultant*."

Marco elbowed Dante in the ribs. "Idiot."

"What?" Dante asked, his eyes wide and innocent.

"An intern." Arianna put her hand over her mouth. "Oh, Leo. Is it serious?"

"*That* is none of your business." He lifted his chin and steeled his gaze, hoping his expression would put an end to the subject. He didn't want to talk about his love life with his siblings, especially since he was still so unsure of his feelings. "And that's all I'm going to say on the matter."

Ari's eyes sparkled with mirth as she passed a knowing glance with Dante and Marco. "Well, you better see to her, then." She patted Leo's arm and kissed his cheek. "It wouldn't do to keep her waiting."

Leo fisted his hands at his sides, but Ari and Dante had already turned toward the restaurant.

"Don't drink too much," Leo called after them. "That wine is for the wedding."

Dante raised his hand and, without turning around, gave his brother the finger.

Marco laughed and patted his back. "Ah, what are we ever going to do with those two, eh?"

"Yeah." Leo frowned and glanced at Marco. "Is everything progressing with the wedding as planned?"

"Oh course." Marco lowered his hand and straightened his tie. "Only—"

"Only, what?"

"Only . . ." Marco cleared his throat. "Have you noticed anything wrong with the staff over the past couple of days?"

Leo looked at him in confusion. "Like what?"

"I don't know." Marco frowned as he glanced at a group talking in the corner. "You seemed so busy going over the new plans and making arrangements. I didn't want to bother you. It's just . . . everyone seems to be on edge."

"Of course they're on edge," Leo scoffed. "Everybody's getting ready for the wedding."

"Yeah, I suppose. I just can't help but feel . . ."

"Feel what?"

Marco tore his gaze away from the group and focused on Leo. "It's nothing, I'm sure." He glanced at his watch. "I'm late for my appointment." He clapped Leo on the shoulder and headed toward the front door. "I'll talk to you later."

"You're not going to drink with Dante?"

Marco glanced over his shoulder and frowned. "Not this time. Like you, I have a personal obligation that I must see to."

Before Leo could respond, Marco walked through the revolving door and disappeared onto the busy sidewalk.

Pursing his lips together, Leo made his way over to the elevators and up to the penthouse suite.

It wouldn't do to keep her waiting. And yet, it seemed as if that was all he and Karin did—wait. Leo was so tired of dealing with the press, but he only had to hold out for a short while more. After the wedding things would be different. With his company out of the papers, he wouldn't have to hide so much anymore. Perhaps, if Karin was willing to extend their arrangement, he could show her off to the world.

As the elevator opened to the penthouse suite, Leo found Karin was not naked and waiting for him in his bed like he had hoped. Instead, she was leaning on the railing of the balcony, staring out over the horizon.

"Ah, there you are," Leo said as he approached. His arms ached to hold her, and as he got closer, he held them out to the sides. "Finally."

Karin's back stiffened as she turned to face him. "We need to talk."

He lowered his arms and noticed a tremor ripple through her body. "You're shivering."

"I'm fine."

"No, you're not." He motioned to the door. "Come inside."

"No, Leo, I'm fine."

"At least let me put my jacket around you." She started to protest, but he silenced her with a look that meant business. Sighing, she let him drape his suit jacket over her shoulders and lead her to a nearby chair.

"Now," he said once they were both settled. "Why don't you tell me what's on your mind?"

She looked down at her hands in her lap. "What's going to become of us, Leo?"

"Excuse me?"

She looked up and met his gaze. "This can't continue."

"Of course it can." Despite his words, his thoughts turned toward how that reporter broke onto his yacht, and his siblings' reactions to Karin a few moments ago.

"No, Leo, it can't, and we're just fooling ourselves if we think otherwise."

"Did something happen?"

Karin shrugged. "Nothing more than usual."

"Then what is it?"

She frowned. "There has been more talk about a strike at the Palazzo. People are choosing sides."

Leo's chest constricted, and he struggled to keep his breathing even. When he regained the ability to speak, he asked the question weighing the heaviest on his mind. "And have you chosen sides as well, *cara*?"

"No, I mean yes." She looked up and met his gaze. "I'm with you." She dragged her gaze down to her lap. "I'm afraid that my choice has alienated me from the rest of the group. They know how close we are—"

"How could they? We aren't together in public."

"But I spend all of my time in your suite."

"It's natural that we spend time together. You're helping me—"

"They don't see that, though. All they know is that I spend every day and night up here with you. I don't go home, and I don't go to a different hotel room at the end of the day. What else are they to think?"

"Karin." He took her hands and leaned forward in the seat. "I'll take care of whatever is bothering you. Tell me, and I'll make it right." He moved to kiss her hands, but she pulled them away.

"That's just the thing, Leo," she said as she stood and started to back away. "You claim you want to know the real me, but I have to confront you about pill bottles before you'll tell me about your childhood."

"Karin—"

"No, look, I have no idea what this is." She motioned between them. "Or where I stand in this relationship. I don't know what you want from me anymore."

"Nothing has changed. We still have the same arrangement we spoke about at Stone Suites—" He moved to hold her, but she stepped out of his grasp.

"Do we?"

"Of course." He took a step forward, desperate to touch her, but not sure if he should.

"I feel as if you are trying to make me into something I'm not."

He furrowed his brow in confusion. "That's ridiculous."

"Is it? You . . . tell me to be open and honest about myself, then put me in expensive dresses I could never purchase on my own and teach me how to eat fancy food."

"I wanted to do something special for you."

"Do something special for me, or make me more acceptable to the press?"

"What do you mean? You know I don't care what those people think—"

"No, but you care what they say. You said yourself that they have hurt your family with their embellished tales."

Leo placed his hand on the balcony's edge to steady himself over his rising panic. "I'd never try to change you—"

"Not even to protect your family?" She took a cautious step forward. "Or yourself?" She let out a long breath. "You never said that I had to change who I was in order to be part of this arrangement."

"You knew what you were getting into . . ."

"Yes, I suppose I did." She wiped a tear from her cheek. "But that was before . . ."

Leo frowned. "Before what?"

Karin shook her head and held up her hand. "We pretend a lot in this suite, you and I, but our little games change nothing." She lifted her chin and met his gaze. "I am part of your staff, Leo." She waved her hand over her expensive dress. "This isn't me." She picked up her small clutch purse. "This, is not me." She dropped it onto the seat. "Nor these." She took off her shoes and placed them beside the purse.

"But *cara,* I gave those to you—"

"To make me more presentable."

"No."

"Then why? My service to you will end in a few short months. Why spend all of this money on clothes and food?"

Leo stared at the tears on her cheeks, unsure of what to say. *Because I can't cope without you.* He opened his mouth to tell her, but his throat constricted, blocking his words. *Because I lov*—No. He couldn't make himself that vulnerable again. Not again.

"I want you to have them," he finally said, desperate to fill the silence. "They're gifts."

"No, Leo, I can't. Perhaps if this was a real relationship . . ." She took in a shaky breath. "But this isn't a relationship, is it?" She met his gaze, and Leo saw the hurt in her eyes. The icy fingers on his chest tightened, making it difficult to breathe. He wanted to say something to ease her pain, but found he couldn't. He had never been in this situation before. He didn't know what to say.

"Of course this is a relationship—a business relationship." The words felt empty as they passed over his tongue. He wasn't sure who believed them less, she or he.

"No promises for the future, no regrets about the past."

Leo nodded.

"And when I'm no longer convenient, I'll be cast aside with the rest of the Palazzo staff—people who now hate me, thanks to you."

"That's not—"

Leo was cut off by the familiar ring of his cell. Karin made a disgusted sound and walked away. He ignored his cell and went after her.

"Karin, please, listen to me. This arrangement—" His cell went off again, cutting through his thoughts.

"You might as well answer that," Karin said as she

headed for the bathroom. "I'm sure whoever you've been texting all week is anxious to speak with you."

"No, wait. Karin."

She entered the bathroom and slammed the door in his face. Tears burned his eyes as he tried the handle and found it locked. His cell rang again, cutting through the soft sobs he heard on the other side of the door. Leo let out a frustrated growl and answered the phone.

"This isn't a good time."

"I know, and I'm sorry, but you better come down and see this," Marco said.

"Why? What's going on?"

"The Palazzo staff has started picketing out in front of our hotel, and they are drawing a crowd."

Karen leaned up against the bathroom door and wiped the tears from her eyes. What a mess. She had no idea how her life had started spinning out of control like this, but it had to stop. For weeks she had been doing things Leo's way, letting him take control both in and out of the bedroom. Her eagerness to please him had gotten them nowhere. She was still the secret he kept behind closed doors, his guilty pleasure.

Karin was so tired of it. She realized that Leo and Jason, while rivals, also were a lot alike. Neither could see past the fact that she was only an intern. She didn't fit into their world, and because of their self-centeredness, they didn't fit in hers.

If things continued down this path, her life would end up a disaster. The only reasonable solution was to let Leo go and find a stable internship at a small family hotel where the owners weren't so obsessed with their image. Unfortunately, she had let things go on too long and now she was attached. Letting Leo go would mean she would no longer be pushed both in and out of the bedroom. She wouldn't discover her true potential, and her addiction for Leo would never be satisfied.

She craved him, not just for what he made her feel, but because she knew that he needed her, too. Since they were first intimate, he had been more pleasant around the staff and less volatile with his brothers. While not exactly friendly, Leo had been more amiable and understanding. Everyone was less on edge. His change in attitude was because of her, she knew. Unfortunately, he was too wrapped up in himself to realize what had happened.

"Karin, please come out. I . . . I have to know you are all right before I leave," Leo said through the door.

"You're leaving?"

"I have to. Something happened downstairs . . ."

Karin placed her hand on the door and fought the urge to fling it open and slap him in the face. He knew that she was hurting, and yet he was just going to walk away. Once again, he was proving to her that she was not a priority in his life.

Leo's heavy sigh filtered through the door. "We're not through with this yet, *cara*. When I come back, we need to talk." His voice was thick and full of emotion.

"What happened downstairs?" she asked through the door. *What's more important to you than us?*

"Never you mind. Just stay up here and don't leave the penthouse suite."

"But—"

"Promise."

There was something final in his voice that gave her pause. "Okay. I promise."

"Good." He cleared his throat and stepped away from the door. "I'll be back soon. Wait for me."

Wait for me. His words rang through her mind as she listened to him take the elevator downstairs. After she knew he was gone, she sank down to the floor and covered her face with her hands.

She was always waiting for him behind closed doors. Sure, he listened to her and was starting to implement her plans, but he had never given her credit, and kept her locked away like some skeleton in his closet. He had taken her out to get new clothes, but just now, when she was wearing a dress he had bought her and had done her makeup just so, he still left her behind. Karin doubted if Leo would ever let her see the light of day again. *You are mine,* he had said. Karin was beginning to fully understand what that meant. She wasn't his girlfriend, or his business partner, but his possession, and like all of his possessions, Leo only took her out when she suited his purpose.

"Karin!" Wes's voice floated through the door. "Karin, where are you?"

She wiped her eyes with the back of her hands and frowned at the black smudges on her hands. *Damn designer mascara.* She scrubbed all evidence of the expensive makeup from her face and opened the door.

"I'm in here," she called to her friend.

"Oh, thank God." Wes strode down to the hallway toward her. "Come on, we have to get out of here."

"Why?" she asked as he grabbed her hand and dragged her toward the service elevators.

He hesitated, taking in her expensive dress. "Where did you get that?"

"Leo got it for me. What's going on?"

He jerked his head up to meet her gaze. "The staff decided to go on strike early, and someone called the evening news. Gloria has been speaking with representatives from Perconti hotels in France and England. Everyone is watching this closely. If Leo doesn't meet their demands, his staff at other Perconti resorts will follow our lead, and all of his hotels will fall like dominoes."

Karin's heart skipped a beat. "You're kidding."

"I wish I was." He dragged his gaze over her body. "That *Whispers* reporter is going to be the least of their problems. Both NBC and the BBC are here."

"Shit." She grabbed his sleeve. "You have to stop this."

"I can't. Everything happened so damn fast. Now it's bigger than me, the Palazzo, or the wedding. Even if I was able to stop the strike here, there's nothing I can do about the other hotels." He pushed his hair back from his face and glanced around the suite. "We're wasting time. Soon there will be so much media out there that no one will be able to do anything. Do you still have your work uniform?"

"Yes."

"Good. Go change, I'll wait by the service elevators." When she just stood there, he made a shooing motion with his hands. "Hurry!"

The urgency in his voice broke through her haze. Karin stumbled to the bedroom and changed as quickly as possible. As she tied her hair up in the familiar bun, she strode through the penthouse and found Wes holding the elevator doors open with one hand and texting on his phone with the other. "What's going on?"

"Marco, Dante, and Leo are trying to defuse the growing mob." He pressed his lips together and shoved his phone in his pocket. "It's not working."

"What do the strikers want?" she asked as he hurried her into the elevator. "And why are we using the service elevators?"

"Because it is too much of a mess out front," he said as he let the doors close behind them. "Karin, you have no idea what I've been dealing with. These people are out of control. I wouldn't be surprised if the crowd grows into an angry mob." At that moment the elevator doors opened and Wes grabbed her hand. "Let's go." He pulled her out the back way.

"Where are we going?"

"To my place, where it's safe." He pulled her along the sidewalk to where the taxis normally waited for guests. As they moved around the building, the noise got louder and the crowd thicker. Karin's steps slowed as they stepped out to the front of the hotel. Wes pulled her away from the building, but Karin could only stop and stare.

"Holy shit."

It was worse than she could ever have imagined.

Chapter 15

Leo stared at the scene before him and tried to comprehend how everything could go so wrong. A large group of Palazzo staff stood out in front of the hotel, all wearing their familiar uniforms. Some carried signs, some held megaphones, but all of them looked incredibly pissed off. News crews from all over the country were piling up, and the traffic outside of the hotel was almost at a standstill.

"What are you going to do, Mr. Perconti?"

"He has no comment," one of his security guards said as he eased the reporter back.

"Did you know that both your London and Paris hotels are rumored to be watching this closely, getting ready to join in if necessary?" another reporter asked.

"How will this impact the wedding?" asked a third.

Amanda Vaughn pushed to the front of the crowd and stuck a microphone in his face. "Rumor has it that you have been sleeping with one of the staff members and giving her preferential treatment, while holding back cost-of-living raises for everyone else. Is this true?"

A flash went off, temporarily blinding him. When he could finally see once more, he spotted a familiar figure in the back of the crowd, staring at him in stunned silence.

"Shit." Leo had told Karin to stay in the room. Did the woman have no sense? These people were dangerous.

"Can I quote you on that?" Amanda asked as she scribbled in a notebook.

Leo shoved Amanda aside and started toward Karin, then paused as a familiar voice rang out over the loudspeaker set up on the sidewalk.

"I'm so glad that you all decided to show today."

Leo turned his gaze to a woman with long, thick black hair. She stood tall and proud at the makeshift podium as she surveyed the chaos in front of her. Leo had seen her somewhere before.

"You, too, Gloria?" Marco muttered from beside Leo.

"Over and over again, the Perconti family has been treating us poorly," Gloria said. "They force us to work overtime without pay and with equipment that is inadequate for our needs."

The crowd cheered as the reporters all moved closer. Pain blossomed behind Leo's eyes and reached out through his skull.

The gathering reporters made the woman bolder, and she beat her fist against the podium as she talked. "We aren't asking for much, just our fair share."

Murmurs rumbled through the crowd as the news crew snapped pictures.

Gloria lifted her chin, her voice getting stronger with each sentence. "When was the last time we have gotten a cost-of-living increase? Or new equipment?"

"Three years," someone shouted.

Soon voices rose up and joined the first, until a sea of cacophony filled the air.

The woman, Gloria, smiled with satisfaction. "I think that we deserve more money, don't you? We can no longer work these long hours and still not be able to put food on the table."

"Yes!" Cheers rose up from the crowd. Leo's heartbeat quickened as he saw another television crew get out of a van. He had to stop this madness before things got even more out of hand. But first he had to get Karin out of there. It was too dangerous, and he'd never forgive himself if something bad happened to her.

He spotted Roberto at the edge of the crowd, looking rather put out. Leo waved him over.

"Get Karin out of here as soon as possible."

"Where would you like me to take her?"

"I don't know, somewhere safe. I'll give you a call when it's okay to bring her back." He motioned to where Karin was standing and arguing with her friend, Wes. "Make sure that she's far away from here."

Roberto nodded and Leo focused on the brunette at the stand. Her vitriol for the Perconti empire fell down on the crowd like rain, and they ate it up as if it was manna from Heaven. With each passing moment, tension grew. If he didn't do something soon, they'd have a public relations disaster on their hands.

As he moved through the crowd, he saw Marco and Dante make their way over to him.

"We've tried to stop this," Marco said as he fell into step alongside Leo.

"They won't budge."

"Where's Arianna?" Leo asked.

"Inside, thank God," Dante said. "Someone needs to say something. We can't have this spectacle out front when Mother gets here with Gio and Gianna. It will kill her."

"Agreed," Marco said. "But what can we do? They aren't breaking any laws—yet."

"Remind me—how long has it been since these workers have gotten a raise of any kind?" He looked up and met Marco's gaze when he didn't immediately respond.

"Three years."

"Three years with no raises," Leo repeated, suddenly feeling ill.

"To be fair, we didn't receive raises, either. It isn't like you've been increasing our funding—"

With a curse, Leo wove through the crowd and made his way up to the podium.

"So nice of you to join us, Mr. Perconti." Gloria said the last words as if they tasted like filth in her mouth. "Are you prepared to listen to our demands?"

He leaned in closer to the microphone. "I'm prepared to listen. But," he added when Gloria pulled out a thick folder. "But not here."

She tilted her head to the side. "Where then?"

"Inside."

"In the penthouse suite?" She turned and faced the crowd. "That's where he brings his favorites, you know."

"Now see here." Leo tried to usher Gloria away from the podium, but she wouldn't be removed so easily.

"Now, let's just stick to facts, shall we? All I know is that he has been bringing our intern, Karin Norell, up to the penthouse suite for the past few weeks. Now all of a sudden, she has a new salary, new clothes, and a new living space."

"The situation with Ms. Norell is private," Leo said through clenched teeth.

"Yeah, I'm sure." Gloria smirked and turned to the crowd. "She no longer has to work in the office, but instead sits and waits for him in his suite. I don't know about anyone else, but I'd personally love a job like that. I'm sure it has many . . ." She dragged her gaze over Leo's body. "Perks that we aren't aware of."

The crowd's laughter sounded uncomfortable.

"She's a consultant," Leo muttered. His chest constricted and he wished to hell that he had his anxiety medication.

"Is Ms. Norell the same woman from your shopping trip on Newbury Street?" Amanda asked.

"Yes."

"And the woman running from your suite in a bed-sheet?"

Leo ground his teeth and fisted his hands. "No comment."

"How about the maid spotted on your balcony?"

"No comment."

As more questions rose up from the crowd, Leo took Gloria by the elbow. "Take two of your organizers and meet me in the main conference room in three minutes," he growled in her ear.

She offered him a smug smile. "Absolutely, Mr. Perconti." She yanked her elbow from his grasp and returned to the microphone. "He has agreed to negotiate not only my position, but everyone else's as well." The crowd murmured their approval as she stepped down into the crowd.

Leo took the microphone. "We will speak with your representatives and listen to your demands. Please be patient."

Out of the corner of his eye, Leo saw another news van pull up and more reporters get out. "There will be no more further comments from anyone until both sides have had their say and an agreement has been reached." He quickly shut off the mic and handed it to Dante. "Get rid of this," he murmured.

"Are we really going to listen to that she-witch's demands?" Marco asked as they started back inside.

"Do we have a choice?" Leo countered.

"I guess not." Marco shuddered. "I'm sorry, Leo."

Leo waved his hand in dismissal and briefly scanned the crowd. To his irritation, Karin was still standing there with Wes.

He stopped walking and scowled. "What the hell is she doing?"

"Who?"

"Karin. I told Roberto to take her away." He scanned the crowd and saw Roberto walking away from Karin—and toward him.

"Why aren't you away from this place?" Leo asked when Roberto got within earshot.

"She won't come with me."

"Why not?"

"She said that she wanted to stay and help."

Leo bit back a snarl and glanced at her once more. Some people in the crowd seemed to recognize her. They waved their hands and shouted obscenities at her. Karin huddled closer to Wes, as if scared. Anger burned inside of Leo's chest. He'd never forgive himself if he let those vultures destroy Karin like they did Sabrina.

He barreled his way toward her, leaving his brothers and Roberto to follow in his wake. As he got closer to Karin, the words of the other staff members became clearer.

"Must be nice to be the boss's pet."

"Tell me, how much does he pay you to sit in his suite?"

Karin pulled out of Wes's protective grasp and slapped the person who'd just spoken. "How dare you?"

"Enough." Leo took her arm and pulled her to one side, away from the crowd. "Why didn't you go with Roberto?"

"I want to help."

"There's nothing you can do."

"But—"

"No buts. It's too dangerous here." He angled their bodies so that he could watch the crowd and swore as he saw Amanda and her cameraman making their way toward him.

"You have to leave."

"Why?"

He forced his gaze to meet hers. "Because what your coworkers are asking now will be nothing compared to what that reporter will ask once she gets her meat hooks into you."

Karin glanced over her shoulder and shivered.

"I'll take her." Wes inched closer to her side.

Leo wanted to argue, but there was no time. He had to get Karin away from the reporters and safe so he could focus on the negotiations.

"Fine. Get her out of here, and don't bring her back until an announcement of a deal has been made."

Wes nodded and threaded his arm through Karin's.

Karin glanced over her shoulder at the crowd. "But—"

Leo cut off Karin's words. "Don't fight me on this, Karin. I can't be worrying about you during the negotiations." He glanced back at his brothers, who were struggling to keep the workers from pushing through the revolving doors and storming the hotel. "I'll have enough to worry about."

Leo frowned as a black limo pulled up in front of the hotel. The driver got out and cleared a path through the crowd, as if parting the Red Sea. He opened the back door of the limo and a tall, well-dressed man with sandy-blond hair emerged. *Stone.* Just what Leo needed. Another problem.

"Get her out of here, now." Leo shoved Karin toward Wes and ran his fingers through his hair as he made his way over to his adversary. *Let the games begin.*

It had been three days since Karin had left the Palazzo. Three days of seclusion and nerves. Thankfully, Wes had offered to let her stay at his apartment while Leo and the others worked through the negotiations. If she didn't have her friend, she probably would have gone insane.

"Another cup of coffee?" Wes asked.

"No, I'm okay for now." They were watching the morning news and so far there hadn't been any word. Leo hadn't called her, and she tried very hard not to be hurt over that fact. The poor man had a lot on his mind, and he probably had just forgotten. Numerous times she had thought about calling him, but she didn't want to seem like a nag. There were more important things going on right now than their relationship, and she tried her best to be patient.

Karin nibbled her nail as she stared at the television screen. The reporter wasn't saying anything new, but Karin couldn't help but watch, hoping that some nugget of information would slip through to let her know how Leo was doing.

Amanda Vaughn was interviewing Jason Stone once more. Karin thought back to when he showed up at the strike, and how after a few tense moments, Leo stormed inside the Palazzo in a huff. Jason had then smoothly diverted the attention of the reporters away from the strike and focused them on himself and his empire.

Damn, Jason loved the camera. The camera loved him, too. Never before had Karin seen anyone so well-suited for publicity.

True to form, Jason had swept in and used the media attention to push his Stone Suites hotel line. When asked about the situation at the Palazzo, he remained politely neutral, even mentioning the charity event he'd co-organized with Leo's sister Arianna several months ago. When pressed, Jason said that it was difficult running a family business. There were certain expectations and sometimes family members let each other down. If one didn't know any better, it would seem that Jason was genuinely remorseful and sympathetic over what was going on at the Palazzo.

But Karin knew better. Jason was a slithering snake. He'd love nothing more than to see the Perconti empire crumble. Behind closed doors the bastard was probably dancing with glee.

"You know, you really should stop watching that." Wes shut off the television and sat down next to her on the sofa. "It isn't healthy."

"Neither is being out of work."

"Yeah, well, neither one of us can help that." Wes sighed and took a sip of coffee. "Damn strike." He shook his head. "I need that job."

"We all do," Karin agreed.

Wes studied her face for a moment. "He'll be okay, you know."

Karin didn't need to ask who he was referring to. Leo had been at the center of most of their conversations.

"I know. I worry, though." She didn't want to tell Wes what she knew about Leo's medications, or how much she missed lying in Leo's arms. "I just wish I could do something."

Wes's cell phone rang, slicing through the tension in the air. Karin jumped, spilling her coffee. As she cleaned up the mess, she tried to follow the conversation.

"Are you sure?" Wes said. Then, after a minute of silence, he continued. "Yeah, we'll be there." He disconnected and grinned at Karin. "Hurry up and change."

"Why?"

"The negotiations are over. We're going back to work."

A few hours later, Karin piled into the large conference room with the other staff members in attendance. Television sets had been set up in separate conference rooms, allowing the entire Palazzo staff to hear what Leo had to say. As the Perconti patriarch stepped up to the podium, Karin couldn't help but notice that he looked ragged and tired. Her heart broke as he shuffled some papers and began his speech.

Despite being exhausted, his voice rang out loud and clear through the PA system.

"Good afternoon . . ."

He continued, outlining the negotiations and what changes were going to be made at the hotel. As he spoke of vacation time, employee incentives, and retirement contributions, Karin looked at the small group behind him, desperate for the type of information she wouldn't hear in his speech.

His brothers looked as tired as he did. Dante's eyes were red, Karin could tell that even from a distance. Marco had fresh wrinkles around his eyes. All three men looked like they could use a long, hot bath and about three days' worth of rest.

Gloria, on the other hand, looked victorious. She stood next to Emily and a few other staff members with a wide grin as Leo read his speech. Hatred burned deep inside Karen's chest as she watched the woman who had made Leo's life a living hell for the past three days. She looked a little too happy, a little too eager.

"Now we'll take questions," Leo said as his brothers moved with microphones throughout the audience. Karin sat and listened to talk about sick time and flex hours until she thought her ears would go numb.

"I wonder when we can go back." Wes whispered next to her.

"I'd imagine soon," Karin said. "They have a wedding to prepare for."

Wes nodded in understanding, and Karin's mind drifted to the penthouse suite upstairs. She could hardly wait to get Leo alone so that she could question him. It worried her that he looked so tired.

"Do you have an answer to the question?" someone from the audience asked.

Karin realized that she had been daydreaming. She sat up in her seat and found that Leo was staring at her. In fact, quite a few people around her were staring as well.

"Mr. Perconti?" the staff member asked. "What will you do about the bias and favoritism that has infiltrated Perconti Enterprises?"

Leo took a deep breath and turned away from Karin to face the person with the question. As he turned away, an uncomfortable feeling settled in her stomach.

"There was never any favoritism at the Palazzo, nor at any of the other Perconti resorts."

A murmur of discontent rose up from the crowd. Leo raised his hand. "Nevertheless . . ." He waited for the staff members to settle down. "Nevertheless, I have agreed to replace Karin Norell as my consultant. She will finish her internship and then go back to school at the end of the month. Her compensation will be appropriate for her new responsibilities."

"Will she be offered a position once she graduates?" someone asked.

"Sadly, no. All of the open positions within Perconti Enterprises will be put on hold indefinitely until we implement the other changes I talked about previously."

"Jesus," Wes whispered beside her. "Talk about kicking you while you're down."

"Mr. Perconti." Amanda Vaughn shoved her way to the front of the crowd. "Will Ms. Norell continue to stay in the penthouse suite?"

Leo's face took on a pained expression for a moment, then smoothed over into an expressionless mask. "No, Ms. Norell will no longer be staying with me in the penthouse suite, nor anywhere else in this hotel. She will report directly to my brother Marco, but I, personally, will not have any contact with her whatsoever." He shifted his gaze to hers. "Neither I, nor any of my brothers, condone workplace relationships and will set an example for the rest of the staff."

Karin tore her gaze away from Leo and focused on Gloria, who gloated from her place behind the podium. Karin's stomach churned and she tasted bile in her throat.

"Oh, Karin." Wes tried to put his arm around her, but Karin stood and shook him off.

"I have to go."

"Let me go with you." Wes started to stand, but Karin was already moving.

I will not let them see me cry. She pushed through the crowd and hid her face as she lunged for the exit.

"Karin, wait."

Karin heard footsteps behind her, and picked up the pace. She didn't want to talk to Wes. She didn't want to talk to anyone.

Karin hailed a cab, threw herself onto the backseat, and motioned the driver to move.

"Karin!"

"Do you want to wait, miss?" the driver asked.

"No, just drive."

It wasn't until the cab pulled into traffic and the Palazzo disappeared behind them that Karin finally let the tears flow.

Chapter 16

After over a year of preparation, everything was finally coming together. The Perconti family's future had never looked brighter, and yet Leo had never been more miserable.

Soon, he'd see his younger sister, Arianna, married to a rich aviation tycoon, thus securing his family's prosperity. His younger brothers had curbed their spending and, with a little coaxing, had united to get the hotel ready for the big event. Leo's mother and the twins, Gio and Gianna, had arrived from Milan and were safely settled into their rooms. Leo had moved out of the penthouse suite, giving it over to Ari and her wedding entourage. He found that the smaller room suited him, and although his sister didn't seem thrilled with the prospect of marrying Landon Blake, she was at least polite and receptive to him. She had agreed that this marriage was what was best for the family, and would keep her charity afloat for many years to come.

He had everything he had always wanted, but it all meant nothing because he didn't have *her*.

Not that it mattered. At the moment, he couldn't be with anyone, let alone the woman he cared about. If he wasn't dealing with the Palazzo staff, he was fielding calls from his ex-wife, which only added to his anxiety.

He leaned against the balcony railing with his morning coffee and peered down into the foyer below. After a quick glance at his watch, he settled in to wait.

For the past week, he had made sure that he was up and perched in his lookout overlooking the foyer at precisely seven in the morning and seven at night. While the rest of his day was more fluid, this habit he refused to change.

As he watched the Palazzo's day shift trickle in through the doors, his heartbeat quickened. Would she arrive today, or make some excuse? He tightened his grip on his mug and tried to appear nonchalant. To everyone else, he was just having his morning coffee before the start of his day. No one could never know how important this moment was to him.

His watch alarm went off, signaling the changing of the hour. The staff at the Palazzo—what was left of it—changed shifts at both seven in the morning and seven at night. Karin's shift was starting, which meant she would be arriving soon.

He scanned the foyer and wondered if she had called in sick. He wouldn't blame her if she did. Leo had thought that keeping his distance would stop the media's interest in her, but Amanda Vaughn had been relentless. Poor Karin had been avoiding the tabloid reporter as best she could, working consecutive shifts just to hide from the woman's relentless questioning. While the other workers had taken their breaks, she had kept going, as if she was almost afraid to stop and breathe. Many times over the past few days Leo had thought about intervening, but had refrained. He had made his deal with the devil. Karin was off-limits, at least for now.

He just hoped she'd understood his motives.

At five past seven Karin came in through the revolving door. She wore a peacoat over her uniform, and her soft hair was pulled back into a bun. A tight smile had been plastered on her face, and her step was purposeful.

Desire sparked in his lower abdomen as he watched Karin go behind the desk to sign in and check her mail. He watched her pull the small, thin envelope from the mail slot. He held his breath as she looked at the front of the envelope and ran her fingers over the writing. *Come on, Karin. Open it.*

Every day since his speech, Leo had written her a note, explaining why he'd said what he did, and why it was imperative that they stay away from each other until after the wedding. In that small envelope, Leo had laid out his heart, telling her how much she meant to him, and how, if things were different, he'd run away with her and leave the Palazzo and this entire mess behind. He wrote about how he longed for their penthouse days, and the closeness they had shared on his yacht. He'd give almost anything to have a secret rendezvous with her once more.

With each passing day the ache in his chest grew stronger. All he wanted to do was lose himself in Karin's warmth, to feel her thighs wrap around his body and trust him with her body like she did before this whole mess began. Karin made no demands of him. Leo loved her for that, but love had a price. Now she was miserable, and it was all his fault.

Little by little, Karin's light had been dimming. He had seen it every morning in the slump of her shoulders, in the weariness in her voice as he eavesdropped on conversations. He wanted to put that light back in her eyes and the smile on her lips.

Leo watched her glance up to where he was standing, as if she knew he was watching her all along. Their gazes met and Leo schooled his features.

Karin frowned, and Leo noticed the dark circles under

her eyes. He had done that to her. She had trusted him, and he'd betrayed that trust. While he had fought hard to have her stay on at the Palazzo, the position was beneath her, and the work tedious. At the time, he had thought that he was helping her, but now he wasn't so sure.

The pain in his chest intensified as she tore up the crumpled letter in her hand. Leo found it difficult to keep his features an expressionless mask as she threw the pieces away and gathered her things. He knew that she would do this, she had been performing the same ritual every morning since his speech, but he couldn't help but hope that this morning would be the one where she would open the letter and read between the lines. He wanted her to understand that he wanted to move beyond the arrangement and into something deeper. Unfortunately, there was just too much at stake right now. He couldn't risk his family's livelihood, no matter how strong his emotions may be.

His entire life Leo had taken pride in the Perconti legacy. It wasn't until now, in this moment, that he felt the full weight of the responsibilities that came with such a powerful name.

Leo let out a heavy sigh as Karin turned away from him to speak to another coworker. As Leo and Karin had been drifting apart, she had been getting closer to her coworker and friend, Wes. The knowledge ate at his gut and made his chest squeeze with anger, but he was helpless to do anything about it.

"Where is he?" A shrill, female voice rose up from the front door to the hotel. Leo cringed as he scanned the foyer. Even now, after all this time apart, that woman's voice still had a way of making his skin crawl.

A tall, sandy-haired woman breezed into the hotel wearing a trendy trench coat, pearls, and a designer dress. Her hair was in a perfect twist, her nails painted a bright red to match her lipstick. "Where is that husband of mine?" Danika yelled as she approached the front counter.

Leo's blood ran cold. He had to go and divert his ex-wife's attention before she made an even bigger mess of his life. Placing his coffee to one side, Leo steeled his emotions as he hurried down the staircase to meet her.

Danika better have a good reason for showing up at the Palazzo, because if she didn't, Leo was going to toss her out on her ear, consequences be damned.

Karin cringed as the woman's shrill voice became louder. Leo grabbed the newcomer by the elbow and took her to the far side of the foyer, out of earshot.

"Looks like there's trouble," Wes said.

"Yeah," Karin agreed as Leo strode purposefully away with the woman in question. "Not that it's any of our business."

"Oh, come on now," Wes said, drawing her attention back to him. "You can put on that 'I-don't-care attitude' in front of the others, but you can't fool me. You worry about him."

Karin sighed. "It doesn't matter, Wes. As long as he puts his business first, then we can never be together."

"You were never really one for casual relationships, were you?" he joked.

Karin grimaced. "I tried, Wes. I really did."

"I know, darlin'." He put his arm around Karin and considered Leo and the stranger for a moment. "His hands are tied, you know," Wes said. "It's not like he left you voluntarily. There's a difference."

"Is there?" Karin frowned at the woman arguing with Leo. She looked as if she had walked off the pages of *Vanity Fair*. Everything about her projected high-class perfection. Karin knew that she could never compete with someone like her.

"Of course there's a difference. Leo cares about you."

Karin wrinkled her nose. "That's impossible."

"Everyone talks about how he has been moping around the office area. Stop being so difficult. After the wedding—"

"After the wedding, something else will come up and Leo will have some other excuse for us to stay apart." She shook her head in dismissal as she turned back to Wes. "It doesn't matter, Wes. If he won't be with me now, then he won't be with me a week from now, or a month. There will always be something standing in our way."

"If you say so." Wes studied her face for a moment. "Let's go out tonight and have fun."

"I'd love to," Karin said, welcoming the change of subject. "But I can't. There's too much work to do."

"Screw work." Wes smirked and slid his arm around hers, locking them together. "Screw all of them. You, my dear, need to get away from this awful place. We'll go to a bar, get drunk, and have wild one-night stands with strangers."

Karin smiled. "I can't, Wes, but thanks." Karin disentangled herself, picked up her purse, and started back to the supply room to start her day.

"You might brush other women off like yesterday's garbage, Leo Perconti, but you can't do that to me."

Karin slowed her steps as the woman with Leo smiled up adoringly at him.

"No one is trying to throw you out," Leo said. "Be reasonable, Danika."

"Come now, Leo. This is no way to treat your wife."

"Ex-wife."

"Details. It's only a matter of time before you take me back."

"What about your musician?"

She shrugged and slid her fingers underneath the lapel of his suit. "A woman gets lonely. Just say the word, and he'll be gone."

Karin dropped her purse as the woman's words burrowed their way into her sleep-deprived brain. *That's Leo's ex?* She looked so different from the pictures in the media. In person she seemed much older and her makeup was much heavier. She also seemed to have lost weight since she and Leo were together. Her thin frame looked slightly undernourished, her skin a little too pale.

Karin glanced at Wes, who seemed to be just as shocked as she was. He mouthed the words "She still wants him?" before he returned his attention back to the arguing couple.

"Danika, you are making a spectacle of yourself," Leo said as he removed her fingers from his chest. "We're never getting back together, so stop creating a scene. As I told you on the phone, after the wedding, you shall have everything you want."

"I've already been waiting months and months, Leo. You ignore my texts and refuse to see me. Is that any way to treat your spouse?"

"You are not my spouse, Danika. If I remember correctly, you were the one who insisted on a divorce. I was the one who wanted to work things out."

"Honey, I never would have asked for that divorce if you knew how to be a proper husband."

"You had a lover—"

She ran a long, manicured fingernail across his jaw. "Had. And I never would have run to Rico's arms if you gave me as much attention as you do your company."

Leo jerked his head away and fisted his hands to his

sides. "Perhaps we should take this somewhere more private."

"And what? So you can tell me to go away? No." She inched closer and ran her fingers over his arm. "We used to be so close—"

Leo grabbed her wrist and pushed it away. "You destroyed that when you cheated on me."

Danika straightened and pulled her hand out of his grasp. "And you are no saint, either, cavorting with the staff. We have both made mistakes, Leo. Let's put them behind us and—"

"Your sources are wrong. I haven't been cavorting with anyone."

"I don't think so." Danika offered him a sultry smile. "Unless you make a habit of buying your interns designer dresses."

"It was a mistake—" Leo stopped midsentence, as if he only just realized what he was about to say. He fisted his hands at his sides and steeled his jaw.

"Have you been following me?" he asked, his voice low and dangerous.

"I'm just checking up on my investment, my dear. I can't get paid if the Perconti name is worth nothing, you know."

When Leo spoke, his voice was tinged with warning. "You have done enough damage here, Danika. It's time to go."

"But I came here to reconcile. I've missed you so much."

"Liar. You don't want me, you want my money."

"But Leo—"

"Out." Leo pointed to the revolving door. "Get out."

Danika smiled and patted Leo's cheek. "I will be back after the wedding to collect double what I asked for."

"Double?"

Danika's smile turned into a fake frown as she slid her

hand from his face. "For my broken heart, Leo." She adjusted his designer tie with confidence, as if it was something she had done many times before. "All I ever wanted was your attention, you know. It's all I still want." She removed her finger and glanced down at his cock. "The choice is yours. Take me back, or double the price." Before Leo could respond, she turned and left the Palazzo.

"Oh, honey." Wes put his arm around Karin's shoulders. "I'm so sorry."

All Karin could do was stare. She felt too sick to speak, too weak to walk. She couldn't seem to get past two facts. One, Leo considered her a mistake. Two, Leo's ex-wife was trying to win him back.

Was that the real motive behind their public breakup? Was he still in love with his ex-wife? Whether she was succeeding or not didn't matter. On one thing both Danika and Karin could agree: Leo focused so much on his family and company that he had no room for anyone or anything else.

Leo slowly turned and caught her gaze. His features paled, and he looked about as sick as she felt.

"Bastard," Wes said. "Come on, honey." He started steering her back toward the front desk.

"No, Wes," Karin said. When Wes didn't stop, she pulled out of his grasp. "Leave me alone, please." Her voice came out no louder than a whisper, but it seemed to have the desired effect.

Wes lowered his arm and searched her features. "Perhaps you should go home."

"No, "I'll be fine." She cleared her throat.

"Karin." Leo's booming voice rose up behind her, but Karin didn't look back. She didn't dare. One more look at Leo and she'd fall into his arms, and he didn't deserve that.

"I'll see you later, Wes." Karin forced herself to put one foot in front of the other. She heard Leo approaching from behind, but she had a head start. Karin made it to the elevators and the doors closed before he could reach her.

"Karin, wait!"

As the doors closed, muffling Leo's call, Karin let the tears fall. She had always known that he had been married, but for some reason she had pushed the knowledge to the back of her mind. Now she could no longer ignore the facts. Leo's ex-wife wanted him back. Danika was the perfect picture of the socialite wife, and Karin had no doubt that the woman could handle herself in front of the media, much better than Karin had been managing the past few days, for sure. Karin couldn't understand why Leo would give her the time of day, when it was so obvious that Danika would be a much better fit for his lifestyle and image.

Only one thing made sense—Leo had used her. With each passing second, Karin was feeling less and less sorry for herself, and angrier and angrier over how Leo had taken what he wanted from her and then cast her aside. She clutched her large tote to her chest, digging her fingers into the fake leather. She wanted to hit something, hard. Something primal and angry was growing inside of her, and she needed to let it out.

When the elevator doors opened, Karin threw her tote with everything she had.

"Bastard!"

It sailed through the air and crashed into the vase on the table along the far wall, spilling both the purple orchids and the contents of her tote out onto the floor.

Let him rot. Let them all rot. With a frustrated growl, Karin swept her arm over the table, sending the candlesticks, small figurine, and lace doilies onto the floor. Still it was not enough.

"Asshole!" She knocked over the table itself, sending it to the floor with a crash.

Great, now I just created more work for myself. With a sob, she fell to her knees and covered her face with her hands. As soon as she was done with this internship, she was so out of there.

Leo used and discarded me, just like Jason Stone did before him. Karin doubled over as pain lanced her body and numbed her mind. She was such a stupid, stupid girl.

"What the—"

Karin looked up to see a long, raven-haired beauty stumble over the fallen table. She landed on the floor in a heap.

"I'm . . . I'm sorry. I'll clean this up." Karin stood and stumbled back toward the elevator door. Her foot landed on something round and slipped out from under her. *The figurine.* She flailed her arms as she tried to regain her balance and stumbled over the body on the floor.

As Karen blinked at the bright white-and-gold tiles, she heard laughter bubble up behind her.

"Well now, I guess we're even."

Karen turned her head and saw a woman about her age giggling behind her well-manicured hand.

"God, I'm sorry," Karin said.

"No, I'm the one who's sorry." The woman wiped the tears of laughter from her cheeks and chuckled to herself once more. "I should look where I'm going." She sat up and brushed her hands over her brown-and-gold peasant skirt.

"I . . . Are you okay?" Karin asked.

The woman grinned and adjusted the gold comb in her hair. "Sorry about that. I heard all of the commotion and thought someone was attacking you. I rushed over to help and didn't look where I was going." She lifted her skirt to show her high platform heels. "These aren't the best for stability."

"No, they aren't." Karin chuckled. "I don't even know how you can walk in them."

"Oh, it's tough, but no tougher than holding onto your purse." She giggled behind her hand and Karen found the sound infectious. Before she knew it, she was giggling, too.

Giggles turned into full-blown laughter. It felt good to laugh again. Karin couldn't remember the last time she had done that.

The woman collected herself and studied Karin for a moment. "Man problems?"

"How did you know?"

"Only a man would make a woman angry enough to destroy things."

Her remark sent both women giggling once more.

"God, I'm a mess." The woman got her laughter under control and rolled her eyes. "Not very becoming for a hotel heiress, is it?"

Karin's laughter immediately subsided, replaced by shock. "Hotel heiress?"

"Yes." The woman sat up and held out her hand. "I'm Arianna Perconti."

Karin stared at the woman's hand. "You're Leo's sister."

Arianna lowered her hand and frowned. "Ah, you've met my brother." She stood and held out her hand once more. "I suppose that would explain the tears and destruction."

Karin wiped her cheeks once more, suddenly embarrassed over her state. "I'm sorry."

"Don't be," Arianna said as she helped Karin up. "My brothers tend to have that effect on women." She helped Karin brush off the dust from her clothes. "What did he do this time?"

Karin swallowed the lump in her throat. "Nothing."

"Oh, come now. He must have done something."

"Not at all. He is a fine boss."

"Hmm." Arianna studied her face for a moment. "You're a terrible liar . . ." She glanced down at Karin's name tag, which peeked out from between the folds of her coat. "Karin."

Before Karin could respond, Arianna looped her arm with hers. "Come, let's take you back to my suite and clean you up. Then we can have a little chat."

"No, I'm fine. Really."

"Nonsense. I, above all people, know how overbearing my older brother can be. This situation calls for some wine and some pampering, don't you think?"

"I couldn't possibly—"

"Nonsense. Come now. And I won't take no for an answer."

Karin's head spun as Arianna swept her back into the elevators and up to the penthouse suite. She wasn't quite sure about Arianna's motives behind her kindness, but she had to admit, it was nice to laugh and have someone friendly to talk to.

Chapter 17

Karin stared at the words "Tiffany & Co." on the champagne flute as Arianna filled it to the top with the most expensive bubbly the hotel had to offer.

"It's not even nine o'clock in the morning," Karin murmured.

"Pish, posh," Arianna said. "It's noon somewhere." She glanced up from the bottle and studied Karin's face. "Although if it would make you feel better, I could call up one of the staff to throw a little orange juice in the glass and make a mimosa."

"No, that's okay." The last thing Karin needed was for one of the remaining staff members to see her kicking back and drinking champagne with Leo's younger sister.

"Okay, then." Arianna grinned as she filled her own glass. "It's settled."

"But . . ." Karin didn't know quite how to protest without hurting the woman's feelings. "I'm working . . ."

"Of course you are, dear," Arianna said as she put the bottle down. "You're working for the Perconti family, which means that you're working for me. Right now, I need someone to drink with, so I'm giving you the order to relax and enjoy yourself."

"But Marco and Leo—"

"You leave my brothers to me." Arianna waved her hand in the air. "They can be overbearing sometimes, but you just need to know how to deal with them." She frowned and averted her gaze. "Unless it comes to marriage. Thanks to my father's affairs and Leo's disaster, they all see marriage as little more than a business deal."

"Excuse me?"

"Oh, nothing. Here." She handed Karin a champagne flute. "Take it."

Karin took the glass from Arianna's hand. "Thank you."

"There," she said as she settled back on the couch. "Now, isn't this better?"

Karin had to admit that it was. As Arianna held up her glass, Karin smiled and raised hers. Together they clinked the stemware and Karin tried not to stare as her new friend downed the entire contents of the glass.

Karin put the glass to her lips and took a sip. The champagne was wonderfully fruity and hit the spot after the horrible morning she'd had.

"So." Arianna set down her glass and folded her hands in her lap. "Tell me, what did my brother do that made you so upset?"

"Ms. Perconti, I can't—"

"Call me Ari."

"Okay, Ari, I'm not sure if I should get into that with you. Leo is your brother."

"Don't worry, you can tell me anything." Ari smirked. "I'm very good at keeping secrets. In fact, I have a secret I've been keeping for quite a while about myself." She leaned forward and placed her elbows on her knees. "And, to be honest, it will be nice to finally tell someone about it. So." She leaned back and offered Karin a friendly smile. "If you tell me what is going on between you and Leo, I'll tell you something that no one in my family knows about."

"I don't know." Karin took another sip from her glass

to hide her confusion. Ari seemed nice, but she was still a Perconti. From what Karin had overheard from Leo and Marco's conversations, she didn't have a firm grasp on reality. In fact, she spent so much time traveling and working for her charity that she neglected most other aspects of her life. According to her older brothers, she lived in a fantasy world, and everyone around her bent over backward to make sure she didn't have to worry about the harsh realities of life.

And yet, all of those snippets of conversation she had overheard didn't add up. The woman sitting before her was a contradiction. Arianna sported thousand-dollar platform shoes, but still wore a peasant skirt and ruffled top that looked like they were bought at a thrift store. Her hair and makeup were done up perfectly, but the nail polish on her fingers was chipped and she had dirt under her nails. When she laughed, her eyes remained troubled, and she'd drained that glass of champagne like someone who was trying to forget, not enjoy herself.

"Okay, I'll tell you." Over a full bottle of champagne, Karin told Ari about her relationship with Leo. How they met, their secret affair, how the staff at the Palazzo had become jealous, how Leo had dismissed her abruptly, and finally, how his wife had shown up downstairs.

"That bitch!" Ari cried as she put down her empty glass. "I can't believe that evil witch dared to show her face around here."

"It seemed like she wanted to get back together with Leo."

"I doubt it." Ari wrinkled her nose. "It's much more likely that she wants the Perconti fortune, or what's left of it." She sighed and leaned back on the couch. "Leo thinks that only Marco and Dante know she's blackmailing him, but the rest of the family knows, too—even Mother." Ari shook her head. "Breaks the poor woman's heart."

Karin's hand shook so much that she was forced to put down her glass. "Blackmailing him?"

"Yeah." Ari sighed and leaned her head back on the couch. "Their marriage wasn't based on love, but rather convenience. Oh—" Ari waved her hand in the air as Karin started to speak. "Leo fancied himself in love at the time, but it wasn't the real thing." She straightened her head and curved her features into a pensive frown. "Everything happened so fast, much too fast. They had started dating and three weeks later they were talking marriage."

"Wow. I had no idea."

"Not many people outside of the family do." Ari pressed her lips together in thought. "Despite the press's romanticizing, the relationship between Danika and Leo wasn't equal. It was obvious that she was using him for his money and status. She cared about his influence more than she cared about him. We tried to tell my brother that she was bad news, but he wouldn't listen to reason. They seemed like the perfect couple in public, but as soon as the doors closed, they fought every chance they got."

Karin thought back to how Danika and Leo had argued downstairs, and how much Leo valued the Perconti image. She knew that she could never be like Danika and put on a plastic smile in public while she was hurting inside. Perhaps Leo was right to call off their arrangement. Karin could never be what he needed her to be.

Ari frowned and picked at a stray thread on the nearby throw pillow. "Danika was brutal, taking his money and emasculating him in front of the rest of the family. Dried up a good portion of our finances on her gambling addiction, for which she blamed Leo, of course."

"How did they break up?"

"I'd like to say Leo wised up and kicked her out on her rear, but it didn't happen that way. About three months into their marriage, she had an affair with a musician and left him."

Karin quickly did the math. "So they were only together for less than a year?"

Ari nodded. "Leo gave her a sizable portion of the Perconti finances to keep everything from the media, but we all knew that she would be back, eventually." She shook her head and waved her glass at Karin. "People like her are always back once the money dries up."

"But they're divorced—"

"Yes . . ." Ari turned to face Karin, as if refocusing her thoughts. "She must have found some loophole in their settlement and now she's exploiting it." She tapped her finger to her lips. "I'm quite sure that's why she showed up downstairs."

"You think so?"

Ari nodded. "That bitch never cared about Leo, or this family. She probably heard about his relationship with you and saw an opportunity to gain the upper hand."

Karin digested everything that Arianna said. If what she was suggesting was true, then yes, Leo's ex-wife was interested in him, but only for his money. It shed an entirely new light on their relationship.

"No wonder he's on medication . . ." Karin murmured.

Ari scowled. "My brother's on medication?"

"Never mind." Karin raised her glass to her lips to hide her embarrassment. "I was thinking of someone else there for a moment." Leo's entire family looked up to him for guidance and support, but when Leo needed someone in his life to lean on, there was no one. He had been forced to deal with things by himself for so long that he didn't know how to rely on someone else.

Arianna nodded to the glass. "Did you like the champagne?"

Karin smiled and put down her glass. "Yes, thank you."

"Good, and I hope our talk helped you understand my brother a little bit. He really is a good guy. He's just had a lot of bad luck where women are concerned."

Because he won't allow himself to trust anyone. Karin nodded. "Thank you." The conversation had helped and, she hated to admit it, the champagne had helped a little as well.

"Now, it's time to share my secret." Ari grinned and leaned in closer. "Want to hear it?"

"Sure."

Ari cupped her hand to her mouth and whispered so softly that Karin had to lean in closer to hear. "I don't want to get married."

Karin raised her brows. "You don't?"

"Well I do want to marry someday of course, just not Landon Blake, aka Mr. Boring." Ari frowned and rubbed her hands on her lap. "This is an arranged marriage, you know." She glanced at Karin. "Leo facilitated it to help get us out of debt."

"You didn't want this marriage?"

"Well, it's complicated. Leo introduced us at the grand opening of one of the hotels last year. Landon mistook my politeness for flirtation and approached Leo with a deal."

"A deal?"

Arianna nodded. "A deal that would expand Landon's aviation empire and quiet the tabloid rumors about his more . . . personal pursuits. At first Leo balked at the idea, but the more he thought about it, the more sense it made, so he approached me and we agreed that it seemed to make sense."

"Why would you agree to that?"

Ari sighed and leaned back on the couch. "At the time my charity was severely underfunded. I was assured that the marriage would be in name only. We wouldn't even have to share the same bedroom or live in the same house. I could continue my charity work, and Landon and my brother would be able to undercut Stone Suites with their vacation deals and run our archrival out of business."

"Wow."

"Yeah."

"It seems like everything was set."

"Tied up in a neat little bow." Arianna frowned. "And those tabloid pictures of Landon wearing a leather collar and a leash would be declared a forgery . . ."

"Collar and leash, like a dog?"

"Yeah. They were taken in a bar in San Francisco while Landon was on a business trip. Later, more pictures came out of him at some local club doing similar things. I was told that clubs have strict privacy policies that include no outside cameras, but I guess rules don't stop a determined reporter."

Karin thought about how a reporter managed to get around the privacy screen on the penthouse suite balcony and take a picture of her and Leo. "I don't see why people are so interested in someone's sexual preferences. Bedroom practices have nothing to do with the ability to make business decisions."

"You'd be surprised at how conservative some investors are. The photos scared them. I mean, how can Landon maintain credibility as a hard-nosed CEO when the board had all seen pictures of him kissing another man while wearing a studded collar and nothing else? Landon needed to quiet the tabloids and bury the pictures, and my family needed the money."

"Jesus. How . . . unromantic."

"I didn't mind too much until about a year ago." Arianna leaned forward and took Karin's hand. "Until I found someone to care about."

"There's someone else?" Karin asked as she put down her glass.

"I didn't realize it at first. We met at one of my charity functions a month or two before my engagement announcement. At first it was just about the great sex, but now . . ." She shrugged. "Now, it's more."

"Is he interested in you as well?"

She seemed to think about that for a moment. "I don't know. Maybe." She glanced at Karin. "But even if he isn't, how can I enter a loveless marriage after knowing that *that* is out there?" She sat up and leaned in closer. "Think about you and Leo. How could you possibly settle for anything less after what you two shared together?"

"Leo and I don't have—"

"Don't be ridiculous. He cares for you, Karin. It's written all over his face."

"It is?"

She nodded. "He's been miserable and ornery for days." She leaned back and slid her arm over the back of the couch. "I've never seen him this upset, not even over Danika."

Karin thought about Ari's confession. If Leo really did care about her, didn't Karin owe it to him, and to herself, to try to put things right? If she walked away now, leaving everything the mess that it was, she knew that she'd never stop thinking about what might have been. She'd never forgive herself for not trying.

Yes, she would give one last effort to setting things right and if that didn't work out, well, she'd cross that bridge when she got to it.

"I can see you care for him, too." Arianna sighed and leaned back on the couch. "Unfortunately, the object of my affection thinks our relationship is still just about sex. Despite this, I believe he has grown to care for me. At least,

I hope he has." Ari frowned and chewed on her fingernail. "You think I deserve happiness, don't you?"

"Of course." Karin studied her for a moment. "You don't have to marry Landon, you know."

Arianna pursed her lips in thought. "If I don't, our family will lose our hotel empire."

"I think Leo would understand."

"Would he? I'm not so sure. My brother has a nasty temper, you know."

"I know. He has a compassionate side, too, though. I'm sure if you explain that you met someone, perhaps have Leo meet him—"

"Oh no, Leo could never meet him!" Arianna's eyes went wide with fear. "That would be disastrous." Ari stood and began to pace. "You must never tell anyone of this, Karin. Promise me." When Karin didn't immediately respond, Arianna leaned closer. "Promise."

"I . . . I promise."

"Good." Arianna sighed and straightened. "Oh hell. What time is it?" She glanced at her watch. "I was supposed to be at the florist an hour ago." She grabbed her purse and jacket. "I don't suppose you want to come with me and argue the value of gardenias over orchids, would you?"

"No, thanks." Karin pointed to her uniform. "I've got rooms to clean."

Arianna sighed. "I don't blame you. I wouldn't go, either, if I could help it." She shrugged on her jacket and stiffened her shoulders. "Wish me luck."

"Good luck."

"Would you mind texting Roberto for me? I don't want to spend any more time with those reporters than I have to." Before Karin could respond, Ari hurried onto the elevator.

With a sigh, Karin texted the front desk to have them bring the limo around and then slumped on the sofa. Without realizing it, Arianna Perconti had given her a lot to think about.

Leo believed it was the media that was ruining his family. He was wrong. Secrets were slowly killing the Percontis—and her. It seemed as if everyone had something to hide. Wes and Marco were hiding their sexual liaisons from the world, Dante was hiding his pain over his breakup with Sabrina by drinking, and Arianna was hiding the fact that she didn't want to get married to the aviation tycoon and her love for a mysterious man. Leo was hiding the fact that his ex-wife was trying to extort money from him. He was also hiding that he was taking little pills so that he could remain the pillar of strength for his family.

Even Karin was keeping secrets. She hadn't told anyone about how her demotion had stretched her already tight budget, and how her demotion wasn't giving her the right kind of job training for her degree. She should have taken another job, one with more professional opportunities, but the thought of never seeing Leo again, even if it was only from a distance, made her physically ill.

She loved Leo. It wasn't until this exact moment that she would even admit that to herself, but the more she thought about it, the more she realized that it was true. She had looked forward to coming into work and finding his letter. She loved looking up and seeing him standing in the balcony above, watching her. She had enjoyed his intense stare, his focus on nothing but her. She craved those brief moments throughout the day when they'd run into each other, or see one another across a crowded room.

She couldn't get enough of him and, on some level, she knew that he felt the same. Otherwise, he wouldn't seek her out. He wouldn't stare or write her letters day after day, letters that she refused to read because her heart couldn't bear the pain again.

There had to be some way to dig out of this mess. She had seen the accounting records when she worked with Leo. If they didn't do something soon, the Perconti family would run out of money, and then they'd all be out on the streets.

"You look like you could use one of these." Wes's Southern accent broke through her silence as a bottle of ibuprofen came into view.

"Thanks." Karin grabbed the bottle and then took the water Wes handed to her.

"What happened in here?" he asked as he rounded the sofa and sat next to her. "It must be intense if you didn't hear me wrestle the cleaning cart through the elevator doors."

"Arianna just wanted to talk. Girl stuff." Karin laughed at Wes's scowl and leaned her head back on the couch. "Can I ask you a question?"

"Sure, darlin', anything." Wes slid his arm over the back of the couch and turned to face her. "Although I'm not a woman, so I'm not sure if I can help."

Karin gave him a playful slap. "This is serious." She knew that she had to phrase her question carefully. Wes loved to gossip, and she had promised Ari that she wouldn't say anything about her not wanting the marriage to take place.

"If you saw a family slowly becoming buried in secrets, and those secrets were tearing them apart, what would you do?"

"Mind my own business."

Karin chuckled. "But what if you were being affected by these secrets?"

"Affected how?" When Karin didn't immediately

respond, Wes placed his hand on her leg and leaned in close. "Girl, you better just spill it. I know I always feel better after I let out whatever is eating me up inside."

Karin swallowed and averted her gaze. "It has to do with Leo."

"Of course it does, honey." He slid his arm around her and had her lean back onto his chest. "Tell me about it."

She glanced up at him. "This is serious."

"Of course it is." He tightened his hug. "Come now, everyone knows how he follows you around day after day, and how you do your best to ignore him but fail miserably."

"It's that obvious, isn't it?"

Wes nodded. "I probably shouldn't say 'I told you so,' but . . ."

"You told me so." Karin smiled, despite her feeling of helplessness. "But this doesn't have to do with us. It has to do with how his ex-wife is blackmailing him."

"Blackmailing?" Wes straightened and raised his brows.

"Yeah. Leo has . . . secrets."

"What kind of secrets?"

Karin flashed him a frown. "You know I can't say. Let's just say that these secrets are at the heart of why the hotel chain is failing."

"You really want to help him, don't you?"

"I do."

He considered her for a moment. "Then the answer is simple." Wes grinned as he shifted in his seat to face her. "He comes clean and tells the reporters everything."

"That's impossible." Karin shook her head and widened her eyes in disbelief. "Revealing all of these secrets might very well create enough scandal to put the Percontis out of business."

"Or it could create enough publicity to push them into the black." When Karin flashed him a skeptical look, he continued. "Think about it. People love an underdog. When there are reality shows centered on restaurants and the struggling owners, people flock to those restaurants to be a part of the action." Wes shrugged. "I'd bring everything out in the open as quickly as possible. Make a clean break and use the media attention to rebuild the Perconti image from the ground up."

"What if Perconti Enterprises can't recover?"

"I can't see how any secret would ruin a company completely . . . unless he is skimming money out of our paychecks." Wes frowned and eased Karin away from him, gripping her shoulders and turning her until their gazes met. "He's not stealing my money, is he?"

"No, God no."

Wes let out a long breath. "Well, then that settles it. He holds a press conference and outs all of the family's dirty laundry. The media will go nuts, and he can direct that attention to make a clean break from his past and build a new future. Problem solved."

Karin sighed. "I wish it was that easy."

Wes patted her leg. "Of course it's that easy. When people keep secrets, it festers inside of them like an infected wound. It changes them, and not for the better." He straightened. "Lance the wound, my friend, and then put salve on it. It will take time, but wounds heal."

"I can't imagine Leo holding a press conference to announce his family's secrets. It goes against everything he stands for, everything he is."

"Maybe, maybe not." Wes sighed. "But he has to try, if not for his sake, then for his family's."

She stood and began to pace as the idea formed in her mind. If Leo held a press conference, could he spin his secrets in his family's favor? It was worth a shot. "You're right. We have to take control of the media, before it ruins our lives."

"That's my girl. I'll go with you." When she gave him a sharp look, he shrugged. "Like I said, this affects me. Besides, I have all day to clean that suite, and you need moral support."

Karin nodded and they both took Wes's cleaning cart into the elevator.

"He's still in the foyer, I think," Wes said as he hit the button.

When the elevators opened on the ground floor, they found Leo striding toward them, looking ready to kill.

"On second thought . . ." Wes slipped out of the elevator with his cart.

"Wes!"

"What?" He shrugged and started walking backward. "It looks like the 'General' is ready to do battle, and I'd like to keep my bones intact."

Karin tried to leave as well, but Leo slipped his arm around hers and tugged her back into the elevator. He stood beside her, holding in his thinly veiled rage until the doors closed.

Seconds passed as the air grew thick with tension. "Is there a reason why you dragged me back into the elevator?" she finally asked.

"Yes." He turned toward her, his features full of anger. "We need to talk."

Chapter 18

Leo knew he was being controlling, but he couldn't seem to help himself. After the ordeal with his ex-wife, he had run into Arianna on her way out and she'd told him how much she enjoyed the company of "his intern." Her knowing smile had put Leo's teeth on edge. Why did the whole world want to know his business? The constant effort to keep his private life out of the public domain was taking its toll.

He had to know what Karin and his sister had talked about. Ari had a way of charming information out of people, and he had told things to Karin on that yacht that he had never told anyone. His siblings didn't need to know about his shortcomings.

"What do you mean, 'we need to talk'? I thought we weren't supposed to talk to each other. Communication is strictly forbidden, and yet you write these letters—"

"Trying to explain what happened and how I really feel, but you wouldn't know that, because you don't read them. Instead, you drink champagne with my sister in the penthouse suite and talk about me. Speaking of which, what did you two talk about up there?"

"That's none of your business."

"When you talk about me, it's my business." He flexed

his fingers at his sides. "You told me that I had your loyalty."

"Of course you do." Karin straightened away from the elevator wall, clearly ruffled by his comment. "This isn't about Arianna at all, is it? What happened?"

Leo stopped the elevator and tried to explain, but was at a loss for words. All he could think about was her scent—champagne and strawberries. It had been days since he had been close enough to smell it. The scent made him instantly hard, and he couldn't help but think that it would be so easy to lead her back to the bedroom—their bedroom—and have his way with her. To sink himself into her warm heat and forget his troubles would be the ultimate fantasy.

Her gaze was intense, and it unnerved him. He averted his eyes as he tried to think of something to say that wouldn't make her worry.

When he didn't speak right away, she moved in front of him until her lovely face filled his line of vision. "I'm battling these reporters and working my fingers to the bone every day to save this hotel—to save you and your family. The least you can give me is a little honesty."

"You're right. I'm sorry." He shoved his hands in his pockets. This wasn't going well at all, and he had Danika to thank for that. She had shown up out of the blue, and had rattled him so much that he wasn't thinking clearly.

"I just need to know if you told my sister anything about what happened on the yacht," he said.

"Like you assaulted that photographer? No, I didn't tell her anything about you that wasn't already public knowledge. You have nothing to worry about."

"Thank you, *cara*."

"I told you that you could trust me, Leo. I meant it."

"I'm sorry. My ex-wife has a tendency to make me rather paranoid." The elevator door opened up at the penthouse suite and Leo realized that, without thinking, he had directed them back to their former sanctuary. It only spoke to how much he needed her.

"Why did you bring me here?" Karin asked.

"So we could be alone for a few moments." She flashed him a questioning gaze, but he ignored it and ushered her into the penthouse suite.

"We shouldn't be alone," she said as she followed him. "It violates the deal you made with the staff."

"To hell with the staff." He stopped in the middle of the living area and tried to pull her into his arms, but she slipped from his grasp.

"The Palazzo is important to you," she said. "It's the flagship hotel of your company, and a symbol of the strength of your family. You can't possibly mean for them all to go to hell."

Unfortunately, he did. Leo wanted Karin with every fiber of his being. He wished he knew the words to soften her heart. He had been so God damn lonely without her. It had been torture thinking of her, day after day. He knew that he shouldn't have followed her around like a lovesick puppy, but he couldn't seem to help himself. She was the one person who could quiet the madness around him. His sanctuary. Without her, he felt adrift and lost.

He didn't know what to say to her to make it all better, so he decided to just tell her the truth. "You're right, of course."

"Of course, I'm right. Besides, your ex-wife wants to get back together with you."

He flexed his fingers at his sides. "Danika doesn't want to get back together. She only wants my money."

"But she was the perfect image for your company." She lifted her chin and stiffened her jaw. "I remember reading about your relationship in the papers. The press loved her."

"She was good for the company, but not for me.

Karin . . ." He took a hesitant step forward, but Karin stepped back, creating distance between them.

"You should get back together with her. She'd help with your image, and her flair for manipulating reporters will be good for your business. She'd be a strong ally . . . And it isn't like we are seeing each other anymore."

"But I don't love her."

"Does it matter? You've made it very clear that your company comes first. With Danika, you'll have everything you've ever wanted."

But I won't have you. Leo took another step toward her and hesitated. He ached to touch her, ached even more to hold her, but he wasn't sure what her reaction would be.

Karen shook her head. "I never should have let you bring me up here. Good-bye, Leo."

Leo fisted his hands as he watched her make her way to the elevators. He felt so damn helpless in this situation. He had never cared about someone so much before, or made such a mess of things.

"Wait." He rushed forward and grabbed her hand before she could push the button for the elevator.

"I don't want to fight, Leo." Her words sounded small and defeated.

"I don't want that, either." He forced himself to unclench his fists.

She turned and met his gaze. "I want to make this easy for you."

He held out his arms. "You know what would make this easy for me? Letting me hold you."

"But the reporters—"

"The reporters aren't here, are they? Please, Karin. I . . . I miss you."

Karin turned away from his pleading expression. Out of the corner of her eye, she saw the painting of the girl swinging in the sunshine behind the bar. She didn't know when it had gotten fixed, but she was glad that it had. As Karin stared at the girl, she thought about the long road they'd gone down to get to this point. It was wrong of Leo to try to make her fit some sort of Perconti mold, but it was equally wrong of her to expect that he would change his life and forsake all of his responsibilities just to be with her. This wasn't about just her and Leo. It was about his family and their survival. He had people counting on him, and the fact that he didn't forsake them spoke a lot about his character.

"I missed you, too." Karin fell into his open arms, and nothing had ever felt so good.

"I'm so sorry, *cara*," he whispered as he pressed his lips against her hair.

Karin closed her eyes and let his sexy accent ripple through her body.

"It was Danika's phone calls that were making you so upset, wasn't it?" she asked.

"I didn't want to bother you with something so insignificant."

She leaned back and met his gaze. "Your ex-wife wanting to get back together with you is a pretty big deal."

"She had never said that she wanted to get back together on the phone. That was something new—for the staff to overhear. She has always played the wounded wife in public, but in private she is much more cold and calculating. Marriage means nothing to her. It's just a means to an end. A business deal."

"Like your sister's marriage."

"Yes."

"Was your marriage to Danika also a business deal?"

"No, she was my choice." He rubbed his face with his hand. "Although now I can see that she was manipulating me. My mother indulged me because Danika was part of a large, wealthy family, and schooled in the proper etiquette of the elite. I had thought that she'd be a good match for me not only because of the money, but because she knew how to perform in front of a camera."

"The media loved her," she said, remembering the *Boston Globe* articles that focused on the couple.

He sighed. "Ah yes, well, I guess I did fancy myself in love with her at the time. The paparazzi noticed us when we went out in public and we got caught up in the limelight. But then, after we got married, the dynamic of the relationship shifted. She became less attentive and started making outrageous demands." He slid his fingers down her back, creating tingles of awareness along her skin. "Evidently, her father had kept her on a tight budget, and never let her do much on her own. Being married to me meant she was finally free." He shook his head and pressed his lips against her forehead. "I didn't realize she was using me as a bottomless bank account until it was too late."

"Is that why you divorced her?"

He leaned back and considered her for a moment before responding. "I didn't divorce her right away, no. I wanted to make it work, not only for me, but for my family. Her family had given us a lot of money and property as part of the marriage and to divorce so soon would have made us look bad." He offered her a wry smile. "But the constant arguing and betrayal took its toll. Eventually I was so desperate to get rid of her that I agreed to an outrageous settlement." He let out a long breath. "The money gave her financial freedom from her father, but put Perconti Enterprises in the red. We've been struggling to get out of it ever since."

"She has a stake in your company?"

"No, but she wants it. She gets a yearly allowance as long as I am able to pay it. If she can prove that I am late or missing payments, then she will take half of all my assets."

"Why not just give her what she wants and make a clean break?"

He shook his head. "Because half of all of my assets would include a sizable portion of Perconti Enterprises. I am the controlling shareholder, but if Danika got half of what I own, I will lose control of the one thing that has kept my family afloat for all of these years. And that's not all." He eased back from her and walked a short distance away. "She has found a loophole in the settlement that allows her to apply for more money if my personal assets increase, which they will after this marriage. As a Perconti Enterprises shareholder, my money will triple with this union."

"Unbelievable."

"She is using that loophole to try to force my hand. She came to remind me that if I don't pay her in proportion to my newfound wealth, not only would I lose my hotels, but she would make all of my secrets public."

"Like the pills."

Leo steeled his jaw and looked down into his hands. "Yes. But that's not all."

"There's more?"

He hesitated a moment before answering. "There are things you don't know about me, *cara*. I'm afraid . . . I'm afraid that if I told you the truth, you'd run away."

Karin slipped her fingers in between his and led him to the couch. "I'm not Danika, Leo. I won't hurt you like she did."

"I know, it's just—"

She patted the seat on the couch next to her, urging him to sit. "I want to help you, but I can't unless you tell me."

He looked down to their joined hands. Karin held her

breath and willed him to answer her question. It was a long
moment before he responded. "I mentioned that my father
committed suicide, but what I never told you was that I had
a brush with death as well," he whispered as he sat down
beside her.

He met her surprised gaze. His mouth ran dry and for
a moment he wondered if he was making the right decision by telling her. *Too late to turn back now.*

"To understand, you must first know more of what
happened to my father," he said. "Soon after I arrived in
Naples, a new article came out about us—we were supposed to be the new father-and-son team who would take
the world by storm, but the article itself wasn't about our
success and hard work. Buried deep within its pages, the
reporter talked but about my father's parties and the women
he brought back to his home. He said that if my father went
over his company books with as much enthusiasm as he
did chasing skirts, Perconti Enterprises would be four
times the company it was." Leo shook his head. "The very
same reporters who had built him up, were encouraging
him to do scandalous things so that they could tear him
down and sell papers."

"Oh, Leo." She moved to hug him, but he eased away.
He couldn't touch her, not yet.

"No, there's more. I wanted you to hear everything, so
I'll tell you."

"Okay." She pulled her hands away. "Tell me."

He took a deep breath. "My father found me reading the
article. When I questioned him about his partying, he told
me that the reporter was lying. When I showed him a second article, backing up the first, he called them all liars,
and told me to stop reading such trash."

"They were tabloids?"

"Not all of them, but to my father, any publication that
spoke poorly of him was considered garbage." Leo sighed.

"I thought the matter was over, but then I caught him the next morning reading the article I'd talked about the night before. He had never read any article before that, said it was useless reading things he already knew. I think that was the first time he realized how he had been manipulated and used by the people he trusted."

"It wasn't your fault."

"He never would have realized what was happening to him if it wasn't for me."

"You're being too hard on yourself."

"Am I? My father read the paper every morning after that and started withdrawing more and more into himself. He committed suicide one year later." He let out a disgusted noise. "It made quite the headline."

"I'm so sorry."

"So I took the reins of Perconti Enterprises, determined to not let the press destroy me like they did my father."

He moved to the window as old memories flooded to the surface. "I threw myself into my work and spent years building Perconti Enterprises up into my father's vision, but running a company is a lonely business." He ran his finger along the windowpane. "Marco tries hard, but he's a little too self-centered to see the big picture. I also think that he blames me a little because Father trained me, not him, to take over the business. After he died, Mother relied on me, not him. I think . . . I think he might feel like I brush him aside, but the truth is quite the opposite."

"Does your brother know how much the business is struggling now?"

Leo shook his head and moved toward the bar. "I've tried telling him that the problem runs much deeper than the Palazzo, but his whole world is this hotel. He has no idea of the extent of the damage. Then there is the issue of his love of the camera."

Karin frowned. "He likes to be seen, doesn't he?"

"Yes." He started rearranging the bottles and decanters, lining them all up in perfect rows. "I think he might have some sort of craving for attention. He lives for the moment, and rarely thinks about the future. He's constantly chasing the next good time." Satisfied that the bar was in order, he moved to the coffee table, arranging the magazines so that they were displayed in perfect piles, parallel to the edges of the table. "At least he knows enough about the business to keep the Palazzo running by himself. It has been a great help to me."

"That's good."

He moved over to sit next to her on the couch. "Like my father, I tend to micromanage the hotels, which lends itself to a lot of traveling and living on the road. It can get lonely." He took her hands and averted his gaze. This next part no one knew about except for Danika. Not even his brother Marco, his closest family member, knew of his struggles over these last two years. "When Danika left, things got worse. I realized that the possibility of having a family, of settling down with someone and leading a somewhat normal life, was gone forever. The depression and anxiety I had kept under control for years started to get the better of me."

"But you never told anyone about this."

"No," he whispered, the full realization of the pain he had been holding inside for years hitting him head-on. "I thought I could manage it with over-the-counter sedatives, but I was wrong. One night in Milan, on the night that would have been Danika's and my one-year-wedding anniversary, the anxiety became difficult to control. I . . . I didn't keep track of how many pills I had taken . . . If Gio hadn't found me, I'm not sure I'd be sitting here today." He shook his head. "I told him that I was just stressed over the business and needed a good night's sleep. After taking me to the hospital, he canceled my engagements and reported that I was suffering from exhaustion, but I think he always suspected something more. At any rate, I started seeing a new doctor, got new medication, and here I am."

"You see a psychologist?"

"Psychiatrist, yes. He's in Milan, which is where I spend most of my time. When I can't meet there, I either fly him out to where I am or we talk over the phone, depending on how badly I need him." He hesitated before continuing. "I need to feel in control in order to keep the depression at bay. This . . . compulsiveness can come out in strange ways."

"Like straightening things on the bar that are already neat."

He glanced over at the bar, where everything had been picked up and neatly arranged. Did he do that? The cleaning compulsion was so much a part of him that he didn't notice.

"This is a lot to take in." She stood and walked over to the fireplace.

"I know. And I don't expect you to want me now that you know the truth. But I needed you to know what Danika was holding over me. It's not just the hotels or things we do in the bedroom. She knows about my condition. She knows my family history and how much damage it would do to our company if my struggles with depression were ever made public. They'd start digging, and find out about my hospitalization. Those vultures would spin the incident to entice readers and make me look unstable."

"Your customers would lose faith."

"In a manner of speaking, yes. Our investors would question my ability to lead, as well."

Karin wrinkled her brow in thought. "So no one in your family knows about this?"

"No one except Danika, and now you."

"You need to tell them. Especially since depression is

hereditary. Some of your siblings might be struggling with depression right now and not even know it."

Leo thought of Dante's drinking and Marco's sleeping around. "You may be right."

"I *am* right." She inched closer to him. "More importantly, you need to go public with this information."

"Haven't you been listening? If I go public, I'll lose half of my shares and controlling interest in Perconti Enterprises. The investors will lose faith and we'd go bankrupt."

"Not necessarily." She smiled as she put her hand on his leg. "Do your siblings have shares in the company as well?"

"Yes, but nowhere near enough—"

"Perhaps separately it isn't enough, but what if you all pool your shares together? Together, you would have more shares than Danika, or anyone else."

"Perhaps, but—"

"For so long you have been taking care of your siblings. Let them do something for you in return."

"I'm not sure they would just give me their shares in the company."

"Would it be so bad if they didn't? You said yourself that you are on the road all the time. Perhaps it's time you spread out the responsibility. I think your siblings are more than ready for it."

He thought about that for a moment. She may have a point. "It may not be enough to dig us out of the hole I created."

"It will be a start. After talking with your siblings, you might all come to the realization that some downsizing might be in order."

"Downsizing?"

"Streamlining. Or perhaps dividing the company up into divisions, each with their own unique focus." She waved her hand in the air in dismissal. "We can work out the details later. The point is that you'd all be doing this together. Your siblings will feel as if they have ownership, and you will have the help you need."

We can work out the details . . . Did that mean she wanted to stay and help? That one small word gave him hope. Leo looked down at their joined hands as he ran through the possibilities. "What about the investors and the media?"

"If you do it in the right way, you could gain sympathy for our cause. I bet if you put in place a plan to the investors, things won't be as bad as you think."

"But the depression—"

"Could be used to our advantage." She leaned in closer. "You are managing the depression, Leo. It's not managing you. There's a difference. If you make a public confession, and they see you are well, it will make a difference, I'm sure of it."

"You think so?" He ran his thumb across her cheek, enjoying the soft feel of her skin.

She nodded and leaned into his touch. "Don't you see? The best way to dig ourselves out of this mess of lies is to come clean with our secrets and start over."

"Maybe." Leo dropped his fingers and squeezed her hand. He desperately wanted to believe her, but there was still too much that was unknown.

"This is right, Leo. I can feel it. You can't continue down the path you're heading. The company will go belly-up. It's time to pull the rug out from under these reporters and use their hunger for a story to our advantage."

Leo thought long and hard about her words. She had a point, but there were so many details to work out. Hours of planning and late-night strategy meetings.

"We would have to time it perfectly," he said. "I wouldn't want the negative publicity to affect Arianna's wedding."

Karin pulled away, slightly. "We shouldn't put so much weight on this wedding."

He ignored her comment and took her hands again, tugging her closer. "With the money from this new marriage, and the streamlining of hotels, we could start over once more. We could build it right, so it can weather the changes in economy."

"Yes." She grinned. "Exactly."

"There's just one thing."

"What's that?"

He laced his fingers with hers. "I'll need someone to help me. Someone who knows the hotel business and can help with the announcement and the reorganization. Someone who can help keep me on the straight and narrow."

"Someone?"

He leaned forward until only a sliver of air separated their lips. "You." When her eyes widened, he rushed to continue. "If you're up for it, that is."

"Of course I am, Leo." She framed his face with her palms. "You can lean on me. I'm here for you."

He closed his eyes and rested his forehead against hers as all of the stress and loneliness of the past few weeks rose to the surface. "I've missed you, Karin."

"I've missed you, too."

He tilted his head and captured her mouth with his own. He had never tasted anything so sweet, so soft. Tears stung his eyes as he moved his head and deepened the kiss. She opened to him immediately, and Leo was rewarded with her addictive taste. He groaned as he snaked his arms around her and pulled her onto his lap. She let out the most perfect feminine squeal as her leg rubbed against his cock.

There had been far too many lonely nights, far too much time apart. Leo couldn't get enough of her. It was probably unwise to take advantage of Karin in his sister's suite, but he couldn't help himself. Leo slid his hand up under her blouse and cupped her breast through her bra.

She moaned against his mouth and threaded her fingers through his hair.

His cock thickened, and he gently eased her breast out of her bra. Her nipple pebbled in his hand, and he ran his palm over it as desire rose up through his veins.

"I need you, *cara*."

"I need you, too."

He pinched and stroked her breast as he invaded her mouth. "Ride me," he whispered against her lips.

She pulled back. "What?"

"Ride me." He undid the zipper of his suit pants. "I want to feel inside of you."

She stood in front of him and slipped off her khakis, revealing white, creamy skin that left him weak and needy. He hurried to free his lengthening erection, but fumbled with his buckle. He swore as he picked at the metal, cursing himself for being more eager than a schoolboy. If he wasn't careful, he'd finish before he even began.

"Let me." She had already stripped from the waist down, and Leo couldn't help but stare at the prize before him.

She was more beautiful than he remembered—and far more elegant. He reached out and ran his fingers through her curls as she undid his pants and freed his cock.

"My pants pocket—"

She slid her hand in his pocket and raised her brows. "Do you always carry a condom around with you?"

He brushed his lips against hers and grinned. "Let's just say that I'm always hopeful."

"Hopeful." She straddled his thighs.

Leo slid his finger through her wet folds. "Ah, *cara*."

"I don't want to wait this time, Leo," she whispered as

she rolled the condom over his length. "Please don't make me wait."

"No." He grabbed the base of his cock and positioned himself at her opening. "We have already waited long enough." He rubbed his swollen head through her folds, preparing them both. She framed his face with her hands and plunged her tongue into his mouth. Never before had a woman tasted so good. Before he realized what he was doing, Leo grabbed her hips and dragged her down on his cock. As her wet heat surrounded him, he groaned his appreciation. Finally, he was home.

Karin leaned back and gasped as he filled her core. She had been dreaming of this, wanting it with every fiber of her being.

"Yes," she whispered. "God, Leo, yes." She started moving her hips, enjoying the wonderful friction between her legs. Desire surged through her lower abdomen, twisting around her muscles and giving her a sense of urgency. Leo slid one hand back up under her shirt and teased her exposed breast once more. She loved it when he did that. Never before had anyone been so attentive to her needs.

"You like pain," he said as he pinched her nipple again, sending another spark of pain through her system.

Karin moaned and leaned her head back as pleasure rolled through her body.

"We shall have to explore this in more depth, *cara*." He pinched her again, then moved his free hand to her clit. "But for now, just ride me. I want you to take control."

She hesitated. "You what?"

He offered her a seductive smile. "You always had the reins, *cara*. I just didn't realize it until now."

His words rippled through her, making her weak with

need. He grabbed her hips to hold her steady as she moved faster. Again and again she pushed him inside her body, losing herself in the moment.

He rubbed her clit and breast in the same manner, first pinching, then rubbing them in a circular motion.

She widened her legs, wanting him deeper. No matter how hard she tried, she couldn't get close enough, couldn't feel enough. She grabbed onto his shirt, holding on as she raced closer and closer to her goal.

On the next thrust, he shifted his position on her clit, sending fresh waves of joy through her system. Her orgasm hit her hard, and she cried out as her body went limp with ecstasy. Leo wrapped his arms around her and held her close as he pushed his hips off the couch and entered her again and again, lengthening her pleasure. Within seconds he buried his face in her neck and groaned as he, too, fell over the edge into oblivion.

She collapsed on top of him, and for a time, they laid together in silence. Each of them was unwilling to move and break the wonderful spell that had been placed over them.

After a few long, blissful moments, he kissed her temple and eased her off him. Karin cringed at the sense of loss, but knew that it was inevitable.

"Come on," he said as he tucked himself back into his pants and stood. "The sooner we get this mess over with, the sooner I can have you all to myself." He let his gaze roam purposefully over her body. "And I will have you all to myself, *cara*. Make no mistake of that."

Karin shivered as she put on her clothes and let him lead her to the elevator. "What are we going to do?"

"First we'll talk to Marco and Dante. Then we'll strategize what to do from there." He squeezed her hand as the elevator doors opened. "Ready?"

"Ready." She smiled as he led her into the elevator. It felt good reclaiming her future. She only hoped that her idea didn't blow up in their faces.

One Week Later

Things were going better than expected. Leo's siblings had taken his confessions in stride and were appropriately outraged at Danika's blackmail. They agreed to pool their shares of Perconti Enterprises together, and Karin's idea that each of them take some control was met with enthusiasm. Leo would remain in charge, of course, but much of his responsibility would be delegated to his siblings, who would each head up their own division of the company.

All of his siblings welcomed Karin with open arms. Arianna even let out a very girly squeal and embraced her like a sister. His mother and the twins were supportive as well. None of them had liked Danika, as it turned out, and all were relieved that he was finally waking up and getting out from under her thumb.

All that was left was planning the announcement. It was Dante's idea to announce the Perconti Enterprises restructuring before the wedding, and when Marco noted that the wedding could mark a new beginning for the family, everyone seemed to get on board. Arianna looked a little pale at the thought of her wedding being so important, but Leo figured that it was just new bride jitters. A phone conference later, and Arianna's fiancé was on board with the plan. After everything was set and the families merged, Leo was sure that he'd be able to bring the Perconti family into a new age of security and prosperity.

Everything was in place for the announcement. Karin had practiced the speech with him numerous times, so Leo didn't really need notes. As the media looked on, he announced the restructuring of Perconti Enterprises and how with this marriage, he hoped to completely change how people bought and viewed vacations.

It felt good having his family behind him as he talked. They were right where they should be, and Leo wondered why the hell he had waited so long to tell them his secrets.

This was all Karin's doing, he realized. He owed her so much. Not only his own emotional well-being, but his family's.

"And none of this would be possible without the help of Karin Norell," he said, concluding his speech. Leo glanced back, took her hand, and tugged her forward until she stood next to him. "Karin has been crucial in this restructuring, and her experience will be invaluable to me and this company going forward." He hesitated, making sure that all eyes were on him. "Therefore, I'm making her a full partner in Perconti Enterprises. She will oversee the day-to-day restructuring efforts, and bring Perconti Enterprises to an even higher standard."

Leo smiled at Karin, who widened her eyes in surprise. He had told his siblings that he wanted to do something grand for his little maid, and was surprised when they had proposed this idea. Each of them would give her some of their shares, giving her a vested interest in the company's prosperity. This new position would not only give her the security she was looking for, but would keep her firmly by his side for the next several years.

He squeezed Karin's hand and returned his attention to the reporters before him. "I'll now take a few questions."

Many of them raised their hands. Leo chose one, who asked about some of the details of the restructuring efforts.

"I think that's a question for Ms. Norell."

Karin shook her head, but Leo urged her forward. She cautiously took the podium and answered the question.

When the reporters raised their hands once more, Leo urged her to take another question. As she did, he took a step back, admiring how, as seconds passed, she seemed to grow more and more confident. He had made a good choice, he realized. With a little coaching, she'd do very well as a Perconti Enterprises partner.

His partner. Leo's cock thickened as he thought of Karin being his partner, not only in business, but in life. There was no question about it, Leo needed her like he needed air. The time they had spent apart had been torture, and he was determined never to have them separated again.

"Next question," Karin said. This time, Amanda Vaughn spoke up before Karin could choose someone, forcing everyone's gaze toward her.

"Rumor has it that you and Mr. Perconti had a sexual relationship in the weeks leading up to this announcement. Is this what led you to be named his partner?"

Leo's happiness turned to anger. He marched up to the microphone and caught Karin before she could respond. "You don't have to answer that." He nudged her aside and took his spot behind the podium. "I'll have you know, Ms. . . ."

"Vaughn."

"Ms. Vaughn, that our personal relationship has nothing to do with this decision. Ms. Norell has long been a valuable member of the Palazzo's team, and during her tenure she has proven herself again and again."

"As an intern."

"Yes, at first it was as an intern. But more recently . . ."

The reporter looked down at her notes. "More recently, she has been cleaning the bathrooms of the hotel suites, has she not? Or has she been doing things not agreed upon during the strike negotiations?"

Leo fisted his hands, too angry to speak. A strong hand touched his arm, easing him aside.

"More recently, she has been involved in making management decisions concerning the logistics and publicity for our sister's wedding." Marco stood by Leo's side and leaned forward so that he could be heard through the microphone. "The decision to promote Ms. Norell was not made by my brother alone, but by all of us. Ms. Norell has become a valuable asset to our management team."

Dante stepped forward and stood on the other side of Leo. "Agreed. She has not only counseled us on the wedding preparations, but has made deals with the local businesses in an effort to keep them thriving as the popularity of our hotel chain grows. She knows the value of keeping the neighborhoods prosperous to attract customers, and holds a lot of the same Perconti values."

"This is a family decision," Arianna said as she stepped up next to Karin. "In fact, I have rearranged my wedding party to make sure she is a part of it. That is how much she has done for this business and this family."

Karin stared at Ari with wide eyes. Leo guessed that his siblings' vocal support was as much a surprise to her as it was to him.

Leo's heart filled with pride as he glanced sideways at his brothers and sister. For so long he had believed that he had to do everything on his own. Now here they were, supporting him, and he couldn't be prouder.

With a smug smile, he turned and faced the reporter. "Does that answer your question?"

Amanda Vaughn frowned and sat down. Other media personnel raised their hands, but Leo shrugged them off. "Now, if you'll excuse us, we have a wedding to plan, and you're all invited." He waved his hand over the crowd. "Richards, make sure that everyone here has an invitation to the wedding." He motioned to his staff in the back of the room. As the crowd murmured with excitement, he took Karin's hand and left the podium.

"Thank you so much," he said to his siblings.

"Don't worry about it," Marco said as he clasped Leo's back. "That's what family is for. We support each other."

"Don't look now," Arianna said, "but here comes trouble."

Leo glanced over their shoulders at Danika, quickly approaching. A fierce frown etched her delicate features.

"We'll take care of this," Dante said as he nodded to Karin. "I think once Danika realizes that we are all standing together, she'll back down and leave us alone."

"Even if she doesn't," Marco added, "we'll handle this for you. It's the least we can do after everything you have done for us."

Leo glanced at his siblings in surprise. "But—"

"You've been handling things by yourself for too long now," Ari said, cutting off his train of thought. She grinned and nudged Karin's arm. "Now, you two get out of here and have some alone time. I think you deserve it."

"Thank you." Leo glanced at all of his siblings. "All of you."

"Go on, get out of here." Marco patted him on his back. "We'll cover for you."

Leo grinned. "I won't forget this."

"Neither will we." Arianna turned to Karin. "Thank you for bringing us our brother back." She quickly hugged Karin and then pushed both her and Leo toward the elevator. "Now go, before that shrew catches up to you."

"Leo," Danika said as she waved her hand in the air. "Leo."

"Right." Leo took Karin's hand once again and steered her toward the elevator. As the doors closed, Leo could see his brothers intercepting Danika as she came barreling toward them.

As they began to move back up to the penthouse suite, he sighed and slumped against the wall. "Thank goodness that's over."

It was then that he noticed that Karin was strangely quiet. He glanced in her direction and frowned. "Is everything all right, *cara*?"

Karin lifted her chin and met his gaze. That was when he noticed the tears in her eyes. "As okay as one can be after her entire life has been planned out for her."

Chapter 19

Everything Karin had ever dreamed about was coming true, and yet it felt as if the walls were closing in around her.

"Isn't this what you want?" Leo asked as he straightened away from the wall. "To help more with the business decisions of running a hotel?"

"Yes, it is. It's just . . ." She didn't know how to put it into words. Everything was happening so fast. "I guess I wanted to do things on my own timetable. My own terms."

"Ah, I see," he said.

"You do?"

"Yes." He took her hand as the elevator doors opened. "You're not in control."

"I guess." She'd never quite thought of it that way, but she supposed he was right. She had always been in control of her future. Now, with one speech, Leo had taken all of that away and planned out every detail, giving it to her tied up in a neat little bow.

"Let me ask you this," he said as he pulled her into the penthouse suite. "Do you want this new job, or do you want to continue as an intern?"

"I haven't even finished school yet," she said as she followed him into the living room. "I can't take this job. I don't have enough experience."

"That's not what I asked." He led her in front of the coffee table in the living area. "I asked if you *wanted* this job."

"Well . . ." She thought about it. "Of course. It's like a dream come true."

"It's me then," he said. "You don't like working so closely with me." He trailed his fingers over the buttons on her blouse.

"No, don't be ridiculous. Of course I like it."

He tilted his head and studied her face as he began to undo the buttons. "Then it's our personal relationship. You don't like our relationship interfering with your work."

"No, it's not that."

He softened his voice as he hooked his finger under her chin. "You didn't have control over the situation. This is true. And I have to admit, this was my siblings' idea, not mine, but the more I think about it, the more I believe it is right for us. We are a team, *cara*, you and I." He lowered his hands to her blouse. "Don't you agree?"

"Yes." She could feel her buttons popping open, one by one. Desire sparked in her lower abdomen, and her skin heated. "What are you doing?"

"Convincing you that it's better to trust the people who care about you, instead of trying to do everything on your own. We can accomplish so much more together than apart." A faint smile touched his lips. "It's a tough lesson, I know, but a valuable one to learn."

"Why should I trust you with my future?"

He raised his brows at her, as if asking, *Don't you already know?* "Because I know what you need, *cara*. Not what you *think* you need, but what you *really* need."

Karin closed her eyes as he pressed his lips to the sensitive spot just below her ear. "And what do I need?"

He chuckled, and his breath brushed past her ear. "Me." He slipped her shirt off her shoulders and kissed a hot, wicked trail down her neck and shoulder.

Karin groaned and leaned her head to the side, giving him better access. "God, Leo, that feels so good."

She grabbed his shirt as he continued to blaze a trail across her skin.

"We deserve happiness, *cara,* and I'm prepared to show you just how good being with me can be."

Leo raised his head and captured her lips. Karin clung to his shirt as he invaded her mouth, kissing her until she felt dizzy. Slowly he removed her shirt, until it hung by nothing but her wrists.

"Let go, Karin," he said as he broke away from her lips.

She did as she was told. He slipped her shirt from her arms and folded it over onto itself.

"What are you doing?" she asked.

He glanced up from his project. "Teaching you how to trust. Now, turn around."

She did. He started to slip the shirt over her eyes, but then changed his mind.

"No. I want your complete and total trust, and for that you must see what I'm doing." He inched her over until she stood in front of the coffee table. "Now, bend over for me, *cara.* Place your hands on the table."

She did as she was told. The table was low, and the position stuck her backside up in the air. Heat raced through her center, making her wet between her thighs. "What are you going to do?"

She flinched as his palm slapped her bare skin. Karin lurched forward, then struggled to reposition herself on the table. The slap hurt, but as the pain subsided, fresh waves of pleasure wound through her core, causing her to groan.

"I thought you might like that." He slipped his fingers under the waist of her skirt and tugged it down her legs. Without thinking, she lifted each foot in turn, allowing him to remove it from her body completely.

"Red, I approve," he said. It took her a moment to realize that he was referring to her thong.

"I'm glad."

"Everything you do pleases me, *cara*." He slid his fingers over where he'd just hit, soothing away her ache. "But as much as I like this article of clothing, I'm afraid it will have to go. It will just get in the way for what I have planned."

Karin's skin tingled with excitement as he removed her thong. She closed her eyes and focused on his fingers brushing over her skin, his breath against her most intimate of places.

"Very good, *cara*. Now." She heard the click of his shoes as he walked away. "Now the real fun begins." He tapped her on her ass. "Don't move."

Karin watched him as he headed over to the bar. "What are you doing?"

"You know better than to ask questions." He searched around behind the bar, then placed the ice bucket on top. Slowly he filled it from the small freezer, placing the ice cubes inside one by one.

Karin's mouth went dry as she thought of all the things he could do with the ice cubes. She imagined them running over her body, of them moving across her lips. All the while, the steady clink of cubes echoed throughout the room.

As seconds passed, she became wetter, hotter. Karin curled her fingers into the coffee table as he slowly filled the bucket.

"Now," he said as he dropped the last cube. "We let this sit." He jammed the tongs into the ice, picked up the container, and moved closer using slow, purposeful strides. With each step, Karin's whole body tingled with anticipation. She watched him as he placed the ice underneath her abdomen. "Don't touch."

She glanced down at the bucket, wondering just what he had planned. As she ruminated, he moved behind her and put his hand on her lower back. "We shall explore new things together, *cara,* and see how deep this affinity for pain goes."

Before she could process his words, he slapped her ass, making her jump. Her belly nudged the tongs and the ice bucket rattled beneath her.

"I said, don't touch." He hit her again, this time on the other cheek. Karin groaned and moistened her lips as both pain and pleasure swirled through her body.

She glanced over her shoulder. "I'm trying."

"And no talking, unless you want this to stop. You don't want me to stop, do you?" He slapped her again, and Karin shook her head as she shivered with need. The connection was firm, loud enough to hear a sharp crack, but not so hard that it felt jarring. Instead of dampening her desire, it added to it, causing moisture to collect between her thighs.

"Now," he said as he rubbed his fingers over her ass. "Face forward."

She did as she was told, focusing her attention on the bar. What was he going to do next? She kind of liked being spanked, but the bucket of ice was intriguing. She wanted to ask him, but didn't dare.

"I love how pink your skin gets, *cara,*" he murmured as he slipped his hand over her ass. "I could do this for hours." He chuckled at Karin's whimper and slipped his fingers down between her legs. When he caressed her folds, she bit her lip to keep from whimpering with desire.

"It seems you like our little play as well." He withdrew and walked slowly around to face her. "Now, let's go over the rules one more time so you don't forget." As he talked, he began to remove his clothing with slow, purposeful movements. He stood directly in her line of sight, giving her an eyeful of male perfection.

"We already said no talking unless spoken to, did we not?" He slipped his shirt from his shoulders, revealing his hard, muscular chest.

"Karin?"

She dragged her gaze away from his washboard abs and up to his face. "Yes." She sounded breathless, but didn't care. All she could think about was all of that strength and muscle between her legs.

"Good." He twitched his lips, as if holding back a smile. "And we said no moving, is that correct?" He undid his belt buckle and zipper. The loud clang of metal-on-metal drew her gaze down to his hips, where she saw his tented khakis.

"Karin?"

"Yes." She swallowed and dragged her gaze back up to meet his. "Yes."

"Good." He stripped off his shoes, socks, and pants, leaving only a pair of black silk boxers that matched the dark hair on his head. Karin focused on the spot in the center, the place where the material bunched and extended. She moistened her lips as she imagined taking his cock into her mouth, of pleasing him until he begged for mercy.

"Karin?"

She jerked her gaze back up to meet his. "Yes?"

"I asked you a question."

Oh hell. What did he say? She tried to think, but couldn't remember. She'd been too busy looking at the bulge in his boxers.

"Excuse me?" He cupped his hand to his ear, as if he couldn't hear her answer.

"I don't know the question." Her voice came out as a whisper.

"Thinking of other things, are we?" He grabbed something off the bar, but she couldn't see what it was.

"Y-Yes."

He chuckled as he slowly approached, palming the item from the bar. "Are you hungry, perhaps?"

She dropped her gaze back down to his cock. "Yes."

"We shall see what we can do about that. But first . . ." He knelt down beside her. "First I want you to look straight ahead at the far wall. Do you hear me?"

"Yes." She did as she was told. Apprehension filled her veins as he removed the bucket of ice and put it next to him on the floor.

"Good. I want you to stay like that, not speaking, not moving. I only want to hear your moans of pleasure. Am I clear?"

She nodded and braced herself, not knowing what he was going to do next.

"Relax, *cara*. Remember our lesson in trust?" He ran his fingers over her back and ass.

"Yes."

"Good. Then you know that I will give you everything you need when the time is right." He slapped her playfully on her backside. "That was for speaking out of turn earlier."

She steeled her jaw and kept her eyes straight ahead. She had no idea what he was going to do next, and this moment of anticipation was thrilling. He was right, she knew that he wouldn't hurt her. She held no fear, only excitement and desire.

"Yes *cara*, that's it." He reached underneath her body and gently tugged on her nipple. Karin groaned as he kneaded her breast.

She closed her eyes as he shifted his weight and flicked his warm, wet tongue over her skin. Pleasure spiraled out through her chest, infusing with her bloodstream and making her dizzy.

"You taste exquisite," he murmured as he took her in

his mouth. Karin shivered as another wave of pleasure spiraled through her system.

"So delicate." He switched to the other breast, preforming the same, sweet torture. First he massaged, then tugged, then took her into his mouth. Karin whimpered as desire roared through her, making her light-headed. Before she realized what she was doing, she bent her arms and lowered her torso to his waiting mouth.

Slap. Pain slammed through her body as he hit his palm against her backside. "I said, don't move."

She immediately straightened her arms and opened her eyes.

"That's it." He massaged where he had hit, sending spirals of pleasure through her system.

When he placed his lips on her nipple again, it took every ounce of her willpower to not sink closer to his waiting mouth. She concentrated on holding her body still as wave after wave of need flooded her system.

Then he eased back, giving her a moment to collect her thoughts. As her mind cleared, something cold rubbed up against her breast.

Karin gasped and curved her back, anxious to get away from whatever was numbing her nipple.

The sound of flesh on flesh cracked through the air as he spanked her again. "Don't move."

Karin glanced down the length of her torso, she couldn't help herself. She saw him use the thongs to hold a cube of ice up against her breast.

"Close your eyes," he ordered. "I don't want you to think, just feel."

She did as she was told. Cold blasted out over her nerves, freezing her skin. Her breath came out in short gasps as her mind filled with panic. She wanted to get away—the thing was so damn cold—but she didn't dare move.

"Relax, *cara*. Trust me."

She forced herself to uncurl her fingers and loosen the muscles in her back.

"That's it. Just relax." He rubbed the ice in circular motions, stimulating her sensitive skin. Around and around he went, until the cold subsided and pleasure blossomed in her chest. She moistened her lips and groaned as he rubbed her flesh. The air around them was still and quiet. The only sounds were of her moans and the dripping of water onto the coffee table.

"Now, *cara,* promise you'll tell me if this is too much." He removed the ice and she glanced back at him.

Leo lifted his hand as if to spank her. "I said don't move."

She quickly turned back around and faced the bar, unsure what he was going to do. Anticipation rippled over her skin and her pussy throbbed.

He picked up an ice cube from the bucket and moved out of her line of vision. Before she could ask what he was doing, she felt something cold press up against her folds.

"Hold still." He placed his palm on her lower back as she hissed and leaned forward. Gently, he pressed the ice cube against her sensitive skin until it dipped just inside her opening.

"You're so warm, *cara,*" he murmured. "Feel how quickly it's melting."

Karin moistened her lips as water from the ice slid down her inner thighs. The sharp cold had dissipated, and she moaned as he rubbed the cube back and forth over her skin.

"Do you like this?" he asked as he stilled his hand.

"Yes." She arched her back, silently urging him to continue.

"Good, then you'll love this." He pushed the partially melted cube up into her channel with his finger.

Karin whimpered and widened her stance. "You are a cruel man."

Slap. "No talking," he commanded, although Karin

could hear the humor in his voice. His spanking was more playful than hard, and Karin imagined him, standing behind her, filling her body and claiming her as his own.

He took a second cube and ran it along her spine. "You are doing well," he said. "Now close your eyes."

She did, concentrating on the ice as it moved over her back. First he slid it side to side, then in circles. Instead of feeling cold, the feel of ice made her hot, and it wasn't long before she wiggled under his touch. When he finally slipped the cube over her ass and into her opening, she groaned with pleasure.

"Soon, *cara*." He left the half-melted cube inside her and picked up another. Slowly, he walked around to her front. "But I want to tease you first."

Karin opened her eyes and noticed her position had put her eye level with his cock. She saw how this erotic play was affecting him. It was affecting her, too. While she liked him being in control, she wanted to see him lose a little of that arrogance and come apart in her arms. She moistened her lips and focused on the bead of moisture forming at the tip of his erection.

"I want to tease you, too."

He took the base of his shaft and slowly stroked himself from root to tip. "Is this what you want?"

"Yes." God, yes. She wanted to give him a taste of his own medicine. She wanted him to lose himself in pleasure, just like he did for her.

"Then take this. Show me what you want to do." He held out the cube to her lips.

Karin held his gaze and flicked her tongue over the edge. As his eyes darkened with lust, she rolled her tongue around the tip, then leaned forward and slowly licked the underside of the cube, tasting his fingers in the process.

He pulled away the cube and pressed his lips against hers. "You're good, *cara*. Very good."

"I can be better," she said, glancing down at his erection. Leo wrapped his fingers around his shaft and brought it to her lips. Karin slipped her tongue over the swollen head of his cock and groaned as his salty taste burst over her tongue.

"God, Karin."

She looked up and saw his eyes close in bliss. Encouraged, she slid her lips down over his shaft, filling her mouth before he changed his mind and pulled away.

Leo dropped the ice and pushed forward, allowing her to run her tongue over the vein on the underside of his shaft. She moved back and forth, quickly advancing and retreating, sliding her tongue over his sensitive vein in order to give him maximum pleasure.

"You little vixen." He grabbed her hair, tugging it slightly as he performed shallow thrusts into her mouth. Confidence filled her as she moved over his cock, taking him a little deeper each time.

Leo moaned as he filled her mouth, and Karin loved every second of it. "Pull harder," she requested as he retreated from her lips.

"Like this?" Pain sliced through her head as he lifted a section of hair.

"Yes." She took him into her mouth again, enjoying how with each stroke Leo seemed to fall deeper and deeper under her spell. She loved how he grabbed her hair in desperation, and how his voice echoed in the small space. She had never felt more desirable, or more wanton. She didn't want the moment to end.

Leo's thrusts slowed as he loosened his grip on her hair. "You're a tricky one," he mused as he retreated.

Karin grinned up at him, but said nothing.

"You thought that you could distract me." He slipped his hand down the side of her cheek, brushing her hair from her face. "But it didn't work." He trailed his fingers over her shoulder and back as he walked around behind her. "I'll have to punish you for this, you know." He picked up another piece of ice and trailed it over her lips. Karin groaned in response.

"Yes, a punishment." He reached underneath her and slid the ice over her nipple.

"Yes."

Leo's mouth covered hers as he rubbed the ice first over one breast, then the other. She felt the cube melting against her skin, and it wasn't long before water dripped off her pebbled nipples and onto the coffee table.

Karin moaned against his mouth as every muscle in her body tightened with need. She was so wet, so ready. All she wanted was for him to fill her and ease her ache. She couldn't imagine waiting any longer.

As soon as the ice melted completely, he pulled away and moved behind her. *Slap.* Karin yelped as Leo's hand connected with her backside. "That's for distracting me." *Slap.* Karin lurched forward as he hit the other cheek. Pleasure mingled with pain, taking her to heights she didn't know were possible.

"More," she pleaded.

He honored her request, alternating cheeks and using just enough pressure to stimulate, but not enough to harm her. Each time he connected with her flesh, her sense of urgency increased until her arms started shaking.

"Leo, please."

He paused in his movements. "Yes, it is time." He soothed her backside with his fingers, then moved away. Karin heard shuffling behind her and the familiar rip of plastic. "It is well past time."

"Wait."

The air around her went still, and Karin could feel the tension rising. She glanced at Leo over her shoulder. "Let me."

He raised his brows. "*Let* you?"

She nodded. "You have shown me the beauty in serving. Let me serve you."

"You already are," he said as he ran his palm over her backside. "You are giving me more than any woman ever has."

"No." She turned herself around so she was kneeling on the table. "I want to do more." She straightened, wrapped her arms around his neck, and pulled him down against her lips. Surprise lit his features as she slid her tongue into his mouth, claiming him for her own. She ran her fingertips over his shoulders and chest, enjoying the ripple of muscle there. He was so hard, so unyielding. It made her hungry for more.

He wrapped his fingers around her arms and gently pulled them away from his neck.

"Show me."

Smiling, she took the condom from his hands. "I'd love to." She slid her fingers down his chest and ran them over his shaft. Leo closed his eyes and fisted his hands as his cock lengthened under her fingertips.

Unable to resist, Karin bent down and ran her tongue over his swollen tip.

"Karin," he breathed as he unclenched his fists and ran them through her hair.

Karin grasped the base of his cock and moved her lips over his length, taking as much as she could. He tightened his fingers in her hair as she retreated, moving her hand and lips together as one.

Once, twice, three times she moved over his shaft. Each time Leo whispered a few more words of encouragement, and she felt a little more brazen. When she fully retreated, she slid her tongue along the underside of his length, then ran it over each of his balls, enjoying his moans of pleasure. She loved pleasing him, she realized, but more importantly, she loved catching him off guard. She wondered what else she could do to both please and surprise him.

Slowly, she took one of his balls into her mouth. He gasped and groaned as she gently tugged with her lips. Murmuring her name, he pushed her hair back from her face, and she glanced up at him as she retreated.

There was desire in his features, yes, but there was something more, something she couldn't quite define.

"Come here." He tugged her up to his lips and kissed her hard, robbing her of her strength. Karin wrapped her arms around his shoulders as he slid his hands down her spine and cupped them around her ass. Karin moaned as he tilted his head and deepened the kiss, stroking and claiming every inch of her mouth.

When he tried to lift her into the air, she placed her palms on his chest, stopping him. "No," she said as she tore away from the kiss.

"No?"

"Let me ride you."

"*Cara*—"

"Please." She slid her fingers down his chest and brushed them against her nipples.

He considered her for a moment, then lifted her in the air. "Very well," he said, turning their bodies. "We shall do it your way—this time."

She smiled as he sat and then leaned back until his entire torso was against the table.

"Thank you." She straddled his hips and gripped his shaft, pushing the tip of his cock inside her body.

Leo grasped her hips. "Wait."

"What?"

He reached up and slid his fingers down the side of her cheek. "Go slow."

"Make it last." She turned and kissed his palm as she retreated a fraction, then pushed down a little more.

"Yes." Leo returned his hand to her hip and closed his eyes. "Just like that, *cara*."

Karin took her time, first easing down, then retreating, taking a little more of him each time. Anticipation built, adding to her desire. When she finally pushed her hips flush with his, she whispered his name.

"I'm right here, *cara*," he said as he opened his eyes. "I'm not going anywhere."

He felt so good, so right. She held herself there for a moment, enjoying the feel of him inside of her, then slowly withdrew and impaled herself once more.

"Yes," he murmured. "God, you're so wet." He grabbed her hips to steady her as she pushed down again and again. Karin leaned forward and placed her hands on his chest to steady herself. Need pulsed through her veins, winding them tight. Her moans became whimpers of pleasure, mingling with Leo's groans as their bodies came together as one. With each thrust, Karin's urgency heightened. She widened her legs, allowing him to penetrate her deeper. Again and again she slammed into his cock, filling her with his passion. Her breathing quickened as she started moving against him, and the world around them faded away. Nothing existed for her outside this man, this moment.

He slid his hands up from her hips and cupped her breasts, pinching her nipples between his fingers. At the same time he raised his hips, changing the angle and hitting a sensitive spot deep inside her core.

"Come for me, *cara*," he commanded as he thrust up and into her body. His voice was like a drug. She couldn't help but obey. One second she was standing on the edge, the next she tumbled over into oblivion. Karin cried out as her orgasm ran through her body, slicing through her system like a thunderclap. Pleasure poured through her, filling every inch of her with bliss.

Leo arched his back and tightened his grip on her breasts. Within seconds, he whispered her name as he, too, tumbled over the edge into oblivion.

They both hung there, suspended in the moment. Karin didn't know when anything had ever felt so good, or so right. Leo was an amazing man. He seemed to know just what to do and say in order to give her maximum pleasure. Not only that, but he respected her. He wanted to make her a partner.

She had no idea how she had gotten so lucky, but she knew that she could never let him go. Ever.

Leo eased her off his cock and gathered her into his arms. In a few purposeful strides, he carried her to the bedroom and placed her on the mattress. Within moments, he was beside her, pulling up a throw blanket to cover their nakedness. As he spooned his body with hers, Karin had never felt more content in her life.

"That was amazing," she said.

"It was." He brushed the hair back from her face. "Did you think about my offer?"

"Offer?"

"To be my partner. In everything."

She turned around and met his gaze. "What are you asking?"

"For now, I just want you to stay on after the restructuring. I want you to travel with me and help oversee all of our hotels around the globe."

She was touched that he asked her to stay with him, rather than assuming she'd say yes. It meant that he had listened to her earlier when she had said that she wanted to make her own decisions.

When she didn't immediately respond, he rubbed his nose against hers. "The position comes with a few perks."

"Perks?"

"Yes."

"Like?"

He frowned. "Like this." He slid his arm around her waist and pulled her close, allowing her to feel every inch of his naked body. "And this."

She giggled and slid her fingers down the side of his cheek. "I like the perks."

"Good." His grin disappeared and his expression became serious. "I need you, Karin. I can't do this without you."

"You have me, Leo." She framed his face with her palms. "You can lean on me whenever you need it."

He raised his brows. "Does that mean you accept the position?"

"Yes, I accept the position." She rubbed her hips against his. "I accept every position you have to offer."

He rolled his eyes and groaned at her bad pun. "Good, this makes things easier."

"Easier?"

"I would've gone to any lengths to keep you at my side. It would have been tragic if I had to kidnap you."

"Kidnapping, eh?" She made a show of thinking about it. "How would you keep me here?"

"I'd tie you to the bed, of course." He turned her over, and settled on top of her. "I'd pin you here until you agreed to stay."

"Sounds romantic," she said, letting her sarcasm show in her voice.

"Ah, but it is." He rubbed his growing erection against her thigh. "It can be very romantic. Let me show you."

Karin squealed as he captured her mouth and showed her exactly what he intended to do with his new prize.

The man was a stickler for details.

Chapter 20

Everything was ready—except the bride.

Leo paced back and forth at the entrance to the large ballroom, waiting for Arianna.

"Where the hell is she?" Marco asked as he passed Leo in the hallway. The brothers were pacing back and forth in completely opposite directions as time seemed to slip through their fingers.

"Ah, relax. You know Arianna. She likes to take her time," Dante said from where he leaned up against the wall. He had half shut his eyes and crammed his hands in the pockets of his tuxedo. He looked about ready to fall asleep, which made Leo suspect that he had been drinking again. If he wasn't so damn anxious about Arianna, he'd go dunk Dante's head in one of the bathroom sinks to sober him up.

But today wasn't about Dante. It was about the Perconti family, and how they were finally going to get out of debt.

He stopped pacing and glanced inside the ballroom once more. Everyone who was anyone had gathered. His mother had already been seated in the front row, and the twins Gio and Gianna were standing around with programs in case there were any late arrivals. The press had prime seats in the front of the room, and the priest was sitting in a decorated folding chair placed on the pulpit.

Flowers were everywhere. Orchids, gardenias, and roses dotted the ends of the rows, each outlined with red ribbon and lace. The plain Berber carpet was hidden underneath a crimson path, rolled out moments before by his brothers. An electronic beep went off behind him, causing him to jump.

Marco swore and picked up his cell. "We better go. The groom is asking for us."

"He's probably wondering if everything is all right," Dante said from behind closed eyelids.

Leo slapped his brother on the arm. "And everything *is* all right." He glanced at Marco. "You tell him that."

Marco texted back to the groom and put away his cell. "He's anxious to get started."

"We all are." Leo ran his hand over his face and pulled out his pocket of pills. His anxiety was climbing and he'd give anything to have all of this over with.

"Can't you text that girlfriend of yours and find out what's going on?" Marco asked.

"I did," Leo admitted. *Three times.*

"What did she say?" Marco asked.

"She didn't reply. I think her phone is off."

"That can't be a good sign," Dante observed.

After a brief moment of silence, Marco stopped pacing. "Well, you should text her again."

Leo was done texting. He hated being ignored. He hated being left in the dark about his sister's welfare even more.

"I'm going to do one better," Leo said as he took his medication then put the pills back into his tuxedo pocket. "I'm going to go up there and find out what the hell is going on." He grabbed Dante's arm and yanked him from the wall. "You two go stall the groom."

"All right, all right, no need to get testy." Dante brushed

off his tux where Leo had touched it. "The ceremony is the boring part anyway." He grinned at Leo. "Everyone knows that the reception is much more fun."

"And keep him away from the liquor," Leo shouted at Marco as his brothers started for the annex to the ballroom.

Marco raised his hand in the air in acknowledgement.

Leo steeled his jaw as he watched his brothers leave. Arianna and Karin should have come down over an hour ago. While it was entirely possible that his sister was still getting herself ready, Leo couldn't shake the feeling that something was horribly wrong.

He signaled the priest at the other end of the room, letting him know that it would only be a few more minutes. After seeing the old man nod, Leo headed for the elevators. As he pushed the button for the floor with the penthouse suite, he hoped that his instincts were wrong. He leaned back against the mirrored wall of the elevator and replayed their last few conversations in his head.

He knew that his sister was less than thrilled about entering a loveless marriage. Leo had asked her if she was involved with anyone else, someone who might object to her circumstances. Her new husband would keep her well-funded and she could do what she pleased. She didn't even have to see him after the ceremony if she didn't want to. Leo didn't care, as long as his family would be pulled out of debt and rise up to its former glory. For far too long he had been under intense pressure to keep everything together. With Arianna's wedding, the pressure would finally be off him, and he'd be free to focus on his own life—and Karin.

Leo thought of Karin and smiled. He was so lucky to have found her. She would be a real asset to the business, and her skills at negotiating would help to keep his selfish siblings in line. She was a real asset to him as well. After sharing some of his secrets with her, Leo felt as if a huge weight had been lifted from his shoulders.

Yes, after this wedding, he looked forward to spending as much time as he could in that lovely woman's arms.

The elevator doors opened, and he strode purposefully out into the penthouse suite, expecting to see a small crowd of women fussing over his sister. There was no one.

"Where the hell is everyone?" he bellowed as he roamed from one room to the next. "Arianna? Karin?"

"I'm out here," Karin called from the balcony.

Leo stormed from the back room out to the balcony. "What the devil are you doing out here? Where's Arianna?"

Karin circled her arms around her waist and sighed. "I'm out here, trying to gather up the courage to talk to you. As for your sister . . . she's gone."

"What?" Leo strode over to Karin and grabbed her arms. "Gone? Where?" When Karin didn't immediately answer, he tightened his grip. "You have to tell me."

Karin averted her gaze. "She left."

"What?"

"She ran, Leo." Karin lifted her chin and steeled it in defiance. "She doesn't want to marry Landon."

"You're kidding." Leo let go of Karin and ran his hand over his face. "This is terrible." He turned his back to her and walked a short distance away.

"I know that you think this is the end of the world."

"End of the world?" Leo turned on his heel and faced Karin. "Without this marriage, we won't get the money we need to get out of debt."

"She doesn't want to marry him, Leo. Try not to be so selfish."

"Selfish?" He raked his fingers through his hair and collapsed into a desk chair. "Hardly. More like surprised. Why didn't she say something?"

"She was afraid to disappoint you."

"So instead she runs from me in the most dramatic, scandalous way possible." He pinched the bridge of his nose. "This won't just affect us, or my siblings. If we don't have that money, it will affect the thousands of people that the Perconti empire employs all over the world."

"I know." She sighed. "But at least it got Danika off your back. She lost interest when she realized that she would have to fight not just you, but all of the Perconti siblings. At least we won't have to worry about her anymore."

"No," he said as Karin sat down next to him. "And I am grateful for that."

Karin put her hand on his knee. "I know that this seems impossible right now, but we'll figure something out. Sell off some more hotels, trim the redundancy."

Leo let out a long breath and covered her hand. "Stone would just love that, wouldn't he?"

Karin shrugged. "Selling your hotels might end up working in our favor. I know Jason. He might parade around like he's made of money, but his finances are tight. He runs a lean ship and buying your hotels might cause him to overextend himself."

Leo cast her a skeptical glance. "Don't try to cheer me up." He let out a long breath and rubbed his hands over his face. "Why, Karin? I had been so worried about my brothers. I had no idea that my own sister would stab me in the back."

"She didn't stab you in the back." Karin pulled her hand away and chewed on her lip. "This had nothing to do with you."

Leo raised his brows. "No? Then what do you call this?" He waved his hand in the air around them. "I have four hundred people waiting downstairs, half of them from the press, one of them the most powerful aviation tycoon in the northern hemisphere, all waiting for a wedding that will never happen."

"It will be embarrassing, yes." Karin chewed her lip as she stood and walked a short distance away.

He lowered his arm and studied her for a moment. "Your mind is working. I can see the gears turning."

Karin turned to face him. "But it won't be any more embarrassing than the announcement about your depression." She sat down next to him once more.

"I don't follow."

"We take the blow and use the money we have in reserve to refurbish our remaining hotels. Then next year we do a grand reopening of the Perconti hotel line . . . and introduce a brand new hotel, called the Phoenix."

"The Phoenix?"

"Yes, because it will rise from the ashes." Karin grinned. "Just like your family."

Leo turned over her words in his head. He liked the idea of his family being a symbol of overcoming adversity. The phoenix was a symbol of strength and power. Perhaps . . . perhaps her idea had merit.

"Our family," he said as he took her hand. "It's a crazy idea, but it has possibilities."

"Possibilities?" Karin pressed her lips together in disapproval. "This will work. We'll just need to hire someone to put a good marketing spin on it when we have our grand reopening."

Karin thought for a moment. "We'll do it in stages. That way, at least some of the hotels will remain open and generate income. We'll also have the income from selling off some of the hotels that aren't making us any money."

"I'll have to talk to my brothers, of course, but I think you might be onto something." He narrowed his gaze. "But don't think for a moment that this will get Arianna off the hook. Once I find her, I'll—"

"Oh, I'm not expecting it to." Karin smiled as she leaned in closer. "She doesn't expect it to, either."

Leo tightened his grip on her fingers. "Where is she?"

"She didn't tell me."

"Karin—" His voice was filled with warning.

"I have no idea. Honest. All I know is that she's hiding out for a while until you cool off and things blow over."

"Hiding out? Where?" He shook her hands. "You have to tell me."

"I swear, I don't know."

"And I don't believe you."

"Leo—"

He leaned closer and raised his brows. "I think I might know a way to get the information out of you." His voice was low and oh-so-seductive.

Forgetting her protest, Karin inched closer. "Yeah?"

Leo nodded. "I might have to bring you back to the bedroom and . . . torture you until you tell me your secret."

Karin shifted her gaze to his lips. "I can't tell you what I don't know."

"You're a horrible liar."

"It's the truth, I swear." Karin shivered. "Besides, we can't do this right now. We have guests to address. *Then* we can find your sister."

"*We*." He offered her his arm. "I like the sound of that."

"You don't have to do things alone, Leo. Not anymore," she said as she grasped his elbow.

"Neither do you." He offered her a seductive smile. "I'll always be right by your side." Leo slid his hungry gaze over her body. "Or on top of you." He tugged her closer.

She flashed him a mischievous smile. "Or underneath me."

"Or inside of you." He turned her hand over and slid his tongue along the inside of her wrist, making her shiver with need.

"Or inside me," she whispered as the elevator doors opened.

"Come. The guests are waiting."

Karin made a feminine squeal as he pulled her into the elevator and covered her lips with his own.

Epilogue

Arianna slammed her palm on the button in the service elevator and slumped against the wall as it started down to the basement.

Holy hell. She closed her eyes and tried to get her heartbeat to settle down. Leo was going to be beyond pissed. She'd thought that she could go through with the wedding. She really did. But as the hour approached, she realized that she couldn't spend her entire life tied to a man she didn't love.

After a breakdown in the penthouse suite, Karin offered to help. She gave what money she could, which was less than the cost of one meal at her reception, and offered to keep her brothers busy while Ari got away.

Now she had no clothes, no place to stay, and less than one hundred dollars in her purse. Where was she going to go? What was she going to do?

Her phone chimed, signaling a text message. Arianna took it out and stared at the screen.

Hey, gorgeous. Got your text this morning, but I was in a meeting. What's up?

Arianna thought long and hard before she responded.

I need to tell you in person. Where r u?

Ari chewed on her lower lip as she waited.

At the hotel. Finishing up a meeting.

She tapped her phone as an idea formed in her mind.

Stay there, I'm coming to you.

What will the groom say?

He'll be fine, I'm sure. She had a feeling that Landon Blake would be relieved to be rid of her.

There was a few seconds' pause before she got a response.

U R crazy.

Arianna smiled as the elevator doors opened. She stepped out into the back hallway and rushed by the laundry rooms and staff offices as she made her way to the back exit.

Maybe, she texted. *Will you be at the room?*

Her fingers shook as she typed. It was a bold move, much bolder than was normal for her. Desperate times called for desperate measures, however. Their relationship was built on sex, nothing more. When she was in town, she stopped by for some fun, no strings attached. Everything was so discreet. If her family found out about her arrangement, they'd be outraged. Leo especially would become angry. Sleeping with his number one rival was an unforgivable sin.

But it wasn't like she and Jason Stone were dating. They were more like friends with benefits. They didn't confide in each other, or have expectations of each other. It was what it was, and she was just fine with that. Until now.

Yeah, she had told her brothers she didn't mind being married in name only, but there was this part of her that still loved to dress up like a princess and had hoped that one day she'd find her Prince Charming.

It was a small part, but as the wedding got closer and closer, that small part began to grow.

She had tried to feel the same excitement with her fiancé, really tried, but there wasn't anything there. In the hours leading up to the ceremony, she couldn't get Jason Stone out of her head.

Not that she expected anything from him. No, long ago they had established the boundaries of their relationship. She would respect that. Visiting him had nothing to do with her feelings, and everything to do with gaining sanctuary from her family.

I'll meet you downstairs in the staff wing. Text me when you arrive.

Smiling, she pocketed her phone and stepped out onto the sidewalk. After doubling around to the main street, she hailed a cab and got into the backseat.

"Where to, miss?" the cabdriver asked as he pulled away from the curb.

"Stone Suites, and take the back roads. I don't want anyone to see you leave . . ."

Don't miss Suzanne Rock's next thrilling book

For His Pleasure

Coming soon from St. Martin's Paperbacks